CAPITOL SPY

A NOVAK AND MITCHELL THRILLER

ANDREW RAYMOND

OTHER TITLES BY ANDREW RAYMOND

GET EXCLUSIVE NOVAK AND MITCHELL MATERIAL

You can keep up to date with my latest news by joining my mailing list. It's rare for me to email more than once a month, and you also get a Novak and Mitchell reading pack with some very cool exclusive content.

If you would like to find out more about the mailing list, head over to:

andrewraymondbooks.com

1

Andrei Rublov had been awake for nearly two days straight, but sleep was the last thing on the thirty-year-old Russian's mind. He had more than enough caffeine gunning through his system to keep him sharp, and he was still feasting on an adrenaline rush after meeting his anonymous source the previous night.

The files the source had supplied him with were comprehensive to say the least. But it was one file in particular – just three pieces of paper slipped into a cream manila folder – that Andrei knew would change everything.

It would unquestionably be the biggest story of his career, and have serious consequences for some very powerful people.

Now he had to get out of D.C. as soon as possible.

It didn't take him long to pile his things into a backpack. In the two weeks he'd been in the rented apartment, he hadn't allowed himself to get too comfortable. He had been in the journalism game long enough to keep a go bag ready for such a story.

As he took the bag to the window he did a final scan of the studio apartment, checking he wasn't leaving anything relating to the story behind.

If his source's file proved right, the apartment would surely be turned over soon.

Now he had to stay alive for long enough to get on a plane. He hadn't decided yet on Ronald Reagan or Dulles. Wherever had a flight leaving for a non-extradition-treaty country in the next hour.

Going home to Moscow wouldn't be an option for quite some time. Maybe ever again.

Andrei didn't want to risk getting cornered in the stairwell, so he went out the bedroom window of the flat-roofed two-storey, ducking and weaving his way down the metal fire escape with panic-filled footsteps.

Now he was out in the open, a sense of dread seeped through his stomach. He felt the unmistakable paranoia of being watched. A feeling he had grown used to in Moscow.

In the darkness he couldn't see far. A grab team could have been parked around the corner for all he knew. There would be a time for euphoria about the size of his story, and that would be once he was safely on an airport runway.

There wasn't much going on in the Garfield Heights district of the nation's capital. Somewhere in the distance a solitary dog barked, followed by the sound of a trash can being kicked over.

It was too late for the dealers, and too early for everyone else, leaving the dark, pre-dawn streets deserted.

As Andrei's breathing quickened, the thick bursts of fog from his mouth came out faster. It was barely thirty Fahrenheit out, but there wasn't enough space in his head to contemplate the cold.

He pointed the key at the Chevy Impala rental he'd been driving – looking all around, expecting someone to appear from the shadows at any moment. The sound of its perky assertive beep as it unlocked seemed to ring out around the surrounding buildings. Much louder than Andrei wanted.

He set off so quickly the back wheels spun on the cold tarmac. He fumbled with his phone as he raced through the endless blocks, managing to get connected to the car via Bluetooth. He tapped "Ronald Reagan Airport" into his Sat Nav.

Ronald Reagan was the closer of the two D.C. airports: Andrei didn't want to be on the road a minute longer than he had to.

He merged swiftly onto Suitland Parkway that took him to I-295, then the Anacostia Freeway. There were quicker ways to get through Capitol Hill, but the major roads were better lit and more liable to have camera coverage.

That provided little solace, though, as Andrei caught sight of a black van slowly but steadily progressing up the slow lane, sitting some four cars back.

Andrei crooked the rear-view mirror to get a better angle on it. As the road gently curved right, he could see a tall silhouette in the driver's seat, no passengers.

Andrei pressed the call button on his phone, then said in Russian, 'Call Natalya.'

It was nearly two p.m. in Moscow, which Andrei hoped would make it likely she would answer. After a few rings it went to voicemail.

His voice cracked with a mix of triumph and fear. 'Talya! It's Andrei.' He took a beat, long enough for a calming breath. 'I've got confirmation. I know who it is.

And they're right here in Washington. I met my source last night and they know everything. They gave me a dossier...' He shook his head. 'I think I'm being followed. They could be after you too. Listen to me, Talya: you've got to get out of Moscow right now.' He glanced in the rear-view mirror, noticing the black van creeping forward, overtaking. Now just two cars back. 'If anything happens to me...You know what to do.'

He hung up, then put his foot to the floor, using all the power his 3.6-litre V6 engine had to offer, taking him up to sixty miles per hour. The van was soon far back and seemingly uninterested in following.

Andrei exhaled. Panic over.

In a bid to stay on roads with some kind of CCTV coverage he took a left off Anacostia onto East Capitol Street, taking him over the Anacostia River. In no time he was on Pennsylvania Avenue.

Wanting to zoom in on the Sat Nav map, Andrei pinched his fingers across the phone screen. 'Weird,' he said to himself, as the screen went black, then seemed to reload.

The directions told him he was only ten minutes away from Ronald Reagan National Airport. He checked his rear-view mirror again. It was still clear.

For a newcomer to Washington, it was easy not to realise you were on a road leading to the epicentre of American political power. The east side of Pennsylvania Avenue coming through Dupont Park was so unassuming, it was like driving through some little Midwest town, with its modest storefronts and tidy hedgerows.

Then something magical started to happen around the intersection of 13th and 11th Street: in the distance, the illuminated white dome of the Capitol Building slowly emerged. The sight of it made Andrei's heart swell, as the scale of what he was about to go public with truly hit home.

The stakes didn't get much higher.

What didn't help was the sudden reappearance of the black van. It was being driven more aggressively now, recklessly swinging right out of Potomac Avenue at too high a speed. The van was following much closer – its lights on a purposely hostile full beam, which also made it impossible for Andrei to make out the face of the driver.

The Impala's interior was flooded with the van's headlights.

Andrei cursed to himself, 'Shit.' He knew he was in it now.

He wasn't going to take any chances, and keyed '911' into his phone screen. All he had to do was hit the green call sign if he got rammed.

The black van was all over his back bumper, but made no move to take him off the road. It was just following malevolently close.

Andrei knew he had to lose the tail somehow or else he'd be followed into the airport and his destination spotted: he'd be starting all over again at the other end. The sort of people that were after him had assets all over the globe. He needed a clean break or he was as good as dead.

He used every inch of the road to make the tight left turn onto Constitution Avenue, touching forty-five as he clipped the apex.

As the road straightened – heading west past the Smithsonian Museums and other grand white buildings that lined the road – Andrei's speed crept up.

Fifty...

Fifty-five...

Sixty...

His knuckles were white on the steering wheel. The buildings to his left a blur in his peripheral vision. He only had eyes for the black van.

Arlington County Emergency Communications Centre – same time

Marcy Edwards was on hour seven of her night shift. Apart from restroom breaks, she hadn't left the 911-police group pen. Dinner had been a large bag of tortilla chips and guacamole.

Such were the demands on emergency call workers in Virginia, the combination of stress and emotional anxiety had left the state with a crippling shortage of operators like Marcy. Even if starting salaries of $35k a year managed to entice qualified applicants, hardly any of them hung around longer than a few months. Having to listen to calls from crying children asking for help because "mommy's been asleep for four days," or talking someone through a call while someone's house was robbed, brought often unbearable stress.

Operators couldn't afford a 'bad call', or be off their game even once. Lives depended on it.

Marcy's call line lit up. She answered, 'Nine one one, what's your emergency?'

She heard the sound of a car engine before a voice.

'My name is Andrei Rublov,' the caller said, voice raised. He sounded scared. 'I'm a reporter for the TV station Russia Now. I'm in a silver Chevy Impala going west on...Constitution Avenue. I cannot control my car.'

Marcy asked routinely, 'Are you under the influence of alcohol or drugs, sir?'

'No! The car is not under my control.' Frustrated at his inability to explain, he tried again. 'The car is...'

In the background the engine could be heard getting louder.

Marcy said, 'Andrei? Are you there?'

'It's the Arlington bridge,' Andrei cried. 'I'm going to go off it...'

Marcy shot a look out the window. Her building was just half a mile from the bridge. 'Andrei, *listen* to me. No matter how bad you might be feeling, take your foot off the gas and slowly pull over to the side of the—'

'I can't! Aren't you listening to me? I'm not suicidal but my car is going to go off the bridge...'

Marcy raised her voice. 'Andrei, there's no reason for you to go off the bridge. Just listen to me—'

Two of Marcy's colleagues, off-call, turned to see what was going on, thinking she had a jumper.

Andrei's heart sank. He knew what was going to happen. It was inevitable. 'Are you recording this?'

'Yes, I am.'

'I need to say something...' The thought of what he was about to say put a lump in his throat. '...for posterity.'

Marcy, trained in keeping despondent callers in a positive frame of mind, said, 'You're not going to die, Andrei, just keep talking to me, stay with me.'

Nearly drowned out by the engine, he said, 'There's a mole in Congress.'

'I'm sorry?'

'There's a mole!' he yelled. 'There's a Russian spy in Congress. Senator—'

The line went dead.

Marcy pressed her earphone in harder. 'Andrei? Andrei talk to me...' Seeing the line was definitely dead, she hit a speed dial on her keypad. 'D.C. dispatch, this is ECC. I need a vehicle response to Arlington Memorial Bridge. I need a visual on a silver Chevy Impala.'

Arlington Memorial Bridge

The black van pulled up just short of the bronze statues of men on horseback – the Arts of War – marking the start of the Arlington Memorial Bridge.

Traffic came to a standstill in a matter of moments.

Drivers on the bridge hurried out their cars and ran towards the gaping hole in the concrete balcony. Down in the river, a silver Impala sank below the surface.

Seconds later at ECC, an operator beside Marcy Edwards took a 911 call.

'Oh my gosh...' the female caller said, struggling to keep her composure. 'He just went off the side of the bridge! He was going so fast...'

There was a conversation in the background of someone having to be dissuaded from jumping in after the car. 'It's already under water. You'd freeze in there before you even reached him...'

Back at the Arts of War, the black van calmly set off again across the bridge.

The man in the driver's seat sent a text message: "*Done. Who's next?*"

2

Judge Pierce Buckley Ellison III said sharply, 'Speak up, Mr Novak.'

Pierce Buckley Ellison III, Tom Novak thought. Only the stock of a federal judge would be crazy enough to give three males in their family such a name. Novak couldn't help but wonder if giving your children crazy names was the key to success in life: you never encountered someone with a name like Pierce Buckley Ellison III flipping burgers.

Novak, sitting in the witness box of Courtroom One, pulled the microphone a little closer. 'I'm thirty-six years old, and I'm the security correspondent for *The Republic.*'

Novak had seen the inside of a few courtrooms in the past, but none like this one in its current state. The public gallery had been cleared on the grounds of national security, relating to the testimony Judge Ellison expected to hear from Novak. There was no press, no photographers, no static, unmanned cameras. Not even any police were allowed entry. All nine people in the chamber had clearance under the emergency powers of the Patriot Act: disclosing so much as a syllable of what was uttered during the case would be a federal offence.

Outside, the national news media huddled together on Cadman Plaza, a narrow walkway outside the courthouse blocked off to all vehicles by anti-terror concrete roadblocks at either end.

Novak had been on the other side of a perp-walk many times over the years. Normally a solemn walk of the accused towards a courthouse, surrounded by news photographers – camera shutters clapping – and TV crews doing their backwards walks while they got their shots; the accused's lawyer leaning in to insist they had 'no comment at this time.'

As the accused, Tom Novak had become used to this scenario over the last year. Now he positively relished it. Novak did his perp-walk with a big smile on his face, stopping to archly check his hair in the reflection of a CNN camera lens, or attempt to chat up the cute redhead from the Pittsburgh Fox affiliate.

It was the kind of scenario Tom Novak was most comfortable with: namely, being the centre of attention, and the biggest story of the day. The question on everyone's lips: was he about to become the first American journalist to be convicted as a spy under the Espionage Act, for disclosing items of national security in a story? And not just any story. The NSA Papers that had made his name nearly a year earlier.

Back in the chamber, Novak looked out at the court stenographer, who appeared tiny in the vast, empty courtroom behind.

Novak missed the adoring eyes of the public gallery. The murmur of appreciation after a pithy political point.

Or the barely restrained giggles from a witty comeback. There wasn't even a jury: the intense secrecy of the material that formed the government's case against Novak made it impossible for civilians to sit in on it. It was a bench trial: Novak's future would come down to one man's judgement. With a potential ten years in jail.

Novak's lawyer, Kevin Wellington, got to his feet and fastened the top button of his suit jacket - which Novak had earlier noted as an exquisitely cut Brioni three-piece pinstripe suit. It was an upgrade from his usual Hugo Boss, which Novak took as a sign that Kevin was close to being named partner. It was impossible not to strut a little wearing a Brioni. And Kevin needed every little boost he could get if he was going to keep his client out of jail.

Kevin began his questioning, 'Mr Novak, this is a clear case of First Amendment rights, which the Espionage Act has long made provisions for. Let's be clear: what's on the line here is potentially setting a legal precedent for prosecuting journalists as spies. As my client, the court must surely recognise your protection under the constitution as a whistleblower regarding classified records being published in your magazine, rather than you *facilitating* the removal of the records from federal computers. And that is the distinction-'

Judge Ellison interrupted. 'Mr Wellington, do you actually have a *question* for the witness? Or would you rather submit a catalogue of speeches in hardcopy to my office?'

Kevin raised a forefinger and turned back seamlessly to Novak, as if it were all part of some grand oratorical plan, and he was on the cusp of a crucial question.

Norm Winter, the government prosecutor, rolled his eyes derisively at his second-chair.

As Kevin and the judge got into a semantic debate concerning when a question became a statement, Novak started to zone out, and wondered how the case was playing outside.

The only courtroom that really mattered to him was that of public opinion. In a way he was rather taken with the notion of ending up in jail for disclosing classified documents. He knew he wasn't exactly going to end up in Rikers Island, and being the first for something so huge brought its own unique cachet. Regardless of Judge Ellison's verdict, Novak's lawyers from Bruckner Jackson Prowse were too good to see him end up in anything other than minimum security alongside a bunch of rich white guys banged up for wire fraud.

Then he got to thinking about Stella, no doubt pacing around outside. Their first story together three months earlier had made the front page of every major newspaper from North America to Europe to Asia. He didn't want that partnership to end yet. To him, it felt like they were only getting started.

Finally, Kevin got to his question. 'Mr Novak: do you believe your source – Stanley Fox – to be the man who presented himself-'

Norm Winter's eyes raised from his briefing notes and he shouted, 'Objection, your honour!' The urgency in his voice was all too obvious.

Kevin continued anyway. '-at your previous hearing in Washington? And do you believe his subsequent disappearance is related to your-'

'*Objection*, your honour!' Norm repeated, seemingly terrified of so much as another word being uttered.

Judge Ellison held his palms out at Winter. 'On what grounds, counsel?'

Struggling for a viable answer, he replied, 'Relevancy, your honour.'

Ellison gave a withering look, then said to Kevin, 'Continue, counsel.'

Kevin said, 'Thank you, your honour. Mr Novak?'

Norm, still not satisfied, said gravely, 'Your honour. May I approach the bench?'

Kevin threw his hands up in the air, then said to his opposite number, 'This can take several weeks if you want it to, Norm...'

On his way to the bench, Winter said quietly to Kevin, 'I want you to know this wasn't my idea.'

Winter's shoulders hunched slightly as he approached the bench. An involuntary reaction to what he was about to say.

As Kevin attempted to follow – as court protocol allowed - Norm said to Judge Ellison, 'I need to approach alone, your honour.'

Novak looked at his lawyer in concern.

Kevin raised his eyebrows as if to say, *I don't know what's going on either.*

It only took about thirty seconds of discussion between Ellison and Winter – but in an empty, silent courtroom it felt like much longer.

Once Winter was through, he retreated to his table and started straightening out his briefing papers as if he was done.

Judge Ellison banged his gavel once. 'The prosecution rests and the case is hereby dismissed. Mr Novak no longer has a case to answer.'

Novak flashed a look at Kevin, incredulous. 'I don't understand,' Novak said.

Ellison stood up, already mentally ordering lunch. 'You're free to go, Mr Novak. The government has dropped its case.'

Norm Winter held his hand out to Kevin and said, 'You're young so you don't realise it, kid. But this is what an easy win looks like.'

Baffled, Kevin shook Winter's hand.

All of ten seconds later, Novak and Kevin were left in the courtroom alone.

'What the hell just happened?' asked Novak, his voice echoing around the chamber.

'We won the case,' Kevin replied, barely able to get his head around it.

'But how? They just walked away from a federal case they've been trying to nail me on for the best part of a year.'

'And now it's over.'

'What did he say to the judge?'

'I've absolutely no idea.' Kevin tried to lead him away. 'Come on. When the other side walks off the field, you call it a win.'

Novak pulled his arm back. 'We don't want it to be over!'

Kevin laughed. 'You're actually mad about this?'

'We want to win the *argument*.'

'There *is* no argument. Not anymore.'

Novak pulled out his phone and saw that he had nearly twenty missed messages and calls – which, considering he had been in court for less than thirty minutes, was considerable even for him on a Friday morning. He had Facebook and Twitter notifications, texts, and emails from colleagues and news anchors:

'Fox is killing you. Come talk to us. You already know we've given you the most sympathetic coverage out there.'

'Hey Tom. Update on our offer: my producer says if you're convicted I can get you 100k for an interview.'

'Hey buddy, it's Seth at WNBC. When it's over we want to do an hour special. But we want to ramp up pressure on the Republicans this week, so if you've got anything juicy for an exclusive we could talk $$$. Sound good?'

Novak couldn't believe these were the people at the top of their profession. A profession that had produced reporters like Edward Murrow, Katharine Graham, Ben Bradlee, Woodward and Bernstein, Dan Rather, Diane Sawyer...

As Kevin led him to the courtroom doors, word had already leaked that the trial had collapsed. The press assembled noisily in the public corridors outside, kept at bay by a dozen cops.

On the move, Novak said to Kevin, 'It's not news. It's sports.'

'What do you mean?' Kevin said.

'These producers sending me messages. It's not about issues, or the truth to them. It's about winning. It's about beating the other side. And if your side is wrong, screw it! You just spin it like your side is right anyway. They're stoking outrage. You know why?'

'Because outrage gets more clicks, and that means more ad revenue. I get it, Novak. But what's your point?'

'What if you don't fit on the right or the left? What if your only agenda is finding the truth?'

Kevin said, 'You might want to think about that another time.'

'Why?'

'Because right now you need to deal with this.'

Kevin opened the courtroom doors, revealing a baying mob of reporters, barking questions like their lives depended on getting an answer.

Kevin spoke on Novak's behalf. 'Mr Novak is very happy at this complete exoneration. I would like to point out that the government has shown more desire in its pursuit of Mr Novak than the criminally corrupt who turned the National Security Agency into nothing short of an American Stasi. At every turn the Justice department has shown that it has a vendetta against Mr Novak for exposing illegal, criminal actions in last year's NSA Papers. Mr Novak has no further comment at this time, but as you might have noticed I still have plenty to say, so give me your best shots...'

Novak grinned. It felt good having someone like Kevin Wellington on his side.

The cops weren't much good at keeping the press back. Stella Mitchell managed to fight her way through the crowd, but a side-on embrace with Novak was all that was physically possible. She was wearing a long black coat, and also a woollen winter hat. Not just because it was freezing outside, but to stay as far under the radar as possible. A task made considerably harder thanks to *Republic*'s exploits since December. She herself had faced constant questions from the press while waiting with them in the public hallway.

Stella was distracted by the sound of an English voice somewhere in the throng of reporters:

'Stella, do you have any reaction to Lloyd Willow's

daughter blaming you on Twitter for driving her father to his death?'

Novak heard the question too. He said to Stella, 'You know, you Brits might drink tea and come across so polite, but some of your reporters are only marginally removed from pond life.'

'Don't be too judgemental, Novak,' she replied. 'It wasn't long ago I was stuck in a pond with them.'

The police yelled at the press to get back and speed up the glacially slow pace towards the main entrance.

Novak guarded his eyes from camera flashes. 'I just don't know why you let them get away with it,' he said to Stella.

'What do you want me to do?' she replied.

'At least deny it.'

'Then they get their clickbait headline: "Stella Mitchell denies driving Lloyd Willow to his death." I get more satisfaction when they have to take a non-quote to their editor, who then bins the story. As soon as you open your mouth you're giving them what they want.'

'Then you're a bigger person than I am.'

'No. Just smarter.' She flashed him a smile.

Novak smiled back.

A reporter shouted, 'Tom, do you think your involvement in the Goldcastle story made the government more eager to prosecute?'

Novak pretended to be confused. 'I was never involved in that. The reason I know is because my name wasn't on the byline. Stella Mitchell was the lead reporter, but she assures me she doesn't talk to the press.'

'Come on, Tom,' the reporter replied. 'Everyone knows you worked that story.'

Novak was relieved to hear his phone ring. 'Excuse me.' It was a withheld number and he couldn't make out the voice at the other end when he answered.

They went through the main courthouse doors, where dozens of protestors and supporters had gathered. There were signs demanding a 'FREE PRESS NOW!' and cheering Novak's verdict, while others wearing stars and stripes outfits yelled 'traitor' and 'fake news' at Novak.

As a quick aside to Stella, Novak said, 'I can't work out if I should sign autographs or put on a bullet-proof vest.' He went back to the call. 'No, look, you're going to have to speak up,' Novak shouted, raising his forearm at the jostling crowd.

The press stayed with the trio all the way to Tillary Street, where a Lincoln with dimmed windows was waiting for them.

'Sorry,' Novak said, climbing into the backseat. 'I can finally hear you.'

The voice at the other end said, 'It's *Natalya*, Tom.'

Novak didn't respond.

Stella thought from Novak's expression he'd just been told terrible news. She flicked her head up slightly to ask 'What?'

Novak shook his head that it was OK.

'I'm sorry to call you out of the blue,' Natalya said.

Novak replied, 'It's been four years, Talya. Is that out the blue? More like a slight mauve. Or possibly teal...'

'I need to see you.'

He squinted, thinking she sounded far away. 'Where are you?'

'Still in Moscow.'

'That's very kind of you to think of me, but I'm going

to have a lot of interviews in the next few days. I don't know if you've been following-'

'Of course I've been following. You were on Russia Now a few seconds ago.'

Novak looked out the back window as their car cleared the last of the news crews. 'Wow,' he said with mock-pride, 'I'm even making headlines on Russian state news. I hope I was the lead.'

'I know I have no right to ask, but I need your help.'

'Help? Why exactly would I help you?'

'It's Andrei. He's in Washington.'

'What's Andrei doing in Washington?'

'It doesn't matter now. But he has a file from a source. I need you to get the file. I can't tell you how much depends on it.'

'Talya, I'm in New York. My trial's just over, I'm going to have a million-'

'Tom.' She took a beat. 'I know I'm probably the last person you care about right now. But my life depends on you finding that file.'

Novak sat up a little. 'What the hell's going on, Talya?'

'We shouldn't talk on the phone about this.'

Novak said, 'OK. Look. Stay calm. Just hang tight. Call someone there. In Moscow. Get Aleksandr to come over. Someone you trust.'

'Right now, Tom...you're the only one I trust.'

Before he could think what to say she'd hung up.

He lowered the phone. He didn't want Stella or Kevin to see, but he was in pieces.

'Who was that?' Stella asked.

Novak replied, 'Someone from long ago.'

Rebecca Fox residence, Central London – Friday, 3.52am

The corner penthouse of the 24 St James building afforded some of the most impressive views in London from its floor to ceiling windows. To the north was St Paul's Cathedral. To the west, Big Ben and Parliament. And to the east, the towering Shard - all gleaming mirrored windows, and a beaming white crown on the top five floors – amongst the other skyscrapers in Canary Wharf.

The skyline was set against a dark-blue twilight, punctuating a thin haze enveloping the tallest buildings - as if something malevolent was taking hold of the city.

Although it was getting on for four in the morning Rebecca Fox was still working hard. Since her promotion out of GCHQ to Ghost Division, which brought her to London just six weeks ago, she'd been on a consistent run of twenty-hour days. Despite her newfound seniority, significant salary bump, and comfortable surroundings, she still thought of herself as that GCHQ junior analyst with a particular talent for crosswords.

Her involvement with *The Republic*'s famous Goldcastle story – covering the Downing Street bombing - had changed all that, of course. Now she was at home amongst City high-flyers, bankers, and lawyers.

The penthouse wasn't about status to her. It was simply the most remote living space she could find in the City: high up, and severely private. She had a video door entry system, and a long hallway before even reaching a neighbour's door. Whenever she took the long elevator ride downstairs, she had her noise-cancelling headphones on, listening to podcasts about obscure data analysis and science.

Friends didn't play a role in her life, as she didn't have any. She had never sought any out either. From a young age she was always happiest on her own. The one person whom she thought of most like a friend was Stella Mitchell, and they had spent all of a few days in each other's company. Most of it on the run for their lives.

The only thing that mattered to Rebecca Fox was work: uncovering the truth, solving the puzzle.

And she had become totally consumed with solving one particular puzzle.

She sat at her glass-top desk, hair scraped back in a ponytail as it had been since having a cold shower around midnight. Her slender face was illuminated by the white/blue light of her email inbox on the screen.

Three emails had arrived at 00.01am: one from her bank; one from Facebook (an inactive account she'd been using to test a new GCHQ data-scraping tool); and one from her old gym in Cheltenham. The subject lines all wished Rebecca variations of 'Happy Birthday'.

Without reading any of them, Rebecca deleted them all. The fact that she had been born exactly twenty-six years ago to the day was of no fundamental interest to her.

She clicked on the newest message which had just arrived. 3.52 a.m. London time. Nearly one p.m. Tokyo time where the sender was.

The subject line read: '*Photo enhancement results*'

The email showed a JPEG taken from a mobile phone. The picture was of an older man – in his sixties – in a packed courtroom, wearing a blue corduroy suit, being led away by police. The man had turned half in profile, but the motion had caused a slight blurring of his face.

Rebecca had been able to speed read since she was a

child. Her above-average intelligence and sky-high IQ were not just the result of blessed genes (although her cryptographer father, Stanley Fox, had certainly helped with that) but also hours and hours of reading.

Her eyes scanned down the centre of the passage, extracting the most salient words and phrases in a smooth motion.

The email was from Kei Yamamoto of the Fuji laboratory in Tokyo. Kei was widely regarded as one of the most gifted photo technicians in the world, with access to equipment worth millions of dollars.

His results were in: even with some of the most complex digital compositing, and reversing the motion flow of pixels, the face of the man in the photo could not be cleared up significantly enough to make facial recognition possible. Yamamoto had, however, provided a slightly clearer – but inconclusive - image.

Yamamoto's expertise didn't come cheap. The two hours' work had cost Rebecca nearly £3000.

She printed it out and attached it to the wall.

She stood back admiring it whilst finishing the dregs of her coffee from a mug that had a picture of Data from Star Trek on the side. She recoiled from the cold taste: after checking the time she realised she'd made the coffee nearly an hour ago.

Yamamoto was the fourth photographic expert she had tried, and they all said the same thing. The motion effects of the photo couldn't be fully reversed. The original image from Stella Mitchell's mobile wasn't high enough resolution.

Beside Rebecca, pinned on the white wall, were several blow ups of the photo in difference sizes, all of them treated in different ways by various experts around the globe in attempts to clear up the image.

Rebecca stood up and stretched by the window, looking out at the gathering haze. A city of eight million, and the only motion in evidence was the slow blinking of aircraft warning lights on top of the taller buildings.

'I know you're out there somewhere,' she said.

Whitehall, London – Friday, 6.59am

The scaffolding was still erected around Downing Street where its iconic front was being rebuilt following the December bombing. Parliament had been under great pressure to ensure the work was completed as soon as possible. The visual metaphor alone of the centre of British politics having been attacked – with collusion from some of its own MPs and inside its own intelligence agencies, no less – was inescapable with each week that went by.

Until the scaffolding was removed and the work complete, the message being sent was that the country still hadn't fully recovered.

It wasn't the first time that such work had been necessary on Downing Street.

By the mid-1950s it became obvious that Number Ten was falling apart. Staircases had sunk, there was dry rot in the walls, and supporting walls were deemed so fragile they had to ration how many people were ever upstairs at one time.

An almost total interior reconstruction was ordered by then-Prime Minister Harold Macmillan. Initially the work was estimated to take two years and cost around £300,000. In the end, it took three years and cost nearer £3 million.

Questions were asked in Parliament about why it had cost so much more, but the government never fully explained. The plans they pointed to should never have come to anything like the sum that was billed.

When the work was completed, the chief architect Raymond Erith was said to be 'heartbroken' that the government had wasted so much money and had so little to show for it.

Like the rest of the country - and hundreds of elected members of Parliament - he just hadn't been told how the money had really been spent: on an underground military citadel beneath Whitehall.

The bunker was named Pindar, after the Greek poet whose house was the last one standing after Alexander the Great raided the city of Thebes in the fifth century BC. Intended as a bunker for conducting government business during a nuclear fallout or a safe retreat in the event of massive civil unrest, Pindar's use had evolved far beyond its original intention.

After nine eleven, the Ministry of Defence never released the details that the bunker had been massively modernised, at a cost that had been extremely difficult to hide in the government budget. But with the spiralling costs of wars in Iraq and Afghanistan, the MoD managed to successfully hide nearly £512 million in costs: creating one of the most advanced underground bunkers in the world.

Connecting Downing Street with the MoD via a tunnel five storeys below ground level, it was now used for government's most sensitive meetings. Given the advances in snooping technology - especially audio, following the recent hacking of several prominent EU leaders' phones by the Americans – it had become critical for the head of the

British government to have a safe room, impenetrable to hacks or leaks.

And also, conveniently, official note-taking.

The PM's official diary never noted Pindar meetings.

Every word uttered there was categorically off the record.

As far as Downing Street and the MoD were concerned, officially, Pindar did not exist. And they planned on keeping it that way.

Prime Minister Angela Curtis strode confidently along the Pindar tunnel linked to Downing Street. Her chief advisor Roger Milton followed close behind, phone in hand as always.

After Milton tutted, Curtis asked, 'What's wrong?'

'That GCHQ overspend we buried last week has broken.'

'How's it playing?'

Milton said, 'Pretty horribly. Just when you think you've got away with something, some smart-arse blogger retweets a week-old press release and suddenly it's picked up by *The Times*. I miss the old days when you knew if a shitstorm was over or not. We've got ministers combing through statements from ten years ago, worried someone's going to find a misapplied gender pronoun and they'll be excommunicated from public life.'

'Do you know why I *don't* miss the old days, Rog?' Curtis stopped outside the conference room doors, keying in her personal passcode. 'I get to do this.'

Milton smiled.

Around a large circular table sat the new chief of MI6,

Sir Teddy King, having been moved across from MI5; the new director of GCHQ Sir Oliver Thorn; the new chief of MI5, Dominic Morecombe; and director of the newly created Intelligence Agencies Internal Affairs – otherwise known as Ghost Division - Rebecca Fox.

The atmosphere in the room was strained, as the new appointees struggled to make conversation with each other. Sir Teddy King was the most experienced in the room, with a decade as chief of MI5 already under his belt. His appointment had been deemed a political necessity by Prime Minister Angela Curtis, following the arrest of former MI6 chief Sir Lloyd Willow for conspiracy to murder, and aiding and abetting terrorism.

With the murder of former director of GCHQ Trevor Billington-Smith, and the arrest of Willow, Angela Curtis had faced the prospect of finding new chiefs for all three of the major British intelligence agencies, just weeks after a landslide General Election victory.

At forty-three Dominic Morecombe was now the youngest chief in MI5's history. But as he had also been King's deputy at MI5, Angela Curtis believed it provided the steadiest pair of hands for both MI5 and MI6.

The most controversial appointment had been Sir Oliver Thorn, a man who had spent most of his time in GCHQ research labs, rather than running government departments. The more cynical suggested Thorn was a political appointee: someone so grateful for the huge promotion that Curtis could easily control him.

By far the youngest in the room, though, was Rebecca Fox, at twenty-six. Her role as director of the agency responsible for conducting anti-corruption investigations behind the scenes at GCHQ now did so on behalf of all three major intelligence agencies.

Sir Oliver Thorn made his way to the breakfast trolley, loading up a plate of pastries for himself. When he realised the cold stare Sir Teddy King was giving him, Thorn asked, 'Croissant?'

King replied, 'We normally wait until the PM arrives before feeding ourselves.'

Morecombe quickly put a hand to his mouth, faking a cough to cover up his stifled laughter.

Thorn put the plate down and returned to his seat, licking jam from a finger. It wasn't much surprise Thorn had grown so portly over the years, grazing on a coder's diet primarily made up of fat and sugar.

Rebecca kept her head down, combing diligently through her notes.

Angela Curtis didn't look anyone in the eye as she took her seat. 'Good morning,' she said.

As a PM, no one had really been able to figure her out yet. Especially in Whitehall. The public loved her: Curtis had pulled the country through a national crisis, and arguably the biggest political scandal in British history. Large sections of the media had suggested she might have single-handedly saved the reputation of Westminster in the eyes of the public.

At a time when confidence in politicians should have been at its lowest, Angela Curtis had steadied the ship.

As had become the trend among politicians, she sipped from a reusable coffee cup. She said, 'I don't know about you, but I went to bed about three hours ago, so let me keep this brief. If there was one conclusion that will come out of any inquiry into the Downing Street attack, it must be that we don't talk enough as one: my office and the intelligence agencies. We talk individually, but rarely in the same room together unless something catastrophic has happened. Like December. That changes today. If we want to tackle the scourge of corruption in our intelligence agencies, then we're going to have to talk openly and honestly about any concerns we have in our agencies. So consider this the first of what will be weekly intelligence-sharing meetings. Let's go around the room. Sir Teddy, why don't you start us off.'

He said, 'Prime Minister, following the suicide of Lloyd Willow in Belmarsh prison last week, I've now concluded my independent report as you asked.' He passed out copies across the table. 'Forensic Services have confirmed a verdict of suicide by hanging. They've found no evidence of foul play.'

Curtis stared at the findings, gently shaking her head. 'I don't understand how this happened. I thought he was on suicide watch, how the *hell* did he get hold of a belt?'

King joined his hands and anxiously tapped them on the desk. 'I...can't conclusively say yet, Prime Minister.'

Curtis flicked angrily through the rest of the report. 'What about Nigel Hawkes and Alexander Mackintosh?'

King replied, 'Mackintosh maintains – as he has from day one - that he knew nothing about the attack or the murder of MI6 operative Abbie Bishop. I haven't seen any evidence that disputes that. Nigel Hawkes has also been very open. He has categorically denied that there were other conspirators, and says that he alone gave out the order to allow the bomber into Downing Street.'

Rebecca Fox pressed down the centre pages of her report to keep it open. 'And that of course has nothing to do with Lloyd Willow dying in suspicious circumstances,' she said.

'Suspicious?' said King. 'That's entirely the opposite of my conclusions.'

'I saw your conclusions, Sir Teddy. I'm talking about the actual evidence. On page thirty-three, the forensics report notes deep bruising on Lloyd Willow's inner thumb.'

'I'm aware of that,' he nodded, wondering where Fox was going.

'That's a defensive gesture.' She demonstrated the motion. 'An attempt to relieve pressure on a source of strangulation.'

King flashed his eyebrows up. 'And if you'd spoken to the experts that I have, you would know that suicides often display defensive wounds.' He looked at Curtis. 'I'm sorry, Prime Minister, it's my understanding that Rebecca's expertise is cryptography rather than forensics.'

Still flicking through the report, Rebecca noted, 'It's Director Fox, actually, but that couldn't matter less.'

Angela Curtis said, 'The interrogation team told me Lloyd Willow might have been willing to name names.'

King was dumbfounded. 'I...don't have that in my report.'

'I know you don't. The interrogators were from Ghost Division.'

'Killing Willow sends a powerful message, doesn't it?' Rebecca said. 'Demonstrates what happens to anyone who even thinks about pointing the finger at another conspirator. Even in Belmarsh they can get to you. It would certainly encourage anyone else thinking of talking to stay quiet.'

King said, 'Nigel Hawkes and Alexander Mackintosh

are both going to die in prison. Why would they lie to protect another conspirator?'

Curtis replied, 'Point the finger and they could be dead next week. Stay quiet and they probably have a good twenty years left in them.'

King raised his hands in acquiescence. 'Prime Minister, these are my conclusions. It's not for me to question how those are interpreted.'

'May I, Prime Minister?' asked Rebecca, beckoning Roger Milton for the video wall remote.

She pulled up a picture of an old GCHQ entry pass from the early nineties. The name on the pass was Stanley Fox.

Dominic Morecombe didn't do much to conceal his frustration, throwing his head back. 'We went over this weeks ago,' he complained to Teddy King.

King sat back, not willing to get involved.

Rebecca pressed on. 'Prime Minister, while we're all here I'd like to find out if any progress has been made in locating Stanley Fox? He was, after all, named as your highest national security priority last month.'

'It's a good question,' Curtis said, turning to King and Morecombe.

'With respect, Prime Minister,' Morecombe began, his tone suggesting that he was about to be anything but respectful. 'There is no hard evidence that Stanley Fox is alive. The man who was arrested at Tom Novak's hearing in Washington, claiming to be Stanley Fox, was never formally identified. In less than a minute, he was taken down to the holding cells of the courthouse-'

Rebecca interrupted, 'Where he mysteriously disappeared and hasn't been seen since.'

Morecombe didn't allow himself to be diverted. 'There were no cameras allowed in the courtroom that day. But I'm assuming that you must have a clear picture of this man to be so sure that he's your father.'

She paused. 'No.'

'In fact, isn't it right that no one present in that courtroom had ever met Stanley Fox before to make a positive ID?'

Rebecca hated having to accept Morecombe's notion. 'That's true, but what about the messages sent to me at GCHQ? Messages that allowed me to decrypt crucial evidence against the men who had conspired in the assassination of former Prime Minister Simon Ali.'

Morecombe opened his arms, sarcastically welcoming the news. 'Wonderful! If you can furnish us all with your hard copies then we can start an investigation...You *do* have hard copies don't you, Director Fox? Because otherwise, how do we know the messages exist?'

'As you well know, the very nature of the messages meant they were untraceable and left no history.'

'Convenient.'

Rebecca fired back, 'My father came out of hiding that day to spare Tom Novak from jail by revealing himself as Novak's source in the NSA Papers story. And it's my firm belief the Americans have now snatched my father to steal the weapon he had spent years perfecting at GCHQ.'

Morecombe appealed to Curtis, 'Prime Minister, I fear Director Fox might be too emotionally involved to see the full facts here.'

Sensing blood in the water, King piled on. 'I have to say, Prime Minister. I have the greatest respect for Director Fox and the work she did for GCHQ in apprehending the conspirators in the Downing Street attack. But...' He looked to either side of him. 'I've been around the block longer than anyone else in this room. And it's my distinct sense that Director Fox has been the victim of a false flag operation. With respect, she had a clear vulnerability that someone exploited-'

Rebecca spoke over him. 'If anyone knows about false flag ops in here it is MI6...'

'-and we're still seeing evidence of that now. I think it's highly likely the Russians could be behind this mysterious man in the courthouse. They're toying with us. And here we are, three months later, still discussing it.'

Curtis turned to Sir Oliver Thorn, who had been noticeably quiet. 'Oliver. You're the only one in this room coming to this relatively fresh. What do you say?'

Thorn, eagerly chewing a pain au chocolat, wiped his hands with a napkin. 'I've looked through the files on Stanley. I think whatever decryption method he created, it was unlike anything anyone had ever seen. His formula could render governments and intelligence agencies like our own totally impotent. Setting aside whether Stanley Fox is alive or not, what isn't in any doubt is that Director Fox was conversing with *someone* who had access to the exact same weapon that Stanley Fox invented. What else isn't in doubt is that CIA or anyone else would be willing to snatch whoever was in possession of such a weapon. Because whoever possesses it has control over any encrypted form of communication in the world, and would have the upper hand on espionage for the better part of the next fifty years.' Thorn could tell he was surprising the others with his analysis. 'It's hard to comprehend how much money is going to change hands in that time. Oil reserves are going to start running low. We're going to run out of viable land to grow food on. The planet is heating up faster than anyone had predicted. That means refugees. And that means a shortage of resources...'

Curtis concluded, 'Which means wars.'

Everyone fell silent, waiting for Curtis as she drummed her fingers on King's report. 'Let's keep all channels open, but for now we need to make some moves closer to home.'

King shared a look of relief with Morecombe. It had taken most of the meeting but Curtis had finally sided with them on something.

'Rebecca,' Curtis said, 'I believe Ghost Division has found a new target.'

'We have,' Rebecca declared. 'MI6 again.'

Teddy King shuffled irritably in his seat. Another corrupt agent was the last thing he needed.

Rebecca pulled up a picture of a man with small, beady eyes, and hair combed forward in the hope of evading rapidly onsetting baldness. His age was listed as fifty-five.

'You can't be serious.' King was aghast. 'That's Colin Burleigh. He was in Moscow for over a decade.'

Rebecca explained, 'He had been reassigned to desk analysis after deteriorating eye test results. A Ghost Division investigation has uncovered evidence of Burleigh channelling intel to the Russians.'

'Is this coming from you?' asked King.

'My deputy director Ant Macfarlane brought it to me. He's been collating metadata on Burleigh's phone calls, emails, and dark web browsing for the past four weeks. We've already built actionable intelligence. His movements and comms track perfectly with known Russian agents. So far, all he's given them are some trust actions.'

Curtis wasn't familiar with the term. 'Trust actions?' she asked.

'Less consequential information to demonstrate that he has access and is willing to do more. Our intelligence suggests Burleigh's giving the Russians more today.'

'What's he giving them?' asked Curtis.

Rebecca replied, 'We don't know exactly what yet. But certain STRAP Three files were compromised in MI6's New York bureau servers late last night.'

'That's news to me,' King said.

'That's why they call us Ghost Division, Teddy.' Rebecca passed proof of the download to King and Morecombe. 'Whatever Burleigh's got now, it's big and it will be damaging. He's arranged a dead drop for this evening. We're going to take him.'

King shook his head. 'I know this doesn't look good but there's got to be some mistake. Colin Burleigh has seventeen years in the field. There's no way he risks his pension now.'

Morecombe joined in. 'I've got to say I echo Teddy's concerns here.'

'What a shock,' Rebecca muttered under her breath.

'I'm sure Ghost Division has full confidence in its intelligence,' said Morecombe, 'but there's something no one has been able to explain to me yet.'

'And what's that?' asked Curtis, peeved at his argumentativeness.

'Has anyone considered what happens if Ghost Division itself suffers a penetration? It's clear that British intelligence has suffered major leaks and double-agents for quite some time. Why are we so certain an internal affairs division is immune to the same danger?'

'*Quis custodiet ipsos custodes?*' King quoted. 'Who guards the guards themselves?'

Not to be outdone in Latin, Curtis replied, '*Auribus teneo lupum.*'

King tilted his head.

Curtis said, 'It means I hold a wolf by the ears. Both holding on and letting go could be deadly. A Prime Minister has to make the choice. Doing nothing isn't a luxury that's available to me.'

'With respect, Prime Minister,' Morecombe went on, his voice trembling slightly from what he was about to say, 'I don't know that you're qualified to do that. And, as well-intentioned as it is, an internal affairs division like Ghost Division is every bit as vulnerable to corruption as the rest of us. Maybe even more so.'

'Do say exactly what's on your mind, Dominic,' Curtis said with an ironic laugh.

Realising he might have gone too far, he said, 'I'm sorry, Prime Minister, but-'

She raised a consenting hand. 'I understand, Dom. Really, I do. To be candid, there's no one I can fully trust right now. Not one hundred per cent. Not even any of you.'

Curtis's frankness brought a chill to the air, with each director exchanging glances with another.

'One step at a time, we'll end this thing. Starting with the apprehension of Colin Burleigh tonight.' She rose from her chair, and the others followed. She said as an aside, 'Hang on a moment, would you, Rebecca?'

The comment didn't go unnoticed by King and Morecombe.

Thorn seemed more interested in grabbing a final pain au chocolat on his way out.

. . .

Morecombe and King spoke in private going back along
the tunnel towards the MoD.

'That was unexpected,' Morecombe said. 'Colin
Burleigh?'

'I don't buy it for a minute,' King maintained. 'I'm
telling you, Ghost Division is going to be the death of us.'

Morecombe checked over his shoulder, seeing the
tunnel was clear. 'How worried should we be about him?'

King glanced back. 'Somewhere between not at all and
sod all. No one in Whitehall knows how he got the job in
the first place.'

Morecombe was less convinced. 'It remains a fascina-
tion to me that people keep underestimating Angela Curtis.
Thorn's going to be so grateful for that job he'll do
anything she asks. Now she basically has full control of
GCHQ. And that means access to phone calls, emails. It
might be the smartest thing she's done yet.'

King said nothing.

'And she obviously has Ghost Division in her back pocket,' Morecombe added.

'They're like her own secret police,' King said.

'So what are we going to do about them?'

King kept looking ahead. 'Don't worry about Ghost
Division. They'll be shut down in forty-eight hours. Mark
my words.'

Back in the conference room, Curtis and Rebecca were left
alone.

'Are you still convinced it's Teddy King?' asked Rebecca.

Curtis snorted in frustration. 'I don't know what to think anymore. He certainly has the connections, the loyalty of operatives in the field. He and Willow couldn't have been closer. If Willow wanted rid of Simon Ali, I don't believe for a second that Teddy King didn't know about it. We just don't have any proof.'

Rebecca said, 'I've got Ant Macfarlane going back over King's movements in December.'

'You trust him?'

'If anyone can catch him it's Ant.'

'That's not quite what I asked.'

'I was hoping you wouldn't notice, Prime Minister.'

Curtis paused. 'Between us,' she said. 'Are you close to finding him?'

'I'm nowhere,' Rebecca admitted. 'But please don't ask me to stop.'

Curtis shook her head. 'I would never ask you to. Right now, though, I need bold moves. Starting with Colin Burleigh tonight.'

3

There were paparazzi waiting at the entrance of the ten-storey sandstone block that housed *The Republic*'s offices. They pounced on Novak, Stella, and Kevin the moment the back doors to their black Lincoln opened up.

Kevin put himself between Novak and the dozens of cameras and mobile phones and microphones being thrust towards him.

Kevin said, 'Mr Novak is now a free man. The government's case has collapsed as we always knew it would. There will be no further comment at this time.'

Security kept the mob from progressing past the glass revolving doors. When it was clear that Novak was gone, the paparazzi lowered their cameras and wandered off, like hyenas after a scavenged feast.

Diane Schlesinger, chief editor of *The Republic*, stood in the doorway of the conference room. 'You two,' she shouted at

Novak and Stella. 'Get in here.' Considering the magazine had just avoided a potentially arduous and expensive trial she didn't sound exactly chipper. She looked at Kevin, idling by Novak's office. 'You too, Kev.'

Kevin might have worked for one of the most powerful legal firms in New York, and was on his way to becoming the youngest partner in their illustrious history, but there was something about Diane Schlesinger's reputation that scared the hell out of him. She was one of only five people in media the attorney general had texted in advance of the public statement that bin Laden had been killed. She once reduced Bob Woodward to tears because of her red pen. And she had the White House Chief of Staff's personal mobile number. When a woman like that talks, you listen.

Kevin scurried into the conference room behind Novak and Stella.

Diane put her arms out in wonder. 'How the hell did you do it, kid?' she asked Kevin.

'I actually didn't do anything,' Kevin said. 'It was the DA who intervened.'

'Why?'

'It was Katharine Gun again,' Novak said with a smirk.

Kevin asked, 'Who's Katharine Gun?'

He was the only one in the room who didn't know.

Diane looked at Stella. 'You tell them. You reported on her.'

Stella answered, 'She was a translator for GCHQ who leaked classified intelligence to the UN in the run up to the Iraq War. When the Brits found out, they charged her under the Official Secrets Act. But moments before the case was due to start, the British government withdrew the charges when they realised the defence could potentially call members of the Cabinet to the witness stand, where they would be asked under oath if they thought the Iraq War was legal or not. Either a Cabinet member would perjure themselves, or they'd call their own government's war illegal. Not a good look either way.'

'So they ditched the case to avoid the debate,' Kevin asked rhetorically.

'This was a closed bench trial,' Diane said. 'No testimony was ever going to be made public. Every word sealed. Why drop the case?'

Kevin clarified, 'Closed, yes. But not technically off the record. Sealed testimony is very different to outright expunging. As long as the records are physically in the recording office, a court, under certain circumstances, could have them unsealed and made public. Something the DA was well aware of. They took a risk, hoping the situation would intimidate us into a plea deal before it got to court. It didn't work.' Kevin held up his hand without looking at Novak, who casually high-fived on his way past.

'That's what *I'm* talking about,' Novak said, channelling his inner jock. 'That's how we do things in Brooklyn.'

Stella said, 'You know it's only other men who think you sound cool when you do that, right?'

Diane said, 'If you two are done with your whole...' she twirled her hand, 'whatever that was. Would you care to tell me what the government was so afraid of becoming public?'

'Stanley Fox,' Novak said. 'That prosecutor didn't flinch until Kevin said the name.'

Kevin concurred. 'They were prepared.'

'Which is why we need to find Stanley Fox. He's the only person who can still fill in the blanks in Stella's story.'

Stella chimed in, 'It's *our* story.'

'Yeah, speaking of which,' Novak complained, 'I want to know who's continuing to brief reporters that I was involved in Goldcastle.'

'Yes, we should definitely stop and spend some time on that pressing issue right now,' Stella said.

'No, you know what.' Novak pushed his sleeves up. 'I'm ready for a goddamn argument about this, Stella.'

Stella just laughed.

'No, I'm serious,' Novak said, which only made Stella laugh more. 'I left my name off that story for a reason. And in the last month Stella's contribution has been reduced to that of a glorified typist according to some articles I've read. It's bullshit. We need to put out a statement clarifying the magazine's position.'

Stella went up to him and squeezed his cheek. 'Look at you getting all upset. I can stand up for myself. I've been a grown woman for quite some time now.'

Diane picked up a copy of Garner's Modern English Usage – which weighed nearly three pounds – and slammed it on the desk. 'Enough!' She exhaled and said to Kevin, 'Unfortunately I need the room with these two.'

Relieved to be leaving, in the hallway Kevin passed Henry Self, the owner of *The Republic*. Henry winked at Kevin and gave his shoulder a gentle fist bump.

'Great work this morning, counsel,' Self said.

Kevin got a lump in his throat whenever Henry spoke to him. 'Th...thank you, sir,' he replied.

Henry strode to the back of the conference room to make himself coffee. Even from a distance he looked made of money: the Mont Blanc watch, suede tan Gucci jacket, one arm of his Tom Ford sunglasses casually slipped behind the neck of his fitted white t-shirt. For a man in his fifties, he was in great shape. But his attire masked something his face could not.

Normally svelte and bright, he looked exhausted and grey.

Without Henry opening his mouth, Stella knew something was terribly wrong.

Diane said to Novak and Stella, 'Sit down, the pair of you.'

'I'm fine standing, thanks,' Novak replied.

With just one look from Henry, Novak changed his mind and sat down.

Diane spoke while Henry came to the front with his coffee. 'As you know, there's been a lot of speculation about the future of the magazine. Henry ploughed a lot of his own cash into this place just to keep the lights on. The Goldcastle story brought in a lot of revenue, for sure. There just hasn't been enough of it since December. It's March now, and we're no better off.'

Novak was baffled. 'Diane, Downing Street and Goldcastle was on the front page of every major paper around the world. The website crashed from all the traffic. What about online ad revenue? The clicks on the site alone-'

Diane said, 'We're not *The Huffington Post*, Tom. We don't make that much from online ads.'

Henry took a sip of coffee, then put his mug down by his feet. 'The revenue didn't come to us in the weeks after the story, Tom. It went to Facebook and Google. Look around town: everyone's making cutbacks. Even online exclusives are making cuts, and they didn't have nearly as much debt as we were already carrying.'

Diane said, 'The days of one publication owning a story, like Watergate and *The Washington Post*, are long gone. Have you seen the half-life of a story these days? Look at Las Vegas: the deadliest mass shooting by an individual in American history, and everyone's moved on a week later. And frankly, we didn't actually sell that many copies of the Goldcastle edition. It was our biggest ever, by miles. But it still wasn't enough.'

'What about subscriptions?' Novak asked optimistically.

Diane just laughed. 'Please. It's the equivalent of turning a few extra lights off each week. I'm afraid what we have is not sustainable.'

'What are you saying?' asked Novak.

Stella made her best guess. 'We're out of cash.'

'We are,' Henry confirmed. 'I've put *Republic* up for sale. The news will break later today.'

Novak felt like he'd been punched in the stomach.

Stella was the same but she wasn't ready to take it without a fight. 'What about a loan?' she asked. 'With your contacts...'

'I'm leveraged up to my eyeballs,' said Henry. 'I've got loans at ten times the value of *Republic*.' He laughed ruefully. 'I'll be lucky if I get a Walmart rewards card after this.'

Stella said, 'Some people out there have got pensions. Are they secure?'

Henry nodded. 'I'll sell everything I have to make sure of it.'

Novak turned his back to the others, hands on hips.

'This is my fault.' He turned around. 'It's the legal bills, isn't it.'

Henry paused, unsure how to answer at first. 'They haven't helped, Tom. Kevin Wellington halved his hourly rate to do this. Bruckner Jackson Prowse would have dropped the case if it weren't for him. It's probably going to cost him a partnership.'

Novak shook his head in dismay. Kevin hadn't said a thing to him.

Henry made his way towards the door. 'In case you're also wondering: I'd do it again if it kept you out of jail. This is all by way of saying: keep doing what you're doing, you two. The rest is on me.'

Henry shut the door behind him. Shellshock. No one's eyes met.

Diane broke the silence. 'What's next?'

Novak said, 'Stella had another question about Lloyd Willow. His daughter's been doing the rounds in the British tabloids, saying our reporting pushed her father to suicide.'

Stella said, 'It was a "gotcha" question from a London hack. It might make for good clicks on social media, but it's certainly not a story.'

'A key player in the Goldcastle conspiracy hangs himself before his trial, and you don't think that's a story?'

Stella countered, 'No, *that's* a story. What *you* pitched was gossip.'

'I'm with Stella on this,' Diane said. 'When something new comes up on Lloyd Willow we'll report it. But we're not responding to members of his family. This is a news magazine, not an episode of Dr Phil.'

Stella took out her pad from her back trouser pocket – always prepared. 'I think there's still legs in the Omar bin

Talal murder. The Swiss police say they are close to a break in the investigation.'

'What are the Saudis saying?' asked Diane.

'They're still in full denial mode. Helped by the White House this morning releasing a statement saying, quote, "We stand united with our friends and allies of the Kingdom of Saudi Arabia, and have full faith that the Swiss police will find the guilty parties."'

'It's the same statement they always issue when the Saudis do something insane. Park it until something else breaks.' Diane turned to Novak. 'What about you?'

Novak looked uncertain. 'I need to go to Washington.'

'What's in Washington?'

'Andrei Rublov,' he answered.

Diane's eyes narrowed slightly. 'I haven't heard that name for a while. Is it work or personal, Tom?'

He didn't reply.

Diane said, 'Natalya called here while you were in court. She said it was urgent.'

'We spoke during the ride over.' Novak took out his phone, which was ringing. 'I have to take this.'

Diane warned him, 'Whoever it is, Tom, no comment.'

'Yes, mother...' he replied over his shoulder.

Once he was out in the corridor, Stella asked Diane, 'Who is Natalya?'

Diane said, 'Natalya Olgorova. She's a reporter for Russia Now. Not exactly cutting edge journalism.'

'More like glorified state propaganda. RN's an international joke. How the hell did Novak get involved with someone like that?'

'It's not that they were working together...' Diane trailed off. 'They were engaged.'

'Really? What happened?'

Diane flicked her eyebrows up, as if pained by the memory. 'He never told me the whole story.'

'What did he do?'

'What do you think? They split up. He took the next flight he could to Congo, and was embedded with an NGO for the next three months. Tom doesn't really do grieving.'

Stella glanced out to the corridor. She couldn't help but look at Novak with different eyes now. All that superficial posturing for the cameras; his obsession with being popular. She could see it now. It was his way of protecting himself. It was the first time Stella had felt sorry for him since she came to New York.

While Novak was on his phone, an intern from the wires desk cautiously approached. Interns looked at Novak and Stella like they were rock stars. It was rare for interns to even get a chance to speak to senior staff.

The intern held out a printout from the latest wires. 'I'm sorry...I thought you'd want to know right away.'

Novak, waiting on the other line, put the phone against his shoulder while he took the report. 'What is this?' he asked testily.

The intern was scared to death. 'It's...they're saying about the car that went off the bridge in Washington this morning. It's Andrei Rublov.'

In a blank, stunned voice, Novak told the caller on his phone, 'I'll need to call you back.'

The intern continued. 'He worked for Russia Now. And your, um...Wikipedia page says you knew one of their reporters. Natalya Olgorova.' The intern was embarrassed to admit that he had basically memorised his idol's Wiki-pedia page.

Novak was too lost in the report to notice the intern leave. When he was finished reading, Novak returned to the room urgently.

'What's going on?' asked Stella.

'I need a flight to Washington,' Novak said, looking numb. 'I need to get there. Now.'

'What's happened?' asked Diane.

'Andrei's dead.' Novak dropped the report on the table. 'His car went off a bridge. Natalya told me she was worried about his safety. Look what happened.'

Diane skim-read the wires report.

Novak shook his head. 'She told me she needs a file, something Andrei had in Washington. They could be after her next.'

Diane said, 'Go. I'll make some calls.' She motioned at Stella. 'You're going as well. Do you have a go bag ready?'

'Always,' Stella replied.

'Good. Because the last thing I need is him going full Dirty Harry in Washington D.C.'

Kensington Palace Gardens, London – Friday, 5.04pm

Kensington Palace Gardens is one of the most expensive streets in Britain, and is certainly the most exclusive. It's home – at least an occasional one – to various foreign double-figure billionaires: the Sultan of Brunei; the steel magnate Lakshmi Mittal; members of the Saudi royal family; and some of the most influential, powerful embassies in London.

Houses for sale there are rarely even advertised. The sort of buyers who can afford such property don't sit at home combing the internet for options.

They have people. Assistants. Staff.

The street is owned by Crown Estate, a corporation belonging to the British monarchy that oversees its various property holdings and estates around the United Kingdom. The monarchy doesn't just own a few palaces in England and countryside estates in Scotland: they also own a vast empire of commercial properties, including entire residential streets across London's West End. Technically, the Queen is a landlord.

Both entrance points to Kensington Palace Gardens are blocked by security bollards that sink into the ground when vehicles are cleared for entry.

As there are often several royals in residence at any given time in Kensington Palace itself, the Palace Gardens entrance is guarded by the armed officers of Parliamentary and Diplomatic Protection - a branch of Specialist Operations within the Metropolitan Police.

From the Kensington Road end it's easy to walk right past the entrance without realising it: a narrow lane with an elegant, subtle brick gateway. The entrance from Bayswater Road, however, is a more ostentatious affair: three cream arches separated by a large plane tree that looks like it has been manicured with nail scissors.

To walk down the street in the modern age is much as it would have been fifty years ago: cars are never parked in the street, and the tree-lined avenue is only dimly lit by Victorian-style gaslights.

It's hard to tell if anyone is at home in any of the residences, as almost all have head-height privet hedges where CCTV systems are concealed, and tall driveway gates impenetrable to camera lenses. But if you listen closely you can hear the sound of service staff on driveways, tending to porch steps, or hosing down golf clubs.

Five houses along the avenue, Yevgeny Belchov was taking dinner in the main dining room of his fifteen-bedroom stucco mansion. Always a faster, the fifty-one-year-old hadn't eaten a thing since ten o'clock the night before. He treated his hunger throughout the day with a steady supply of coffee and cigarettes, before gorging himself in the evening.

On the table in front of him was a laptop, showing a live feed of the thirty cameras that covered all possible access points to the building.

The driveway entrance was one of the most imposing on the street: sitting on top of white pillars were two bronze eagles, each facing away from the other. The left held an imperial sceptre, the right an imperial orb. Forming a replica of the coat of arms of the Russian Federation.

It was more impressive even than the actual Russian embassy down the road, which, with its iron bars on the ground floor windows, looked more like a prison. And Belchov's house was as well-protected too.

Out of sight from the street, behind a ten-foot-high solid iron gate, were four security guards dressed in close-fitting technical wear, black bodywarmers, and combat boots. Each carried a Heckler & Koch G36 assault rifle: the shorter barrel making them the perfect weapon for close-combat situations - like protecting a walled property, or firing from a car.

Belchov didn't care about the cost of such security. He simply told his team to choose weapons that would make getting up the driveway 'problematic.'

Belchov was on his second packet of cigarettes of the

day - the minimum he would intake before even thinking about eating.

The financial papers were spread out in front of him. A bit of good news, but mostly bad news for his stock portfolio.

He understood that the British public frowned upon Russian billionaires like him. Back when Roman Abramovich moved from Russia and bought Chelsea Football Club there was an air of glamour. That had now been superseded by an image of crassness – of buying whatever happened to be the most expensive, rather than the most tasteful, in a given situation. Many oligarchs and billionaires and their families were sucked into a lifestyle of competing for the most extravagant spending. And there were so many of them now, it became harder and harder to outdo each other. The sight of an overweight oil tycoon struggling to get out of a super-lowdown Lamborghini Huracan outside a restaurant was not so rare anymore.

What most people didn't understand was that obscene wealth like Belchov's brought problems of its own. It required twenty-four-hour armed guard, and that was just for starters. You couldn't simply jump in your car and go to the supermarket. It required planning with your head of security to arrange routes, diversionary tactics, and a decoy vehicle in the event of a chase. You had to be sure the guy who fitted your cameras hadn't sold the plans of your property to a well-funded gang of elite burglars.

A huge bank balance seems like a great idea, until you realise you're one Russian presidential election away from having your entire assets seized if you haven't greased the right hands along the way. Perhaps that guy you screwed over twenty years ago now has a fortune of his own, and is hell-bent on revenge. Maybe the market tanked because of totally unforeseen circumstances, which meant between going to bed and waking up you had twenty million wiped off your net worth.

Belchov's dinner consisted of plain pasta sprinkled with black truffle shavings, accompanied by a pint glass of skimmed milk.

Each chink of his cutlery reverberated through the cavernous dining room. Only Belchov was at home. His girlfriend Svetlana was on her way back from a day at the Ascot races. Not that she ever ate dinner with him anyway. At barely seven stone, Svetlana rarely ate anything.

Belchov didn't own a television or any kind of speakers for music, as he never watched movies and found music to be distracting. What he did have lots of were bookcases: dark oak ones that stretched far up the walls, requiring numerous ladders on runners to reach the top shelves. There wasn't a single novel in any of the cases. Belchov couldn't stand fiction. It was something about growing up dirt-poor on the outskirts of Moscow: you don't need any extra help with imagination. When you dig yourself out of poverty, your life becomes your escape.

A message came through on one of the three burner phones in front of him: '*There was a file in his car. Recover ASAP. Your man will need to go in dark. Could get v wet. Second District station.*'

Belchov mumbled, 'Shit.' He texted back: '*In motion.*'

He searched the news tab on his laptop, typing in "Washington".

The first result was:

"*Russian journalist dies in car crash off Arlington Memorial Bridge – Washington Post.*"

Belchov pushed his plate back, a smile spreading across his lips.

He picked up a different burner phone and dialled the only contact on the SIM – there was no name, only a number.

A man at the other end, Gaspar, answered in French, '*Oui.*'

Belchov said, 'You need to stay in Washington. You're not finished yet.'

Gaspar switched to English. 'What is it?'

'There was a file in the car. I need you to recover it.'

'But the police...'

'I know.'

'It will get wet. You want this?'

'It must be done,' insisted Belchov.

Gaspar added with no emotion, 'You should expect headlines. It will be unavoidable. At night, at a police station, the rain could be torrential.'

'I know,' Belchov said. 'So don't get wet.' He hung up.

They weren't talking about the weather. For two men with military experience, wet meant it would be bloody.

Arlington Memorial Bridge, Washington D.C. – Friday 3.42pm

The afternoon Delta from JFK to Ronald Reagan National Airport got Novak and Stella into Washington in decent time - just a short cab ride from the airport to the still-active crime scene.

The bridge was closed on both sides, cordoned off by D.C. police.

The taxi driver dropped them as close as he could, short

of the west side of the bridge on George Washington Memorial Parkway. The Lincoln Memorial stood imperious on the other side of the river, but the tourists weren't focussing on the iconic statue. Their cameras were pointing at the police divers still dragging the river.

The sun was setting behind the Capitol building, leaving the Arlington Bridge in shadow. Stella had spent little time in D.C., and it was a reminder that it had a good case for being the prettiest city in America, but only for two hours of every day: at sunset. The harsh full light of day was almost too much for the white architecture, and late night brought a vague seediness to everything. There was little glamour to be found in the Georgetown bars, where lobbyists and lawmakers talked shop into the small hours. But in between those times, D.C. was a postcard.

As Novak and Stella neared the bridge they pulled their coat collars up against the chill easterly wind.

Novak was reasonably tall at six-foot-two, but with her boots on, Stella was nearly the same. While Novak was a languid mover, Stella's footsteps were fast, as if trying to keep up with the speed of her thoughts.

Andrei Rublov's Impala rental was being pulled from the river by a tow truck in the middle of the bridge, near the gap in the pillared wall where the car had broken through. The recovery had been a logistical nightmare, and dragged out the spectacle – to the delight of the local news producers who had covered it live all afternoon.

Once the Impala was back on the bridge, river water still poured out through the door and window seals. The wheel arches were covered in weeds.

Camera crews had set up all along the river bank, and there were three network choppers in the air. Andrei

Rublov's identity wasn't the story yet. For now, the visual of the car in the Potomac was making good television for the West coast midmornings.

At the police cordon an officer with the Metropolitan Police Department of the District of Columbia (MPDC) was busy directing some French tourists back over the Roosevelt Bridge to get to the Lincoln Memorial. He seemed to think sheer volume could compensate for not being able to speak French. 'No, no, *Roosevelt*,' he barked, pointing wildly at the bridge a little down river.

Stella was a fast talker anyway, but in French, she sounded even faster. Particularly to Novak who had grown somewhat used to her brisk Katherine Hepburn-esque delivery.

After a brief back and forth, Stella explained to the cop, 'They're not trying to get to the other side. One of them has lost their passport. They're asking for help.'

The cop motioned at the cordon, 'What do they want me to do about it? I'm busy here.'

Stella explained to the tourists that they should go to the French consulate in Georgetown, then apologised about the cop, explaining, '*They're not all like that here.*' She then said to the cop, 'We're looking for Agent Shapiro. Do you know if he's here?' She showed the cop her United States press pass.

The cop took one look at the pass. 'All I know, lady, is that my shift ended an hour ago, and if this happened two hundred yards up the road this would be USCP's problem.'

There wasn't much love lost between D.C. and Capitol Police. Not only were USCP on a slightly higher pay scale, they got to hobnob with politicians around the grounds of Congress. Day to day, it was seen as the cushier end of D.C. policing.

The cop whined, 'I should be sitting at home right now watching the Final Four.'

'I have no idea what that is,' Stella replied.

'March Madness.' He waited for a reaction. 'The NCAA. Basketball?' He looked to Novak in appeal, then did a double-take. 'Hey...ain't you that guy? You were on the news this morning.'

Novak said, 'I'm on TV all the time.'

'So are you one of these lame-stream media guys the President's always talkin' about? One of the guys at the precinct says you're fake news.'

Stella couldn't help herself. 'Excuse me, we do the real stuff, thank you very much.'

Novak caught sight of who they needed: a man in a brown mackintosh coat, standing in the middle of the bridge on his own. Novak waved at him.

The man wandered over, looking around himself while taking sips from his takeaway coffee cup.

The man said to the cop, 'Hey, officer. Give us five minutes, would you.'

The cop made his way further along the cordon, muttering to himself about 'the Feds'.

Novak held his hand out for Shapiro to shake. Shapiro looked away.

'Good to see you too, Dave.' Novak retracted his hand.

'It's not the best look for my career right now to be seen talking to you. I've got superiors who pushed hard for that espionage charge.' Shapiro looked around again. 'Make it quick.'

Stella said, 'I'm Stella-'

Shapiro replied, almost embarrassed, 'I know who you are, ma'am.'

'What's the Bureau doing down here?' asked Novak. 'A car going off a bridge is hardly a federal issue.'

'Officially, I'm not here, Tom,' Shapiro said. 'A buddy in D.C. homicide gave me a call when they ID'd the victim. A Russian reporter dying like this is probably going to make some waves.'

'Was he run off the road?'

Shapiro clocked Stella reaching for her notepad. He touched her arm then shook his head. He checked over his shoulder again. 'I'm going to tell you what they have, but you can't quote me on any of this. You can refer only to sources close to the investigation.'

'OK,' said Novak.

Shapiro kept his voice down. 'The victim is Andrei Rublov, thirty years old. His passport was in his jacket. At around six forty-five a.m. he was approaching the bridge at speed. Witnesses on the bridge say he accelerated to somewhere between fifty and sixty miles per hour. He appeared to lose control halfway across, when the car skewed across the opposite lane and busted through the bridge balcony. He would have been lucky to survive the fall, but with the temperature down this low, he didn't stand a chance in the water.'

'Was there anything in the car?' asked Novak, trying not to press too hard. 'Notes, papers...files. That kind of thing?'

'There was a laptop in the car, but the divers say it's pretty smashed up. It doesn't look like we'll get anything from it but we can try-'

'Yeah, what about *files*, Dave? It's important.'

Shapiro had never seen Novak wound so tight before. 'MPDC took away a couple of bags earlier. I don't know what was in them.'

'What do you know about the car?' asked Stella.

'It's a rental. Not many miles on the clock. He couldn't have strayed far outside D.C. at all.'

'And no one ran him off the road or anything?'

Shapiro took out his phone. 'Technically...no.'

'Technically?'

Shapiro navigated to a recording, then held the phone out for them to hear:

"*Nine one one, what's your emergency...*"

Novak and Stella shared a startled look when the call ended abruptly at the mention of a senator.

'*That,*' Shapiro explained, 'is why I'm here.'

It took a lot to impress Novak and Stella, but Andrei Rublov had managed it.

'That was fast thinking,' Novak said.

Shapiro said, 'I'll give you three guesses what MPDC are saying about the call being cut off, but you're only going to need one.'

Stella didn't even blink. 'They're saying Rublov was cut off before he could say more because the car hit the water.'

'Except?'

'Except there was no sudden change in the pitch of Rublov's voice,' said Stella, 'which would definitely have happened if he was in a car crashing through a bridge. Also, if the call was cut off by the car hitting the water, you'd be able to hear the crash through the bridge a few seconds before. All you can hear in the background is the engine.'

'Meaning?'

Novak looked at Stella as the penny dropped. 'He was still up on the bridge when the call was cut off. It wasn't the crash. Someone else cut him off.'

'Now you're in my world,' Shapiro said.

'But who would be in a position to cut off the call?' asked Novak. 'And how?'

Stella remained troubled by something else though. 'Rublov didn't say the car was out of control. He specifically said the car was out of *his* control. That's very different.'

Novak suggested, 'He was in a scary situation. He wouldn't have been thinking clearly.'

Stella countered, 'He had the presence of mind to call nine one one to ensure there was an audio witness to what was happening. Not to mention trying to get on record vital information. He did what any good reporter would do in that situation: don't get buried with the story.'

An MPDC detective near the Impala shouted for Shapiro.

'Give me a second,' Shapiro told them.

Stella craned her neck to see what Shapiro was being shown at the front seat of the Impala.

Novak was checking his phone for messages. From Diane. From Natalya. Anyone with news. But there was nothing.

When Shapiro returned he pulled off the latex gloves he'd been wearing to examine the car.

'You know what this is?' Shapiro asked, holding a small plastic evidence bag.

'Looks like an old phone charger or something,' Novak guessed.

'Actually, that's not far off,' he replied. 'The steering column was all smashed up. It exposed the OBD port – it looks like a small SCART socket. The kind you used to get on the back of VCRs or an old television. It's under the wheel. You could have a car for decades and never realise it's under there. The port looks pretty innocuous, except for these little pin connectors here,' he pointed at a tiny pair of prongs, 'they're linked to every computer protocol in your car. One operates the radio and car locks. And there are two others that connect to the engine and steering mechanism.'

Novak and Stella could feel a break coming.

'With this port attached, you have access to the car-'

Novak added, 'And anything else connected to it.'

Shapiro nodded.

Stella asked, 'Are you saying the car was *hacked*?'

'This isn't exactly NASA technology,' said Shapiro. 'But it's enough to give total remote access of that car to whoever controls this chip. Steering wheel, gas, brake, doors, ignition, you name it.' He looked at Novak and Mitchell in turn. 'This is a murder weapon in this bag.'

'How easy is it to hack a car?' Stella asked.

'You wouldn't believe,' Shapiro replied. 'Anyone with physical access to the car, an internet connection and the inclination, could do it in about an hour.'

Stella started thinking of the bigger picture. 'The State Department's going to have a diplomatic nightmare on its hands once this goes public. A Russian reporter murdered in D.C.'

Novak had a thought. 'That could explain the phone call being cut off, then.'

'How?' Stella asked.

'He had a suitcase in the car, right?'

'Right,' Shapiro confirmed.

'So he was going to the airport,' said Novak. 'That means he would have been using Sat Nav. But Rublov would have been more likely to use the Sat Nav on his phone so it was in Russian. Sat Nav via his phone means a Bluetooth connection...

Stella could see where he was going. 'Whoever controlled the car could also control Rublov's phone.'

Shapiro started to smile.

Novak said, 'Whoever hacked the car didn't want anyone hearing, and managed to cut the signal before Rublov named the spy.'

'We at least know the spy is in Congress,' added Stella.

'Dave, I need to find something for a friend of Rublov's. I have reason to believe she's in danger too.'

'In D.C.?' he asked.

'Moscow.'

Shapiro flicked his eyebrows up. 'I don't know how much I can help there.'

'It's a file that Rublov had here in the city. I'm running out of time, Dave.'

'Anything belonging to the victim will be in evidence at Second District Station by now.'

Novak grimaced. 'Dave, you know I wouldn't ask if it wasn't important.'

Shapiro shook his head in exasperation. 'You don't want much, do you...' He checked his watch. 'Meet me at the station in an hour.'

Cabs were the great equaliser in Washington, D.C.: it didn't matter if you were a political lobbyist on K Street, a senator running late for a caucus, or two New York reporters. You could still find yourself in a taxi that stank of pastrami and had Bon Jovi blasting from a classic rock radio station. The driver was drumming his fingers on the steering wheel to 'Livin' on a Prayer.'

Novak pinched the top of his nose in frustration as he tried to knock out a message to Diane back in New York. He couldn't think straight with the music.

Stella had to cover her other ear whilst on the phone, struggling to hear. 'Yes, thank you, I hope you can. My brother is staying in D.C. and he rented a car from your company recently. The thing is, he's lost his phone and can't get into his bank records. He's trying to remember what date he began his rental with you and how much longer it's paid up...'

Novak mouthed, 'What are you doing?'

She raised her forefinger while she continued to speak. 'No, I don't, sorry. But I can give you the postcode he would have registered it under...Oh, I'm sorry, I mean zip code. It's two zero zero two zero. Apartment is three B, at fourteen twenty-two Providence...'

Novak rapidly bounced his leg up and down while he texted Diane: '*Any word from your guy in Moscow?*'

Stella snapped her phone cover shut. 'Incredible what some people will give you over the phone when you have a license plate and a story.'

Novak was smiling at something.

'What is it?' Stella asked.

'Nothing. It's just...' His smile got bigger as he looked at her notepad. 'You're very thorough.'

Stella had filled an entire page from a phone call that lasted ninety seconds, noting everything from background noise to irregular pauses from the customer service rep. One question she put in a box was '*Has anyone else called about this account?*'

Stella said, 'So Rublov took out the car rental two weeks ago to the day. And he had it paid up for another two weeks.'

'So the decision to go to the airport must have happened fast.'

'I also checked: no one else has called about the account yet which is good.' Stella could see Novak didn't get the point. 'It means we're ahead of everyone else. Andrei didn't exactly go off that bridge in secret. Once his ID is made public we're going to be looking over our shoulders.'

The cab driver called back. 'Hey. You want me to come in from Suitland Parkway or Southern Avenue?'

Distracted, Novak said, 'I don't mind. Parkway's probably fastest, I guess.'

The driver switched routes on his Sat Nav.

Something about it set off a thought in Novak.

'Of course,' he said to himself. 'Andrei had been here two weeks. He wouldn't know the roads. Wherever he went in D.C. I'd bet all the money in my pocket he used Sat Nav to get there.'

Stella said, 'Which would mean...'

'If we can access his phone, we could get a map of everywhere he'd been.'

'If only we knew someone who could help with that.' Stella took her phone out and searched for a contact - "Rebecca Fox" – then sent her a secure OTR (off-the-record encrypted) message.

Up front, the music switched to a news report.

Novak leaned forward.

Stella asked, 'What's wrong?'

'They cut in in the middle of the song.' Novak asked the driver, 'Hey, man. What's the news?'

Stella's phone pinged with a news alert from Reuters. As she read the alert she put her hand up, about to cover her mouth. 'Oh, bloody hell...'

The driver called back, 'Something's happened in London again. That damn city just can't catch a break.'

Stella showed Novak the alert, highlighting the phrase 'active shooter'.

4

THAMES HOUSE, LONDON – FRIDAY, 5.28PM

Ghost Division's headquarters were located in an anonymous grey five-storey building in the City: the heart of the financial centre of London.

Rumours had been circulating since January about some new outfit in the basement of GCHQ, but everyone assumed it was a standard research project, perhaps testing new software. Ghost Division's real mission – to investigate and capture corrupt intelligence agents - was still a closely guarded secret, known only to those with STRAP Three clearance.

Ghost Division had uncovered more cases than it could handle, and it soon became apparent that GCHQ's cramped basement and limited technology could not be a permanent solution. Operationally, it was proving vital for Rebecca and her team to have physical access to London where the majority of their field work was taking place.

After £29 million in renovation and upgrade costs, for the modern age Ghost Division's new home was a bargain.

They called it Thames House.

For a building to meet government requirements for holding material classified "Secret" or above, the whole interior had to be ripped out and upgraded by List X contractors: a government database of approved companies who work on contracts that require classified information. The only way to even get on the database is to be recommended by an existing List X body, a government body, or someone in NATO.

The computer and phone-networking logistics were mindboggling, and required ripping up the main road outside for a week to lay the necessary cables.

Thames House drew little attention due to its modest size in relation to the corporate offices that surrounded it near the river. Even the security staff that manned the entrances didn't know exactly what they were protecting up the stairs.

Officially, the building was classed as "a GCHQ research facility".

Rebecca entered the ops suite, reading the latest tracking information on the target.

The suite fit fifteen people at computers all linked to GCHQ's systems, with access to all the essential database tools like ECHELON and TEMPORA. All landline phones were military-grade modified Sonim XP8s for secure, encrypted communication. The same standard as what the Prime Minister used to talk to foreign leaders. For a tech nerd like Rebecca, it was a palace.

The team of twelve of the most brilliant minds Rebecca had hired from GCHQ hung on for her orders. Rumours of her almost single-handed dismantling of the

Downing Street bombing conspiracy within MI6 and GCHQ had already approached the stuff of legend. That she was still twenty-six years old only served to heighten her mystique.

Rebecca stood at an adjustable desk that was raised to waist height. She had her notes on Burleigh laid out in front of her.

One half of the video wall at the front of the suite had a live feed of Greater London's CCTV system, which the Metropolitan Police granted Ghost Division full access to. The other half of the wall displayed details on the 'street team' that would be following Burleigh.

Rebecca asked her deputy director, Ant Macfarlane, 'Ready?'

He nodded.

Without any preamble, he announced, 'This is our target. Colin Burleigh of MI6. He's a level two with seventeen years' experience. You don't last that long in the field without impeccable tradecraft. Trust me when I tell you, the moment we underestimate this guy, we lose him. Is that clear?'

'Yes, sir,' came the unified response.

Ant was Scottish, in his mid-thirties and had achieved more in his ten years at MI6 than most field agents did in their entire careers. He could have gone anywhere, done anything. He chose to come to Ghost Division, purely to work with Rebecca.

Just as she had found her perfect team for analysis, Ant had put together his own team of field operatives. Agents he trusted, who, like him, had shown a determination to flush out rotten apples in the British intelligence services.

With Rebecca's analytical and technological expertise,

alongside Ant's operational experience and tradecraft, after a dozen missions they'd proven themselves a perfect team.

Ant continued, 'Burleigh penetrated MI6's internal database two nights ago, and we believe he's supplying STRAP Three documents to Russian agents today. That constitutes a national security threat. We have no idea what's in the files but if we don't take Burleigh today, this could be the last we ever see of him. Our mission is to observe the file exchange, which we expect to happen at the National Gallery, Trafalgar Square. We will then follow the suspect back to Mayfair, where the grab team can take the suspect quietly along with the documents. All at rush hour in central London.'

Although GCHQ or MI5 had the power to collect intelligence relating to domestic criminal offences, only Special Branch of the Met Police were authorised to actually make arrests on UK soil. At least that used to be the case, before Angela Curtis rushed through new powers for Ghost Division at the turn of the year, burying it in the middle of a dense intelligence budget. Ghost Division agents were now granted legal authority to detain and hold suspects, before handing them over to Special Branch for formal arrest.

Ant paused to let the scale of their task sink in. 'This is what we train for. This is what we do best.'

Rebecca pulled up a live feed of the street team's location on the video wall's map. 'Someone get me the tick-tock on Burleigh for today.'

Ghost Division had pinged Burleigh's phone a week ago, and had been scraping data from the phone provider since. Phones are in constant contact with the nearest signal tower, even when the phone is switched off. That history is kept, giving agencies like Ghost Division - or GCHQ and

NSA – full visibility of everywhere a phone has been, with any request to a phone provider.

Calling them 'requests', however, was putting it rather gently. The providers faced harsh legal consequences if they failed to comply. Essentially, the intelligence agencies had a private door giving access to the data of every major phone provider.

Burleigh was on Savile Row in Mayfair, following the path that Rebecca's metadata had predicted.

Street One, wearing the pinstripe suit of someone in finance, was on a mobile phone to talk to Thames House. 'Heading for Bond Street underground.'

'Grab team, stand by,' said Ant, watching the icon for Burleigh disappear as he went underground.

There were five in the grab team, sitting in a white panel van just off Savile Row. They weren't dressed to blend in like the street team. They were dressed purely for action. They now had to do what they hated most: sit and wait.

Ant said, 'Street Two and Street Three, you're up.'

They responded with double-taps on their radios to confirm message received.

They followed Burleigh into Bond Street underground.

Street One had gone ahead and was already on the Central Line platform.

Burleigh was in a long tweed coat, and carried a battered brown briefcase. Coupled with his thick-rimmed glasses, he was easy to keep track of. He took the escalators on the left side, walking briskly past the other commuters. When he got to the platform he took subtle looks to his left and right, carefully clocking the faces of those around him.

Street Two had a fake baby bump underneath her coat,

and had a badge on that said 'Baby on Board'. She carried a tote bag that said 'VEGAN' on the side, and had a rolled-up yoga mat sticking out of it like a baguette. She had always been Ant's most trusted operative. There was nothing she couldn't do convincingly, and made great play of holding her 'bump' as someone gave up their seat for her on the crowded underground.

Street Three was an early-twenties male, carrying a backpack on both shoulders and wearing a trendy sports jacket: his legend being a student. He was further down the carriage and had to stand. Now both exits of Burleigh's carriage were covered.

Ant reminded them, 'Remember, don't look in his direction on the train. He could have spotters with him. Just wait for him to pass you when he gets off.'

Rebecca said, 'So far so good.'

Even Ant had the feeling that the stage was set for a textbook action.

During the change at Oxford Circus to the Bakerloo Line, Burleigh left it to the last moment before making for the doors. It was a classic old-school move he had used throughout his career: get on a train for one stop, then another for one more stop. The chances of one person following you on both legs of such a journey were slim, and helped dial in which faces you should keep track of.

But Ant's team had played it beautifully this time: Burleigh had no suspicions.

An analyst raised her hand in the corner of the room.

Ant harangued her, 'I'm not your teacher. If you've got something: speak.'

The analyst was now even more scared. 'We don't have Street Three,' she said.

'What do you mean?' Ant asked.

The analyst told Ant, 'Street Three never made the change at Oxford Circus.'

'Fuckin' hell,' Ant cursed, his full Scottish brogue coming through. 'Street Three, single cough to confirm missed change. Double cough if-'

Analysis said, 'Sorry, sir. We don't have Street Three's radio. We can't always guarantee a signal on the underground.'

Ant turned to the analysis desk. 'Find out where he is and tell him to go ahead to Street Four and Five at Trafalgar Square.' As far as Ant was concerned, Street Three's career with Ghost Division had just ended.

Rebecca saw Street One and Street Two's signals return on the map, but they were now in front of Burleigh. She asked Ant, 'Do they-'

Ant said, 'They know.' He then radioed, 'Street One and Street Two, you both need to do dead stops.'

Seamlessly, Street One stopped to give a homeless man some change. Once Burleigh overtook him, Street One confirmed with a double-tap on his radio. Street Two then stopped at a ticket machine, pretending to check her Oyster card balance. Using the reflection in the ticket office's window, she saw Burleigh head up the stairs. She double-tapped her radio too.

Rebecca remarked, 'They're good, I'll give them that.'

Burleigh climbed the stairs out of Piccadilly Circus underground, but instead of turning right towards Trafalgar Square as the metadata history predicted, he turned left to Piccadilly.

Rebecca watched the map carefully. 'He's changing.'

Ant shook his head. 'Why now? Why today?'

'Has he made us?' asked Rebecca.

The analysis team told Ant, 'We've lost the target's phone, sir.'

'Battery?' Ant asked.

'It looks like it, sir,' they replied.

Rebecca said, 'Set a pattern for two weeks, then break it on the day it matters. Very nice.'

'We still have eyes on the ground,' replied Ant.

'Should we send Street Four and Five for backup?'

'We need to keep our composure. Give it a minute and let's see where he's going.'

Rebecca said, 'Get TfL on the wall.'

Analysis brought up CCTV images from the surrounding streets, taken from Transport for London's system.

'There he is.' Rebecca spotted Burleigh across the road from the famous Piccadilly Lights advertising screens.

The state-of-the-art LED screens illuminated the pale dusk descending on the capital. The screen showed the temperature was down to a brisk three degrees Celsius – thirty-seven Fahrenheit. Though it felt colder than that on the ground.

Burleigh glanced at a passing double-decker bus window, catching the reflection behind him of a blonde woman in a leather jacket, and a broad man with a shaved head, wearing a dark-blue fleece. There was a steeliness to their faces that raised a flag - and not just for Burleigh.

Street One had spotted the man too. 'I think we've got company out here,' he told Thames House. 'Blue fleece, my three o'clock.'

'We see him,' Ant replied, already zooming in on the video feed.

Street Two, keeping a safe distance from Burleigh, radioed in. 'He's going into Waterstones.'

'Great,' said Rebecca. 'The biggest bookshop in Europe.' She asked analysis, 'Can we get their cameras?'

'They'll be on a network,' came the reply. 'I can get them.'

Street One said, 'I'll follow.'

Ant replied urgently, 'Negative, Street One! Do not pursue.'

'Why not?' Rebecca asked him.

Ant scoured the CCTV images, seeing Burleigh wandering the ground floor. 'He's not doing a dead drop in there. He's using the lobby.'

'I don't understand.'

'He's already changed his pattern. He's being extra careful. If I was him, I'd hold off on the next step until I made an SDR.' Ant could tell Rebecca didn't know the acronym. 'Surveillance detection route.' He pointed at Burleigh on the screen. 'Look: he's positioned himself right in between the two entrances, which means he can clock every face that comes in after him. He'll have a list in his head of every face from the underground, and who changed trains with him. If he sees even one of those faces follow him in there, he'll know he's got a tail. He might abandon the drop altogether.'

Sure enough, after a few laps of the tables at the front, Burleigh made his way back onto the street.

Ant nodded to himself. 'OK, street team. Stand by.'

But just as they thought Burleigh would head back towards Trafalgar Square as planned, he dashed across the main road, into a short lane leading onto Regent Street.

Street One confirmed, 'Target heading north to Regent Street.'

Street Two, cradling her baby bump, followed, worming her way through the static traffic. 'I have him,' she said.

Rebecca said, 'This drop is too important for him not to have scouted it out at some point.' She told analysis, 'Somewhere in Burleigh's metadata there's a history with this area. Sometime in the last month. I want a location on where he's going.'

Ant said, 'Grab team, start making your way towards Regent Street. I don't think he's coming back to Mayfair this time.'

Rebecca said to Ant, 'It's going to take them ten minutes to get through rush hour traffic.'

Ant shook his head. 'You've got to admire the prick. Burleigh's planned this entire thing beautifully.'

A call came up from analysis again. 'Sir, Street Three is still on the underground.'

'Forget him,' Ant said.

'No, sir. I mean, he never made it off at Oxford Circus.'

'What are you talking about?'

'The train is still sitting at Oxford Circus, and Street Three is still on it.'

Ant came towards the analysis desk. 'Have you radioed him?'

'No response.'

Rebecca looked closely at the wall. 'Bring up CCTV for Oxford Circus, Central Line.'

The video wall showed the tube train was stopped, and all the doors were open. Two policemen in fluorescent jackets were crouched over a body on the platform. Passengers stood back, hands at their mouths in shock. Para-medics dashed down the platform towards the body.

'Zoom in!' Rebecca demanded. 'Quickly!'

The shot revealed a policeman holding his hands against a knife wound, blood pouring from Street Three's stomach.

'He's been stabbed,' Rebecca said. She could imagine how easy it would have been in the packed carriage. 'We need to abort,' she told Ant.

Ant looked with horror at the map, showing Street Two's location going through the lane in pursuit of Burleigh. Ant said to himself, 'We're being ambushed...' He radioed, 'Street Two, get out of there!'

The map didn't show the appearance behind Street Two of the blonde woman in the leather jacket, who had peeled off from the man in the blue fleece.

Street Two's audio was still going. There was the sound of a physical struggle, then a muffled groan.

Her vitals on the video wall showed a sudden heart rate spike.

Panic.

Fear.

Pain.

'Is she down?' Rebecca asked analysis.

Ant shot his hands up. 'Quiet!'

The decibel range on Street Two's audio feed was still moving.

'Is that traffic?' Ant asked. 'Background noise?'

A whisper from Street Two came through. 'Female...blonde hair...leather-'

Her feed went to static and the audio cut.

'Street Two?' Ant called out. 'Street Two, do you read me?'

Her vitals on the wall flatlined.

Analysis confirmed. 'She's dead.'

There was silence in the ops suite.

Ant wiped his face.

Rebecca told him, 'We have to abort.'

'What about the files?' asked Ant.

'Forget the files! The mission is compromised.'

Street One was still pursuing Burleigh up Regent Street, and could hear the disagreement on his radio. 'What's going on?'

Ant replied, 'Street Two and Street Three are down. You are staying with Burleigh. Street Four and Street Five, I want you on Regent Street in six minutes.'

'Received,' Street Four replied, his voice already shaking from running. 'Street Four and Five are en route.'

They abandoned their position in Trafalgar Square, and set off up the middle of Haymarket, bounding through the solid traffic.

'What are you doing?' Rebecca asked Ant in confusion.

'We can't abort,' Ant insisted. 'We still have three active agents on the ground in pursuit of stolen STRAP Three documents.' He stepped close to Rebecca. 'This is why you brought me in here. This is why you gave me operational authority for experience in the field that you don't have.'

Still staring at Ant, Rebecca asked the room, 'Is Street Two still in that lane?'

An analyst changed the satellite map to a heat sensor. It

showed the lane was empty. Two vans that had been there were now gone.

'They've taken her away,' came the reply.

Regent Street was like a car park, with traffic solid on both sides. Dusk was falling, making a clear ID all the tougher.

Burleigh couldn't have picked a bigger surveillance nightmare.

An analyst called out, 'I think I have something on Burleigh's history.'

Rebecca came round.

The analyst showed her the metadata log. 'Twenty-two days ago, Burleigh received a call from this phone. Later that night, Burleigh's phone was tracked to this building off Textile Place. The next night, the phone that called Burleigh also ended up at Textile Place.'

Ant nodded.

Rebecca agreed. 'That's the meet.' She told the room, 'We have a link, people.'

Ant said, 'Grab team, what's your ETA?'

'We're still two minutes out,' they replied.

Ant mumbled, 'Shit,' under his breath. 'Street team, you're going to have to detain the target in Textile Place until grab team gets there.'

Burleigh ran across the road into Textile Place, a quiet cobbled lane leading to a cul-de-sac. To the right was a shuttered garage door leading into a building with boarded-up windows.

Rebecca had a drone feed from five hundred metres above Oxford Street up on the wall, showing a direct overhead of the lane.

Burleigh was keying in a code for the shutter door when Street One entered the lane. His gun was out. He had him.

'Down on the ground,' Street One yelled. 'On your knees! Hands on your head!'

Burleigh didn't know what had hit him. He went straight to his knees. 'What the hell is going on?' he cried.

Street Four and Five arrived, their chests heaving from their sprint. Four kept his gun on Burleigh, while Five covered the exit back onto the main road, waiting for the inevitable arrival of whoever had taken out their colleagues.

Street One manoeuvred Burleigh flat on his front, then put his knee into Burleigh's back as he searched him.

Ant consulted the live map feed then told Street One, 'Grab team still two minutes out.'

Street One snapped his fingers, then motioned at the large dumpsters at one side of the lane. 'Pull them over.'

Street Four and Five pulled two large dumpsters across the lane to block the public's view from Oxford Street. But it was dark, and Textile Place was only sparsely lit.

Street One took out a roll of papers from the inside pocket of Burleigh's coat. 'Is this everything?' Street One asked.

Burleigh winced as Street One dug his knee harder into his back. 'It's everything,' he groaned.

'Stay still. This will be over soon. How many others are out there?'

'Others?' asked Burleigh.

'Fine. Play it that way.'

Back in the ops suite, Rebecca said to Ant, 'I don't understand. If Burleigh's getting help, where are they?'

Ant's face was etched with tension. 'Something's not right here.'

Both he and Rebecca were relieved their vitals weren't up on the video wall. Their heart rates would have shown definite spiking. Rebecca made fists with her hands, stretching them out. Her palms were clammy.

Losing patience, Rebecca got on the radio. 'Grab team, update.'

'Ninety seconds out,' they replied.

They were so close they could have made it on foot. But they couldn't drag Burleigh down Oxford Street. They needed the van inside Textile Place.

Burleigh kept his hands behind his head, smiling ruefully. 'You're Ghost Division, aren't you? Christ, I should have known...'

While keeping his gun trained on Burleigh, Street One eyed the buildings on each side. All windows with a view were boarded up. He called to Street Four and Five, 'We good?'

They had blockaded the lane. Four signalled back a thumbs-up.

Back in Thames House, an analyst asked for Rebecca's attention. 'I've been looking for other angles on Air Street to get the plates of the two vans that were in there.'

'Don't bother,' Rebecca said. 'They'll be fakes.'

'I know. But there was a food delivery cyclist who went through a few moments after Street Two went down. I searched for anyone on Strava in the area: it's a phone app that logs your journey. Someone went through the lane at the same time. We have the helmet camera.' The analyst hit playback on her computer screen.

It showed the cyclist going quickly through the lane, then as he passed two vans parked on the side, he glanced to the right where Street Two had gone down.

The analyst hit pause.

Street Two wasn't lying in a heap from a stab wound, or any other type of wound. She was sitting up against the front of one of the vans, helping the blonde woman remove the sticky dot monitoring her heart rate.

Rebecca felt all the breath leave her body. She called Ant over to show him.

Once he saw the pictures, he grabbed the radio. 'Street team, brace brace brace. You have imminent heavy incoming. Street Two is with them. Repeat, look out for Stacey...Grab team. I need all feet on the ground, *now*. We have an imminent threat. Go go go...'

The grab team piled out of the van. As soon as they reached the pavement rifle shots rang out from somewhere above. Two of the grab team went straight to the ground with head shots. One of them collapsed into a screaming commuter whose face was now spattered with blood.

The call came back from the grab team van, 'Shots fired! Sniper! Sniper!'

Within seconds, Street Two had reappeared, now without her baby bump. She ran up the central reservation between the two lanes of traffic, crouching down to stay out of sight.

She sneaked up on the grab team driver's window, holding a silenced Glock 17 9mm.

She popped the driver and the two other passengers, before disappearing back into the crowd on the pavement.

The driver behind the grab team van was so stunned by what he had just witnessed he could barely move.

The drone footage had caught it all, relaying it to the stunned ops suite.

'Get me SCO19,' Ant told the comms operator. 'This is

GD1, we have active shooters on the ground at the corner of Oxford Street and Regent Street, and at least one active sniper above ground.'

He was patched through to the Met's Specialist Firearms Command, whose sole duty was armed response. In a matter of minutes they would be on the scene in BMW X5 armed response vehicles. Each carrying a driver, one operational officer, and a navigator. All three carried Glock 17s and Tazer X26s. Even the driver. And each ARV had two MP5 carbines and two G36 assault rifles.

They knew what they were doing. The question was whether they could get there in time.

Back in Textile Place, Burleigh and the other members of the street team could hear screaming from down the road - a long wave of cries and shouts from hundreds of people now fleeing the murder scene.

'They're going to kill us all,' Burleigh said, still on his knees. 'They set me up. I thought I was meeting your director, Rebecca Fox!'

Street One grabbed Burleigh and pressed him against the wall to get him out of the open.

Street One shouted at Four and Five, 'What's going on back there?'

They'd taken a few steps back from the lane entrance, as commuters and tourists ran east along Oxford Street. Then two rifle shots rang out from above, knocking down Street Four and Five with a clean head shot on each.

Street One could tell from the way they fell that the shooter was up high. But he couldn't see a thing. He radioed, 'Where the hell is SCO19? They're picking us off one at a time.'

Burleigh leaned his forehead against the wall, one thought in his head: *this is how it's going to end.*

'Street One,' Rebecca said, 'We're running out of time. Ask Burleigh how he arranged the meet.'

As he relayed the question, Street Two emerged from behind the two dumpsters blocking the lane. She took aim at Street One and got off two quick shots into his forehead.

He fell straight back against the wall, dropping Burleigh's files on the ground.

Burleigh's face was somewhere between a grin and a grimace as Street Two stalked towards him. He knew he was done this time. Not like when he thought he was done fifteen years ago in Vienna, when he was subjected to a mock execution by his captors. And not like when he was staring down the barrel of a Beretta M9 in Berlin in eighty-eight.

This was different. This time there was no hope.

Street Two stood over him, aiming at his head. 'You're smiling.'

Burleigh looked over at Street One, noticing his radio had fallen out of the inside of his jacket.

'This is what it's come to,' Burleigh explained, as if he was just talking to Street Two.

Listening to the exchange, Rebecca held her arms out for continued silence in the ops suite.

Burleigh went on, 'Seventeen years. After everything I've given. What the hell could they ever pay you to make this worth it?'

'Enough,' Street Two replied, then looked behind her, wondering what Burleigh was glancing at. When she caught sight of the radio sticking out of Street One's jacket, she scowled as she realised what he was doing.

The next thing the ops suite heard was two suppressed gunshots going into Burleigh's forehead.

Street Two picked up the files on the ground, then took out an old Nokia 3310 - a 2007-era 'dumb' phone with no internet access. It could only do calls or texts. She slid the phone into Burleigh's coat pocket then walked quickly back onto Oxford Street.

She sent a text to her colleagues. '*Merchandise is secure.*'

5

Rebecca and Ant got a police escort to Textile Place through the chaos of Oxford Street, which was closed for nearly a mile around.

SCD-4 forensic investigators from the Met's Specialist Crime unit were already on the scene, tenting off the entire lane.

SCO19 had been in mobile units around Westminster, and arrived barely a minute after Street Two's escape. They were still on the ground, securing the crime scene.

'What's the final body count?' Ant asked, numb at the sight of his dead colleagues.

'Nine,' Rebecca answered. 'All our guys, plus Burleigh.'

'What's the story?'

'The press is being told it was related to an armed robbery. The Met's about to release a statement backing that.'

'There will be an enquiry,' Ant said. 'We're taking care of all CCTV footage of Burleigh and the street team.

Thames House is monitoring everything in the area.' Ant circled cagily around her, lowering his voice. 'Why did Burleigh think he was there to meet you?'

'You're not giving that any credence, are you? Dragging my name into this is obviously part of the setup.'

'It's hardly going to play well when Ghost Division's had a massive intelligence leak. Stacey Henshaw going rogue from the street team doesn't give us the whole picture.'

Rebecca pulled back. 'Are you suggesting I'm involved in this?'

Ant handed her a plastic evidence bag with a Nokia 3310 inside. 'That was in Burleigh's coat pocket.'

'I thought we had all his phones.'

'Apparently not.'

Rebecca asked, 'Have we run the numbers on it yet?'

Ant pressed buttons through the evidence bag, navigating to the phone's call log. He showed her the screen. 'This is the last call Burleigh received. From this morning. Thames House has just sent me tracking on the phone's location.'

'Where was it?'

'It's a payphone. Fifty yards from 24 St James.'

Rebecca could see what was happening. 'Ant, you know that I would never...I'm being framed. Stacey could have easily planted that on Burleigh after she shot him.'

'Yeah, *I* know that, but how are you going to convince Teddy King and Dominic Morecombe?'

'Just give me a minute,' Rebecca said, trying to clear her head.

'If you want...' Ant looked around. 'This phone can still disappear. It's bagged but it's not been-'

'No,' Rebecca replied. 'I won't do that.'

'Then you better prepare yourself for what's coming,' Ant told her.

6

38TH STREET, WASHINGTON, D.C. – FRIDAY 6.12PM

Two beat cops, Jason Ferragio and Mike Stoltz, were on the final hour of their foot patrol, only a few blocks away from Second District Station, when they took the call for a 'residential four five nine Sierra' - a silent burglar alarm going off. Burglaries weren't common in the early evening: there was a higher risk of people arriving back from work, or making dinner. Most burglaries take place between ten a.m. and three p.m., and take an average of ten minutes. Catching a burglar in the act would be a nice collar for two eager young patrol officers looking to get onto the next pay grade as soon as possible.

The property in question was a four-bedroom detached on 38th Street, with a 'For sale' sign pitched on the front lawn which was slightly overgrown. Although an untended lawn drew attention to a potentially empty property, the owners weren't worried: there was nothing to steal inside. The whole house was an empty shell.

Still, for their own peace of mind, they had paid for an alarm company that was linked to the local Alarm

Receiving Centre for D.C. police, opting for a silent alarm to spare their neighbours any potential false activations.

It was growing dark already, but most of 38th Street was already in shadow, the sidewalks and most of the driveways and gardens covered by low-hanging camperdown elms and golden curls willow trees.

When the cops reached the property, Stoltz checked the front door – locked – while Ferragio went to the back. Which was open.

Stoltz couldn't hear it from the front. A 'thwift' sound. Like a burst of highly compressed air.

Gaspar, hiding in the kitchen and dressed head to toe in black – wearing latex gloves - caught Ferragio's falling body before it hit the bare wooden floorboards, and guided him silently down.

Stoltz called out his partner's name as he crept towards the back garden, his radio buzzing with static.

The back door was flapping open a few inches.

Stoltz got on his radio. 'Jase? What's your location?'

He heard Ferragio's radio inside, but no response.

That was as Gaspar intended.

He needed to draw Stoltz inside for the plan to work.

Stoltz repeated, 'Jase?' He drew his weapon, keeping it trained low at the ground, as he slowly entered the kitchen area.

When Stoltz saw the faint outline of a body on the ground he knew he was in trouble. He whipped around with his gun but it was too late.

Gaspar was using a Walther P22 with a SilencerCo Sparrow suppressor, and subsonic ammunition – eliminating the loud crack a bullet makes as it breaks the sound barrier. The suppressor also, crucially, reduced the muzzle flash which, in the growing gloom outside, could have been noticeable even to a neighbour's peripheral vision.

There was one 'thwift' as the first bullet hit Stoltz's forehead, then another in almost exactly the same spot.

Gaspar didn't bother catching Stoltz.

He took Ferragio's radio and quickly made his way out the back door.

The next stage required some misdirection.

He removed his Lycra facemask as he would have to be out in the open for a minute or two. Once he reached 39th Street, he waited until he was under adequate cover in the copse behind the tennis courts. He had already checked in advance that there were no floodlights there. As freezing as it was, and given what was at stake, a detail like that couldn't be left to chance.

A good assassin bases plans on what's most likely.

A brilliant assassin bases plans on what's certain.

He removed the suppressor from the gun and pocketed it. He would be needing it again in a few minutes.

He swapped out the subsonic ammo for regular rounds, then got on Ferragio's radio. After waiting to hear the buzz of dispatch online at the other end, he fired two shots up between the trees.

The sound cracked through the evening sky, echoing all around. It was more than loud enough to be heard by anyone in the Second District police station just one hundred metres away.

Gaspar, channelling as much panic and terror as he could, shouted into the radio in his best American accent, 'This is Officer Ferragio. Code thirty! Shots fired at twenty-one ninety, thirty-eighth street. I got an officer down. Repeat officer down with multiple GSWs.'

Gaspar ran through the woods, behind the vacant tennis courts, conveniently allowing him to simulate heavy breathing and a chase in progress with a suspect. He had to fight his natural French accent, but in the circumstances it was more than good enough.

While he spoke, he loaded the subsonic ammo back into his gun.

'Suspect is a BMJ, early twenties, on foot. Headed east towards Woodley Road...'

The diversion would make the next part of Gaspar's plan easier. But only marginally less bloody.

Two minutes earlier

It was completely dark by the time Novak and Stella reached the Second District's police headquarters on Idaho Avenue. Novak checked his watch. They were five minutes early for Shapiro.

It was a relatively small HQ as the city had been broken up into seven police districts. The Second was one of the easier to work, taking in luxurious areas like Wesley Heights, where property regularly sold for eight or nine figures. The most common offence they had to deal with was auto theft.

But their comfort was about to be rudely disrupted.

The desk sergeant sat alone in the reception area, diligently going about his paperwork.

Novak and Stella were halfway across the lobby when two gunshots went off outside. They whipped around, thinking that they sounded very close by.

The desk sergeant came out from behind the desk with his weapon drawn. 'Get back, please,' he told them, waving them away from the entrance. It was clear from the sergeant's demeanour and darting looks around that he wasn't entirely sure what the situation was.

Then what seemed like the entire station's armed personnel came charging down the stairs.

When a call comes in for an officer down with multiple gunshot wounds - who happens to be reachable on foot in around a minute - word gets around a station pretty damn quick.

'Shots fired,' a detective shouted to the desk sergeant. He threw off the mustard-stained napkin he had tucked into his shirt collar. 'Black male, early twenties. He's only out on Woodley Road...'

The desk sergeant holstered his weapon and retreated to his desk. He grabbed a radio to hear the commentary from his colleagues out in the street. Within thirty seconds there were three separate calls of apprehending the suspect – three entirely innocent, young black men.

Agent Dave Shapiro had nearly had a heart attack as he approached the station and saw over a dozen cops with their guns out running past him.

'What the hell is going on?' he asked Novak when he reached the station lobby.

'Someone hit a cop,' Novak replied.

'Should we come back later?' asked Stella.

Shapiro starting saying, 'I don't-'

All the lights in reception went out. Including the short candle lights lining the pathway outside the station.

The heating overhead went off with a diminishing whimper.

'Everyone stay calm,' the desk sergeant said, 'nobody move.'

Shapiro held his badge up. 'Sergeant, I'm Agent Dave Shapiro, FBI. Are your phones out too?'

The sergeant tapped on the phone plunger. 'Yeah. There's nothing.'

Shapiro mumbled, 'Shit.'

It was loud enough for Novak and Mitchell to hear, and the first indication that something far more dangerous was going on.

It was one thing having the electricity go out. But the phone lines too, coupled with the failure of the backup generator, was more suspicious.

Shapiro said, 'OK, everyone stay calm. And stay low.' He reached under his coat for his service weapon.

The next sound was a 'thwift-thwift' of two silenced bullets.

Novak and Mitchell's eyes had adjusted enough to the light to make out the silhouette of Shapiro being thrown backwards. He'd taken two shots in the chest from someone outside the open front door.

Gaspar was much closer for the next shots - inside the building now – and landed two in the desk sergeant's head.

The sergeant fell straight to the ground like his knees had collapsed on him. Novak grabbed Stella out the way, pulling her behind the long leather banquette in reception.

Somewhere through the lobby there were soft-soled running steps.

A lieutenant appeared near the top of the stairs, calling out, 'Hey, Joe, are your phones-'

Before Novak or Stella could shout a warning there was another 'thwift' sound. The lieutenant tumbled down several steps, landing on his back, legs pointing back up the stairs.

Stella told herself to calm down, to breathe, but all of her senses were telling her that that was impossible. In a flash, all she could see in her mind was the image of Jonathan Gale being shot in the middle of the road in London back in December. As her chest thumped, she felt herself tumbling back into that nightmare.

Upstairs, there were gunshots from regular police issue .40 calibre Glock 22s, but the firing didn't last long. Gaspar was taking down targets with ease, stalking from room to room.

Stella eyed the front door. 'We should run for it,' she whispered. 'While he's upstairs.'

Novak didn't want to go anywhere. 'As long as we don't get in his way...he didn't see us.'

'We can't sit here and just hope to not die.'

Novak slid to one side and stole a look around the banquette, seeing Shapiro lying on his back, motionless.

He stared up to the top of the stairs, seeing nothing and hearing nothing. He waved Stella towards him at the end of the banquette.

Knowing they'd slow her down, Stella slid off her boots and held onto them.

The coast was still clear.

Novak clambered to his feet, but pushed off too hard with his back foot, which immediately slid out. Stella managed to stay on her feet and pulled Novak back up. Both tried to stay focussed on the front doors as they ran.

When they got outside there were police sirens going off everywhere around a two-block radius.

Upstairs, the cops were still trying to fight back against Gaspar, sending out white flashes like strobe lights all across the second floor, that were visible from the sidewalk.

With nowhere else to go, Novak and Stella ran towards a low wall at the front of the building. Stella dropped one of her boots but didn't even think about stopping for it.

Fearing the shooter might emerge at any moment, they both vaulted the wall, not knowing there was a sharp downslope on the other side, and a drop of around ten feet.

They both landed awkwardly on a worn patch of bare grass that the freezing temperatures had turned rock hard. They huddled together with their backs against the wall, as what seemed like endless gunshots went off.

Some of the detectives and beat cops who had run out to answer the call from Ferragio's radio had started to run back to the station. They'd received desperate messages about a shooter working his way up the stairs, clinically dispatching anyone who got in his way.

One of the cops pointed his gun at Novak and Stella for a moment, then saw their hands in the air and their looks of terror.

'I think he's still inside,' Novak said.

SWAT, which had been dispatched from the Capitol, poured into the building, doing a floor by floor sweep.

The gunshots finally relented.

It was over.

They had survived.

But Gaspar was gone.

A back-up generator kicked in, lighting up the lobby first, then the rest of the station. The bright tube lighting made the carnage upstairs all the more unbearable, high-lighting every drop of blood on the magnolia floor.

With all the sirens out front, no one had heard a patrol car in the back parking lot speeding out onto Newark Street with its lights and siren going. It would be nearly ten minutes before anyone even realised it was gone.

The car would be found abandoned in a side road in Georgetown. By which point Gaspar was making his way across the city on foot, now wearing a reversible gilet from his backpack, round glasses, and looking every bit like a casual student.

When the medics had finished checking them over, Novak and Stella stepped off the back of one of the many ambulances on Idaho Avenue.

A cop handed Stella the boot she'd dropped, and had still forgotten about until that moment.

News crews were everywhere, and there were numerous choppers overhead. The survivors looked shattered. Uniform and detectives gathered together on the front lawn. There were some barely hidden tears from a few.

'How many people are dead in there?' Stella asked an EMT.

'We got seven so far,' they replied. 'About a dozen more wounded.'

Novak shuffled his blanket off his shoulders.

'It's freezing out here, Novak,' she said, breath steaming in the air.

'I'm fine,' he said.

A detective, one of the lucky ones to have left the station before Gaspar's attack, held out two Styrofoam cups of coffee to Novak and Stella. 'I thought you guys could do with some heat,' he said.

Apart from some scrapes on her legs from the wall

jump, Stella had emerged pretty unscathed. Novak had cut his head during the wall jump, and was holding a bandage to his temple.

'Thanks,' Novak said.

Stella asked the detective, 'Is there any MO? That seemed pretty clinical and professional to me.'

'It sure was,' the detective agreed. 'He cut everything before entering. We even lost the camera feeds, and they run off a backup supply. This guy knew what he was doing.'

Novak said, 'This wasn't a guy with a grudge and a shotgun trying to take out as many cops as he could. It was a mission. This guy had training.'

The detective said, 'This is off the record. But it looks like the evidence room was the target.'

'The evidence room?' said Novak.

'The only people hit were on the route to the evidence room. The gunman went past bags of impounded heroin and piles of cash.'

'What did he take?' asked Stella.

Novak already knew what he was going to say. 'An evidence bag removed from the scene of Andrei Rublov's homicide this morning.'

'Yeah,' the detective squinted, 'how did you know that?'

Novak's phone started ringing. Seeing Diane's name on the caller ID, he turned away quickly to answer. 'Diane? What's going on?'

The detective turned his attention to Stella. 'How did he know that...'

Diane was trying to speak but Novak just talked over her.

'Has Talya called yet?' he asked.

'My God, Tom,' Diane said. 'I just got your message. Are either of you hurt?'

'We're fine,' he said, taking away the bandage from his head. He covered the mouthpiece while an ambulance sped past with its siren going. 'Is there anything from your guy in Moscow yet?'

Diane paused. 'He's at Natalya's now, Tom.'

Before she could continue, Novak sighed in relief. 'Ask him to tell her I-'

'Wait, Tom...' Diane said. 'He couldn't get through because of a police barricade. He got there as fast as he could. The police were barely there a few minutes ahead of him.' She took a breath. 'It was too late. She had already been...She's dead, Tom.'

'How did it happen?' he asked.

Diane wasn't sure how much to give away.

'How did she die, Diane?'

Stella was able to hear, and started walking towards him.

Diane said, 'She was shot as she was leaving her apartment.'

When Novak turned, Stella had removed the blanket from her shoulders.

'We're not stopping, Diane,' Novak said. 'Get me on the next flight to Moscow.'

Stella pointed back and forth at her and Novak, mouthing, 'Us.'

7

THE EASTSIDE OF MOSCOW – SATURDAY, 10.17AM

Stella braced herself against the cold. Even though she and Novak were in the back of a taxi she could still see her breath. The cold had hit them the second they cleared the doors of the Aeroflot 747 from JFK, eliciting groans and startled chuckles from the passengers who had never experienced Moscow in March.

Trying to keep Novak distracted, Stella jested, 'I thought I knew what cold was after a winter in the north of Scotland. That was the Caribbean compared to this.' She corrected herself, saying it the American way. 'Sorry, I mean the Ca-*rib*-bean.' She thought that would at least ignite a smile in him.

Novak pursed his lips then went back to looking out the window.

The taxi made its way along a narrow road on the edge of the Sokolinaya Gora district on the Eastside of Moscow, lined with high-rises and warehouses, all claustrophobically close to the road.

The traffic system was as anarchic as Novak remembered it. There always seemed to be a horn being blasted somewhere.

Novak had spent much of the ten-hour flight wondering how he would feel being back in the city again. Now he was there, he hated it. When he'd first come to Moscow he could sense the history on every street corner. The city that had once seemed vast and romantically decadent now felt small and seedy. He'd been helplessly naïve on his first visit. He knew too much about the inner workings and corruption of Moscow now.

Stella figured Novak needed to actually talk about Natalya for a while, rather than avoiding it. She said, 'You haven't told me how you met Natalya. Russia Now only started broadcasting back in two thousand and five. I was trying to figure out how your paths crossed.'

'Before RN she was a foreign affairs correspondent for *Rossiyskaya Gazeta*.'

Stella knew it well from her time in foreign affairs in London. The *Gazeta* was one of the more transparently pro-Kremlin newspapers.

Novak went on, 'We met in Sevastopol where we were covering the Russia-Ukraine conflict. I'd been with *Republic* a few years and was striking out more on my own. One night she let me use her satellite phone to call New York, and we got talking. I told her how the Russian military had black-balled me. Then on her last night, Talya passed on an interview with a prominent Russian general and gave it to me.' Novak shook his head wistfully at the memory. 'Her producer nearly sacked her for it. When I got back to New York we started emailing each other. Then a few months later Diane set me up at her friend's desk at CNN's Moscow bureau. I told Talya I was in the city and she showed me around, the places to go, places to avoid. Taught me Russian. Before I knew it we were in a relationship.'

Stella said tentatively, 'Diane said you guys were engaged. It must have been pretty serious.'

'Saul Bellow once said, when two people say they love each other, there's always one person who means it more. With Talya and me, I was always the one who meant it more. Deep down I think I knew it was never going to work.'

Stella asked, 'What went wrong?'

He took a long breath. 'She told me she had a source who was leaking internal memos on corruption within the interior ministry. Civil servants paying for hookers and coke with public money, that kind of thing. When she took the story to her editor he didn't believe her and demanded she give up the name of her source. She did. And within twenty-four hours the source had hung himself in his jail cell. Two days after that the source's lawyer happened to die of a heart attack while out running.'

'I think I remember that,' Stella said.

'There's an old communist proverb: there is no difference between the person who loads the gun, and the one who fires it. The way Talya saw it, she put more lives in danger by trying to change things than by toeing the party line.' He shook his head despondently. 'She wasn't the same after that. *We* weren't the same after that. It was more important to her to stay alive than tell the truth. Then Russia Now came calling, offering her the biggest salary of her career. She knew what she was signing up for: everyone knows what Russia Now is like. We argued about it, then it was over.'

'What did you say to her?'

Novak looked sheepish. 'I might have said something along the lines of she was selling her soul to protect murderers and thugs, and that if Joseph Goebbels were alive he would have taken a job at Russia Now.'

Yeah, Stella thought, *that sounds like him.*

'That was four years ago.'

The headquarters of Russia Now, the most popular TV news network in the country, was set behind a copse of trees just off the main road in Perovo district on the eastside of Moscow.

Funded entirely by the Russian government, it claimed to provide "a fair and balanced Russian viewpoint on global events." But RN – as it was also known – had been widely accused of spreading disinformation, even by some of its former reporters. RN's editor-in-chief, Viktor Karpov, had proudly compared the network to the Russian army, waging a war against "the Western propaganda machine".

But RN was no longer just a Russian enterprise. It now had English, Spanish, and Arabic-language channels, which had become a popular platform for fringe political figures. Especially in the U.K., where it had attracted mostly right-wing commentators. There had even been tentative talk of branching into America.

Karpov was believed to have personally come up with RN's slogan: "Face the facts."

. . .

Novak and Stella's taxi pulled into RN's car park. While the driver calculated the fare, Novak noticed a gleaming Mercedes that had double-parked outside the main doors. A cop was talking to the driver, who was wearing a black suit and smoking a cigarette. The driver slid a five-thousand rouble note into the cop's hand.

It was the same grift Moscow cops had been running for years: anytime they saw a flash car anywhere, they'd pull them over and see what minor traffic violation they could nail the driver for. If there wasn't any immediately obvious violation, they'd just put their foot on one of the tyres and tell them their pressure was too low, and issue an on-the-spot fine. It was all part of the grift of Moscow - everyone in every line of work had one, or knew of one.

The taxi driver turned off the meter. In gruff English he said, 'One thousand.'

Novak took out five hundred roubles and handed it to the driver.

He looked at it in disgust then snapped at Novak, this time in Russian, '*Are you deaf?*' He wrote the number in the air with his finger as he spoke. '*One thousand.*'

Novak knew the driver thought he could play them as he and Stella had been talking in English the whole time.

'*Come now, my friend,*' Novak said in flawless Russian. '*Don't bullshit me. The going rate from the airport to here is never more than three-fifty, four hundred tops. Consider the extra fifty your tip.*'

The driver took the money with a grumble. '*Bloody American.*'

In the lobby there were three smiling blonde receptionists, all in their late twenties. They were stick-thin - bordering on unwell - wearing grey trouser suits and white shirts with the first three buttons open. They had all been discovered by the same modelling agency a decade ago, but that was a long time in modelling. By twenty-five, most models in Russia were practically on the scrapheap. There was always a fresh batch to be found on the streets of Voronezh or further afield in Almaty, Kazakhstan. It wasn't uncommon for girls to be found there then end up on catwalks in Milan or Paris a few weeks later. For the older ones, many had to resort to hanging out in the many night-clubs that Moscow's wealthy, older men frequented.

Novak said to the one receptionist not on the phone, '*I'm looking for Viktor Karpov.*'

After consulting a diary in front of her she shook her head dismally. '*I'm sorry. Mr Karpov is in a meeting until-*'

Then a man coming through reception stopped, imme-diately recognising Novak.

'Tom,' he said. He had a crestfallen expression and looked like he had slept – albeit briefly – in his horribly creased clothes. 'Have you heard?'

Novak went over to the man and hugged him. 'I heard. I'm sorry, Aleksandr.'

He nodded, trying to hold back tears.

Novak held his arm out towards Stella. 'Aleksandr, this is Stella Mitchell. My partner at *The Republic.*'

Aleksandr shook Stella's hand. 'Of course. A pleasure to meet you. Sorry for my English. It's been a while since I last used.'

'It's better than my Russian,' Stella replied.

Aleksandr led the way upstairs. 'First Andrei and now Natalya. Who could do such things?'

Novak glanced up the stairs. 'Is Viktor here? We need to see him.'

Aleksandr hesitated. 'Now might not be a good time. The minister is here.'

'Minister?'

Aleksandr was sure to lower his voice. 'Minister Ivanov.'

'Is he here in his capacity as General of Police or Minister of the Interior?'

Aleksandr sounded evasive. 'I'm not sure. Viktor's always meeting ministers these days.'

From the look of the newsroom floor it was clear that the government was ploughing plenty of money into RN. Every desk, even for junior copywriters, had top of the line, highest-spec iMac Pros. The chairs were ergonomic and the place generally felt like it belonged to the headquarters of a Silicon Valley tech firm rather than a TV news network.

'That's the great thing about state sponsorship,' Novak whispered to Stella. 'It comes with great office equipment.'

The whole place felt strange to Stella. She'd never been in a newsroom so devoid of energy or grit or fire. It looked more like data entry than journalism. Everyone cranking out their two-thousand words for the day on whatever the government desired.

Stella muttered, 'It's like, if the Kremlin is a drug cartel, then these guys are the dealers on the street.'

'That's about the sum of it,' replied Novak.

The editorial offices all had glass walls, including Viktor Karpov's. A man in a black suit with a shaved head stood outside it. He held his hands in front of him in the familiar pose of a bodyguard. He looked like he threw trees around in his spare time.

Inside the office, a man in his sixties sat across from Viktor, smoking a cigar.

At that moment Viktor looked out across the newsroom.

When he noticed Novak – eyes lingering for a moment while he placed him – he went to the blinds and snapped them shut.

Aleksandr took Novak and Stella to Natalya's office, glass-walled like all the others.

'I see she hadn't changed much since I last saw her,' Novak remarked. There were piles of notes and papers everywhere on Natalya's desk, in no discernible order. How she had made any sense of it was a mystery.

On the entire side of one wall was an enormous Russian flag.

'Very patriotic of her,' Stella remarked.

Pens were still on her desk. Notes written out about meetings she would have had that day. A half-finished cup of coffee. All as if she might return at any moment.

Aleksandr didn't know what to do with himself. He stood in the centre of the room with folded arms, too uncomfortable to look too closely at anything. 'It will need to get cleaned away eventually, but the police have asked us not to remove anything.'

Stella was struggling to see anything of relevance without knowing Russian. It all looked very normal to her, though she couldn't fathom working in such a chaotic mess.

Novak stood over her desk, looking for clues. 'Did she say anything to you? About being in any danger?'

It seemed to take Aleksandr by surprise. 'No. She never said anything to me. I saw her Thursday night. No problem.'

'What was she working on recently?' asked Stella.

'The usual,' Aleksandr said. 'She had been doing some political profiles.' He looked out at the newsroom, then closed the door slightly. 'They were, how you say it...puff pieces. Public relations jobs. Ministers, they dress in nice suits, go and shake hands with some workers, then they sit down with Talya and talk about the need for reform and political transparency. The same they have been saying since Yeltsin.'

'Who was the next profile on?' asked Stella.

Aleksandr looked worriedly towards Karpov's office. 'It doesn't look good. Me talking to you here.'

'It's just us, Alek,' Novak insisted.

Aleksandr swore under his breath, then whispered, 'Ivanov.' He moved towards the door but Novak stopped him, putting his arm across him.

A few reporters looked over in their direction.

Novak asked, 'Did she say anything about her research?'

Aleksandr just wanted out of the room now. He spoke more quickly. 'Talya didn't say anything, and no one was supposed to know. But she and Andrei were working on something. Talya did what she was told. But Andrei...he was more difficult. Viktor thought he pushed too hard. Asked too many tough questions.'

Novak asked, 'What was he doing in Washington?'

'Officially, he was writing about candidates for the next U.S. Presidential elections. Before he left, he and Talya were always in each other's offices. Mostly late at night after Viktor was gone. I tried to find out what they were working on, but she wouldn't tell me. Tom, we both knew Talya wasn't a crusader. Why would someone do this to her?'

Novak asked, 'Was she taken to the European Medical Centre or GMS?'

'The Central Clinic,' Aleksandr said.

'Why would they take her there?'

Stella asked Novak, 'Is that strange?'

'It's the most exclusive and expensive hospital in Moscow. It's open to anyone, but at outrageous cost. It's where they take politicians and celebrities.'

Aleksandr shook his head. 'I also think this was strange.'

Novak said to Stella, 'We'll never get in there. They guard that place like a prison. Anyone other than close relatives would struggle to get in.'

Ivanov's bodyguard made a slight move towards Karpov's door.

Aleksandr said, 'We need to go.'

Novak slid a business card into Aleksandr's pocket. 'That has my OTR address on it. It's completely secure. You can message me anytime.'

'OK,' he replied. 'I'll talk to Viktor about seeing you. I didn't expect him to be in today.'

'Why's that?'

Aleksandr reacted like he'd said something he shouldn't have. 'Did you not... Of course.'

Novak had a horrible feeling. 'What is it?'

'Natalya and Viktor... They were together.'

As they descended the stairs, Stella said to Novak, 'You were a little rough with him, don't you think.'

He had a dark expression on his face. Unrepentant. 'We're working, Stel.'

'Yeah, which is why you should have waited for a quieter moment. Now everyone in that office knows he was talking to us.'

'No one has a clue what he told us.'

'That's the point, Novak. You didn't give him a chance

for deniability. As far as anyone else is concerned, he could have been in there with us singing "The Star Spangled Banner".'

If it was anyone else, Novak would have kept arguing, but he knew Stella was in the right. 'It looks pretty clear to me: Talya does research on Ivanov, finds out something she shouldn't have, then someone is sent to kill her. If you throw Viktor into the mix-'

'Whoa, let's slow down a bit...'

'If we were in any other city, Stel, I'd call myself para-noid. But this isn't any other city.'

'For all we know Ivanov is there giving a personal briefing to Viktor about the police report on Natalya's murder. Which, you know, given they were together shouldn't be that surprising: a little gesture from a political ally. You're jumping straight to government conspiracies.' She paused. 'Can I ask you something?'

Novak sighed. 'No, this is *not* about Viktor and Talya being involved.'

Stella thought it best to drop it.

Novak was away in his own world, having a conversa-tion with himself. 'This thing with her and Andrei doesn't feel right. Andrei's been a loose cannon for years. I'm amazed he's lasted as long as he has. If he did get onto a story, of all the people to bring in why would it be Talya?'

They were about to exit the lobby when one of the receptionists called out, 'Mr Novak!' She held a small note up and brought it over. She said, 'Mr Karpov asked me to give you this.'

Novak opened the note then smiled. He passed the note to Stella.

'*Talya's place. One hour.*'

'What do you think?' asked Stella.

'I'll message Diane to tell her where we're going,' he replied, taking out his phone. 'In case we happen to disappear. I didn't trust Viktor back then, I certainly don't trust him now.'

8

———

The Meshchansky district of Moscow housed some of the city's most iconic architecture. Not least the Kremlin and its fortified walls, St Basil's Cathedral with its famous coned spires, and the Bolshoi Theatre. Much more significant for Novak and Stella was a few streets back from Lubyanka Square, up a tight road with three-storey apartment blocks on either side. 7 *Milyutinskiy Pereulok*: Natalya's home address.

The taxi driver dropped them at the end of the street. There was no police tape marking off Natalya's front door. In fact, there was no indication that anything at all had taken place the day before let alone a murder.

Novak had some of the local news reports on his phone. As he scrolled through them, he walked through the positions he imagined Natalya would have, starting at her front door. 'According to an eyewitness, Natalya came out of here in a hurry. Then a man ran past the eyewitness – so running up behind Natalya - then shot her from a metre away. The man ran to the end of the street there, and turned right towards Lubyanka Square.'

Stella looked up around the balconies and windows. 'No CCTV.'

Novak said to himself, 'He was on foot...'

'What are you thinking?'

'These are narrow streets...' Novak quickened his pace, walking to the end of the road. 'Why didn't he just shoot her from inside a car? It's easier. Safer.'

Stella jogged to catch up.

He stopped at the T-junction at the join of the main road. It had been a while, but he got his bearings. The building he had in mind couldn't be seen from their position, so Novak went into Apple Maps on his phone. Unlike Google, Apple didn't keep histories of map searches, and added random map fragments to routes saved on their servers, so no one could ever know who searched for what, or where someone was going.

He zoomed in from their location and showed Stella the phone screen. 'Look what's only nine hundred metres away.' He tapped on the image preview.

It was a huge Neo-Baroque building with a dark-yellow façade.

'The Lubyanka Building,' Novak said. 'The former headquarters of the KGB, now the FSB. The Russian security services.'

Stella didn't look convinced. 'You're reaching,' she said. 'From this spot you could just as easily say the shooter was headed for the St Regis hotel. Or how about any of the five metro stations. He could have been out of the city in fifteen minutes.'

'You don't understand the mentality of these people,

Stella. They're a glorified state police. They have a budget twice that of the CIA and most of that is spent on domestic espionage. Killing a reporter is nothing to them. Hell, an agent could have shot Natalya here and just walked back to Lubyanka.'

A green Jaguar slowly entered Natalya's street. The driver kept the engine running as it pulled up outside Natalya's house.

Stella turned around. 'Is that him?'

'That's him,' Novak said.

A man with medium-length pushed-back silver hair and a smart suit got out the back of the car. He looked out of place for the neighbourhood. Too sharp. Too slick. The landmarks nearby might have been famous but the housing was cheap.

'Here we go,' said Novak. 'I'm gonna have to find a way to be civil to this guy.'

'Try,' Stella urged him. 'Try hard.'

Viktor waited for them at the front door. His English was faultless. 'Tom Novak. It's been a long time.'

Novak folded his arms as a defence, in case Viktor wanted to shake hands for any reason. 'I'm sorry about Talya,' he said.

'Yes...It was a terrible shock.' Viktor looked down at his hands and turned them over. 'I don't think it has hit me yet.'

'It's hit me.'

'We...' Viktor stopped himself. 'I have to get used to saying things in the past tense with Talya now: we were divorced. It had been coming for a while. We wanted different things. But the hospital wouldn't even let me see

her. Only immediate family, they told me.' His eyes started
to fill.

Novak understood how humiliating that was for a man
of Viktor's standing in Moscow.

Viktor composed himself. 'Shall we go up?'

On the way up the stairs, Stella realised Novak wasn't
about to offer introductions. 'I'm sorry for your loss, Mr
Karpov. I'm-'

Viktor said, 'I appreciate your humility, Ms Mitchell,
but I know who you are.'

While Viktor unlocked Natalya's front door, Novak
asked, 'You still have a key?'

'A spare,' Viktor said. 'For emergencies.'

Upon entering the flat the feel of the place all came
rushing back to Novak. The decor was still the same, the
furniture, the wallpaper.

A jacket Natalya was wearing in a photo was still
hanging from the wooden stand in the hallway. Viktor
seemed to pause at it, then guided Novak and Stella to the
living room.

Viktor was tall and broad-shouldered. An intimidating
presence to be in a relatively small room with. It was easy to
imagine him being forceful in editorial meetings – a man
used to getting his own way. His face still had a faint tan
from a holiday at the turn of the year.

Novak sat beside Stella on the sofa. He felt odd not
sitting in his usual spot across the room. He couldn't work
out how Viktor and Natalya ended up married. When
Novak was on the scene, Viktor had been just another sube-
ditor like Natalya. He'd always shown a keen desire to get
on, and was adept at office politics, which in a Russian news
agency was especially complex. He'd clearly honed those

skills, or there would be no way of making it to editor-in-chief so quickly.

'You didn't want the minister to see you talking to me,' Novak said.

Viktor stood at the bar, making three vodkas. 'A lot of what I do is about appearances. Ivanov's a private man. He came to offer his condolences.'

Stella asked, 'Did he say if the police have any leads?'

'A witness said it looked like some street kid, but I don't buy it. It wasn't a robbery. It was an assassination. Ivanov assures me he has his best men on it.'

Novak asked, 'Do you have any idea who might be responsible?'

Viktor handed them their vodkas. 'Isn't it obvious? This was a political act against a prominent journalist designed to undermine our democracy. It's an attack on RN's values.'

'What exactly are RN's values?' asked Stella.

'We believe in sovereign democracy. That the one-party system makes for a stronger Russia, which means more material wealth and greater freedoms.'

Novak nodded along. It was a classic case of what Novak called 'word soup', which politicians were especially talented at. Words and phrases that sounded fine on their own, but became meaningless when put together.

Novak said, 'You know, I get very nervous when I hear qualifiers put before democracy: managed democracy; people's democracy; socialist democracy. It seems to me the more words you put in front of democracy the less it ends up looking like it. Democracy in Russia is a fiction.'

Viktor retorted, 'Democracy in Russia is under attack from people like you. I thank God Talya got away from you when she did.'

'Yeah, things worked out really well for her.'

Normally Stella would have tried to intervene, but she didn't want to take Novak's legs away from him in front of Viktor. She had a feeling they were on a hiding to nothing with him anyway.

Novak stayed on the attack. 'Talya contacted me yesterday morning. She said she was in fear for her life because of a story she was working on. Is that why you asked me to come here? Is there something I should know about?'

'It's complicated...' Viktor took a drink. 'She'd been working with Andrei, the mad fool. He never knew the half of what I shielded him from. He had some crazy notions once in a while, but he was an experienced reporter. And he was great for ratings. I thought it would be good for Natalya to work with him a while.'

Stella decided it was time to find out how honest Viktor was willing to be with them, and that she might be the one he preferred to be honest with. 'Viktor, what was Talya researching? Was it something on Ivanov?'

Viktor finished his drink, giving him an excuse to leave his chair. 'You didn't hear this from me,' he said, pouring another vodka. 'But Talya told me last week that something came up in her research.'

'About Ivanov?'

Viktor didn't even want to confirm verbally. He just nodded. 'She didn't go into specifics. It concerned a file that Andrei had. A dossier.'

'A dossier on who?' asked Stella.

'I tried to find out,' Viktor replied. 'But she wouldn't tell me. She said she didn't want to put me at risk. She wouldn't even work on it in the office.'

'Where would she go?'

'An office across town somewhere.' Viktor pouted. 'She said it was safer for me if she didn't tell me.'

Novak made a move to get up, which took Stella off guard.

'Are we going?' she asked.

Novak said, 'We're wasting our time. He doesn't know anything.'

Something about Novak's abruptness spurred Viktor into a sudden admission. 'I lied before,' he said.

Novak stopped at the living room door.

'We didn't just grow apart. She realised she didn't love me as much as she loved you.'

Novak didn't know what to say.

Viktor said, 'Find the people who did this, Tom. You might be her only hope for justice.'

Novak strode towards the main road, hunting for a taxi.

Stella called after him. 'Novak! Where are we going? And why the hell did we just run out of there?'

'I know something Viktor doesn't.'

'You can't lash out like that, Novak. I know why you did it but-'

'I know where Talya's secret office was. And I don't want him to know that. I wanted him thinking we left there with nothing.'

'But we didn't, did we. Think about it. He admitted there was something about Natalya's Ivanov story, and he confirmed she was after Andrei's dossier. We gave him nothing. He gave us nearly everything. Why?'

Novak didn't have an answer. He just shook his head.

'OK, that's not a good explanation. This is a guy who's helping the Kremlin with public relations.'

Novak threw his arm out at a taxi on the other side of the road. 'I'm not slowing down now that we've got the upper hand on him.' He dashed over the road.

Stella struggled to keep up with him, holding her hand out at oncoming traffic as she followed him.

Novak ducked inside the taxi and told the driver, '*Kapotnya.*'

The driver set off, muttering, '*It'll cost you an extra two thousand roubles to get to that shithole. In advance. Some kids smashed one of my windows last time I drove through there.*'

Novak handed him three thousand.

The driver shouted something to them through the perspex divider.

Stella hated not understanding what was happening. 'What did he say?' she asked.

Novak reached over her and pushed down the door lock on her side and then his.

'He said we should lock the doors in case someone tries to carjack us.'

'That doesn't happen in Moscow, does it?' asked Stella.

'It does in Kapotnya,' Novak warned her. 'It's the most dangerous district in Moscow.'

9

DOWNING STREET - SATURDAY, 6.43AM

It was early for tourists to be congregated at the front security gates of Downing Street, cameras snapping in the
direction of Number Ten's famous black door which was
still shrouded by scaffolding.

The tourists were mostly from the Far East. Jetlagged
from their cruel time difference with the U.K., they had
taken to the streets early – enjoying the rare peace around
Whitehall.

It didn't last.

Prime Minister Angela Curtis was getting into her
armoured, bombproof Jaguar XJ Sentinel from the
entrance to 12 Downing Street, almost out of sight – unlike
Number Ten, which was visible from the main road at
Whitehall.

The retractable roadblock disappeared into the street,
then two armed Parliamentary and Diplomatic Protection
officers opened the black gates leading out of Downing
Street.

The tourists taking photos were startled by sudden shouts of 'Get back!' from the PDP officers.

When someone holding an MP5A3 semi-automatic carbine shouts at you, it doesn't entirely matter if you know the language or not.

The tourists backed away from the gates.

Once the path was clear, two motorcycle outriders went ahead to halt what little traffic there was.

The PM's Jaguar made the turn onto Whitehall at speed, followed closely behind by a Specialist Operations unit in an unmarked black Range Rover, then a people carrier with an emergency medical team inside.

This was what Angela Curtis had come to think of as her 'low key' escort.

That morning, St James's Park was unusually busy with joggers going up and down Birdcage Walk. Except they all had in clear ear-pieces, and were keeping close tabs on anyone else around.

The PM's convoy pulled up at a quiet spot on the road, then Angela Curtis got out with the rest of her bodyguards. After just a few shakes of each leg, she broke out into a run. One thing about protection detail for the Prime Minister: they were much happier when she did her stretches and warm ups in Number Ten's back garden.

After a minute of running alongside the lake, Curtis was joined by Rebecca Fox as planned.

Curtis was in all black with a cap pulled down low. Her protection noticed that her pace was faster than usual.

'Good morning, Prime Minister,' Rebecca said, trying to mask that she was losing breath already.

The conversation would have been hard enough sitting

down at a table, let alone taking place at ninety-five beats per minute in a freezing cold park at dawn.

Curtis said, 'Roger Milton is back at Number Ten, drafting a statement condemning the brutal violence that took place on Oxford Street last night as a result of an armed robbery. We've cleaned up the mess at Textile Place too.'

'I don't know what to say,' Rebecca confessed. She had never seen Curtis so mad.

'What the *hell*, Rebecca. We lost Burleigh, we lost Ghost Division agents, and to top it all off you've given Teddy King all the ammunition he needs to shut you down. Tell me you've made progress since we last spoke.'

'We've started with the agent we called Street Two. Her name is Stacey Henshaw. She was clear all through MI6. They posted her in Vienna, Berlin, Paris. Passed every polygraph she ever sat. Financial records are clean.'

'What about Ant Macfarlane? He was the one who handpicked this dream team.'

'Ant's distraught. He trusted his life with Henshaw - with any of that team.'

Curtis checked her time on her watch. 'You're Ghost Division. You're Rebecca *Fox*. Give me *some*thing.'

Rebecca was having to work hard to keep up. 'Burleigh was carrying a burner. One we didn't know about. There are phone calls to and from a payphone outside my building. I think I'm being set up.'

'By King?'

'Probably. We know there's still a conspirator out there. It has to be someone with the muscle to have taken out Lloyd Willow in Belmarsh. That requires high-level clearance, access with total control of CCTV. And Willow would also have needed someone within MI5 to help pull off the Downing Street conspiracy.'

Curtis checked her watch. Her pace had slipped. She picked it up. 'Teddy King has called an emergency meeting at Pindar in an hour.'

'I didn't know about this,' said Rebecca.

'You're not supposed to. There's one topic of discussion: who is to blame for the Oxford Street shooting. You know what to expect, right?' Curtis checked.

'Teddy King will call for a closed-doors enquiry, and he'll likely suggest that I be suspended, along with all other Ghost Division operations.'

Curtis replied, 'And you understand why I have to agree to it.'

'I do, Prime Minister,' Rebecca puffed. 'You have to show Whitehall you're doing something within the intelligence community. Suspending me and Ghost Division will mollify King and Morecombe.'

'It's a bruising defeat I didn't need in my first hundred days. Thank God it's one the British public will never know about.' Curtis did a shoulder-check to see how close her bodyguards were. 'It's both our necks on the line here, Rebecca. With Lloyd Willow dead and Dominic Morecombe now at MI5, Teddy King has got himself a close ally at the stern of British intelligence. Morecombe was practically King's secretary at MI5: there's nothing he wouldn't do for him. If we don't nail King now, the British government will only face more of these plots from the intelligence community. I need you to keep investigating who the main conspirator is: there's a ringleader still out there, Rebecca.'

Rebecca wondered, 'Can't you just sack King? The

Home Secretary appoints the director of MI6, and the Home Secretary works for you.'

'I used up all my political capital on Oliver Thorn. I needed someone soft in there, someone I could be sure of. I need King thinking he's safe. That's how we'll catch him.'

'What about Burleigh?' asked Rebecca.

Curtis checked her watch again. Seeing she was still way off pace she slowed to a stop. 'Get to Thames House and find out everything you can about Colin Burleigh. I won't be able to keep the doors open there much longer. Once you're suspended, you'll have to go undercover on this. And I mean deep.'

Rebecca leaned on her knees, catching her breath. 'My father did it for decades. So can I.'

As her bodyguards kept a respectable but safe distance, Curtis turned Rebecca away from them. 'Someone wanted Colin Burleigh dead, and they went to great lengths to ensure it happened. They were willing to go through four other members of Ant's team to get to him.'

Rebecca stood up straight again and nodded.

'It's going to get worse before it gets better. We need to be prepared for that.'

'Yes, Prime Minister,' replied Rebecca.

Curtis set off again, leaving Rebecca standing on her own.

Rebecca ran all the way along Victoria Embankment, then through the financial district in Blackfriars to get to Thames House.

She was pleased to see her entire analyst team in the ops suite. What had driven them to seek a place in Ghost

Division was the same thing that got them out of bed after two or three hours sleep the night before: a need to solve the puzzle.

Specifically, who was Stacey Henshaw?

Her team were excavating Henshaw's past, setting up a tick-tock – a complete rundown accounting for every hour, and everywhere she'd been in the last week. A video analysis team combed frame by frame through every CCTV angle they had to reconstruct the tragic events.

'Have you seen Ant?' Rebecca asked an analyst.

The analyst replied, 'He came in about twenty minutes ago, but he went straight back out again.'

Rebecca inhaled deeply as she retreated to her office. Now was not a good time for her deputy to go AWOL.

Still wearing her running gear - sweat rappelling down through her hairline – she grabbed a towel from her sports holdall and dried her face. There wasn't time for a shower.

She knew she had nearly cracked it.

She entered her computer password, then carried on from where she'd left off fifty minutes earlier.

GCHQ's TEMPORA computer system had access to hundreds of fibre-optic and landing station intercepts, creating points where GCHQ could simply hoover up any data that passed through the intercepts. Of interest to Rebecca had been her old department at GCHQ, Global Telecoms Exploitation (GTE).

In front of her, Rebecca had metadata – who called whom, at what time, where, and for how long - on every phone call and text message from any phone number she entered.

Tom Novak might have built his career on exposing government spying on the public, but it hadn't meant the intelligence agencies had actually stopped. They just got better at keeping it secret. GCHQ and NSA had actually increased their surveillance on the public since Novak's infamous NSA Papers story.

Rebecca had a note of Burleigh's phone number – the one he'd been using in the run up to the Oxford Street operation – and tapped it into the search bar.

When the results came back she mumbled to herself, 'That's weird.'

The metadata showed a number of phone calls and messages sent and received in Washington, D.C. over the past two weeks. Then Rebecca realised the number on the note she'd read had been Andrei Rublov's. She hadn't yet had a chance to run the number that Stella sent her on OTR.

Except, for some reason, further down the list a number was highlighted in green. Which happened when a number corresponded to one found on a previous search.

Rebecca told herself, 'This can't be right.'

But after looking at it every which way, and double- and triple-checking both numbers, there was no denying it: a week ago Andrei Rublov and Colin Burleigh had spoken to each other on the phone on three separate occasions.

Delving deeper, every app Rublov had used on his phone was wide open to GCHQ, as they had a secret, under-the-table contract with Rublov's phone supplier to leave backdoors open to GCHQ. The government had used anti-terror legislation to strong-arm the phone supplier – and dozens of others, as well as various internet search engines – who was powerless not to comply. Rublov's Sat Nav app was basically a digital breadcrumb trail of every-where he went. Every day, millions of people were leaving the same kind of records, all of it stored on a server that the government could access with a simple email request via the Home Office.

Now Rebecca wondered if Rublov's location might reveal more about the nature of his relationship with Colin Burleigh.

Judging by the activity on Rublov's phone he hadn't gone many places while in Washington. He had tapped in the address in Garfield Heights a number of times, a local Papa John's (Rebecca could even see what he'd ordered), and little else.

The one that stood out, though, was Rock Creek Park just north of Woodley Park. Rublov had gone there on four separate occasions.

Why go there so often in a two-week window? He was in D.C. for the first time, yet not once did he venture into Capitol Hill, and take in the Jefferson or Lincoln Memorials. Or any of the other dozen world-famous sights D.C. had to offer.

It was an anomaly. And Rebecca liked those.

Even better, though, was that NSA had collected more than just metadata on Rublov. And as NSA was partnered with GCHQ in the TEMPORA surveillance program, Rebecca had access to it as well. Part of TEMPORA was designed to record a target's actual phone conversations if a certain keyword or phrase was used by the target. The common assumption after the NSA Papers revelations was that anyone saying 'President' and 'assassinate' would find their calls being recorded. But NSA and GCHQ were much more specific than that.

Rebecca could see Rublov had triggered one particular

keyphrase, and it had been triggered at the same time as one of the calls between Rublov and Burleigh.

The keyphrase was: *"STANLEY FOX"*

Rebecca stared at the screen, almost in disbelief. Time and time again all conspiracies seemed to lead back to her father. The fact that the NSA were still monitoring mentions of his name only encouraged her further.

She opened another tab, bringing up Rublov's phone location data. It showed he had driven to Connecticut Avenue NW, stopped briefly, then driven in a circle around Woodley Park for the next twenty minutes.

Woodley Park again, she thought.

She then pulled up a list of phones that had been switched off during that twenty-minute period in that area, but also – crucially – had been kept off during Rublov's visits to Rock Creek Park, and had come within twenty metres of Andrei's phone signal.

The odds of finding more than one number that qualified for all those parameters were astronomical. And so it proved.

Only one number was a match.

It fit perfectly with what Rublov had told Natalya on the phone the night before he was killed: a number of meetings in a remote spot with no cameras. Trust was acquired. Then the source went all in and gave Rublov a dossier.

With the phone number it didn't take much more digging for someone of Rebecca's talents to identify the source that Andrei Rublov met the night before he died.

The phone belonging to the source had been switched on and off throughout most days during business hours. The location confined almost exclusively to the Hart Senate Office in Capitol Hill.

At night, the consistent location of the phone when it was switched off was a clear giveaway as to the source's address.

Which brought up a match against the NSA's internal database.

Andrei Rublov's source was chairman of the Senate Intelligence Committee, Senator Tucker Adams.

10

ADAMS RESIDENCE, WOODLEY PARK, WASHINGTON, D.C. –
SATURDAY, 9.13AM

Sharon Adams awoke slowly, stretching her hand across the empty space on the mattress where she had expected her husband to be. She felt the mattress was cold, and realised he must have been up for a while.

Senator Tucker Adams was in his study across the landing of their sprawling five-bedroom Tudor home. The outside world normally felt miles away, at the end of a long driveway with secure entrance in a gated community. But not that morning.

A copy of that day's *Washington Post* sat out on Adams' oak desk. Only one story covered the front page above-the-fold: the mass shooting in the Second District police station the previous night.

Adams, however, had the paper turned to a story hidden away on page three: '*Police investigate 'suspicious' Arlington Bridge crash.*'

The first paragraph identified Andrei Rublov as the victim.

Adams had a glass of whisky in his hand, which was

trembling. He finished the drink then took out his burner phone. He opened up the back cover and removed the SIM card. The situation was far beyond merely deleting messages. They had to be destroyed completely. He took the SIM to his drinks cabinet and mashed it up in the pestle and mortar he used to make cocktails.

There was a gentle knock on the study room door.

'Tucker?' Sharon asked gently. 'Are you OK?' She knew better than to enter without his permission.

Adams tried not to sound frantic as he dashed across the room to dispose of the SIM card. Straining, he called back, 'Yeah, I'm fine. You can come in.'

She opened the door gingerly. She took one look at the desk, then at him. 'You never work on a Saturday.'

'I'm not working,' he said, trying to be cheerful.

A wife always knows, though. She knew his expressions better than he did. And he looked scared. Spooked about something.

She thought it best to leave him for now. Eventually he would come clean.

Once she was gone, Adams picked up his landline and dialled his secretary. 'Janice, it's Tucker. I'm sorry to call so early on a Saturday. I've changed my mind about the Germany trip... No, I'm going to go alone instead. Tell Josh he can stay home. Something's come up.'

No point getting his young chief of staff mixed up in all this, Adams thought. The only comfort Adams had was that he would be far away from his family, the safest place for them given the circumstances.

If they were going to take him out like they had Rublov, it would have most likely been at home. They wouldn't think twice about taking out Sharon too if it made getting to him easier.

Adams knew that was the kind of people he was dealing with. People willing to do anything to protect their secrets. Now he would have to go to Germany and face those people head on.

11

The south district of Moscow was dominated by the enormous Moscow Oil Refinery. The air all around was filled with a noxious odour of gas – just breathing was enough to make people light-headed and caused all sorts of respiratory and vascular problems.

Smoke puffed out of six huge chimneys twenty-four hours a day. From a metal tower, a flame several metres high constantly burned, like a lighthouse marking the end of affluent Moscow and the miserable beginning of Kapotnya.

A vast network of pipes ran from the plant grounds out through the neighbouring fields, carrying superheated oil and other gas by-products, the temperature of which could reach hundreds of degrees Celsius. It brought a steady stream of warmth to the outside of the thick pipes, which were a haven from the cold for miles around for Moscow's plentiful homeless population.

Some left fish out on top of the pipes to slow cook, or draped blankets over them to dry out the overnight rain.

Capitol Spy   131

The district was made up of dozens upon dozens of apartment complexes, all five storeys high. They were decrepit. Grey. A signature of Russia's communist past, when everything was supposed to look the same.

No one was visible at their windows or balconies. There was little to look at.

Some of the local *Bratva* – mafia – stood around on street corners, waiting to sling dope through the windows of BMWs and Mercedes from the affluent Arbat and Tverskoi districts. They might have called themselves mafia, but there was no glamour in the *Bratva*. They worked fifteen-hour days for shit money. There was nothing too seedy or extreme they wouldn't push if it meant more cash than they started the day with.

After getting a few streets into the district, the driver asked Novak, '*What address?*'

'*Just drop us here,*' Novak replied.

'*You speak good Russian but I can tell you're an American. There are some crazy sons of bitches around here. You want to be careful, cowboy.*'

'*Yeah. I know where I'm going from here.*'

The fact that Novak wasn't translating what the driver was saying didn't make Stella feel any better. In the circumstances, she resolved she'd rather not know what was being said.

Once the taxi was gone she had never felt more vulnerable in her life. They were at least two miles from anything you could call civilisation. She trusted Novak, but that wasn't enough to drain away the fear that was charging through her body.

Standing in the middle of Kapotnya, Stella felt like she

and Novak were on the edge of the world. The streets were wide but there was no traffic.

Across the road was a girl with long blonde hair, no more than thirteen. She was walking hand in hand with a man in his fifties. She had on a black PVC miniskirt and high heels. In an attempt to make herself look older she'd put on a bright red lipstick, which only ended up drawing more attention to how young she was.

Novak could feel Stella staring. 'Don't look,' he warned her. 'Her pimp will probably be watching from one of the windows.'

Stella shuddered, as Novak led the way towards one of the high-rises.

Some Krokodil addicts raided through bins, oblivious to Novak and Stella's presence.

'We don't need to be worried about them, right?' Stella asked, concerned at the wild-eyed look about them.

'We're fine. They're looking for things to cook their codeine with.'

Stella noticed patches of scaly, rotting flesh on two of the addicts' arms. 'Does the drug do that?'

'That's why they call it Krokodil. It was just taking off when I was last here. In four years it's killed more people than heroin has killed in thirty. And it's about to hit the United States.' He added sarcastically, 'The wonders of globalisation.'

When they reached apartment block 128, Novak said, 'This is it.'

There were three teenage boys passed out on a couch on the grass outside the main door. They'd been buzzing a can of lighter fluid, which now lay on the ground with its nozzle busted off. The filthy duvet that had been covering them had slid off one of the boys' laps. Thinking about how freezing it was, Stella gently pulled the duvet back over the boy.

As they went inside, Stella asked, 'What is this place, Novak?' She recoiled as a greasy leak from the stairwell above landed on her head.

'It used to be Talya's grandmother's place. When Talya inherited it, we used it as a safe house back in the day. Moscow centre was too dangerous and too public to do the kind of work I was doing. This made a great place to do interviews. Sources didn't have to worry about the cops ever showing up. Talya started doing the same. It sort of became our office.'

They reached a door on the third floor landing.

Novak tried the door handle. It was locked.

'How do you know she didn't give the place up?' asked Stella.

'I don't.' Novak reached up to the ledge above the door where there was a rusting tin can with Boris Yeltsin's face on it. Before looking inside it he shook the tin, which rattled. 'Right where she always left it.' He took the key out and unlocked the door.

The apartment was bare-boned to say the least. In the living room, the floorboards were exposed and untreated, and the plaster on the walls was cracked. A large wooden desk with two chairs remained in the same place Novak remembered.

'I used to sit in that one,' he pointed, sounding melancholy.

On the largest wall adjacent to the living room window was a sentence written in Cyrillic in black graffiti.

Novak touched one of the letters. A little paint residue was left on his finger. 'It's fairly recent.'

Stella jested, 'My Cyrillic alphabet is a little rusty...'

Novak squinted. 'It says,' he paused to translate, '"the thief who steals three kopecks is hung, while the thief who steals one thousand is praised."' He turned to Stella. 'It's an old Russian proverb.'

'Does that sound like Natalya?' asked Stella.

'Not exactly.'

Stella went to the wooden desk, which still had notes and paperwork out on it. 'Her last story?' she speculated.

Novak picked up a memo from the CNN bureau. 'No,' he said. 'This is from four years ago.' He gave a gentle exhalation when he realised the date. 'That was my last day in Moscow.' He picked up the rest of the notes underneath. 'I didn't think I'd ever see these again.'

'You must have left in a hurry if you didn't take them with you.'

Novak put the notes down again.

Stella paused. 'What was this place really for, Novak?'

'What do you mean?' he asked.

'This isn't where you come to write in private. There isn't even an internet connection in here. This is a place to disappear. To stay off the grid. Or am I wrong?'

Novak sat down at the desk and took out a pack of Marlboro Gold. It was his first cigarette in over a week, but he was sure he needed it. The heaviness of the smoke after the first drag came as a surprise to him.

'This was Talya's safe house,' he said. 'She was a spy.' He let it linger in the air while he exhaled. 'That's how her source ended up dead. When she joined Russia Now the FSB recruited her to drop fake news into the agenda. Every week, they fed her stories they wanted broadcast on her segments: she was a mouthpiece for the Russian security services. That's why we split up.'

'How did you find out?'

Novak slowly tapped his cigarette ash on the floor. 'Diane's friend at the CNN bureau told me a source had shown them an FSB file on me. They were worried I was getting myself into trouble, drawing that kind of heat. The source managed to get me a copy. The file had been signed by Natalya Olgorova. She wasn't having a relationship with me. She was spying on me.'

'How long had it been going on?'

Novak realised he wasn't actually enjoying the cigarette but he persevered. 'It went all the way back to Sevastopol, when we first met.'

Stella could see it now. 'That was why she gave up her interview. She was working you.'

Novak seemed nonchalant about it now. 'The Russians thought *Republic* was pro-Ukraine, and they wanted to know what we knew. When I came to work full-time in Moscow, then I became an asset and she stepped things up a notch.'

'Who proposed?'

He paused. 'It makes me look so stupid now.'

Stella smiled sympathetically. 'She did. Right?'

'I knew it was fast, but I was...' He trailed off. 'I'm sorry I didn't tell you everything. Honestly? I was embarrassed.'

'It's OK, Novak,' Stella said. In the silence that followed, her instinct was to do what any English person did when in need of comfort. 'I'll see if there's some tea.'

Novak could no longer stand the cigarette. He dropped it on the ground and mashed it into the bare floorboards.

Stella stood by the kettle next to the sink, but she wasn't moving.

When Novak realised, he said, 'Stel?'

She reached down to the worktop, touching a bed of condensation under the kettle. She rubbed her fingers together. It was lukewarm. Still not moving, she said in a normal voice, 'Yeah, fine. Sorry, I couldn't find the switch.'

She motioned for him to come over, then held a finger at her lips. She took his hand and pressed it against the kettle.

It still felt warm.

That was when they heard the metallic click from back across the room: the sound of the hammer cocking on a handgun.

The woman holding the gun said in disbelief, 'Tom?' She was holding a Heckler & Koch P30 like she knew what she was doing. She lowered it. 'Jesus...I thought they'd found me.'

Stella didn't know where to put herself.

Novak turned around, then said almost breathlessly, 'Talya?'

12

On the video wall was a digital fact file on the Oxford Street shooting: all known details on Colin Burleigh, forensics photos from the crime scene at Textile Place, and CCTV images showing the orchestrated attack on the grab team.

Sir Teddy King was coming to the end of a considerable monologue. Having consulted with Morecombe in advance, King was careful not to come across like an eager executioner calling for volunteers for the gallows. He and Morecombe had thought that would only make Curtis defensive.

Little did they know, she was way ahead of them.

King pulled up a new slide on the video wall. 'You can see here the transcript of the last minutes from Street One's radio. Colin Burleigh, quote "They're going to kill us all. They set me up. I thought I was meeting your director, Rebecca Fox." First of all, who is "they"? Secondly, why did he think he was meeting Rebecca Fox?'

Sir Oliver Thorn, who had retreated to the tea trolley,

suggested, 'How do you know someone isn't trying to frame her?'

King tried to look magnanimous. 'True. It's possible. But either she really did arrange for him to be there so she could then ambush him and steal the documents he was in possession of. Or she's being framed as Ollie pointed out.' King held his hands up a little, trying to look utterly reasonable. 'Until we come to this.' He pressed the remote, bringing up a picture of a Nokia 3310 inside an evidence bag. 'This was found in Burleigh's coat pocket. The metadata since extracted by Thames House's very own analysts, traced several calls to it – including one yesterday morning - from a payphone right outside Rebecca Fox's building. Fox has no alibi at the time of the call.' He paused for effect. 'At best, she has some serious questions to answer. At worst, the evidence suggests she could be responsible for organising this ambush.'

Thorn pointed sharply at the video wall. 'Why would Rebecca be involved in *any* of this? To steal some STRAP Three files? There would be nothing inside those files she can't access remotely from Thames House.'

'It was never my job in MI5 and it's not my job now in MI6 to explain whys, Ollie.'

'What about Ant Macfarlane?' asked Curtis. 'Where is he in all of this? He put together the intel on Burleigh. He handpicked that street team. A member of which was the one who led the ambush against Burleigh and Ghost Division.'

Morecombe looked quickly from Curtis to King, then back again. 'We haven't quite been able to locate Macfarlane, Prime Minister.'

'You haven't "quite"?' she fired back. 'What the hell does that mean?'

Morecombe cleared his throat. 'He's gone, ma'am. His phone is off, and he failed to call in this morning. We have our best people working on it.'

Curtis raged, '*You're* supposed to be my best people!'

Morecombe tried to play it cool, but his face flushed.

King shut off the video wall. 'Prime Minister, I think the picture that's emerging here is that Ghost Division is not fit for purpose. It was a good idea, and I agree, possibly a necessary one. But we've now got the internal affairs department of the British intelligence services with a mole in its ranks.' He used the remote to switch off the video wall. 'It highlights something of an inevitable vulnerability in our line of work, and that is the human factor. I appreciate your efforts and noble intentions in creating Ghost Division, Prime Minister, but there is a gritty reality to intelligence work in the field: no matter who you are, no matter what you do, there are times when you will be betrayed. And no special divisions, elite units, or internal affairs can evade that.'

Morecombe spoke up, 'I agree. What's next? We create a division to investigate the internal affairs team? We're not solving the issue at hand.'

'And you have a solution, I expect,' said Curtis.

'We need to bring this problem closer to experienced hands like myself and Teddy.' He made a point of not mentioning Sir Oliver. 'Let *us* deal with this mole investigation. We have the expertise, the training, and the experience. Three things you never had with Ghost Division.' He raised an apologetic hand. 'Despite your best efforts, Prime Minister.'

Cheeky bastard, Curtis thought.

'Thank you, Dominic,' Curtis said. 'I appreciate the offer.' She turned to Oliver Thorn. 'What do you think, Ollie?'

Thorn couldn't see any other way. 'They've lost their entire operations team. They can't function in the field. And there are certainly inconsistencies here that need addressed. Maybe Rebecca should come back in-house at GCHQ with me for a while. After a leave of absence until we can see which way this is swinging.'

King and Morecombe exchanged the briefest of glances, pleasantly surprised that Thorn was backing their motion.

Thorn added, 'Maybe it was a little early for her.'

Curtis gave nothing away, so King decided to push harder.

He said, 'There's a lot here that's highly irregular, and frankly very suspicious about this whole Colin Burleigh debacle. I don't think it's unreasonable to have serious concerns about Rebecca's conduct during this operation.'

Curtis zoned out for a moment, lost almost in admiration of King's seamless construction of events - how beautifully he had orchestrated it all.

She laid her hands down on the table with finality. 'Special Branch will take up the Burleigh investigation from here. I need clean hands on this thing. Take the whole deal outside of the intelligence services.'

King and Morecombe hung on in anticipation, wondering if that was it.

'In the meantime...' Curtis hesitated a little, for effect. 'Rebecca Fox, along with all Ghost Division operations are hereby suspended, pending Special Branch's investigation into the Oxford Street shootings.'

It was all King and Morecombe could do not to high-five each other.

King nodded sombrely, followed by Morecombe.

As the men rose from their chairs, Curtis added, 'And Dominic, I want updates every hour on Ant Macfarlane.'

'Yes, ma'am,' he replied.

Teddy King rose, then rapped his knuckles appreciatively on the table.

Curtis stayed back, waiting until the others were gone. Then she dialled Rebecca's secure video line at Thames House.

Rebecca's face appeared on the wall. She was in her office, looking exhausted.

Curtis told her, 'King did exactly as we thought.'

'How hard did he push?' asked Rebecca.

'He stopped short of calling for your arrest. But I gave him what he and Morecombe wanted: Ghost Division is shut down and you're suspended.'

It was only when Rebecca heard Curtis actually say the words that she understood the gravity of her situation. Curtis might have been available for secret meetings in the park, but when it came down to it, she was on her own.

'Have you been able to find any sign of Ant Macfarlane?' asked Curtis.

Rebecca said, 'He seems to have taken off. I have someone staking out his home, I'm covering all the usual channels, online, phone, family contacts - but he's too experienced to fall into any of that.'

Curtis wanted Rebecca's verdict before committing herself. 'What do you think?'

Rebecca said, 'I think it's safe to say that Ant has chosen which side he's on and it's not ours. He gave me the Burleigh intel, he chose his ops team. Speaking of which...' Rebecca broke off to pull up an image from her laptop.

Curtis got out her seat and moved closer. 'What am I looking at?'

'This is an offshore bank account in the Cayman Islands, linked to an MI6 slush fund. They use it for buying off-the-books weapons. When an asset shows up in Italy, they can't walk off a plane carrying a loaded weapon. It's essentially an MI6 expense account.' She highlighted one withdrawal. 'This is a payment from two weeks ago of two hundred thousand pounds to an account linked several steps down the line to Stacey Henshaw. Otherwise known as Street Two in Ghost Division. She and Teddy King go way back.' Rebecca pulled up each related file one at a time. 'This is Henshaw's recruitment documents. The first department she was assigned to was Anti-terror division. Whose director at the time was...' She zoomed in on a document signed by King, with his name printed underneath. 'Then there's this, which was filed under Henshaw's operational duties from her first two years of service.' Rebecca clicked to a blank operations log.

'Deleted?' Curtis asked.

'No, just empty. Like she was sitting at a desk doing nothing the entire time. Then, six months later, suddenly she's being sent everywhere. This is a list of destinations her cover passports show her as being sent to, along with the dates. MI5 might be our domestic intelligence agency, but their actual operations aren't confined to within our borders...' Rebecca broke off as she noticed Curtis folding her arms purposefully, a wry grin on her face. Rebecca felt her face flush slightly as she realised her mistake. 'Which, as a former Home Secretary, you know all about of course...'

Curtis smiled nonchalantly.

Rebecca moved on quickly. 'The times and places of Henshaw's movements match up to significant operations at the time. There are field office locations in the Bahamas, India, Malaysia, Japan, and Germany. Almost as soon as she was hired she was protected like no other agent. As far as I can see, Prime Minister, Stacey Henshaw was operating as Teddy King's personal fixer in the field.'

Curtis asked, 'How would he come to trust a rookie like her so quickly?'

Rebecca clicked to an old photograph from the exclusive Tonbridge School, where fees started at fifty thousand pounds a year. Two faces were circled. 'This is Teddy King and Gordon Henshaw at Tonbridge boarding school when they were sixteen. They went on to Sandhurst together. Gordon Henshaw was Stacey's father. He was killed in the field in unexplained circumstances during a botched operation in Berlin in the mid-eighties. Stacey Henshaw might have been a rookie, but she was also the daughter of the only man Teddy King ever trusted. And apparently she's willing to do whatever is asked of her.' Sensing Curtis was about to speak, Rebecca said, 'There's one more thing.' She pulled up a metadata record, with several phone numbers highlighted, alongside a map showing the location of those numbers. 'These are phone numbers associated with the hit team that killed Abbie Bishop back in December. This map shows one other number in the same location as those assassins. Look at the time and date.'

Curtis read it back to herself as Rebecca zoomed in on it. 'The seventh of December.'

'The night Abbie Bishop was killed.'

'I was told we caught all the people involved in that hit team.'

'And it was MI5 that was in charge of that operation...'

Curtis closed her eyes, seeing the pieces falling horribly into place. 'It was Teddy King who made the call that everyone was caught, when Henshaw was still out there.' She stepped back, leaning against the edge of the conference table. 'What about Colin Burleigh?'

'That's where it gets really interesting,' Rebecca teased, pulling up another call list. 'Yesterday Stella Mitchell from *The Republic* sent me a message, asking if I could find her and Tom Novak information on Andrei Rublov.'

'They just don't know how to do a quiet story, do they.'

'When I was searching, I accidentally put Colin Burleigh's mobile number in the search bar instead of Rublov's. Except, ECHELON found a link with Rublov's phone. Burleigh called Rublov a week ago while Rublov was in Washington.'

Curtis rubbed her temple. 'I don't follow. What does this have to do with Burleigh being shot in London?'

'Right now? I can't say for sure. What I do know is that someone, somewhere, knows what Burleigh sent Rublov and why.'

'Would you be comfortable going to Washington to find out?' asked Curtis.

Rebecca replied, 'I have an asset over there who's pulling some strings for me.'

Curtis nodded slowly, deliberately. Weighing up their options.

'How much time do I have left before I have to go undercover?' asked Rebecca. 'Forty-eight hours?'

'Less, I think,' Curtis replied. 'How quickly can you go?'

Rebecca lifted up a backpack into shot. 'I'm ready for anything.'

13

Camp Metro was for high-value, short-stay detainees. Its location was a closely guarded secret to only the very top tier of CIA personnel. The President himself and high-ranking officials in the Pentagon weren't even aware of its existence. Some detainees were only partly through journeys halfway around the world: going to or coming from Central Africa, Southeast Asia, Northern Europe. The detainees brought there didn't even know they were in the United States. Their captors' accents were no giveaway: America had black sites on five continents.

Detainee Triple-X's room was technically a prison cell, but he had been made more comfortable than some of the others. He at least had a bed with a thin mattress. And a desk with crossword books. There was certainly little else he could do in a windowless room. A sixty-two-year-old man he wasn't exactly going to start doing bodyweight dips on the bed frame, or push ups and burpees to keep his blood flowing.

The room comprised a single bed, a small writing desk with blank paper and biro pens. The bare walls were painted grey.

The only light was a buzzing strip light controlled from outside the locked door.

Triple-X turned to the final clue of the crossword. The last one in the book.

'Seven letters,' he announced to himself, wracked with boredom. '"Two girls. One on each knee."' He nodded. 'Not bad,' he said. It took him all of twenty seconds to get it.

With his pen – he never needed to rub anything out when he did crosswords – he wrote the medical name for the kneecap, 'PATELLA.'

He closed the book over and placed it on top of two others: Cryptic Crosswords volumes 1-3.

Triple-X called out, 'Too easy. Next!'

On the desk was an untouched pot of Earl Grey tea and an empty cup. It had been delivered an hour earlier.

There was a knock on the door, then it opened slowly.

A man wearing a navy suit entered. He was in his early forties, with thinning hair in a side-parting to fool himself he wasn't going bald. 'Good afternoon, Stanley,' he said, closing the door behind him.

'Deputy Director Fallow,' Stanley replied, sitting back in his chair. 'I see you haven't died in a horrible car accident on the way to work this morning.' He smiled at Fallow. 'That's unfortunate. But how pleasant to actually hear my name spoken out loud again. For some reason, everyone else here seems to think my name is Triple-X.' He peered at Fallow. 'You're keeping me off the books. Disappearing me.' Stanley tutted at him. 'There's very little inducement for me to give up the one piece of information that's keeping me alive when it's so obvious that you'll kill me as soon as I give it up.' He tilted his head, as if trying to make a small child understand him. 'I've been locked up for nearly twenty years by various authorities and black ops hatchetmen, so I know better than most: you really aren't very good at this, dear boy.'

Fallow couldn't help but laugh. 'You know what I don't understand? For someone so smart, why you decided to confess in a courtroom full of people to being Tom Novak's source on the NSA Papers.'

'It's something you wouldn't know anything about,' Stanley said. 'It's called loyalty. And the fact is, if I hadn't gone to that court and announced myself you would still be looking for me.'

'No,' Fallow said, 'we were closing in on you.'

It was Stanley's turn to laugh. 'Of course. You were just biding your time.' He wagged his finger at Fallow, still laughing. '"Closing in"! That's good, Fallow. You're the funny one, I can tell...'

Fallow didn't rise to the bait, changing the subject. 'If you look around this room, Stanley, you can see we've made life easy for you. But we can make things harder. Much harder. Because the thing is, everyone has a breaking point. No one can hold out indefinitely. The British? They just wanted you hidden away. So don't make the mistake of thinking you've survived the last twenty years. You haven't *survived* anything.'

'I don't care what you do to me,' Stanley blustered. 'It's all in my head.'

'But it's not just in your head, is it, Stanley. It's in the phone we took from you at the courthouse in December. And that phone has a password that will give us your formula.'

'I'll never talk.'

'Stanley. I'll be honest. Some of the guys we have working for us: they're sadistic. I don't know what it is about them. Maybe they don't get enough sunlight or something. But they just. Like. Hurting people. And they're really good at it too. So why don't you give us the password to your phone, we can get the formula, and you can go home to your daughter again.'

'The moment I give you that password, I'm dead.' Stanley turned back to his desk and opened another crossword book. 'If it's all the same to you, I'll carry on here.'

Fallow came closer, crouching down beside him, then turned Stanley's chair so he faced him. 'Imagine the worst pain you've ever felt in your life. How long did it last? A second? Minutes? What if it lasted weeks? Years? I promise you, Stanley: we'll never kill you. We'll keep you in such a state of agony, that you won't be able to withhold the password. You won't even want to go on *living*.'

A feeling of dread consumed Stanley's body from head to toe. He could actually feel it washing through his veins like ice. He couldn't bring himself to look at Fallow.

Fallow knew he was getting through to him. 'See, they'll bring you right to the point at which you think you're going to die...Then keep you there. For days.' He conceded, 'Weeks if they have to.'

Fallow called for the door to be opened.

In the doorway, he said to Stanley, 'We're going to move

you to another room now. Somewhere without any cross-word books. Or a bed. Somewhere a little more persuasive.'

As Fallow turned to leave, he told the guard, 'Take him to the Black Room. We're going to have to exert a little more force than I thought.'

14

'What the hell, Talya?' Novak exclaimed.

She stood there, almost sheepishly, and lowered her gun. 'I'm sorry, Tom,' she mumbled. 'It was the only way.'

Her slender figure was swamped in faded black jeans and a baggy grey sweater, and her fair, chin-length hair was unkempt from her having neither a hairbrush nor a mirror in the apartment. In any case, appearance had been the least of her concerns in the last twenty-four hours.

Novak turned his back and exhaled. 'The only way was making me think you were dead?'

'That wasn't for you. That was for the media. The FSB. Viktor.'

Novak now realised the extent of what Natalya had set up. 'Viktor doesn't know either?'

'Of course not,' Natalya replied. 'He's the reason I've had to do this. Him and Boris Ivanov. I had to make them stop looking for me. Even for a few days.'

Novak stormed past Natalya to the living room. Stella was surprised that he seemed angry rather than relieved.

It took a moment for her to work it out: it wasn't because Natalya had fooled him. It was because she'd made him care again.

Natalya turned her attention to Stella. 'I've read a lot about you since December,' Natalya said. 'Nice to meet you, Stella.'

'Yeah,' Stella said, holding back from the sight of Natalya's gun. 'I'm glad you're alright.'

Natalya depressed the magazine lever, and let the magazine drop into her other hand. She then locked the slide open, making sure there were no empty cases still to be ejected. She was definitely not a gun novice.

Novak took a seat, trying to calm down. 'Was there ever a threat against you, Talya? What's going on?'

Natalya put the empty gun down. 'The threat was very real, Tom. It still is. That's why I've had to do this. I'm sorry I couldn't tell you, but after Andrei...I panicked.' Her hands were trembling, and she was bouncing her leg rapidly up and down from the ball of her foot. 'I don't know where to begin.' She took out a cigarette.

'Try,' Novak snapped.

Stella passed Natalya a glass bowl for her ash. 'How about you and Andrei?'

Natalya took a long drag on the cigarette. 'I was the only one who knew Andrei had been writing anonymous articles for *Exile*.'

'What's *Exile*?' asked Stella.

'It's a blog that covers stories the government doesn't want made public: corruption, election fraud, criminal behaviour of the political elite. Not the sort of thing RN will ever broadcast. A source in the Kremlin told me Andrei was being watched, so I tried to warn him. Then he told me the story he was really chasing.' She paused for another drag. 'He had a source who told him there's a Russian spy in Congress.'

'We heard about that. Do you think it's true?' asked Stella.

'He called me on Friday and told me. He met his source the night before, and they gave him a dossier identifying the spy.'

'That's what you wanted me to get,' Novak realised. 'I thought that file was what got you killed. Stella and I risked our lives for that.'

Natalya's head dropped. 'I know. I'm so sorry. To both of you. When I saw what they did in that police station in Washington I knew I had made the right decision. These people will do anything.' She looked at them in turn. 'You. Stella. A dozen cops. Or a reporter in Washington. It's nothing to them. I've been surrounded by these people my whole life.'

'Who is *they*?' asked Stella.

Natalya looked down into her hands. Plainly terrified. 'The powerful. Very powerful, very rich people.'

Novak leaned forward on his knees. He wanted answers now. 'So you decide to disappear.'

Natalya nodded. 'Andrei brought me in to help with his story. We were working for weeks behind the scenes, researching late at night while doing our regular stories for RN. It seemed to work - until Andrei went to Washington.'

'So how did it work? Making it look like...' Stella trailed off, unsure what to call it.

'When Andrei was killed, I knew they would come for me next. So I had to make it look convincing: I couldn't just disappear. I had to die.' Natalya stubbed out her cigarette then held her hand out to Novak. 'Could I have one of yours?'

Novak took out a Marlboro and lit it for her.

Natalya exhaled. 'A few months ago I helped keep a problem for the police chief out the papers. He owed me a favour, so I came to him. He set up everything so quickly: the ambulance, the police, everything. We paid off a local *baklany* - you know, a street kid - to shoot me with a blank in the street. It was important that there were witnesses. Word would get back to the FSB if anything was suspect. I had on a bullet-proof vest, because a blank can still hurt, you know. The police chief fitted the vest with a...how you say...' Natalya gestured at something coming out her chest.

'A squib,' Novak offered.

'Right,' Natalya said. 'The paramedics were all in on it. And they took me to the Central Clinic so the police chief could control access.'

'What about Viktor?' asked Novak. 'What if he wanted to see your body?'

'Viktor and I are divorced, and it's highly irregular for an ex-husband to be allowed access before an autopsy.'

'So he has no way of realising you're not dead?'

Natalya explained, 'He'll find out eventually. But the police chief can hold a body for up to three days until an autopsy is complete. Enough time for me to get out of the country, at least.'

'Where will you go?' asked Stella.

'Ukraine.' Something about mention of this made Natalya shift in her seat. 'That's where Magdalina is.'

Novak raised his eyebrows. 'You have a kid?'

'With Viktor. A little girl.' She smiled warmly at the thought of her. 'She's two.'

'Where is she?'

'With my parents in Kiev. I sent her there last week so she would be safe. While I did this.'

'Doesn't Viktor have joint custody?' asked Stella.

Natalya said, 'Most Russian men expect women to be married by twenty-one. They think there's something defective with you if you're not - no surprise our divorce rate is so high. The Russian Family Code says children are better off with their mother, and they almost never grant joint custody. Viktor was happy to cut the cord. He has plenty of money for child support. That's all the court cared about.' She stubbed out her cigarette.

Novak appeared irked by something. He spoke whilst rubbing his eyes. 'What changed, Talya? Four years ago you sold out a source to the government. Now you're thumbing your nose at the FSB, and,' he gestured at the graffiti on the wall, 'painting Bolshevik slogans on the wall.'

Natalya bowed her head. When she lifted it again her eyes were full of tears. 'You don't understand what it's like to have your life be about the worst thing you have ever done. I worked for RN because it's all there was. You had an audience, Tom. You could travel the world and report on whatever you liked.' She gestured out the window. 'Who out there hears anything? I don't want to raise my child in a country like this. I want people to hear. And they'll hear Andrei's story. If you want to help me.'

Novak looked across at Stella.

She said, 'First, we need to get out of here. Your face is all over the news.'

Natalya sprang up out her chair. 'I'll get my things.'

'Hey, Talya,' Novak called to her. 'Bring your gun.'

15

When Aleksandr excused himself from RN's offices – as
Novak had asked him to - he only expected to find Novak
and Stella waiting for him. He found them on the stairs
outside his one-bedroom apartment.

He kept his voice down so the neighbours wouldn't
hear. 'Is everything OK? What's going on?'

Novak beckoned him onto the landing. He held both of
Alek's shoulders. 'I want you to stay very calm, Alek. Everything's fine. Whatever happens, don't scream, OK.'

'Scream?' Aleksandr recoiled. 'You are freaking me out,
Tom.'

From the landing above, Natalya cautiously descended
the stairs.

Aleksandr made a rapid sign of the cross then kissed his
hand. '*Mother of God!*' he cried in Russian. He put his arms
out, then threw them around Natalya.

She was nearly knocked off her feet by the embrace.
'*Not quite, Alek,*' she groaned.

Novak looked around worriedly. 'We should get inside.'

Rebecca's office, Thames House

With the suspension of Ghost Division operations, Rebecca was left in Thames House on her own. She logged in to her Darkroom account, then clicked on the account she was attempting to video-call: Stella Mitchell.

Darkroom used end-to-end encryption, making it impenetrable to either GCHQ or NSA. There were no vulnerabilities. All trace of the chats - even the metadata – was deleted from the Darkroom servers as soon as the calls were over.

In a world without privacy, Darkroom was a rare sanctuary.

Stella and Novak were huddled around her phone in Aleksandr's bathroom.

As soon as Rebecca's face appeared in the chat window Stella could tell something was wrong. She looked tense and she was hunched over her desk.

'Are you OK?' Stella asked.

Rebecca had been watching the CCTV feed showing the main entrance downstairs. The security team were still on duty. But Rebecca knew it wouldn't be long before Special Branch arrived to take her for questioning.

'I don't have a lot of time,' Rebecca said.

Novak had notes ready, eager to press on. 'You said in your message you've found Rublov's source.'

'I think so,' Rebecca replied. 'His name is Colin Burleigh, an MI6 agent. He was suspected of selling secrets to the Russians. So Ghost Division was assigned to bring him in. But there was an ambush. Burleigh, along with four other Ghost Division agents, were shot and killed on Oxford Street.'

'Hang on,' Stella chimed in. 'That's what the shooting was?'

Novak was horrified. 'You gave disinformation to your own country's media?'

Rebecca glanced again at the CCTV. 'It wasn't my call, Tom,' she said with slight irritation.

Stella didn't want to lose her, so she said, 'Let's move on.'

'After checking Andrei Rublov's phone records, I found a match between him and Colin Burleigh from a week ago. Burleigh had transferred him a file via encryption.'

Stella looked at Novak. They were thinking the same thing: Andrei's dossier.

'That seems to mean something to you,' said Rebecca.

Novak hesitated. 'We're with Natalya Olgorova in Moscow.'

'What?'

'She's here. She's alive. The shooting was faked. She'd been secretly working on the same story as Andrei Rublov. Now the FSB are after her.'

'You guys have to get her out of there. I mean, out of the country.'

'We're working on it.'

'Does she know anything about the file?'

Neither Stella nor Novak knew how to answer.

Novak said, 'Burleigh seems to have got his hands on a dossier identifying a member of Congress who's been spying for Russia.'

Rebecca froze. 'The United States Congress?'

'Yeah.'

'For how long?'

'We don't know yet.'

'There's a lot we don't know yet,' added Stella.

Rebecca said, 'You've maybe got more than you realise. You were right about his Sat Nav: Rublov did meet someone the night before he died. It was Senator Tucker Adams.'

Novak clicked his fingers like the whole thing was solved. 'He's chairman of the Senate Intelligence Committee. He must have been Rublov's second source.'

Stella tried to put Novak's brakes on a little. 'Hang on. All we know is that Rublov and Adams had some kind of meeting.'

'Where is Adams now?' Novak asked Rebecca.

'There's nothing on his office phone, which you would expect at the weekend. Although I found a number of internet searches on his home computer first thing this morning.' Rebecca read off the list from another tab on her computer. '"ANDREI RUBLOV WASHINGTON." "ANDREI RUBLOV NEWS." "ANDREI RUBLOV CAR WASHINGTON."'

'Sounds like the senator has something on his mind,' said Novak.

Rebecca agreed. 'He's probably worried he's next.'

Stella said to Novak, 'It could take us days to get out of Russia safely with Natalya.'

'I might be able to help you out there,' Rebecca offered. 'I can get to Adams, but right now, you two need to focus on getting Natalya out of Russia. You should know I'm going to have to go dark for a few days.'

'Why?' asked Stella.

'I'm being framed for the Colin Burleigh operation and Ghost Division is being suspended.'

'Suspended? By Angela Curtis?'

'Technically, yes. But her hand is being forced by Teddy King of MI6. King wants Ghost Division - and me - out the way, because we're the only ones who are close to exposing him for what he is: the last remaining conspirator behind the Downing Street attack.'

Novak's mind was racing. 'Lloyd Willow. That wasn't really suicide, was it?'

Rebecca took a long pause. 'I can't comment on that.'

'But Willow was going to name names, right?'

'I think so. But King is the head of the snake here. We need evidence that finally implicates him.'

Stella said, 'The key to this has to be the Burleigh-Rublov connection. If we follow that...it's game on.'

Rebecca looked down at her phone which had suddenly illuminated.

A message from Angela Curtis flashed up:

'*Get out. Get out NOW.*'

On the CCTV, Rebecca could see a grey SUV pulling into the car park. Five men in suits came out swiftly, followed by three uniformed police.

Special Branch.

Rebecca told them, 'I have to go.'

Before Novak or Stella could say goodbye, Rebecca disappeared from the chat window.

16

Downstairs, Natalya had been filling Aleksandr in on her secret life, and what she'd been up to with Andrei.

Aleksandr raised his glass. 'To his memory.'

He and Natalya downed their drinks.

Stella declined an offer of the bottle from Natalya. 'I need to stay sharp,' she said, hoping Natalya would take the hint.

Natalya put her glass back down.

Aleksandr had drunk too quickly and was already a little tipsy. 'I can't believe you actually faked your own death.'

Natalya quipped, 'A piece of theatre even Viktor would have been proud of.'

'Wasn't it stressful at RN?' Stella asked. 'Feeling watched all the time.'

'Yeah,' Natalya said. 'Andrei and I would leave fake notes lying around on our desks. We'd even have conversations in each other's offices lying about where we were going to go, and when.'

Aleksandr didn't pick up on it at first, but Novak and Stella certainly had.

'Your office was bugged?' asked Novak.

Natalya was spooked by the sudden change in tone. She stammered, 'Well... yeah. Viktor was giving the FSB every-'

Aleksandr looked horrified. 'I didn't...I didn't know! You mean they heard everything I said?'

Novak put his laptop into his backpack then stood up. 'We need to go.' He motioned for Natalya to get up. 'Right now.'

Natalya asked, 'What's happened?'

Stella picked up her bag. 'We were talking to Aleksandr in your office earlier. If it's bugged then the FSB might come here.'

Aleksandr stood in the middle of the room, too terrified to move.

Novak slung his bag over his shoulder then told Aleksandr, 'Listen to me. You haven't done anything wrong. But Stella, Talya, and I can't stay here.'

His head was spinning. 'What have I done?'

Novak reassured him, 'Hey. It's not your fault. It's mine. I screwed up.'

'What should I do? If they come here?'

'Just tell the truth,' Novak said. 'Blame me. Tell them you felt pressured. It's the safest way.'

Stella got both straps of her backpack on, then looked towards the kitchen. 'Is there a back way out of here?'

17

The Lubyanka building in central Moscow was home to the feared Russian Federal Security Services - formerly the KGB, now known as the FSB. The front of the yellow brick building still bore remnants of Russia's Soviet past: on the façade above the ground-level windows were numerous hammer and sickle carvings in the stonework. In fact, the building had changed very little since the early twentieth century.

At least on the outside.

In a windowless room on the third floor, a man sat at a computer terminal with headphones on. He was listening to catalogued conversations from earlier that day.

Under the tag "Natalya Olgorova office", he clicked on the most recent entry. The bug in the room was prompted to record only when conversation started within a certain decibel range. The range for the most recent conversation was barely above the minimum threshold.

After some equaliser adjustments, the operator was able to make out the conversation.

He shouted his supervisor over, who didn't have to listen
to much before taking control of the computer.

The supervisor pulled up CCTV feeds from Russia
Now's lobby. Scanning through the few minutes before the
time of the recording, he paused as Novak and Stella
walked into frame at reception.

The supervisor picked up the phone. 'Get me Viktor
Karpov,' he demanded. 'Tell him I have the two journalists
he wants.'

Novak, Stella, and Natalya sneaked out the back door into
a long row of gardens separated by low fences. Snow was
falling gently, and the temperature had plummeted since
they had got to Aleksandr's.

Natalya led the way, holding them back at the alley
leading to the main road. Her breath steamed from her
mouth as she spoke. 'Follow me,' she said. 'Stay low.'

They crouched behind a battered Volvo.

Natalya pointed in the direction of a saloon car cruising
onto Aleksandr's street. 'That's them,' she said.

'How do you know?' asked Stella.

'I've seen that car before at RN.'

The car parked across from Aleksandr's front door. Two
tall men in turtle necks and suit jackets came out.

'We need to keep moving,' Novak said.

Inside the apartment, Aleksandr tried not to tremble as he
answered the door.

The two men showed him their FSB badges. Although
technically a military service, FSB officers generally didn't

wear uniform. The men introduced themselves as 'civilian investigators'.

As they entered the dimly lit living room, one of the men turned the main light on. The harshness of the light coupled with the men's ominous, piercing stares made Aleksandr feel like they could see right through him.

Aleksandr sat down in his regular seat and turned his palms up. 'How can I help?'

One of them asked questions, while the other sat silently, looking around the room.

The questioner held out a phone screen showing an image of Novak and Mitchell from RN's CCTV system. 'We're interested in speaking to these two people. They're reporters with *The Republic*. It's our understanding you know them?'

Aleksandr was smart enough not to go into 'deny everything' mode. But before he answered, he looked above the cheap gas fire that was burning.

Natalya had left her glass up there. It was still half-full.

The FSB officers hadn't clocked it yet.

'Yes,' Aleksandr said, trying to seem casually perplexed by what the issue was. 'I knew the American from several years ago. We talked about my colleague Natalya. You must have seen the news.'

The men said nothing.

Aleksandr got to his feet, staying as far away from the mantelpiece as he could. He put his hands in his pockets and rocked back and forth on his heels. 'We didn't talk for long. A minute or two.'

'Three and a half,' the previously silent officer added.

The officer's bewildering answer was intentional. Among the FSB's tactical arsenal was a technique perfected

by the Stasi. They called it *Zersetzung*. A kind of psychological warfare against enemies of the state, to constantly
remind them how much access they had, and crucially how
much power they held: they knew everything.

The other officer took over again. 'We cannot arrest
everyone who is an enemy of Russia, Aleksandr. But we can
paralyze them. By taking their lives and squeezing them.
We could do that to you. If we needed to.'

Aleksandr gulped in such a way that he was sure the
officers could hear it from across the room. 'I'm sure...that
won't be necessary.'

'We know they were here,' the officer said. 'The glass on
the mantelpiece you've tried to distract us from by moving
away from it. There's a ruffled cushion over here. And as
you've clearly been sitting over there tonight, it tells me
someone else has been here, and recently. Your shoes in the
hallway are still wet from the snow. Beside them are faint
outlines of melted snow from three other pairs of shoes.'

The other officer said, 'Do you like your job,
Aleksandr?'

He nodded.

'Viktor Karpov is a reasonable man. A forgiving man.
He'd be willing to let someone keep their job, provided they
told the whole truth. It wouldn't be easy for a queer like you
to get another job in the media, would it? Not in Moscow.
Not if Viktor Karpov blacklisted you. Because you *are* a
queer. Are you not, Alek? A man your age, living alone.'

A tear rolled down Aleksandr's face, feeling his entire
future evaporate in front of him. He wiped it away as
quickly as possible. He didn't want them enjoying the satisfaction that they'd broken him.

'What do you want?' Aleksandr asked.

'Tell us where they went, and who else is with them.' The officer leaned forward on his knees. 'Then we won't need to squeeze you.'

Alek closed his eyes for a moment. 'I don't know where they were going. I swear. They left five minutes ago.'

The officers stood up together.

'What direction did they go?'

Novak, Stella, and Natalya made their way quickly through Taganka Square, staying immersed in the crowds making their way home from work. It was dark now, and the street-lights were weak.

Natalya had on a baseball cap of Novak's. She said, 'I don't think there are cameras here, but keep your heads down anyway.'

Novak mumbled to Stella, 'Says the most famous dead person in Moscow.'

The entrance to Taganskaya Metro was one of the grander ones in the city: three huge archways under an intricate roof balcony. It looked more like an opulent court-house than a metro station.

The self-service machines were out of order, resulting in long lines at the ticket office. Natalya slid in between Stella and Novak, four back from the front of the queue.

Back at the main doors, two police officers were showing commuters pictures of Novak and Stella on their phones. The same ones the FSB had.

Stella reached forward, tapping Novak's arm.

'I see them,' he said.

The queue had moved rapidly with two clerks in the

booths, doling out tickets with the kind of ease that comes from hundreds of hours of repetitive motion.

As Novak asked for three tickets, a security alert popped up on the clerks' computer screens showing the CCTV image from FSB. The woman serving Novak – a heavy-set woman with red cheeks - didn't notice it at first as the tickets printed, but the clerk beside her did.

Novak could tell from her expression what had happened. His heart skipped a beat.

The ticket clerk got the other's attention, pointing out – not very subtly – that her colleague was serving the man on the computer screen.

Novak told Stella and Natalya quietly, 'We've been spotted. We need to run.'

He reached under the plastic screen and grabbed the tickets off the printer. He said, 'Go go go!' at Stella and Natalya, who ran with him towards the turnstiles.

Novak's clerk stood up and waved her short arms above her head trying to get the police officers' attention. '*Over here!*' she yelled, pointing at the turnstiles.

The police officers shouted, '*Out of the way,*' as they barged through the queue.

Novak, Stella, and Natalya got through the turnstiles quickly, but the escalator was so busy that everyone stood still on their step. Novak pushed through, drawing shouts and insults at him, as Stella and Natalya followed.

The police jumped the turnstile and made significant headway as the crowds parted.

Once they cleared the escalator, Novak and Stella shouted a mixture of English and Russian at the startled commuters as they ran full tilt down the checkerboard granite corridor, leading to the platform.

The corridor was lit by gilded chandeliers, lighting everything a bright white.

The wind created by an approaching train, coupled with running so fast, blew the baseball cap off Natalya's head.

'Leave it!' Novak shouted.

Despite the crowds still funnelling up the corridor from the most recent arrival, one of the cops took aim at the trio in desperation.

His partner yelled 'No!' at him, deflecting his arm upwards.

The bullet struck the marble wall, then ricocheted into one of the chandeliers, tagging a bulb which blew out all over the ground.

The shot sounded like a cannon in the confined space of the corridor, unleashing a wave of terrified screams from the commuters. A lot of people hit the deck, while others ran in panic back towards the platform.

The other cop yelled, '*You could have killed someone.*'

There was one final, short staircase down to the platform.

Novak, Stella, and Natalya spared nothing to get there in time. Novak was up front and could see the train doors starting to close. He knew if they didn't get on it they would be in all kinds of trouble.

He took the last five stairs in one massive leap before grabbing the train doors before they closed.

The train driver was oblivious to the action behind with his protective foam earplugs in, and the ancient engine chugging.

The train set off slowly while Novak ran alongside it, still barely holding the doors open.

A passenger inside helped prise the doors fully open. Novak jumped in, then waved at the others to follow.

Stella could see Natalya was flagging, struggling with the weight of her backpack. Stella held her hand out. 'Give me your bag! It's more important that you make it.'

Natalya handed it to her. Now she was free of the extra weight, she caught up with the train and jumped inside while Novak held the doors.

Stella was still a few paces short, and running out of platform as the train gathered speed.

Stella threw Natalya's bag into the train, then managed one last burst to catch up to the doors.

The two cops fired freely down the platform, missing Stella by inches as she dived into the train. She managed to pull her legs in with barely a second to spare.

The cops leaned over their knees, cursing as the train disappeared into the tunnel.

Novak, Stella, and Natalya lay in a heap on the carriage floor, sweating, trying to catch their breath.

Natalya reached out to touch Stella's leg. 'Thank you,' she puffed.

Some of the other passengers were on their feet to get a look at the fugitives.

A woman pointed in shock. '*That's Natalya Olgorova.*'

Some passengers started taking pictures of her on their phones.

Still gasping for breath, Novak said to Natalya, 'I think your cover might be blown.'

The trio decided to get off at Kuznetsky Most, as Natalya's car wasn't far from there. But as the metro train pulled into the platform, the police were already arriving up on the street.

Natalya stayed between Novak and Stella, heads down as they followed the natural flow of the crowd.

When they got to the top of the escalator they could see the gathering police presence outside, struggling to keep eyes on all the passengers exiting the station.

The problem was that Natalya's presence had prompted some passengers to get off and film her on their phones. One of them further back in the crowd shouted out, '*Hey, that's Natalya Olgorova! She's alive!*'

The police couldn't hear, but they could see some sort of commotion going on at the centre of the crowd.

The sergeant on the scene waved his officers to wade in.

'Should we go back?' Stella wondered.

'I have an idea,' Natalya said. 'Follow my lead.' She reached into her bag and took out her pistol. She screamed, '*Terrorist! He's got a gun!*' then fired three rounds into the ceiling.

The reaction was instant, with panic spreading like a virus through the crowd.

Novak and Stella were as confounded as anyone else.

Almost as one, the crowd charged towards the door, screaming and yelling. Given the history of terror attacks on the Moscow metro, the fear was very real. The crowd surged onto the street, bringing Natalya, Stella, and Novak with them.

The police were forced back, and for a moment they thought there might actually have been an attack in progress.

Trying to keep track of all the faces outside was impossible.

When the FSB commander - running directly from Lubyanka - heard the gunshots, he knew his suspects must have pulled something.

Novak, Stella, and Natalya drifted to one side, as the police went up on tiptoes, now also looking for a gunman.

By the time the yelling and shouting dissipated, a man who had been next to Natalya described to the police what she had done.

The FSB commander came haring up to one of the officers, showing his badge. The cop immediately straightened his back.

'*Where have they gone?*' the commander yelled. '*They were on that train.*'

The trio dashed between the stationary traffic at the edge of Lubyanka Square, and were soon into the quieter streets near Natalya's house.

Once a fresh squall of police sirens passed on the main road around the corner, Natalya led them to her Lada Granta hatchback, still parked where she'd left it the day before.

Natalya took out her keys and made for the driver's side. 'I think I had better drive,' she said.

Once they had merged with the other traffic heading out of Moscow, the trio finally felt safe.

'Follow your lead?' Novak exclaimed.

'Sorry,' Natalya replied. 'It was instinct. Anyway, we'll need to ditch the gun before we get to border. So hopefully no more shooting.'

'Yeah,' Stella wheezed in the back. 'No more shooting. That definitely works for me.'

. . .

Once he returned to FSB headquarters, the commander was shown an enhancement of the image of Novak and Stella getting off the metro train.

The commander squinted. 'Who is that with them?'

The analyst panned slightly to one side and enhanced the image again. This time clearing up Natalya's face.

An analyst called out, 'Commander.' He showed him a post on Twitter. It was a photo of Natalya taken on the metro. Beside her, Novak flapped towards the camera, trying to block the shot.

The commander told the analyst, 'I've just seen a dead woman rise from the grave.' He moved to a quiet corner of the office and took out his mobile phone. He selected the contact, "Yevgeny Belchov."

Once Belchov answered, the commander said, 'We've got a problem.'

18

Rebecca fled along Victoria Embankment, keeping a close eye on any possible tails.

She had escaped Thames House by the slimmest of margins, sneaking out a back exit she had asked to be left off the official schematics: Special Branch didn't know it was there.

Although there wasn't a warrant out for Rebecca's arrest, she was at least a person of interest now in Colin Burleigh's murder, as well as the deaths of the rest of her team.

In the distance she clocked a dark Jaguar speeding towards her from the direction of Thames House.

Rebecca looked all around, but there was nowhere to go: the River Thames was on one side; a twenty-foot-high brick wall on the other.

The car pulled up beside Rebecca, then the passenger door was opened by the driver.

'Get in,' he said.

Rebecca ducked down to see inside the car. 'Sir Oliver?' she said. 'What's going on?'

'I'm saving your bacon,' he said. 'Special Branch is sending an unmarked car this way.' He held up a police radio that he had been listening in on.

Rebecca took one look back down the road, then decided to get in the car. She had barely got her door closed when Oliver sped off.

'What on earth is this about?' Rebecca asked.

'I'm taking you to a safe house.'

'What safe house?'

'GCHQ.'

'Terrific,' said Rebecca. 'GCHQ has a great reputation for safe houses in London.'

Thorn said, 'Your father would never forgive me if he knew I didn't help you.'

'My father? What do you know about my father?'

Sir Oliver's eyes darted between the road ahead and the rear-view mirror. He said, 'I was a junior researcher in your father's cryptography division. Back in seventy-nine.'

'I didn't know you were in cryptography.'

'You won't find it on my official CV. I know what people say about me, but I'm fine with it. I know what I'm really capable of. It's actually not the worst thing in the world to be a good deal smarter than anyone realises. It lets you get away with things like this.'

Judging by the proficiency of his car handling, he showed signs of having taken an advanced driver's course at some point. Even at speed he was nonchalant, careering through the traffic. He seemed like a different person to Rebecca.

'Do you believe he's still out there?' asked Rebecca.

'I'm certain of it. You're much closer than you realise.'

'What do you mean?'

'I don't trust Teddy King or Dominic Morecombe any more than you do. But if you want to prove anything, you've got to find your father. To do that, I've got to keep you out of the hands of Special Branch. That's what Teddy King wants, to keep you out of his hair. What little of it of it he has left.'

'Why are you doing this?' she asked.

'You're still technically GCHQ,' Sir Oliver said, gunning a traffic light as it changed to amber. 'We take care of our own.'

Rebecca held onto the door as they took a corner at speed, marvelling at the ease with which Thorn was handling the pressure. 'You're not what everyone thinks, are you, Sir Oliver?'

The road ahead was clear, so Thorn floored the accelerator. 'That's just as I like it,' he said.

19

The trio's path out of Russia via the Belarus border wasn't without risk. But the extra two or three hours it would have taken to reach Latvia or Ukraine could have been critical.

Once they were safely over the border – thanks to Natalya's passing of $200 to the border guard whilst wishing him a nice weekend – Stella finally relented to her jetlag and fell asleep in the backseat.

Novak lit a cigarette and cranked his window down a little to let in the cold night air.

Natalya, now on her second driving shift, held her hand out, fingers apart. 'Thomas?'

He passed her the cigarette. The sound of her saying his full first name brought back memories. Not all of them good.

'No one calls me that anymore,' he said.

'Why not? It's your name.'

'Everyone calls me Novak.'

'Why is that?'

'I don't know.'

'Thomas was your father's middle name.'

Novak looked at her. 'Even I don't remember that.'

She exhaled. 'Still diffusing with humour, I see.'

'What are you talking about?'

'I bring up your father and you deflect. Why don't you use your first name?' She waited for him to answer, but nothing came. 'You still don't think you're worthy of it, do you. That's why you do this. *The Republic*. The NSA Papers. Goldcastle. Downing Street...Your father's dead, Thomas.'

'Yeah, thanks for that. I heard.'

'I mean, you're never going to get his approval now. The question is, how big a story do you have to catch before you-'

Novak snapped, 'Will you stop!'

Stella twitched slightly in the back.

Novak lowered his voice. 'It's just a name, Talya. You've gotta turn it into a therapy session.' He snatched the cigarette back off her and passed her one of her own. 'This right here,' he gestured back and forth at himself and then her, 'this is why we split up.'

She looked straight ahead. 'No, it's not.'

'In any case, you saying "Thomas" reminds me of when we were together.'

'And you don't want to think about that.'

'Correct.'

For a few moments, there was only the sound of the road and air rushing in through Novak's window.

In the backseat, Stella held her coat tightly around herself. When Novak noticed, he closed his window.

'Why couldn't you have been like this five years ago, Talya?' he asked.

'Like what?'

He tried to choose his words carefully. 'Someone who does the right thing?'

Natalya replied once she had checked in the rear-view mirror that Stella still looked asleep. 'Yes, when we were together, I did what I was told and I kept my mouth shut. I made mistakes. But I'm not the same person you knew before. I *have* changed. Maybe if you had a child of your own you'd understand that, Thomas.'

'You spied on me for the Russian security services, Talya. For eighteen months.'

'They threatened me,' she pleaded. 'You know this. You saw the messages they sent me.'

Novak stubbed his cigarette out in the ashtray. 'You seemed to get over it quickly enough. I had to go to a war to get over you. You married Viktor within six months.'

'I was confused. I *did* love you, Thomas.'

Novak didn't reply.

She didn't want to take her eyes off the road. 'Did you hear me?'

'I heard you,' he grumbled.

'I still love you.'

'I told you not to call me that.'

She reached across for his hand.

Novak pushed hers away. 'Talya, don't-'

'I'm sorry I hurt you.'

The alarm on Stella's phone suddenly went off.

Stella stretched as far across the backseat as her legs would fit. Through a long yawn, she said, 'My turn.'

Natalya eyed her in the rear-view mirror. 'I can carry on. I don't mind.'

'No.' Novak reached for his seatbelt. He wanted the distraction. 'I'll do it. It's not far to Minsk now.'

Stella sat up to check her phone. 'Rebecca's sent another OTR message.'

Novak turned around in his seat. 'Does she know where Adams is going yet?'

Stella said, 'Some hotel in the middle of nowhere...the Grand Hotel von Hoffenheim?' She looked it up on her phone map. 'It's in the Black Forest and about ten miles from anything.'

'Why's he going there?' asked Novak.

Stella went back to the message. 'Something about a meeting...the Hilderberg Group...'

Novak reached out like a Venus Flytrap and grabbed the phone. 'Did you just say Hilderberg?' After checking the message, he broke into manic laughter. 'My God...I've been trying to prove their existence for years.'

Natalya looked over her shoulder, wondering what the fuss was about. 'What is Hilderberg?'

Novak held his head, trying to gather his thoughts. 'No one really knows for sure, but there have been rumours since the Second World War of secret meetings with the wealthiest, most powerful elites in politics, business, finance, media. The rumours were that they would meet somewhere remote every year or two and discuss international problems. That's led to a number of conspiracy theories about who the people are that actually attend, and what they decide there. I've had vague sources about it in the past, but nothing I could run.'

Stella said, 'He's got a lot of experience on the Senate Intelligence Committee, but why would Tucker Adams be invited to something like this?'

'We can add that to the list of questions we have for him. But this could be the breakthrough we need.'

'How much security will there be at this place?' Natalya asked.

'I don't know,' Novak replied. 'Probably a lot.'

'How will we get in?'

'I don't know.'

'What if Adams doesn't want to talk to us?'

'I don't know.'

'And what happens if-'

Novak repeated again, 'I don't know.' If anything, his enthusiasm only grew with each question. 'I don't know about any of this, Talya. But if we get in, we'll be the first journalists to see something no one has ever seen before. And get one step closer to nailing whoever's behind all this.'

20

Senator Adams took his suitcase out to the car with a hastiness that his wife Sharon couldn't understand.

She stood on the front step, arms folded. 'Your plane doesn't leave for another three hours. What's the rush?'

'I told you,' he said, handing the case to his driver, 'I have to stop by the office.' He came back and slid his hands around her waist.

'You're never out that place.'

Adams told her, 'I'll make it up to you.' He pushed her hair aside with the back of his hand to expose her neck for a kiss.

Sharon knew this was what she had signed up for when she married a congressman. But that was a long time ago, and his days weren't getting shorter. If anything, she saw less of him now.

'Stop...' She pushed him gently back. 'Tucker, what's going on? You've been holed up in your study all day. You've been going out for meetings late at night. I've barely seen you all week, and now you're leaving for a three-day trip to Europe. I want my husband back.'

'I know, Sharon. And I'm sorry.' He swallowed hard. 'I wouldn't be going if it wasn't important.'

'It's a security conference in Germany. What's so important about that?'

He kissed her cheek. 'I need to clean up a mess someone's made.' As he went to the back door, he added, 'Oh...remember to lock the gates at night. And put the alarm on before bed.'

After nearly two decades of marriage, and countless trips abroad, Sharon couldn't think of one other time her husband had reminded her about security before leaving.

As Adams' driver waited for the electronic security gate to open, the senator looked out the back window. He kept thinking of Andrei Rublov. And whether Rublov felt the same way he did right now: unsure if he would still be alive the next day.

As the Hart Senate Office Building was closed on weekends, Adams' driver, Max, had to park outside on 2nd Street NE. Adams dashed from the car, holding his collar up against the pouring rain that had started suddenly. He looked all around him, scouting for solitary, suspicious figures.

He had called ahead to alert the security team that he was on his way, so a guard was waiting at the door when he arrived.

Adams' nerves weren't helped by the guard fumbling the keys and dropping them. He didn't want to be outside any longer than was necessary.

The guard finally got the door open. 'Working late, Senator, huh.'

'Evening, Freddie.' Adams shook the rain off his coat then set off for the elevators. He gestured at the front doors. 'You're locking them again, right?'

'Yes, sir,' Freddie replied. As he locked the doors, he noticed a dark Audi crawling past along 2nd Street. Slowly enough that it was obvious someone in the car was scoping out the building.

Freddie peered through the rain but couldn't make out a face inside.

Adams got off on the fifth floor then walked quickly down the arcade overlooking the vast atrium below. When he reached his senate office at room 509 he went straight for the filing cabinet in the corner. He had prepared the files days earlier after first being contacted by Andrei Rublov. Adams had warned him of the dangers of possessing such information. But that ship had sailed. This was the best Adams could do now.

He put in the code to unlock the cabinet, then took out a manila envelope headed 'Senate Intelligence Committee voting records', along with a lengthy dossier he had compiled on the suspect. He opened the dossier to check all the contents were present and correct. They were. Adams had everything required to utterly bury the congressional mole. From details of various meetings and dead drops - all meticulously dated and noted - to voting records.

It was often said that senators were never the same after serving a term in the Intelligence Committee. They were exposed to so much sensitive, head-spinning classified material, that going back to real life with their newfound knowledge was a hard thing to do.

Being part of the committee was like being invited to look behind the curtain of politics itself, and see just how dirty everyone's hands were: secret wars; extrajudicial assassinations; warrantless wiretapping; extortion; blackmail; deals with drug cartels, arms dealers, and dictators; torture; coerced confessions; CIA black sites; incarceration without charge. The list was endless.

To be chair of the committee required fortitude. But the conspiracy Adams was about to reveal was more than even he could stomach any longer.

He was going to blow the roof off the entire upper house of Congress, and probably the White House along with it.

On his way to the door he took a look around his office, his gaze fixing on the American flag, and the state flag of Maryland, standing tall and proud on either side of his desk. To someone like Tucker Adams, politics had always been a very glamorous pursuit. He had told his friends in high school – quite proudly – that he wanted to be President one day. Standing in his senate office, politics no longer felt so glamorous.

The office furniture was cheap and worn. The carpet was coming up around the edges.

Then he thought about all the crappy deals and compromises he'd made there. All the rotten handshakes he'd given to get deals passed, and depressing phone calls to tell constituents their sons or daughters had died in a war halfway across the world.

He'd tried to be an honest man. To raise the level of debate in the country. To do right by his constituents and the American people. Decades he'd been doing it. And here he was, rummaging through his office in the dark like a burglar, smuggling out evidence of the biggest political conspiracy since Watergate. He didn't even know if he'd survive the night, let alone get a chance to tell his story.

He'd gone to Washington hoping to drain the swamp. Instead, he'd let himself get drowned in it.

Adams jogged to his car, clutching the files under his raincoat. He slumped with relief once Max got them onto the freeway for the airport. Adams felt safe for the moment.

But that was only because he hadn't noticed the black Audi tailing them two cars back.

A call came through on Adams's phone.

"*Glen Fallow*".

Adams let it ring a few more times before answering reluctantly. 'Glen. Taking a break from waterboarding tonight?'

'That's good, Senator,' Fallow replied. 'It was nice to see some of that wit make it into your Online Privacy Bill. The last I saw on CSPAN it was getting laughed out the senate by only seventy-three votes. So close.'

Adams wasn't in the mood. 'What do you want, Glen?'

'I know what you're doing, Tucker.'

'What are you talking about?'

'I know that you met Rublov.'

Adams said nothing.

'Yeah,' Fallow sneered, 'I know all about it. What did you tell him?'

'I don't know what you're talking about. And who the hell is Rublov?'

'You should know, Senator. You Googled his name five

times this morning. What, did they not send a clear enough message with him? You want to be next?'

Adams lowered his voice. 'Are you actually dumb enough, as the CIA Deputy Director for Counterterrorism, to threaten a sitting U.S. senator on the fucking phone?'

'I'm trying to protect you, Tuck. This is how the real world works. I thought you'd at least understand what's at stake for them here. Do you think they're just going to walk away, now that they're *this* close?'

Max raised his hand like a patient schoolchild.

Adams covered the mouthpiece while Fallow continued.

'Sorry, Senator,' Max said. 'But you wanted me to check for a tail.'

Adams looked out the back window.

'Two cars back. Black Audi,' Max said. 'He's been on us since Constitution Avenue.'

Adams went back to Fallow. 'Have you got a tail on me, you piece of shit?'

'You've got a tail?' Fallow asked.

'Max is the best driver in Washington. There's a reason I don't take one from the pool like everyone else.'

'Tuck, I haven't sent anyone to tail you.'

Something about Fallow's voice told Adams he wasn't bullshitting.

'Get off the road,' Fallow instructed him, panic in his voice. 'Now. Go somewhere public. A diner. A bar. Something. But get off the road. Believe me, I'm trying to help you here.'

Adams hung up then called forward, 'Let's go, Max.'

Max obliged. 'You got it, boss.'

As the Lexus saloon powered through the deep surface water on the I-395, the Audi behind made an aggressive overtake to keep up. Max accelerated again, swinging an S-shape through one lane to another, squeezing through a gap.

Adams wasn't wrong about Max's driving skills.

The Audi followed with the same manoeuvre, now three cars back and struggling to keep up.

Max kept a keen eye on the rear-view mirror. 'He wants us to know he's there now, sir.'

'I can assure him, he has my attention,' Adams replied.

The Audi flashed its lights as it sharked through traffic, which was slowing from the increasingly torrential rain.

With a bus trundling ahead there was nowhere for Max to go. He looked on helplessly as the Audi prowled around the Lexus' bumper.

'Hold on, sir,' Max said, seeing a gap in the traffic in the opposite lane.

He swung out hard and fast. The lane opposite had looked clear, but the spray from the road had masked an oncoming Toyota, now flashing its headlights and blasting its horn.

Max held his breath as he gunned for the gap ahead of the bus, swinging back hard right, missing the Toyota's front wing by inches.

The Audi was still stuck behind the bus, ducking and diving out every few seconds trying to overtake.

While they had the gap, Max gunned it towards the 14th Street Bridge. He was up to fifth, then sixth gear, the speedometer teasing sixty.

Having lost so much ground, the Audi simply barged into the opposite lane to overtake the bus, the oncoming traffic forced out the way.

Ahead, Max had been slowed by yet more traffic. The

weather was making visibility impossible, and everyone bar Max and the Audi had slowed to a crawl.

The Audi's straight line speed was much faster than the Lexus, and it was soon all over the back of the senator's car.

First came a gentle nudge. Then constant headlight flashing.

Adams reached for the grab handle and held on for dear life.

He thought about phoning Sharon, just to hear her voice possibly one last time. Judging by how the Audi was being driven, they weren't going to let him get away.

In desperation, and with the bridge coming to an end soon, the Audi went deep on the revs and overtook Max, charging down the wrong lane.

Not wanting to cede ground, Max accelerated too.

With the Audi driver's window alongside Adams in the back, Adams could make out the driver pointing frantically to pull over.

Adams sat up. 'Max,' he called, 'I think we should pull over.'

Max took his foot off the gas.

The Audi swerved gradually right, guiding the Lexus to a section of run-off grass.

Max reached across to the glove compartment where there was a .38 semi-automatic pistol locked up. 'Just say the word, Senator.'

Adams put his hand out. 'No, Max. I think it's OK.'

The driver ran towards the back of the Lexus, but was met by Max.

'Who the hell are you?' Max demanded. 'You any idea who that is in there?'

The man, already soaked through after barely five seconds, held out a badge. 'You any idea who *I* am?'

Max read the ID. 'What the hell is American Intelligence Internal Affairs?'

The man was six-three, with a forty-four-inch chest. He had the arms of someone who did weighted chin-ups three times a week, and the steely, frozen green eyes of someone who had seen far too much in his life.

His accent was Midwest, and his voice sounded like he gargled gravel every morning.

'I'm SSO Walter Sharp, I'm with Central Intelligence. I need to speak to your boss. Get back in the car, please.' Sharp held the front door open and looked off to the side, unfazed by either the rain or the situation.

It didn't even occur to Max to argue.

Senator Adams got out the car, holding his raincoat over his head. He had to raise his voice to be heard over the passing traffic beside them.

'What the heck is going on?' Adams asked.

'Sir, I need you to come with me. For your own safety,' Sharp instructed.

'Are you with Fallow?'

'No, sir. I'm working in conjunction with Director Rebecca Fox of British Intelligence Internal Affairs.'

Adams smiled. 'You're with Ghost Division. So it *is* true. Angela Curtis got it up and running.'

'We don't have much time, Senator. Director Fox has uncovered evidence of an imminent threat on your life. You need to come with me.'

21

Gaspar arrived in Berlin Tegel airport wearing an olive corduroy jacket, black roll neck sweater, and round frameless glasses. He carried a battered leather document case and kept a copy of that day's *El País* (turned to the culture pages) under his arm.

He was unusually clean-shaven, and made sure to spend a good fifteen minutes browsing the book aisles of an airport newsagent. A woman came over to browse near him, hoping he would strike up conversation with her. But Gaspar was working, and he would never jeopardise a job over a woman. Every interaction only increased the risk: it meant someone asking questions, which could mean exposing holes in your cover.

Gaspar didn't know a thing about literature, modern or otherwise. A fact that would be brutally obvious within a few minutes' conversation.

All Gaspar needed to do was look the part of a Spanish intellectual, and answer to the name of Sergio de la Pava that was on his passport.

The passport showed him coming from Paris to Barcelona, and now to Berlin. His legend being that he was an editor for a small poetry publisher in Madrid. The only people he might end up speaking to were Customs and Immigration. Poetry wasn't exactly a common source of conversation in glass booths processing hundreds of passengers every hour.

While he browsed the high-end literary magazines, an older man to his left picked up a copy of *Paris Review*, then placed it back in slightly the wrong place, close to Gaspar.

Gaspar opened it and took out the envelope slipped inside by the man.

Expressionless, Gaspar made his way swiftly to the short-stay car park, heading to the space marked on the envelope. Inside the envelope was the key for a BMW 1 Series Sports Hatch. With its powerful eight-speed Steptronic transmission and M Sports steering, it was an ideal choice for the sharp, twisting Black Forest roads that he was destined for.

The car had been parked in a camera blind spot, so there was nothing to fear in taking out the sports holdall from the boot into the front seat.

In the holdall was a 4" Emerson Super Commander folding knife – designed for Navy SEALS - that could be opened with one hand; a Marathon General Purpose Military Field Watch, made in Switzerland, and designed for infantry use (Gaspar normally wore one, but it didn't fit with his Sergio de la Pava cover); a change of clothes for the next morning.

Hanging from the backseat grab handle was a Hugo Boss suit bag.

Gaspar's burner phone pinged with a message alert: '*Target: Joachim Deckelman. Bar Mono, 08.00. Baden-Baden.*'

22

SOMEWHERE OVER THE IRISH SEA – SUNDAY, 5.03AM

Walter Sharp had a thing about sleeping on planes that Senator Adams would never understand.

For Adams, sleep wasn't on the cards. He had his tie loose and top button undone, a picture of exhaustion sitting opposite Sharp in their four-seat booth.

Adams had drifted in and out of microsleeps for an hour, then taken to staring out the window of the CIA-owned Learjet Global 5000.

A man can get a lot of thinking done at a cruising altitude of thirty-two thousand feet, and travelling at six hundred and fifty miles per hour. They were flying high above a bed of clouds which had been gradually changing from dark blue to light purple as the sun rose. Something about it made Adams think about his mortality.

Despite the khaki cap pulled down over Sharp's face, Adams suddenly asked, 'So what did you say you were? A Specialized Combat...' He trailed off, expecting Sharp to correct him.

With his cap still over his face, Sharp said, 'Did you

know that every major disease in the developed world can be linked to a lack of sleep? Cancer, diabetes, Alzheimer's, obesity, you name it.'

Adams paused. 'I didn't know that.'

'Did you also know that the human body can't catch up on sleep? Once it's gone, it ain't ever coming back. Sleep repairs parts of your brain that nothing else can.'

'You know a lot about sleep.'

'I sure do, Senator. I love sleep. For me, sleep is a goddamn religion. The best orgasm I ever had ain't got nothing on the best sleep I ever had. I once slept for sixteen hours after a mission. Thought I'd died and proceeded directly to heaven.' Sharp removed the cap from his face. 'So remind me: what did you want to know that was worth waking me up for?'

Adams stammered. 'I...uh...your position...A Specialized-'

Knowing he was done with sleep, Sharp sat up. 'I'm a Specialized Skills Officer.'

'Then you're trained in paramilitary operations for the CIA.'

'Specifically, clandestine tradecraft, acquiring sources, and gathering intelligence that threatens the United States.'

'Honestly,' Adams said. 'Would I be dead right now if you hadn't found me?'

'It's probable,' replied Sharp.

Adams had never really noticed the enormous difference between possible and probable until that moment.

'They wouldn't hurt my wife, would they? To get to me?'

Sharp, realising he wasn't going to be left in peace, took the cap off his face. 'They don't need to do that.'

'What made you even want to find me?' asked Adams.

Sharp took out a caffeine pill from his pocket, and washed it down with some water from his plastic cup. 'When a reporter for Russia Now comes into the country, that doesn't go unnoticed at CIA. Especially when you realise they've come without a cameraman, a sound guy, or anyone else, then rent a room in Garfield Heights instead of a suite at the Hyatt. So you do a little digging. And it turns out the reporter isn't quite what you think he is, because he's left a bit of an online trail to a series of articles published in Russia which suggest he's not quite as pro-Kremlin as his employer might think. So you check where he's going, where he's been. Turns out in two weeks the place he drives to most often is a park on the edge of the city, where he stays for ten minutes, before making the half-hour drive back to Garfield Heights. Three days later he goes back there half an hour before the park closes. This time he stays for fifteen minutes. So you get a friend at NSA to cross-reference metadata from the reporter's phone and find the number of a prominent senator.'

For all the precautions Adams thought he took, he now felt like he was completely transparent to Sharp.

He went on, 'And when the reporter ends up dying in suspicious circumstances, it makes you really want to talk to the last person who saw him alive, and ask them, quite bluntly, in the hope of a God's honest answer: what did you talk to Andrei Rublov about and what did you give him?'

Adams was now keenly aware of having a lump in his throat. 'Andrei told me he had been passed documents by a Saudi dissident reporter called Omar bin Talal.'

Sharp squinted. 'He was killed six weeks ago.'

'And for exactly the same reason Andrei was killed:

Omar had a dossier showing there was a Russian spy somewhere senior in the U.S. government. They've been delivering classified intelligence to the Kremlin for years now. But that was all Omar and Andrei had. They didn't know for sure if the dossier was fake or not. So they needed another source to back up their story. That was where I came in.'

'You knew there was a spy?' asked Sharp. 'How did you know?'

'I'm the chair of the Senate Intelligence Committee. I know when a committee has a leak, and we had one. It didn't take long for me to work it out.'

'I can tell from your choice of words you're not going to tell me who it is.'

Adams gave nothing away, taking a pause to drink some water. 'With respect, Officer Sharp. These days, I wouldn't trust CIA with so much as a grocery list.'

The captain announced overhead, 'Officer Sharp, we're now beginning our descent to RAF Brize Norton. ETA twenty-three minutes.'

Adams recognised the name. 'That's a Ministry of Defence airfield. I landed there once on a U.S. delegation to-'

Sharp interrupted, 'GCHQ? Yeah, it's barely an hour from there.'

Adams shot a look out the window, then checked his watch. 'I thought we were landing at Ramstein Air Base? Officer Sharp, I *have* to get to Germany.'

'We're picking someone up,' Sharp told him.

Adams' heart jumped. 'Who?'

'The person who found out that you met Rublov. It'll give you a chance to thank her for saving your life.'

23

The trio had been travelling through the night, arriving in Minsk at one a.m. where they stopped for a wash at a truck stop. Novak had caught Natalya stealing a look at him while he took off his shirt at the wash basins.

When they were together Novak had been whippet-thin – the result of a travelling reporter's diet of coffee for breakfast and some potato chips for dinner. Now he was about ten pounds heavier, almost all of it muscle.

When Novak spotted her checking him out, Natalya looked away quickly, blushing slightly.

After they got back on the road, Novak floored it all the way to Warsaw where they had to abandon Natalya's car to make a flight to Stuttgart. Then a car hire into the depths of the Black Forest.

It had been nearly an hour since they last saw another car.

Sunlight was breaking through the trees to the east.

Natalya was out for the count in the backseat, her first sleep in nearly two days.

'What exactly is the plan here?' asked Stella.

Novak was a picture of indecision. 'Uh...there isn't one? Rebecca said she'd call, right? She's on the plane with Sharp and Adams.'

'Yeah, but what if there's a roadblock. What are we going to say?'

Novak said, 'I was hoping you'd think of something.'

Stella smiled.

Novak stayed focussed on the road. 'I know it was you, Stella.'

She played dumb. 'Me what?'

'Who's been briefing the media that I was involved in the Goldcastle story.'

It took her all of three seconds before giving in. 'Well, you were! People deserve to know what you did on that story, Novak. We did it together.'

'I know we did.' He put out a fist. 'Put it there.'

Stella looked at it, mystified.

'What?' asked Novak.

Stella said, 'I suppose I don't understand why this is preferable to, say, a handshake.'

Novak rolled his eyes and retracted his fist. 'OK, forget it.'

'No, it's just, people shook hands for hundreds of years. Is this another American attempt to improve things there's nothing wrong with?' She reached for his hand, wanting to play along now.

'No, forget it, Stella,' Novak said, pulling his hand away. 'It's a little something we Americans call camaraderie.'

While laughing, she managed to grab his hand, making

a meal of touching knuckles with him. 'There. Look. We're bros again.'

Natalya stirred in her sleep from the pair's laughter.

As their laughter subsided, Stella kept her voice low. 'You know, I heard your conversation earlier.'

'When?' asked Novak.

'Before Minsk. I wasn't really asleep. Not the whole time.'

Novak didn't respond.

'You really don't see any holes in her story?' she asked.

'Like what?'

'Like why the only reporters in the world who latched onto this "spy in Congress" story happen to work for a Russian state news channel.'

'I know,' Novak conceded. 'We don't have all the answers yet.'

'Two things I do know for sure are that Natalya is a proven informant to the FSB, and that she spied on you for them.'

'I know, Stel. But that was a long time ago. And the FSB are clearly after her for something now...'

'You're not at all worried she's playing you?'

Novak paused. 'No.' He didn't sound convinced.

Stella's phone started ringing with a Darkroom video-call.

'It's him,' Stella said.

In the backseat, Natalya was woken by the noise.

Stella answered the call, holding the phone up to be seen on the other end. 'Hi, Artur. My signal's pretty weak out here, so I might drop out.'

'That's cool,' he replied.

Natalya held the back of Novak's seat while she leaned forward. 'Who is this guy?' she asked groggily.

'Someone we trust,' Novak answered. 'He'd tell you we saved his life a few months ago. I'd tell you he helped us break the Goldcastle story.'

'You're talking to Artur Korecki? Of the TruthArmy podcast? That's so cool.'

'If anyone knows anything about the Hilderberg Group it's him.'

Stella pointed the phone in Novak's direction.

'Hey, Artur, buddy,' Novak said. 'Sorry, I know it's late back in NYC but we're looking for some information. You were the only one on our list.'

Artur was sitting in front of his laptop. He was wearing a New York Knicks jersey and eating from a box of Krispy Kreme donuts. 'Anything I can do to help,' he said.

'What can you tell us about the Hilderberg Group?'

Artur's eyes went wide. 'Gee...where to begin. When you hear people talk about the deep state, this is the epitome of it. You're talking about a group of people with power, privilege, and connected in ways that verge on the incomprehensible. In simple terms: you might elect Presidents or Prime Ministers, but it's people like the Hilderberg Group that are really in charge.'

Stella asked, 'How far back do they go? Are we talking Cold War?'

'The start seems to be all anyone knows for sure: the group was founded in the late forties by an industrialist called Friedrich Hilderberg. Almost all of Hilderberg's family had been wiped out in Nazi death camps across central Europe. Having barely escaped himself, he swore that he would never again allow the world to burn in such a way. He gathered the most powerful and influential people he could find. We're talking financial titans, politicians, newspaper publishers, business leaders. It started as an annual meeting to discuss politics and economics, taking a real European and American approach to both. They were hardcore capitalists, free-marketers, what we would probably call neo-conservative these days.

'The only meeting anyone really knows about – possibly the first one - took place in 1954 at the Hotel Hilderberg in the Netherlands. Since then, the Group has operated in total, obsessive secrecy. Members are through invitation only, and approved by an all-powerful steering committee. Even members of royalty and billionaires have been rebuffed.'

'We're hardly still on a path to world war,' Novak said. 'What does the Group want now?'

Artur threw his hands up. 'Depending on who you ask, they either want the complete global dominance of Western capitalism, or they want to create a world government run solely by private interests. Me? I've been researching the Hilderberg Group for over ten years. And anyone who tells you they know for sure is either lying or wrong.'

'How on earth do they keep all this secret?' asked Stella.

'You're talking about people with unbelievable power, Stella,' Artur said. 'They're also fiercely loyal to each other. In their history there has never been a single leak from a single meeting. In a world of few secrets, and almost instant comment and opinion, Hilderberg is exceptional in every way. They own a whole network of hotels, security, law enforcement. They can shut down entire estates and staff them with all their own people.'

Natalya leaned forward so Artur could hear her. 'What would you tell someone trying to break into a Hilderberg Group conference?'

Artur started to laugh, then realised Natalya was serious. 'I'd say you were on the cusp of seeing something very few people have ever seen. No one knows how many people who have got close to the Hilderberg Group have been killed to protect their secrets. And I would think long and hard about turning back.' Artur paused. 'But you're with Tom Novak and Stella Mitchell, so you're not going to do that.'

The phone screen started to freeze up.

Stella said, 'Artur, I'm losing the signal. We should go.'

The picture broke up completely. 'Godspeed, my friends,' Artur said, giving a wave.

'Look,' Natalya pointed towards the trees.

There were CCTV cameras high up on camouflaged stanchions between the trees. The cameras looked brand new.

'Well,' Novak said. 'We're in it now.'

24

The Grand Hotel von Hoffenheim was set deep in the heart of the forest, and was every bit as grand as its name proclaimed. To say it was a five-star resort was like saying going to the moon was "far away". Technically true, but nowhere near the reality.

Set on a remote private estate at the foot of rolling hills, the hotel was a traditional Germanic 'burg' (castle), far away from the winding mountain passes favoured by bikers and car enthusiasts.

There was only one road that made the hotel accessible, and it now had a security gate blocking access from one mile outside the hotel.

The roadblock was manned by three security guards, each with the physique of army personnel, and the attitude of vipers.

When Novak saw the security gate in the distance, he pulled the car over at a bend in the road to stay out of sight.

'What are you going to do?' Stella asked.

'Send an SOS.' Novak tapped out an OTR message on his phone to Rebecca. Once it had encrypted, he hit send.

A reply quickly came back.

He tossed Stella the phone and started the engine again.

Stella read the message Rebecca sent back:

'*120954*'

'Are you sure about this?' she asked Novak.

He kept his eyes forward. 'Absolutely not.'

At the roadblock a guard waved at them to stop. He was wearing a tailored Hugo Boss suit over a black shirt buttoned all the way to the top, with no tie (ties were a disaster waiting to happen in a potential combat situation). As the guard indicated for Novak to roll his window down, his jacket flapped open a little, revealing a glimpse of a holstered pistol inside.

The guard spoke first in German.

Novak replied, '*Guten tag. Sprechen sie Englisch?*'

He replied in flawless English, 'I'm sorry. This road is closed for a private event.'

'Yes,' Novak said, 'we're attending with Tucker Adams.'

The guard presented a little handheld device with a number pad on the screen. 'Please enter the passcode.'

Another guard went round to Stella's side, peering in through her window, and then Natalya's. He had the same solid gold ring with an 'H' on it as the other guard.

Novak entered the code: '120954'

The guard nodded in appreciation as the passcode was accepted, then spun around as he heard tyres on the gravel track behind. It was a black, unmarked SUV with tinted windows. It pulled up by the roadblock.

A man wearing the same outfit as the guard got out. By the way he carried himself, he looked very much in charge.

The man called to the guard, remonstrating about something.

Natalya whispered, 'What language is that they're speaking?'

'It's not German,' said Stella.

Novak listened closely. 'It's Flemish. They must be from Belgium. Artur said Hilderberg always use their own people.'

The man from the SUV strode toward them, removing a pair of aviator sunglasses. He had a military buzzcut, and the burly physique of special forces.

He spoke in English. 'I'm Ulrich Schöll, chief security officer. Senator Adams called to say he was sorry you were left behind at the airport. He is not long here.'

Novak nodded like he knew exactly what was going on. 'Great. Thank you, Mr Schöll.'

Schöll wore a fixed grin that suggested he wasn't actually happy or pleased. 'The senator has quite an entourage. A man and a woman already with him, and now three more.'

Novak tried to snigger along. 'Yeah...the senator feels lost without his staff.'

'We didn't see you at the last meeting in Austria.' Schöll remarked.

Novak didn't show any outward sign of panic, but inside he was churning. He had a feeling Schöll was trying to trick him, but couldn't think what other answer might work. 'Oh yeah,' Novak said, 'There was some business on the Hill we had to attend to then.'

Schöll just kept on smiling. 'What a shame.'

Novak couldn't tell if he'd got away with it or not.

Schöll held his arm out towards the open security barrier. 'Enjoy your stay.'

They set off down the single-track road, Schöll watching them the whole way until they turned the corner, winding through the enormous trees on either side.

'That's a cute touch they have with the passcode,' Stella noted. 'The date of the first Hilderberg Group meeting?'

'Probably,' Novak said, worried about Schöll.

Back at the roadblock, Schöll told the guard, 'Keep an eye on them.'

'Something wrong, sir?' the guard asked.

'He doesn't know that we've never held a meeting in Austria.' Schöll slid his sunglasses back on. 'That's interesting to me.'

25

For Joachim Deckelman, the spa town of Baden-Baden in the southwest of Germany, at the border of the Black Forest, wasn't where he had imagined he'd still be at twenty-four years old.

Each day before he started work he came to Bar Mono because it was the only place in town that had Pink Floyd, King Crimson, and Yes on the jukebox.

It was also open from eight in the morning. Germany had some of the most lax licensing laws in Europe, with a lot of states not even bothering to set closing times. The state of Baden-Württemberg only insisted on a *Putzstunde*, a cleaning hour between six and seven, where no customers were served.

Which was fine by Joachim, as Bar Mono had excellent clean toilets where you could roll a joint in peace. They even had a quiet alley out the back to smoke it without the *Polizei* giving you trouble.

He returned from the alley, pleasantly high, to find a

stranger at the jukebox cueing up 'Her Eyes Are a Blue Million Miles' by Captain Beefheart.

The guy sat alone with a roll-up cigarette behind his ear. He was wearing a white t-shirt with the cover of Pink Floyd's The Wall on it, under an old denim jacket.

Joachim took a sip of his lager on the way over, his mouth dry from the joint. Without invitation he sat across from the guy and announced, 'We must be the only two people in Baden-Baden with decent musical taste, my friend.' He held his hand out to shake. 'I'm Joachim.'

The man shook back. 'Daniel.'

Joachim squinted slightly. 'Are you from here? I would have thought I'd have seen you before.'

'Just passing through.'

Joachim nodded. 'Cool. It's just...I couldn't place your accent.'

'Yeah, I'm from Strasbourg.'

He laughed. '*Mais oui*! A Frenchman. I should have known. Your German is good, though.'

'So what do you do, Joachim?'

Joachim rolled his eyes. 'I'm a bellhop.'

'Oh, yeah? In Baden-Baden?'

'No. The Grand Hotel, out in the forest. I'm working later. Sucks, man.'

'Why's that?'

Joachim looked around, then leaned in and whispered, 'I'm not supposed to talk about it.'

'Oh yeah?' said Daniel, eyes narrowing with intrigue.

Daniel knew everything about Joachim. From his musical taste, to his lack of friends and family, and especially where he worked.

Daniel took the roll-up from behind his ear. 'You know anywhere I can get some decent grass?'

Joachim grinned. 'Man, did you ask the right person...'

When they were back at Joachim's apartment just a few streets away, Joachim put down two cans of lager on the coffee table. He put on 'Like a Rolling Stone' by Bob Dylan (his favourite getting-high song), then took out his special wooden box where he kept his stash.

Daniel wandered around the vast, modern living room. It had some of the best views in the whole town. All the furniture was new, and the technology on display was impressive: top of the range Sony Bravia 4k television; Bowers and Wilkins speaker units; hundreds of Blu-rays stacked on the floor.

'This is some place,' Daniel gushed. 'You said you work at a hotel?'

Joachim wasn't used to explaining away the relative wealth on display for a bellhop. 'My employers pay very well.'

Joachim picked through various bags of grass, weighed out in ten-euro increments.

Daniel picked up both cans and asked, 'Do you mind if I get a glass?'

'No problem, dude.'

Daniel went to the kitchen, and stood in front of where he knew the glasses were: this wasn't the first time Daniel had been in Joachim's apartment.

For appearances, Daniel shouted through, 'Which cupboard?'

'Top one on the left,' he replied.

Daniel slipped a white powder into one of the glasses then swirled it around. He noticed a fingerprint on the glass, but that didn't matter: he was wearing false prints.

Daniel returned to the living room, and casually placed the glasses down.

Realising Daniel had also got him a glass, Joachim said, 'Thanks, dude. You didn't have to do that.'

'No problem.'

'How much did you want again?'

Daniel rummaged through his pocket, then produced a crumpled twenty-euro note. 'That much.'

Joachim passed him the bag, then checked his watch. 'Shit,' he said. 'I need to get ready for work soon.'

Daniel nudged Joachim's lager towards him. 'Forget about those assholes. They don't own you.'

Joachim shrugged, then took a drink before setting off for the bedroom to get changed.

He didn't notice much at first, but it was already too late.

He had imbibed a fatal dose – in powder form - of highly poisonous inland taipan snake venom.

Daniel dropped the bag of grass back in Joachim's box then slightly raised the volume on the speaker. In the other room, Joachim reached for his throat, gasping for air.

He fell to the floor, reaching out desperately towards Daniel who could see him from the living room. Joachim couldn't understand what was going on – he'd only had a sip of lager - and especially why Daniel wasn't helping.

'Don't try to figure out why it's happening,' Daniel said. 'Just accept it. It will go faster that way.'

Joachim's shoulders popped up and down a few times as his body tried to find some oxygen. His blood was experiencing the hemotoxic effects of the venom. It felt like he was suffocating, but actually his blood was turning to sludge. And quickly too. Now his heart wasn't able to transport oxygen around his body.

Daniel checked his watch as he walked towards Joachim.

'People try to fight it,' said Daniel. 'Don't fight it. It's just your life slipping away. It's nothing.'

Face-down on the carpet, Joachim gurgled and then went silent.

Daniel stepped over him, then opened the wardrobe, taking out Joachim's work uniform. Joachim wasn't quite the same Euro-size fifty as Daniel was, but close enough. To go to such lengths only to find out he was the wrong size would have been an unforgiveable operational error.

He took Joachim's grounds pass, ID badge, and uniform, then turned the music off. The sight of Joachim on the floor didn't move him in any way. Death no longer even penetrated the emotive part of his brain. Like the army recruit who doesn't ask why he must march up and down the hill with a heavy pack, he never asked why someone had to be killed.

He simply did it.

From his backpack, he changed into a sweatshirt bearing the logo 'Universität Stuttgart', put on a green baseball cap, and changed into clean, white trainers.

It was as if Daniel never existed.

Now he was Horst, an eager Sports Science student with an Airbnb in town.

But tomorrow, clutching a SIG SG 550 rifle in the Grand Hotel von Hoffenheim, he would be Gaspar again.

There were thirty Hilderberg Group attendees in total, most of whom had arrived the previous night. In the lobby, Novak, Stella, and Natalya found that they were the only other guests in sight. Like rock stars who were driven right to a concert stage a matter of minutes before a show started, the other Hilderberg guests wouldn't leave their luxurious suites until they were required.

They were busy tending to their business empires, monitoring the markets, buying and selling. Some had turned their suites into mobile offices, with satellite uplinks and conference calls, video projector screens for presentations by their staff.

Very few assistants with the guests actually knew that their boss was a member of the Hilderberg Group. As far as they were concerned it was just a private meeting of mutual interests. A chance to drink expensive wine in the company of some similarly wealthy acquaintances. It happened dozens of times a year at other conferences and expos. The staff just didn't know the vast infrastructure behind the scenes at the Grand Hotel.

The hotel staff were all Hilderberg's people, almost all born into family who had worked for Hilderberg interests through the years. And they were rewarded in kind. A concierge could earn twice what a bank manager in Baden-Baden earned. And a bellhop could afford a plush apartment in a building full of executives and wealthy retirees.

That was what secrecy cost Hilderberg, but it was worth it.

Novak went to reception. 'We're with Senator Adams. He's expecting us.'

The receptionist bowed slightly, as if greeting minor royalty. Her accent was hard to place as she spoke six different languages, all fluently. 'Yes, of course, sir. Senator Adams made us aware of the situation. He said he will be down very shortly.' She made her way around the desk to collect the bags. 'I'll be happy to take your bags to your room...'

Novak said, 'No, no. Thanks, we're good. It's just a couple of backpacks.'

The hotel manager, on the bottom steps of the sweeping marble staircase, noticed the irregularity of the receptionist having to offer to handle bags. He called the lobby manager over.

'Where is Joachim?' he seethed.

'I'm sorry, sir,' the lobby manager replied, holding out his phone impotently. 'There's no answer.'

Over at the silver elevators, a door pinged open. Out stepped three men in the finest suits Novak had ever seen in real life. One was president of the world's largest insurance company. Another was CEO of Italy's most famous car manufacturer. And the other was the Grand Duke of Luxembourg.

As they sauntered past without a care in the world, Stella overheard them talking in French about the upcoming Russian elections.

Senator Adams followed behind them. He put his arms out. 'Better late than never...' he quipped, quickly walking them to the elevators. 'Josh, it's about time. And...ladies, glad to see you too.'

'Good to see you, Senator,' Novak said, trying to appear comfortable with him.

Stella took out her phone, pretending to show Adams something on it. 'You'll be pleased to know we managed to clear that meeting from Tuesday...'

Soon the elevator doors closed and the three reporters could finally relax.

Novak leaned against the wall. 'Tell me you actually have a staffer called Josh, Senator.'

Adams stammered, 'I...no, I do. My chief of staff back in D.C. Sorry. I was trying to improvise.'

'What happens if the hotel manager makes a few phone calls and finds out your chief of staff is back in Washington? I guess Walter hasn't told you yet to never tell a lie you can't back up.'

Chastened, Adams replied, 'No improv. Got it.'

27

ROOM 77, THE GRAND HOTEL VON HOFFENHEIM

Adams' suite was as classically Germanic and luxurious as the hotel's exterior suggested. The walls were panelled in dark oak, supplemented with original oil paintings of the Romantic era. Antiques were scattered liberally around console tables and sideboards. A huge log fire burned in the centre of the living room, adding to the gothic intensity.

Adams went straight for the bar, fixing himself a glass of Highland Park: thirty-year-old single malt Scotch whisky at nine hundred euros a bottle. 'Everyone help yourselves,' he said, slurping about fifty euros' worth in one go.

Novak's eyes lit up at the sight of Walter Sharp standing by the breakfast bar in the kitchen, drinking a black coffee.

Knowing Sharp wasn't big on hugs, Novak settled for Sharp's typical 'bro' handshake, grabbing it like they were going to arm wrestle. As always, Sharp's grip was crushing.

Novak stepped back. 'Don't take this the wrong way, but you look weird in a suit.'

'I know, right.' Sharp tried to direct things back to business, leading Novak to the leather sofas in front of the fire.

Rebecca stayed sitting at a desk outside the bedroom, busy with her laptop. Inside, she was pleased to see Novak and Stella again, but she didn't let much of it show.

'With you in a sec,' she told them.

Natalya drifted towards the sofas, taking in the vast grandeur of the suite.

Adams said to her, 'I'm sorry, I don't know you.' He tilted his head slightly. 'But I recognise you.'

'Natalya,' she said.

That was all Adams needed. 'You're Natalya Olgorova.'

She nodded.

Adams looked urgently to Novak and Stella then back to Natalya. 'You should probably know, you were in my morning security memo. The FSB is looking for you.'

Stella sat beside Novak. 'We had a suspicion,' she said dryly.

Rebecca closed her laptop then joined the others, staying standing behind the sofas.

Sharp stood beside Adams in front of the fire, Adams staring into his whisky as he swirled it around.

Sharp said, 'As we all have a history – Natalya excepted – Senator Adams has agreed to talk with you about certain information he has. But he has asked me to make clear that everything that is said in this room is strictly off the record until he says otherwise. I'm not here to broker deals about any news stories. I'm here to get to the bottom of the credible threat against the senator, and nothing else. That clear?'

Novak nodded.

Stella said, 'Perfectly.'

Sharp stood beside Rebecca behind the sofas, giving Adams the floor.

Novak led off. 'First things first, Senator. You were willing to talk to Andrei Rublov. Why not us? We at least have experience with this level of story.'

Adams said, 'And Rublov ended up being pulled out the Potomac River.'

Stella's years in Westminster politics had given her a talent for being able to read a room. And she could sense Adams was about to clam up. He hadn't quite put up the wall yet, but he'd gathered enough bricks at his feet. If they didn't tread carefully Stella knew Adams would start building.

'Senator,' she said. 'Presumably you chose to speak to Andrei Rublov because he knew something you also did. Something you disapproved of. Enough to risk your position and career to meet him.'

Adams finished his drink and turned towards the fire. 'That was different. That was in D.C., not a goddamn Hilderberg meeting. If they knew what was going on in this room right now they'd have me killed, and that would be just for starters.'

Natalya leaned forward on her knees. 'Senator. I worked with Andrei for nearly ten years. In an impossible climate of fear, he was the bravest reporter I've ever known. There's nothing I want more in this world than to find the people who killed him, and the people who ordered it.' She looked at Novak and Stella. 'I think I speak for us all on that.'

Adams turned his back, unconvinced.

Natalya went on, 'If it *is* the FSB that's behind all this – the spy in Congress, the cover-up, the murder - I promise you they will never stop. We cannot run the rest of our lives. I want to get back to my family. And I'm sure you do too.'

Adams went back to the bar. This time fixing himself a long glass of water.

'It started a few months ago,' Adams explained, dropping ice cubes into his glass. 'First, files from my office would go missing for a day at a time then mysteriously reappear. Then we were in talks-'

Stella, eager for clarity, cut in. 'Sorry, Senator. Who's "we"?'

'Sorry, yes. The Senate Intelligence Committee. We were in talks with various embassies in Washington, assuring them that the NSA wasn't tapping any phones or monitoring internet traffic. Which was a lie. The NSA was and is still doing those things. They've just got better at hiding it...'

Despite the initial warning, Novak couldn't help trying his luck at taking out a notepad.

He showed Adams a fresh page. 'Don't worry about this. It's just for my own memory. This is still off the record for now,' he assured him.

Stella liked the cagey addition of 'for now'. A pure Bernstein manoeuvre he'd picked up from his dozens of viewings of *All the President's Men*.

Adams stared at Novak, then said, 'Fine. The only country that had a problem with our official denial was Russia. They accused us of lying to them.'

'Because they had proof?' wondered Novak.

Stella put her hand to her face then made a coy 'slow down' gesture to Novak. Like a good therapist who lets their patient talk themselves towards the truth, Stella knew good journalism was as much about staying silent at the right times as asking the right questions.

Adams said, 'They sure did. They had our own

briefing documents from NSA. But the Russian ambassador must have taken his notes too literally, because at one point he used a direct line from the NSA. Word for word. When the meeting was over, everyone was in a panic: either the Russians were spying on us...or the committee had a leak.' Adams went to his briefcase and took out a stack of files. 'I started doing some digging. Senate voting records on bills with implications for Russia. Some of them tenuous, others very clearly connected. We're talking diplomatic and financial implications. Relieving sanctions and whatnot. Pretty soon I had a shortlist.' Adams placed his glass of water down on the coffee table. He sat down on the edge of the fireplace, enjoying the warmth on his back.

Novak was scared the senator would stop short of revealing the name. He needed to keep him talking. 'You have more than a shortlist, though. Don't you, Senator? How did you figure it out?'

Adams said, 'If I wanted to be sure, I had to get records going far enough back. What I found was, the mole was never really turned in the traditional sense. In a way, the Russians always had him.'

'What do you mean?' Stella asked.

Adams said, 'Picture the scene: it's his first congressional race. He's barely thirty years old. He's a hotshot prosecutor with an immaculate conviction record, so nobody can hang "soft on crime" around his neck. Yet for a young guy with basically zero business connections, his campaign is curiously well-funded. Then after two terms he makes it to the Senate. But he doesn't spend the next ten years holding his thumb out for a bullshit subcommittee placement like farming or agriculture like the rest of us. Right out the gate he lands the jewel of the crown: Senate Appropriations.'

'What is that exactly?' asked Natalya.

Adams answered, 'It decides how the trillions of dollars at the United States government's disposal is spent. Naturally, as a member of Appropriations, you're in high demand from lobbyists. Your decisions could make their employers millions in government contracts.'

'They must have had admirers,' Stella pointed out.

'Admirers? This guy was protected from upon high. Because no other senator consistently got the job done like him. When lobbyists saw him walk into a restaurant, they'd make cash register noises to each other.'

Novak asked, 'So Russia was funding this spy from the start?'

'The long game is the only way this works,' Adams explained. 'You didn't have to turn a U.S. congressman into a traitor. They made him a congressman in the first place. That's much easier to manipulate. Maybe you don't use them for months or even years. But you let them grow dependent on you. And your money.'

'How dependent are we talking here?' asked Novak, struggling to keep up with his notes.

'Every six years, a senator has to raise about five million dollars just to get re-elected. And if you happen to piss off a special interest group with almost unlimited funds like the gun lobby or big tobacco, you could be looking at ten million dollars and still lose in a blowout. Four billion dollars was spent on the last Presidential election. Twice that will be spent on next year's. That's how dependent, Mr Novak.'

Novak slouched back in the sofa. 'But a congressman

risks jail for that? Job security? They could make just as much hawking their ass to big pharma or the auto industry. Last time I checked, there's no shortage of money in the private sector.'

'Yes, but cash can only get you so far. That's not enough of a reward to take such huge risks.' Adams leaned forward. 'What if there was a much bigger reward on offer that mitigated those risks?'

'Beyond cash,' said Stella, sensing Adams closing in on some kind of revelation.

'Think about it,' Adams said, getting to his feet. 'You take a guy from nowhere. You get him elected. As compensation he tells you things. Secrets. Classified information. Things that help you make back more cash than you've ever given him. What if you were able to use your money and influence to get him higher up the chain? What if you were able to conspire with others to help make that happen? What if your spy had access to the sort of intelligence that could make an assassination look like a terror attack?'

Novak and Stella could only think of one thing.

'The Downing Street attack...' Stella said.

Adams paced back and forth in front of the fireplace. 'You two did an amazing job on Goldcastle. But you missed the other half. There were forces in the U.K. that wanted Simon Ali out of Downing Street, and forces in the U.S. that wanted Secretary Snow out of the Defense Department, because they both opposed the Freedom and Privacy Act. But the killer move wasn't getting Bill Rand into the Secretary's chair. The killer move was where they were going to put Bill Rand *next*.'

Walter and Rebecca had already extracted the story

from Adams on the plane between RAF Brize Norton and Ramstein Air Base. But even hearing it for the second time they got chills.

'The White House,' Novak said in wonder.

Stella wasn't convinced. 'Could the Russians really make that happen?'

Adams smiled at her.

Suddenly, Stella saw how the pieces clicked into place. 'The spy isn't working for Russia, is he. He's working for Hilderberg.'

Novak leaned forward. 'Senator...even off the record. We need a name. You've gotta give us a name.'

Adams' reticence was starting to get to Novak.

He tried to talk gently, but couldn't help his natural pushiness bubbling to the surface. 'Come on, Senator,' he said, getting to his feet. 'You told Andrei, now Andrei's dead. I get that you want to protect us, but you're standing here with three investigative reporters, a CIA SSO, and the director of Ghost Division.'

Adams wasn't used to being browbeaten, and started to move away from the fire.

Novak didn't let up. 'I know this situation right here isn't what you wanted, but it's all there is now.' He held out his notepad. 'One name, Senator. That's all we-'

Adams finally cracked. 'Bill Rand!' He looked to the ceiling then sighed. 'The spy is Secretary of Defense Bill Rand. The reason Hilderberg called this meeting is to discuss how they're going to make him the next President of the United States.' Hands on hips, Adams sniped at Novak, 'Do you need to write that down, or do you think you'll remember?'

SERVICE ENTRANCE, THE GRAND HOTEL VON
HOFFENHEIM

Accessing the grounds of the Grand Hotel was light work
for someone like Gaspar. It was no secret to Hilderberg
security that no matter how much members of staff were
paid they remained Hilderberg's biggest vulnerability.

What Gaspar had done to Joachim had been speculated
about in the past, specifically by Ulrich Schöll. But with
over one hundred members of staff in dozens of properties
across multiple countries, it was always likely someone
would slip through.

The worst case scenario had always been thought of in
terms of a journalist sneaking in and getting photos, or
possibly video footage of Hilderberg members. That alone
wouldn't be fatal. It could also be dismissed as a random
one-off.

Gaspar was about to radically redefine their worst case
scenario.

The photo in Joachim's ID was easily replaced for one
of Gaspar. So when the guards swiped the card through a

scanner at the roadblock, it confirmed his authority to be on site for the next twelve hours.

With the floor-by-floor map of the hotel on his phone, Gaspar made his way quickly to the back staircase reserved for workers. His cardio work was in top condition, and he easily bounded up to the fourth floor wearing Joachim's bellhop uniform, carrying the large black holdall and Hugo Boss suit bag.

A room service attendant on his way down passed Gaspar on the third floor.

Gaspar had hoped not to run into anyone. That was why he'd figured out a way on the drive over to combine an excuse with a little information gathering.

'Hey, man,' Gaspar said in German. 'You don't happen to know if Senator Adams is on the fourth floor, do you? He left his bag in the bar.' Draping the suit bag over his arm, he acted like he had a scratch just below his left collarbone. Conveniently covering Joachim's name badge.

'There's no one on the fourth floor,' the attendant replied. 'They're only as high as the third this weekend.'

Gaspar nodded like it was all coming back to him. 'That's what I thought. Cheers.'

With so many members of staff in such a big hotel, Gaspar was right that one new face wouldn't arouse much suspicion. Stopping to talk to a member of staff was still a risky move, but it was worth it to know that no one else should have been on the fourth floor. Now if Gaspar heard a noise in the middle of the night, he would know he had to take evasive action.

Gaspar didn't have a key card – for any room – but that wasn't an issue. He stopped at a room that was close enough to the elevator and the staircase to hear anyone coming, but also far enough away to give him time to respond.

The Grand Hotel von Hoffenheim was not alone in using the same manufacturer for their door key cards as most other luxury hotel chains. And there was a very simple exploit in their system.

Underneath the slot where a guest slid their card, was a DC socket – much like an old phone charger socket – which charged up the lock's battery, and programmed the lock with the hotel's unique site code: a thirty-two-bit key that identified the hotel. All Gaspar had to do was plug in a small Arduino microcontroller to the socket, and it simply read what the key was right out of the lock's memory.

It was as dumb as leaving a clay mould of your house keys sitting on your front step - except this was real.

And it got Gaspar access to room ninety-seven.

He stayed in the bellhop uniform, sitting on the floor near the door. If he needed to run, it would be easier to blend in if he was in uniform.

Had Gaspar stuck it out in the military he would have made a fine special forces officer. A lot of other less-disciplined assassins would have given in to the temptation of at least having a shower. Not Gaspar. He was committed to doing whatever the job demanded. Even if that meant sitting on the hard wooden floor all night instead of the luxurious bed, covered in five hundred thread-count Egyptian cotton sheets, just a few steps away. He wouldn't even turn the heating up or down in case it was monitored.

He hung the suit bag on the back of the door. Then he opened the black holdall, taking out the Pelican case fitted to the rifle inside. He then took out the SIG SG 550 rifle, checking the optics in the Hensoldt Wetzlar ZF1.5-6x BL scope, adjusted the hand rest once again, checked the folding buttstock, then disassembled and reassembled the whole gun from scratch.

After doing it ten times he was satisfied.

So he did it another five, this time with his eyes closed.

The shooting location would also be dark. But there was nothing he trusted more under pressure than a SIG SG 550 in his own hands.

It seemed like all of the oxygen in Senator Adams' room had been used up.

On the sofa, Novak and Stella were dumbstruck. They each were compiling so many questions in their heads they didn't know where to start.

Stella was first to break the silence. 'You're one of the most respected members of Congress, Senator. How are you even involved with these Hilderberg people?'

Adams sighed. 'It wasn't always like this. My father, and his father before him were Hilderberg members. In their time it was about solving the biggest issues of the day. Now it's been taken over by Silicon Valley billionaires and media tycoons who want to make the next President. But there's a strong sense of tradition among the upper tier. So they keep some of the old hereditary members like me around, for all the influence we have.'

Novak could see Stella was already about to rebut, so he raised his hand in apology. 'Sorry, but if you were Andrei

Rublov's source confirming that Bill Rand has been spying for some bat-shit Illuminati-type group, why have they not shot you on sight here?'

Adams replied, 'They don't know I'm Rublov's source. They don't know I've been talking to anyone.'

'So who are you running from?'

Walter Sharp stepped forward, holding out his phone. He had a picture of a man dressed like an Hassidic Jew. 'This is one of this man's dozens of identities. CIA believes he is responsible for the murder of Andrei Rublov, and at least three other assassinations in recent years. One of his many passports was last flagged in Geneva six weeks ago.'

Natalya turned to Novak and Stella. 'Who was killed in Geneva?' she asked.

Stella's arm involuntarily drifted up to her head. 'No!'

Sharp nodded. 'Omar bin Talal.'

'I thought that was the Saudis? The entire *world* thinks it's the Saudis.'

Couching his language, Sharp said, 'There's reliable evidence this assassin was responsible.'

'Who is he?' asked Novak.

'The only name CIA or NSA have managed to glean from intercepted communication is Gaspar. He's French and is fluent in several languages. We only have a handful of his identities, and he doesn't seem to use any more than once. He is an absolute ghost. And, frankly, as good as I've ever come across.'

Novak asked, 'If he's an assassin, who does he work for?'

Rebecca had put the intel together on the plane with Sharp. 'The Russians,' she answered. 'Most likely he's a contractor for the FSB.' She held out her phone to Novak and Stella. 'We think this might be Gaspar's handler.'

Novak invited Natalya to look at the image. The man was shaking hands with the Russian president.

Novak asked, 'Do you know him?'

Natalya knew him immediately. 'That's Yevgeny Belchov. He was CEO of Gazrus. When the Soviet Union collapsed he was given control of it. I haven't seen him for years.'

Rebecca pocketed her phone. 'He moved to London around twenty ten. All told, he's worth about three billion dollars and not a cent of it is in Russian banks.'

'Why would it not be in Russian banks?' asked Novak.

Natalya answered, 'Because most of it is laundered. And if it remained in Russia it could potentially be seized by Interpol. When oligarchs like Belchov move abroad, their cash is still tied up in the shares of their business interests. Like Belchov's is with Gazrus. So if Moscow ever decides that he is in fact an enemy of the state, they can freeze his assets and put him out on the street.'

Stella asked Adams, 'What I don't understand is why the *Russians* want to kill you, Senator? Surely if anyone had motive to harm you it would be Hilderberg.'

Adams looked helpless. 'That's what I've been saying to Officer Sharp and Director Fox.'

Novak still had unanswered questions noted on his pad. 'Andrei couldn't have been clearer: he said in his phone call to the emergency services that there was a *Russian* spy in Congress. But you're saying Rand has been spying for Hilderberg?'

Adams sat down disconsolately on the sofa. 'Andrei's

dossier never mentioned Hilderberg. I confirmed to Andrei that the dossier – according to my own evidence, that I have with me now – was accurate, and that Bill Rand has been passing intelligence to foreign agents. But I purposely stopped short of saying who Rand was spying for. I was already going out on a limb confirming that much, and I believed telling him more would only put him in greater danger. Somewhere in that dossier, Andrei concluded that Rand must have been working for the Russians.'

Stella wanted to keep pressing him. 'Why did Andrei come to you?'

'The dossier described me as a possible threat to Rand's cover, given my position in the Senate Intelligence Committee, and the access I had to certain documents and evidence.'

'Like what?'

'Voting records. Details of dead drops, secret meetings between Rand and his handlers.' He looked up tearfully at the five faces all looking to him for answers. 'If I'd just denied everything to Andrei he'd still be alive. But I couldn't stand to see Rand get away with this. Time's running out.'

Novak said, 'The Presidential election isn't until next year. There's plenty of time to punch some holes in Rand's sails before then.'

'I'm not talking about the White House,' Adams snapped. 'My life isn't the only one hanging in the balance right now.'

'Who else are you talking about?'

Rebecca, her hands cradling the underside of her coffee cup, spoke up from across the room. 'My father.'

Novak asked her, 'Do you know where he is?'

'Not yet,' Rebecca said, taking a drink. 'But I will.'

Neither Novak nor Stella had seen Rebecca in person since New Year. There was a new steeliness to her. The kind that comes to a person when their entire lives has, for too long, been about one thing. Obsessed wasn't a strong enough word anymore for what Rebecca was.

Adams said, 'I told you that this whole summit is about getting Bill Rand into the White House. Stanley Fox is how they make that happen. Everyone wants him. Hilderberg, the Russians, the Saudis, the Chinese. He has a weapon that will secure the future of digital intelligence.'

Rebecca said, 'Imagine: every single encrypted email, phone call, messenger service, all wide open and totally transparent. This isn't just about the next election cycle. This is about who controls the next fifty years of covert intelligence.'

Sharp said, 'So far, it doesn't appear that anyone at Hilderberg knows about the senator's involvement with Andrei Rublov. But that could all change. Once the senator finds out where Fox is, we can formulate a plan to keep him safe.'

Rebecca didn't want that to be the final word on her father. She said, 'This is a man who was imprisoned by the British government, then abducted from a Washington courthouse last December. I won't speak for anyone else here, but I'm not here to keep him safe. I'm here to take him home. I'll accept any help that I'm offered, but I'll do it on my own if I have to.'

'How did you find out that this involves your father, Rebecca?' asked Stella.

Rebecca said, 'The dossier that Andrei had was written

by an MI6 agent called Colin Burleigh. He was killed in London on Friday. Burleigh had been in contact with Rublov last week, and during a conversation someone used a keyphrase that logged on NSA's TEMPORA system.'

'What was the phrase?' asked Novak.

'"STANLEY FOX".' Rebecca waited a moment for them to absorb the detail.

Novak said in disbelief, 'It's not enough that Stanley's abducted. They want everyone else who knows about him too.'

'He's not a prisoner to them, Tom. He's a weapon.'

Stella asked, 'So the dossier Andrei had. Did that come from Burleigh?'

Rebecca put her laptop on her knees, screen facing Novak and Stella. 'This shows a transfer of an encrypted file to Andrei. No doubt, that was the dossier on Bill Rand. Walter and I were able to find these on the way here.' She was never more in her element than when explaining computer security. 'He was using the Tor network to access the dark web and chat securely with Burleigh. Tor's like Google for people who don't want to be found. But there's a vulnerability in the Tor network. Your data goes from your computer through a series of nodes. Each node only knows where your data has come from and which node it's going to next. But eventually the data needs to find an exit node. That's where the data is decrypted and someone can read it at the other end on their computer screen. Anyone who has control of that node can read the information being sent. I found Rublov's exit node.' Rebecca clicked to a new tab, showing the messages between Burleigh and Rublov. 'Burleigh had everything you have been trying to find since the Downing Street attack. He said the dossier proves that there was a conspiracy between Lloyd Willow *and* Teddy King to assassinate Simon Ali.'

Novak ruffled his hair. 'All we've got to do is find the dossier. Somehow.'

'Yeah,' Stella flashed her eyebrows up. 'That's all.'

Outside, there was a distant thrumming sound. Sharp moved towards the window and saw the branches of the elm trees outside the window being blown hard in one direction.

'What is that?' asked Natalya, craning her neck to see.

Novak stood up. 'A helicopter.'

'It's not just any helicopter,' Sharp corrected him, observing the helicopter landing on the hotel's helipad. 'It's a Sikorsky UH-60 Black Hawk.'

As the rotors wound down, a huddled figure emerged.

Adams crowded behind Sharp, doing a quiet, mock introduction. 'Ladies and gentleman, the United States Secretary of Defense. And apparently your next President.'

Senator Adams managed to arrange for two other rooms to be opened up on the third floor - directly above his room. Novak would have his own room while Stella and Natalya shared. The reality was that Novak and Stella were too recognisable to be seen downstairs. And Natalya's story had been blowing up all over social media since their Moscow metro escape.

Sharp would share with Adams, insisting he be as close to the senator as possible.

By late afternoon, Novak and Stella were particularly struggling - their body clocks ravaged by crossing and backtracking through all of the time zones Europe had to offer in the last twenty-four hours.

While Natalya was in the other room, Sharp joined Novak and Stella in Novak's room for a debrief.

If there was one person's judgement the pair trusted it was Walter Sharp's.

'What are you thinking, Walt?' Novak asked.

Sharp had his arms folded. They looked like two intertwined Redwood tree trunks. 'I'll tell you this: he went through several parts of the story separately to Rebecca and me. He used different language with you and with us, and he spoke through things in a different order. That's good. That means he hasn't just remembered rote facts. Liars can't think laterally through a series of events. He's also consistent. He used phrases like "I confirmed to Andrei", rather than what we call a diminished confirmation like "All I did was..." He takes ownership of the part that he *has* played. I think he's solid.'

Stella said, 'All we have to do is get him on the record somehow.'

'And how are we going to do that?' asked Novak.

'That's up to you guys,' Sharp replied. 'As far as I'm concerned, I couldn't give a sweet damn whether he talks or doesn't talk. The second he finds out where Stanley Fox is being held, I'm out of here. Until that happens you two need to stay out of sight.' Sharp grinned in the doorway. 'The perils of international fame, huh.'

Once they were alone, Stella asked Novak, 'Should we tell Diane yet?'

'Let's hold off for now. Diane doesn't care if you've set the table. She just wants to know that dinner's out.'

Stella paused for a moment. Then she shook her head. 'Did that sound better in your head?'

'Yeah,' Novak quickly agreed, 'I think I'm gonna stick to baseball analogies.'

'Good idea,' Stella said, heading for the minibar. She muttered under her breath, 'That way I'll still have no idea what you're talking about...'

30

Bill Rand was the last of the guests to arrive. In a room full of billionaires, moguls, and tycoons, he was the one with the biggest swagger, basking in the glory of the most private launch of a presidential campaign in American history.

All told, there were twenty-seven members of Hilderberg present, spread around the study. Some sat in the many single leather chairs or stood by the fireplace clutching crystal glasses of brandy, discussing geopolitics and economics – and occasionally sports. The air was tinged with the smell of cigars.

Everyone was relaxed, dressed down for the evening. What seemed to put everyone most at ease was the fact that they were surrounded by equals. In day to day life they spent so much time around subordinates it was something of a relief to not have all eyes on them as the most powerful in the room.

The only one not feeling at home was Tucker Adams. He sat alone, watching the easy smiles and casual grace of the others. He couldn't help but envy the glint in their watches as they caught the light. The tans they had after holidaying in Costa Smeralda in Sardinia, or taking their boats down to Monaco. It was all so simple to them. The world at their feet.

And now Bill Rand was one of them.

Adams jumped at the sudden feeling of a hand landing on his shoulder.

'Adams! What are you drinking?' Rand blared, taking the chair next to him.

Adams showed him his glass. 'Highland Park.'

Rand bobbed around in his chair. 'The hell are the waiters?'

'There aren't any. You have to buzz.' Adams held up a beeper.

As much as Hilderberg trusted their staff, as meetings were so rare, it was important that members felt free to talk openly when they got together. Which meant evacuating the room of any non-essentials. Not even PAs or secretaries or bodyguards were allowed in to the informal gatherings, let alone the actual meeting.

'This is a heck of a place,' Rand said, admiring the chandeliers, oak-panelled walls, and German Romantic oil paintings.

'I remember my first meeting.' Adams stared wistfully into his amber glass. 'Seems a long time ago now.'

Rand had never known what do with small talk. He didn't speak it. And he certainly didn't care to hear it. 'Tucker, I know there are a lot of folks here think it should be you getting ready for the hot seat. I also know that there's been an Adams in Hilderberg since the beginning. So you have a lot of sway with these people. I know there's a bunch of times you could have lobbied against me. Hard. But you didn't. And I respect that, Tucker, I really do. And when I'm in the White House I'm going to need a man of your integrity, your experience. Nobody knows the intelligence game like you. You understand the Senate inside out.' He leaned forward, speaking in hushed tones. 'I want you to be my Secretary of Defense, Tucker.'

Adams sat back in his chair, reeling. 'I don't know what to say, Bill.'

Rand dipped his head to maintain eye contact. 'You say, thanks, then you say you'll take it.'

Adams put his glass down. 'It's tough, Bill...'

Rand's smile slipped. 'Look at us. Would you just take a look at where we're sitting? It doesn't seem that long ago I was at fundraisers begging used car salesmen for donations to my Congressional campaign. Now I'm sitting in a five-star hotel run by the Hilderberg Group, there are the heads of three of the biggest investment banks in Europe over there, and tomorrow everyone here is going to pledge their absolute support to my candidacy for President of the United States. With Hilderberg's help this campaign's going to be unstoppable. You throw Stanley Fox into the mix and from what the tech guys at CIA tell me, there's nothing we can't get.' His voice was full of wonder. 'Emails. Phone calls. We'll have a front-page-above-the-fold leak every goddamn day until I'm the last one standing come November.'

Trying to be subtle, Adams took a drink then asked, 'Boy, they must have that guy locked up somewhere tight.'

Rand looked from side to side, checking no one was close enough to hear. 'If you only *knew*. CIA take plenty of shit when things go wrong, but my God, Tucker, they're a bunch of goddamn geniuses sometimes. They tell me the President himself doesn't know about this place.'

'What place?'

Rand sat back with a chuckle. 'I shouldn't even be telling you this much.'

Adams tried to keep a lid on his desperation. 'Who would I tell, Bill?'

Rand looked like he'd been won over, then he slapped Adams on the leg. 'They'd kill me,' he said with a wink.

Rand got to his feet, leaving Adams alone with his whisky.

'Damn it,' Adams whispered to himself.

Room 87

While Natalya was in the shower, Stella sat in bed, miles away from sleep. She had been Googling Bill Rand for the past hour on her phone, and was now so far down the rabbit hole she didn't even know what she was looking for anymore.

Even just re-reading her own stories on Downing Street and the Goldcastle conspiracy illustrated how much Rand had gained from Secretary Snow's demise.

Her eyes were burning from the endless blue and white light of her screen, so she cast her phone to one side.

Then she noticed Natalya's phone, tantalisingly close on the other bed.

Straight away she made the calculation about how long Natalya had been in the shower. But then she would surely have at least a minute or two after hearing the shower stop before Natalya actually came back into the bedroom.

Stella had been aware of Natalya unlocking her phone

in the car with a super-fast stabbing motion of her finger.
Then Stella remembered what Rebecca had told her was
the most common phone password.

It's worth a try, surely, she thought.

In an impulsive moment, Stella lunged across her bed
and onto Natalya's. When she woke the phone screen up it
asked for the password.

Stella typed in '1111'.

It worked.

But then the water from the shower stopped.

All of Stella's reasoning about having time instantly
disappeared, and in flushed a huge wave of panic. If
Natalya found her rummaging through her phone she had
no excuse prepared.

As the adrenaline pounded through her, Stella opted for
the call log.

There were several calls in and out to the same number
in the past week, though nothing since Friday.

She looked to her bedside cabinet. All she had on it was
a glass of water.

Across the room, near the door, was a set of hotel
stationery.

If I run, I can make it, she told herself.

But she lost her nerve.

It was lucky that she did. Stella finished mouthing the
last digit of the phone number to herself, and threw the
phone back roughly to the same spot on Natalya's bed.
The instant it landed, Natalya returned from the bathroom
with a towel wrapped around her and a smaller one in her
hair.

Stella had her own phone back, keying the number
she'd memorised into her phone's notes.

'This place is amazing,' Natalya said, making the Z sound like three Ss.

Stella scrolled through her phone for nothing in particular, trying to appear relaxed but occupied. 'How are you doing? Now that it's out there?'

Natalya shook her hair loose, seemingly unfazed. 'It's like Thomas says. It was going to happen eventually.'

Stella kept scrolling on her phone.

'You're being careful with that, right?' asked Natalya, gesturing at Stella's phone.

Stella replied, 'I'm always careful.'

An hour after they'd switched the lights off, Stella was woken by the sound of soft footsteps across the wooden floor. Then the room door creaked open, letting in a crack of light from the hallway.

Stella turned over just in time to see Natalya's trailing foot then the door closing behind her.

A second later she heard light knocking on Novak's door, then Novak opening it.

Room 88 – An hour later

Natalya was lying across Novak's chest, which was rising and falling as he gradually got his breath back. His arms clung on around her back, not wanting to let go.

She sat up a little, noticing the packet of Marlboro Golds on Novak's bedside table.

'Do you want one?' she asked.

Novak replied, 'We can't smoke in a hotel room, Talya.'

'What are they going to do? Add it to our bill? You're so meek sometimes.'

She slapped his side, trying to be playful, but the tone masked a deeper truth: this was how they used to talk to each other when things were bad.

Novak had come to dread hearing that voice when they were together, and he hated it more now.

Wanting to prove her wrong, he reached out for a cigarette. 'Give me one of those,' he said.

He felt himself speaking more quietly than he otherwise might have. Conscious that Stella was in the other room.

As much as he'd wanted Natalya back – as early as hearing her voice on the phone back in New York – there was a bit of him that was ashamed of Stella finding out. He was the one who had done all the forgiving. There was an inescapable power in that, and it all belonged to Natalya.

She lit two cigarettes at once and gave him one.

'I never thought I'd see you again,' she said, exhaling. 'Did you think about me?'

Novak thought for a moment. 'The first year, I thought about you every day. As soon as I woke up. And when I turned out the light every night. No matter where I was.'

'And after a year?'

'After a year, I forced myself to think of anything else.'

Natalya reached for one of the empty beer bottles on the bedside table, using it as an ashtray. She offered it to Novak.

He took a drag. 'Did you think about *me*?'

'Of course.'

'I don't believe you.'

'You have no idea what I've been thinking about the last four years,' she said. 'How hard it's been.'

Novak saw her arm reach out in the dark and move towards her face. She was crying.

'Talya?' he said. 'What's wrong?'

She pulled her knees up to her chest, face pointing down between her legs. 'I'm so sorry, Thomas...'

Novak tried to comfort her, but she showed no reaction when he put his arm tenderly around her.

'I'm such a terrible person...' she cried.

'Hey, don't say that. You're not a terrible person.'

'I've just...I've thought so often about what I would say to you if I ever got another chance. And now we're together, and I don't know if we'll both live through this...I have to tell you.'

Novak moved around to face her. 'What? What is it?'

'After I tell you, I need you to remember the circumstances. How complicated it was...'

'*Tell* me, Talya.'

'I'm not a bad person, Thomas. You know that. I've done terrible things. But I'm trying to put that right, now.' She could feel her chest trembling with nerves. 'I lied to you before. About Magdalina.'

'What about her?' Novak lightly touched her chin.

She looked up again, meeting his eyes. 'She's not two years old.'

'I don't understand.'

She said, 'Magdalina is four.'

It didn't take long for him to work out the timings. And what Natalya had been leading up to. He said, 'You mean...'

Natalya said, 'Viktor isn't Magdalina's father, Thomas. You are.'

31

THE LOBBY, THE GRAND HOTEL VON HOFFENHEIM –
MONDAY, 8.12AM

Since seven o'clock, Werner the shift supervisor had found himself checking his watch every few minutes, waiting for Joachim's arrival. It had been strange enough for him to have missed the previous day's shift, but never two in a row.

He resolved to try Joachim's phone one more time.

It rang three times, and then to his surprise someone picked up.

'Hello?' came the answer at the other end.

It certainly didn't sound like Joachim.

'Hi? This is Werner at the Grand Hotel von Hoffenheim. Is Joachim there?'

There was a long pause at the other end.

Werner could hear murmuring in the background - several voices - then the unmistakable static of a radio.

'Werner, this is *Polizeikommissar* Berger with Baden-Württemberg *Kriminalpolizei*. May I ask how you know Mr Deckelman?'

'He works at the hotel. I'm his manager. Is everything OK?'

'I'm sorry to have to tell you this.' He paused. 'I'm afraid Mr Deckelman is dead, sir. It looks like an overdose.'

Werner sat in his office behind the reception area, hand over his mouth. He couldn't fathom how he was going to get through the day being the 'face' of the hotel. Today of all days.

The detective hadn't said anything about relatives, and as far as Werner knew Joachim didn't have any.

Feeling a sense of responsibility, Werner tapped into the hotel computer for personnel files. After bringing up Joachim's file and searching for emergency contacts, he noticed an entry that didn't make any sense.

The computer was saying Joachim had swiped into the hotel the day before.

Curious, Werner went to the security suite to find Ulrich Schöll. After explaining the situation, Schöll brought up CCTV images from the security gate from the day before. Schöll sped through the long gaps in traffic. After a parade of Mercedes, Aston Martins, top of the line SUVs, and 4x4s, Werner told Schöll to stop when he saw what he recognised as Joachim's car: a three-year-old Volkswagen Beetle.

'Zoom in,' Werner urged, feeling adrenaline building in anticipation.

Schöll zoomed in, then paused with a clear, high-definition image of Gaspar.

'*That*,' Werner said, 'is not Joachim Deckelman.'

Schöll sprang to his feet and grabbed his radio. 'I'm calling a code blue.'

Werner nodded his approval.

Blue meant a subtle, but urgent and comprehensive, sweep. Schöll's men were the best at going about their work without any guests ever noticing.

Schöll put the call out. 'All posts. We have an intruder on the premises. Everyone to the security suite, and for God's sake keep it quiet.'

'What do you think?' asked Werner.

Schöll thought for a moment. 'The overdose might be unrelated, but I don't want to take any chances.' He reached for a Heckler & Koch .45 USP Compact Tactical with a suppressor. If he needed to shoot someone he damn well didn't want anyone hearing a fully unrestrained gunshot.

Schöll snapped a magazine into the gun. 'Where do you want to check?'

'I'll do a sweep of the rooms,' Werner said. 'If anyone's hiding here, they must be above the third floor. What about you?'

'I'm going to talk to Senator Adams' guests.'

Novak awoke with a start when he saw dawn light breaking through a sliver in the curtains.

'Talya,' Novak whispered, nudging her awake. 'We fell asleep.'

She slid her arms around him. 'Is that so bad?'

He reached for his watch on the bedside table. 'You should go back.'

She reached towards his chest, planting a kiss on it.

There was a thud from the room above.

The pair froze.

'You heard that too, right?' she whispered.

'I thought no one else was on this floor let alone above.' Novak jumped out of bed. He clamped his phone between his cheek and his shoulder while he got his trousers on. 'Walt,' he said. 'It's me. I think you should check something out.'

Within twenty seconds, Sharp was at Novak's door. He'd been awake all night monitoring traffic in Adams' hallway.

When Novak let him in Sharp saw Natalya at the end of Novak's bed straightening out her hair.

'What is it?' Sharp asked, keeping his voice hushed.

Stella, who had been awake for the last two hours anyway, appeared in the doorway behind Sharp.

It didn't take a forensics expert to see that Natalya and Novak had spent the night together: the head imprints on both pillows, the empty bottles of beer on each side of the bed, both of them wearing only underwear and t-shirts.

Novak whispered to Sharp whilst pointing upwards. 'I heard something.'

Sharp turned around to Stella, taking out a SIG SP 2022 .40 compact pistol from the back band of his trousers. 'Get in here. No one stays on their own, understood? Lock the door.'

Stella came in and stayed by the door, keeping her back turned while Natalya and Novak got dressed.

Sharp went up the stairs, peeking over the bannister, ready to pull his head back if necessary.

There was an eerie silence on the fourth floor, which only heightened his senses.

There was no reason for there to be anyone above

Novak's room: there were no cleaners required up there, and as late an addition as Stella and Novak were there was still plenty of space on the third.

Sharp knew whoever made the noise wasn't meant to be there.

Halfway down the hallway, he noticed a door not closed all the way. Without realising it – working on instinct – he let his forefinger slide gently, smoothly, off the trigger guard and onto the trigger.

The closer he got to the open door he realised it was a foot sticking out through the doorway: someone was lying face-down.

Sharp nudged the door open with his right shoulder, covering his blind spots as he stepped into room ninety-seven.

A pool of blood lay around the man's throat, the blood advancing along the cracks in the wooden floor. Sharp checked optimistically for a pulse, but it was long gone. A full paramedic team could have been standing by the victim's side when the wound was inflicted and not been able to save him. It wasn't an act of savagery: it was a clinical act of murderous efficiency. Death in as few moves as possible: slashing of the carotid artery.

Sharp turned the man over enough to see his face.

It was Werner, the shift supervisor.

Sharp recognised the uniform as managerial.

A long stream of blood – as if from a hose - had sprayed across the floor.

Sharp started piecing it together in his mind: someone in the room was disturbed by Werner. Having to act quickly, the killer didn't have time to put on gloves, which explained the sound of a body dropping: they couldn't risk leaving DNA on the body.

There was one deep swipe across Werner's neck. There would have been probably two, maybe three, seconds of unbridled agony. Then a very quick peace. In Sharp's line of work, there were certainly far worse ways to go.

Sharp could come to only one conclusion: it was the work of a professional. Someone who at a moment's notice was not afraid to rock and roll.

Sharp knocked hard on Novak's door. The tension in his voice spread panic around the room.

Sharp shouted, 'Tom, it's Walt. Open up. Quickly now!'

When Novak opened the door Natalya gasped at the sight of Sharp's hands, which were covered in blood so fresh it was still dripping from his fingertips.

'Are you alright?' asked Stella.

'We've got company,' Sharp said, kicking the door shut after him, and striding towards the bathroom with his hands held vertically. 'One of the managers has been killed in a room upstairs. Lock the door. If anyone...'

Before Sharp could get his hands washed there was rapid knocking on the door.

A German voice called from behind it. '*Hallo?*'

Sharp reappeared in the bedroom with his finger to his lips.

Stella backed slowly towards the bedroom, gesturing at Natalya to do the same.

Sharp pointed for Novak to follow them.

Sharp went to the door, one hand on the handle, his gun behind his back.

'*Ja,*' he said.

'This is Ulrich Schöll, security manager.'

Sharp's shoulders dropped in relief. He put his gun back in his waistband and opened the door.

Schöll said, 'I need to see your passports and...' He broke off as he noticed the blood on Sharp's hands. Schöll took a step back and pulled out his gun.

Neither Novak, Stella, nor Natalya saw it happen. They just saw Sharp backing up with his hands in the air.

The three of them grouped tighter together.

Sharp said, '*Herr Schöll.* It's alright. I'm-'

'Who are you?' he demanded.

Sharp spoke slowly and calmly, knowing any rash movement could be fatal. 'I'm Officer Walter Sharp. I'm with CIA on a protection detail for Senator Tucker Adams.' Sharp motioned that he was reaching for his ID. 'He's secure in his room, but I've just found a hotel employee in room ninety-seven. I'm sorry, but he's dead. I think you have an assassin on the grounds.'

'Upstairs?' asked Schöll, reading Sharp's credentials.

'One floor up.' Sharp put his ID away.

'*Scheisse*, Werner...' Schöll lowered his gun, cursing himself for not going with him.

Sharp asked, 'Can you take me to your security suite?'

Once Schöll and Sharp had the CCTV system up, Schöll brought up a still of Joachim Deckelman's car entering the hotel grounds.

'Mother of God,' Sharp said, recognising the driver. Knowing he was actually within the hotel grounds was overwhelming.

'You know this guy?' asked Schöll.

'That's Gaspar Nolé.'

'Who is he?'

'A French assassin.'

'Is he good?'

Sharp didn't know where to begin. He could have told Schöll that Gaspar made his first kill when he was ten years old. Or that a source in Russia credited him with over fifty kills by the time he was eighteen.

Instead, Sharp said, 'He's very, very good.'

'Can you get back-up?'

'Yeah, if you want to wait forty-eight hours.'

'What do you want to do?' asked Schöll.

Sharp took out his gun and checked the mag. 'Get every man you have, and every gun you have. We don't stop until he's on his back.'

Gaspar caught his breath making his way down the service staircase. He was now wearing a Hugo Boss suit like the security guards, and carrying the holdall with his SIG SG 550 inside.

The suit was important to his immediate plan. It was for the getaway. Which, as had been drummed into him from a young age, was the most important part of a hit. Almost anyone can make a hit. Only a select few can get away afterwards. Without the getaway, an assassin is worthless. Without the getaway, there's no next job.

A ton of assassins carried out successful hits. Only a select few made it into a career.

He passed a maid and a kitchen porter making out in the basement corridor. They didn't notice him until he was right beside them. Keeping his cool, he told them sternly, 'Move along, please.'

Like most people in life, they did as they were told simply because Gaspar looked the part.

After that, he had a clean run all the way from the service entrance to the opening of the air conditioning maintenance shaft. Climbing and crawling through, it led to a vent above the main library, giving a perfect view of the four leather wingback chairs arranged in a row in front of the fireplace.

He slid himself into position, then assembled his weapon and scope.

Next time, he would be firing.

32

THE LOBBY, THE GRAND HOTEL VON HOFFENHEIM –
MONDAY, 8.12AM

The Grand Hotel library was restricted purely for private events – and it didn't get more private than a Hilderberg Group meeting.

The bookcases that lined two of the walls and all of the mezzanine above were filled with rare books, antiquarian volumes, and clothbound first editions. In many ways the room was both a delight and a travesty to a booklover: so many beautiful books, and none of them read. They were like mere furniture.

The group of thirty separated into small groups of three to five, some standing, some sitting in the leather chairs spread around the room.

The attire was noticeably more formal than the previous evening. The men had shifted from open-necked shirts and cardigans, to double-Windsor ties, double-breasted bespoke suits, and pocket squares. The women were equally formal in skirt- or trouser suits. It was definitely a display of power dressing.

Conversation was hushed, the mood one of anticipation. There was not a moment when someone's eyes didn't drift towards Bill Rand. Everyone knew the importance of what was going to happen there, and the international implications.

Senator Adams stood in a group of three, the oldest men in the room whose membership went back to the days of Adams' father. Adams looked over at Rand, seeing the wide smile on his face. Adams felt like his world was slowly crumbling, his stomach churning with dread.

He turned away from the others to adjust his tufted pocket square. Behind the pocket square was a small microphone supplied by Rebecca.

At the front of the room, a fire roared underneath a huge hand-carved wooden mantel, salvaged from a crumbling castle in Munich and painstakingly refurbished.

The only wall not lined with bookcases had thirty-feet-high windows, covered by blackout blinds. The library was softly lit by copper table lamps placed on small nineteenth-century side tables.

The only door in and out was hidden behind a panel of false books, and behind that a soundproofed oak door.

As always, no expense had been spared to make the members comfortable. Canapés and the finest drinks were laid out on a table, served by an experienced Hilderberg sommelier who had been with the organisation for forty years.

But even he wouldn't be privy to the actual meeting.

The chairman, Jozef von Hayek, walked to the front of the room, backlit by the flames licking up into the chimney. All he had to do was raise his hand for silence to fall.

He waited for the sommelier to make the walk from the

back of the room to the library door, and only started to speak once the door was closed.

Von Hayek, wore a double-breasted silk suit by Henry Poole of Savile Row. From suit to watch and shoes, he was wearing about six thousand dollars' worth of attire. He was approaching seventy years old, but still had a full head of hair: silver, medium-length, wavy. He spoke with a vaguely western European accent that had lost its original patois many years ago from having to converse mostly in English, as he would today.

'Ladies and gentlemen, it's my great pleasure to welcome you here today. We find ourselves at a moment in time where the future appears uncertain. For many of us, the foundations of what we have become accustomed to are no longer so solid. Whether that be economic uncertainty, militarily, or politically. The great Friedrich Hilderberg started this group to solve the great problems of the world. He understood that these problems cannot be solved by governments alone. Or indeed by democracy. We only have to look at events in recent years to see that democracy has not always provided the security and stability we strive for.' He opened his arms out to the room. 'That's where we come in. We are the market correction. That invisible force that restores and keeps balance. And my friends, I have never known a time where it's been more crucial for us to exist.'

A round of polite applause rippled through the room, like the response to a professional golfer holing a putt.

Room 88

Novak and Stella sat at the coffee table in the suite's living room, listening to the chairman's speech via Adams' microphone on a small speaker.

Stella had noticed Novak spacing out sometimes, staring at the carpet. Assuming it was from the earlier fright with Schöll, she nudged his leg. 'You OK?' she mouthed.

Novak broke a smile, but it was gone again almost as quickly as it had appeared.

Natalya paced around behind them, muttering to herself in Russian.

Rebecca sat alone, listening intently on a set of Bluetooth earphones.

Natalya said to Stella, 'What if Gaspar kills Walter? How will we protect Adams then?'

In a way that Novak and Stella had never heard before, Rebecca snapped, 'Quiet!'

Natalya went to the sofas and sat alone.

Rebecca clicked her fingers at Stella and Novak. 'Adams is up.'

The chairman held his arm out towards Bill Rand near the front. 'So it is with great pleasure, I introduce one of our most esteemed colleagues, the senator from the great state of Maryland, Tucker Adams...'

Up above the mezzanine, through a small grate in the air conditioning unit, Gaspar made the last adjustments to his sight as Adams made his way up front.

· · ·

Adams, holding a brandy glass, reluctantly faced the audience. 'I'd like to thank the chairman for his invitation to say a few words here today. It has certainly been the privilege of my life to serve in this group. There are a lot of names for what we are. Some might call us the deep state. The – *mostly* – unelected who pull the strings of power. But someone has to pull them. And no country understands the consequences of abandoning those strings more than the great country in which we now stand. And it's a great source of pride for me to stand here amongst you all, seeking to continue the great work of the men and women who have gone before us.' Adams raised his glass. 'A toast: to doing what is necessary.'

There was a sound of clinking glasses being toasted, along with calls of '*Santé*', '*Salute*' '*Salud*' and 'Cheers'.

Rebecca had one earphone pressed in to hear more closely. She said through gritted teeth, 'Come on, Adams. Get to it...'

Adams waited for quiet again. 'We stand at a real turning point. The decisions we make in rooms such as these are not about the next year, the next five, or even ten years. They are about the next fifty. The next century. And after the vote taken at our previous meeting, we have decided,' Adams cleared his throat, 'in our wisdom, to choose Bill Rand as our next candidate.' He had to wait for enthusiastic applause to quell before continuing. 'We all know what a valuable commodity we have in Stanley Fox, and the opportunities he opens up for us. But some of us know more about Stanley than others - and indeed some of you have asked for reassurances about where Stanley is being held, and whether, given how valuable he is to our mission, that that place is safe enough. I'm sure these matters will become clear at some point in today's proceedings, but for now, it is with pleasure I welcome forward, Senator Bill Rand.'

Rand made his way forward to more applause.

Gaspar's shot was clear. The situation perfectly within his control. He couldn't have asked for more ideal surroundings.

At such close proximity – roughly fifty metres away, and from a height – a head shot would be more than expected. But with only a single door for thirty people to get through, Gaspar was confident he would have far more than one shot to get it right.

Ulrich Schöll was keeping guard outside the library door, his weapon drawn, staying in close contact with his security team. A sweep of the building hadn't revealed any further clues as to Gaspar's whereabouts. Until a call came from the service entrance.

One of Schöll's guards had found something suspicious.

'What is it?' Schöll asked on the radio.

'It's the maintenance shaft,' the guard explained. 'There are two screws on the ground here. The door's just flapping open.'

It was the one part of his plan Gaspar hadn't been able to find a solution to: reattaching the screws that fixed the opening of the shaft while inside the shaft itself.

It was a calculated risk that no one would notice it. And it hadn't paid off.

Schöll barked, 'Get in there, son. And keep your weapon drawn. That shaft leads to the library and the meeting's already begun.' He started running. 'I'm on my way now.'

Bill Rand made his way to the front, shaking the chairman's hand, and then reached out to Adams. But Adams was looking up towards the mezzanine, noticing the exposed front panel of the ventilation shaft.

Rand turned around to see what Adams was squinting at.

'What is that?' Rand asked.

Adams could now see the tripod legs of a rifle rest, then the light reflecting off a rifle scope pointing in his direction.

Once Gaspar pulled the trigger, the suppressed crack of the shot from his SIG SG 550 broke out over the heads of the audience, followed by the thump of the rifle firing.

It was a direct shot to the front of Bill Rand's head, sending a stream of blood like an arrow onto Adams' face and all down the front of his suit.

Rand fell onto both knees.

Gaspar quickly recalibrated then got off two further shots: another to the head, and one to the chest.

· · ·

Everyone in Novak's hotel room heard the gunshot a second before it registered on Adams' microphone. The screams that followed told them what had happened.

Novak exclaimed, 'Jesus Christ!', then instinctively jumped to his feet.

Rebecca threw off her earphones and ran to the door.

Novak and Stella immediately followed, leaving Natalya – who was much slower off the mark - trailing behind.

As they charged down the hallway towards the stairs, Novak asked Stella, 'Was that Adams?'

'I don't know!' she replied.

Adams stood covered in Rand's blood, frozen to the spot. He kept waiting for a shot to land on him, but it didn't.

In the chaos and screaming that followed, Adams was the only one in the room not moving. Side tables and chairs were knocked over in the surge towards the door, people scrambling and grabbing to get there first.

Eventually the chairman hauled Adams aside, leading him towards the crush at the door. 'Keep your head down,' von Hayek shouted.

The wall of people at the door blocked Ulrich Schöll from being able to get through.

The chairman saw Schöll and yelled at him, pointing wildly to the back of the mezzanine, 'Shooter! The ventilation shaft!'

Then Adams noticed a bunch of folded papers in Rand's hand, now covered in blood.

Up on the mezzanine there was a muffled explosion, coming from somewhere within the ventilation shaft, prompting another wave of screams and everyone crouching as low to the ground as they could.

Overhead, the fire alarm went off – a deafening high-pitched siren.

Adams wrestled free from the chairman and dashed towards Rand.

'What are you doing?' von Hayek yelled.

Adams paid no attention to him, taking Rand's papers and stuffing them inside his jacket pocket.

Gaspar recoiled from the blast of smoke blowing towards him. The result of a booby-trap laid further back in the ventilation shaft.

The missing screws at the opening were a calculated risk. A calculation mitigated by a tripwire which set off a flash-bang and a smoke bomb.

Gaspar left his rifle behind, taking out his Beretta 92FS sidearm, staying crouched as he made his way back towards the opening of the ventilation shaft. Halfway back he found one of Schöll's men clutching his eyes in agony. The flash-bang had activated every single photoreceptor cell in his eyes, temporarily blinding him. His sight started to return after five seconds, but the afterimage of the flash made aiming his weapon a lottery. The bang not only left his ears ringing to the extent of being totally deafened, but the disruption to the fluid in his ears left him shaking and unbalanced.

He felt a body push past him, but was powerless to stop them.

. . .

Sharp had one of Schöll's radio earpieces in, and sprinted for the service entrance. Kitchen porters and waiters and bellhops, prompted by the alarm, streamed past him, desperate to get outside via the nearest fire exit.

Sharp didn't have to speak German for them to understand he wanted them to get out of his way.

He forced his way past the staff, reaching the entrance to the ventilation shaft, finding the guard sprawled on the ground. He was blinking wildly, trying to figure out why he felt so nauseous.

'Where did he go?' Sharp yelled, struggling to hear himself over the alarm. He tugged the guard's arm. '*Wo ist er?*'

The guard shouted back, '*Ich weiss nicht.*' – ('I don't know.')

Sharp let go and set off back towards the lobby.

There, through the last escaping guests, Sharp spotted a security guard in the middle of the crowd heading for the front doors: Gaspar.

Ulrich Schöll was standing on the front steps, waving everyone forward to the gravel driveway so he could see each and every face exiting the hotel.

When he saw Schöll, Gaspar immediately turned back towards the lobby.

Sharp pulled his H&K pistol and shouted at Schöll, 'Shooter!' The aim of Sharp's gun showed him where to look.

Gaspar took out his Beretta and grabbed the nearest person from behind, a member of the French banking contingent.

Schöll didn't have a clear enough shot, and wanted

Gaspar to know he wouldn't risk the hostage's life. Schöll lowered his weapon.

Gaspar then aimed at Sharp and shook his head 'no' at him.

Sharp, always looking to preserve life, lowered his gun also.

As soon as Gaspar was through the double doors, he let the Frenchman fall through his arms, then took off through the kitchens.

The stoves had been deserted, with pots of water boiling over on the hobs. The extractor fans couldn't clear the abundance of steam, as water met open gas flames all across the kitchen.

Sharp kicked his way through the double doors.

Knowing Sharp wouldn't waste a shot on anything other than the biggest target area – the torso - to ensure a hit, Gaspar grabbed an eight-millimetre-thick aluminium skillet and turned in profile to narrow the target area.

Using the skillet as a shield, Gaspar stopped one of Sharp's bullets, which cracked into the aluminium base, sending shrapnel in multiple directions.

Gaspar was sent staggering back from the force of the shot, landing on his back. Before Sharp could take another shot, Gaspar tossed the skillet at Sharp's wrist, sending his gun flying.

Sharp ran at him before Gaspar could get on solid ground, but Gaspar was faster than anyone he'd ever seen: he pumped his legs towards his chest, then kicked forward and up. With a squeeze of his abs, the momentum sent Gaspar back onto his feet, ready for Sharp who was advancing swiftly towards him, bare-handed.

Gaspar flicked a towel off an oven door rail, then

wrapped it over the handle of a pot filled with potatoes in boiling water.

Sharp knew what was coming, and grabbed a baking tray from the worktop. It wasn't perfect but it was enough to at least shield his face from the scalding water being thrown his way. His right hand copped the majority of the water, making Sharp yell in agony and drop the tray.

Gaspar kept moving quickly backwards, shuffling side-foot like a fencer. He used his position in the narrow corridor between the stoves on either side to his advantage. He grabbed a bottle of olive oil and doused the tiled floor in it, leaving it slick and impassable.

Sharp boosted himself up onto the row of stoves, stepping over boiling pots and sizzling pans, and open flames on exposed hobs.

Gaspar couldn't help but be impressed at Sharp's agility – and bravery - which gave Sharp the upper hand with a preferable angle of attack.

Sharp picked up any pot or pan that came to hand and hurled them at Gaspar.

Gaspar turned completely and ran into a different aisle, a food prep area where there were no stoves, only worktops. And plenty of knives.

Gaspar grabbed a Wüsthof Pro ten-inch cook's knife and brandished it.

Having reached the end of the stoves, Sharp ceded his prime position. He knew his opponent would be proficient with a knife, so Sharp decided that he would work at him in pieces.

First, he grabbed a handful of red powder from a large mortar and pestle – betting it was paprika, which it was – and threw it in Gaspar's face.

It was enough of a distraction for Sharp to get closer. Gaspar was semi-blinded, slashing his knife wildly around. Sharp thrust his hips back to avoid contact, then grabbed a knife of his own and sliced across Gaspar's forehead.

The resulting wound wasn't intended to incapacitate Gaspar. It was to merely impede him, and it worked perfectly.

The wound was deep enough to bleed immediately down into Gaspar's right eye.

Gaspar cursed at him, '*Putain!*' understanding how clever Sharp's strategy was.

He could either leave the wound and it would keep pouring into his eye, reducing his vision by half. Or he could wipe the blood away every few seconds, which meant taking one arm out of action.

Maddened by the blow, Gaspar lost his composure and lunged at Sharp with wild swipes: a throwback to Gaspar's undisciplined early days in street fighting.

It was exactly the response Sharp had hoped for.

He leaned back to escape the blade - chin down so as to not expose his throat - then sent his boot into Gaspar's groin. The blow made Gaspar involuntarily jolt forward, lowering his head with a groan.

Sharp drove his knee repeatedly into Gaspar's face, then picked up a heavy wooden chopping board. While Gaspar leaned forward, trying to reorient himself, Sharp smashed the board on the back of Gaspar's head.

He collapsed face-first on the floor, out for the count.

Sharp could have killed him if he wanted to. And given what had taken place just a few rooms away and what had ensued in the kitchens, Sharp knew it was unlikely anyone would ask too many questions.

But that wasn't the job. And more importantly to him, it wasn't the *position*. He was there now to protect the others and to hope against hope that Senator Adams was alright.

He took two kitchen rags and tied them together to use as makeshift handcuffs. He repeated the process for Gaspar's feet.

Given who he was dealing with it wasn't much. But if Gaspar showed signs of coming to, Sharp would strike him below the chin with the heel of his palm, pinching the nerve at the top of the spinal column and causing a blackout. A technique that had saved Sharp on three other occasions.

Covered in sweat and blood, Sharp dragged Gaspar – in a sort of modified hog-tie - through the lobby to the security suite, then locked him inside.

The fire alarm was still going. In the distance, emergency sirens were approaching.

On the driveway, the rest of Schöll's security guards circled the illustrious guests.

Schöll spotted Sharp walking gingerly down the front steps. 'Are you OK?' Schöll asked him.

Despite his exhausted, battered condition, Sharp paused to tuck his shirt in. 'Fine,' he replied, taking out the radio earpiece. 'Where's Senator Adams?'

Schöll pointed towards Novak, waving from the centre of the crowd, standing alongside Adams, Stella, Rebecca, and Natalya.

'How many are dead back there?' asked Sharp. He flexed the fingers of his scalded right hand, then pursed his lips from the pain.

'Just one,' said Schöll. 'Bill Rand.'

33

Sharp and Novak stood on the front steps, watching the *Kriminalpolizei* take Gaspar – now with proper cuffs on - into the waiting van.

Before the van doors closed, Gaspar called to him in English, 'You think you can hold me, Langley? I'm going to walk out this van in five minutes. Wait and see.'

'It's important to dream, Gaspar,' Sharp retorted. 'Keep those spirits up.'

Stella couldn't take her eyes off Gaspar's thin-soled shoes, recognising them from the D.C. police station shooting. Her stomach turned at the thought of it again.

The other Hilderberg guests were inside, packing. They weren't going to hang around before more police and inevitably the media arrived.

The American Secretary of Defense being gunned down was one story they couldn't keep a lid on.

Senator Adams was upstairs packing too, along with Natalya.

Once the van doors closed, Novak asked Sharp, 'What will you do now?'

'I've got calls to make to the State Department. The news will probably break back home in an hour or two. And it's not going to be good for me.'

'An investigation?' Novak pondered.

'There's only one fall guy for anyone to point to here. And that's me.'

Stella came over with Rebecca, who handed Sharp a SIM card.

'What's this?' he asked.

'I cloned Gaspar's SIM card,' said Rebecca. 'That's everywhere he's been, everything he's said. And I swapped it out for a new one. The phone's back in his pocket. It will give us everywhere he's going. And everyone he's going to talk to.'

'We should follow,' Sharp said. 'I don't take anything he says as an empty threat.'

'You don't think he's actually going to escape do you?' asked Novak.

'I don't know what to think anymore,' Sharp replied.

Stella asked, 'Why Rand? We've been scared for Adams this whole time.'

Rebecca speculated, 'Someone in Moscow really didn't want Bill Rand to get to the White House.'

The *Kriminalpolizei* had asked for statements from Sharp and the others, but instead of taking them there at the hotel, Sharp insisted they be taken to the police station in Baden-Baden. That way they could travel behind the van carrying

Gaspar, and Sharp could monitor it until Gaspar was safely locked up in a police cell. He wouldn't rest until he saw it.

Novak, Stella, and Natalya went in the car at the back, behind Sharp, Adams, and Rebecca in another.

The U.S. ambassador in Berlin had been notified of what had happened, and was sending a delegation to Baden-Baden to recover Rand's body.

The story had broken to American networks thanks to a leak in the German police. No mention was made of the Hilderberg summit, thanks to the *Polizeidirektor* having close ties to the group.

The narrative on American news was of a senseless, opportunistic attack during a Cabinet member's diplomatic visit.

Natalya, sitting in between Novak and Stella, whispered to him, 'We need to talk.'

'I don't wanna,' Novak replied, looking out the window.

Stella turned away, but it was impossible not to hear.

Natalya said, 'Why don't we find a phone in Baden-Baden and you can talk to her?'

Novak didn't respond.

In the front car, Adams told Rebecca, 'I'm sorry I couldn't get you Stanley's location. I know how much it means to you. I did my best.'

'I know,' Rebecca said. 'Thank you.'

'It's not over yet,' Sharp reminded them. Then he noticed something dark and murky coming over the hills from the east. Low clouds had moved in and it was hard to tell what it was in the darkening light.

'What's wrong?' asked Rebecca.

'Son of a bitch was right,' Sharp said to himself, before

telling the others, 'I know how Gaspar is going to get out of here.'

In the car behind, Novak saw the same thing as Sharp.

'Stella,' Novak said.

She leaned across. 'What is that?'

Novak called Sharp's phone.

Before Novak could say anything, Sharp told him, 'I see it. Put your seatbelts on and keep your heads down. This might get rough.'

A helicopter swooped in through the clouds at a swift velocity, its front end dipped forward.

Stella called in German to the two cops in front. 'Hey, hey! *Achtung. Hubschrauber!*' ('Helicopter')

The cops got straight on their radios to the car in front, who replied with worse news.

'What's going on?' asked Novak, his German a little rusty.

Stella bobbed her head around to see further along the road.

'There are cars coming towards us.'

About half a mile ahead was a convoy of five GMC Sierra 1500 All-Terrain X pickup trucks. All in black. Their windows blacked out. They were travelling at close to sixty miles per hour.

The passenger cop told the driver to back up, but he couldn't because of the helicopter swooping in at the rear.

The convoy of trucks came to a stop ahead, blocking the road. A dozen men all in black, with black visor helmets, got out. They all had the same SIG SG 550 semi-automatic rifles as Gaspar.

They wore thick black gloves, prepared for the freezing temperatures outside. As the SIGs allowed for this, they had shifted the trigger guards to one side so their gloved fingers could fit on the trigger.

The helicopter landed behind Novak and Stella's car, and several men in the same gear got out.

They forced all the car passengers out onto the road, issuing all their instructions through stern gestures: zipped mouths, followed by hands on heads.

They forced everyone onto their fronts.

Novak stared hard at Natalya: trying to tell her 'It's OK. We'll get out of this. Stay calm.'

Novak's legs were shaking so hard he couldn't have stood up even if he'd been allowed. He looked over at Stella, who had her face down on the tarmac, eyes closed. Her body was shivering, waiting for a bullet in the back of her head at any moment. All she could think about was Jonathan Gale again. She'd heard her share of gunshots since then, but none had sounded like the one that went into Gale's head that horrible night in London.

Rebecca and Sharp were beside each other on the ground.

Sharp whispered a reminder to her, 'Breathe. Breathe.'

One of the men got the keys to the back of the police van and opened it up.

Realising what was happening, Sharp instinctively shouted, 'No!'

That got him a swift boot to the kidneys from one of the men.

Gaspar grinned as he was led towards the helicopter, rubbing his wrists once his handcuffs were removed.

The sight of it made Sharp feel physically sick.

'I tried to warn you,' Gaspar shouted.

There were enough rifles to be pointed at each and every person on the ground, ready to neutralise any threat.

Once Gaspar was near the helicopter the whole ordeal appeared to be over. Then the man who'd been directing things so far – terrifying, and almost inhuman behind his helmet – pointed sharply at Natalya, then at the helicopter.

The man closest to her picked her up with ease.

Novak yelled out her name.

Sharp looked back, warning him, 'Don't move Tom! They'll kill both of you.'

Sharp got another boot for that.

Natalya kicked at the air as she was carried away. 'Thomas! Help me!' she screamed.

Novak yelled back, 'Do as they say, Talya! I'll find you, I promise!'

The man nearest Novak slammed the butt of his rifle into Novak's face. It wasn't enough to knock him out, but his yells deteriorated into meagre groans.

As the men backed off to the trucks and the helicopter took off, Sharp called out in his novice-level German to the cops, then in English, '*Bleib, wo du bist, und keine Bewegung*! Stay where you are and don't move!'

Once the helicopter and trucks had gone a safe distance, Sharp was the first to get to his feet.

Stella went straight to Novak, who was still dazed from the rifle blow. 'Novak, are you alright?'

He was woozy, struggling to come to.

Sharp ran up to check on Novak.

Stella said to him, 'It must be the Russians.'

Novak managed to sit upright, 'Natalya...'

Sharp assured him, 'If they wanted to kill her they would have done it here.'

Adams appeared behind, hands on hips. Still gathering his breath. 'Why would they take her?'

Sharp watched the helicopter disappear into the low clouds. 'Whatever it is, we don't have the full picture yet.' He looked back to Rebecca, who was combing through a mobile phone.

'He's active,' Rebecca announced. She brought Sharp the phone. 'He just sent a text.'

'What does it say?' asked Stella.

Sharp held the phone out to Novak. 'It's in Russian.'

Struggling to his feet, Novak read the message. 'This doesn't make sense,' he said. 'How could they know...'

Losing patience, Stella said, 'What does it say?'

Novak told her, 'It says he knows where Stanley Fox is.'

'How has he found that out?' she replied.

'Can we trace who that message was to?' asked Sharp.

'I'll need some equipment.'

'There's a safe house in Frankfurt,' Sharp said. 'We can do analysis there, and wait for a pick-up team for the senator.'

Adams staggered forward, tie undone, hair dishevelled. 'Hang on,' he complained. 'I'm not going anywhere unless it's with Tom and Stella.'

Sharp began, 'Senator, we have to-'

'Officer Sharp, Andrei Rublov is dead because of me,' Adams said. 'I can't just limp back to Washington. Not now. Not after everything. I've got to see this thing through.' He turned to Novak and Stella. 'You can't take an anonymous source to Diane Schlesinger on this.'

Novak and Stella didn't dare interrupt him.

Adams said, 'You can quote me as a senior member of Congress with access to classified intelligence. I know you would never name me as a source, even under oath. And I know the White House has shown considerable resolve in prosecuting leakers of classified material. To answer your next question: yes, I am prepared to go to jail to help you break this story. I'll do whatever it takes. Now if you want me on the record, we better get started. Because I got plenty to say. So where are we going?'

Novak looked at Stella. 'There's only one other person who knew as much as Colin Burleigh and Andrei Rublov.'

Adams said, 'Omar bin Talal.'

Stella agreed. 'And he was killed by Gaspar too.'

'He got Andrei onto the Bill Rand story to begin with. If Omar was writing for *Provocateur* we should go talk to Romain.'

'Who's Romain?' asked Adams.

Stella said, 'The editor of *Provocateur*.'

'He's eccentric,' said Novak.

'Certifiable,' Stella clarified. 'But right now we need him.'

'So where are we going?' asked Adams.

Novak told him, 'Paris.'

34

The ICE train was careering west across Germany after
leaving Berlin's HBF station nearly two hours earlier. At an
eight-hour travel time to Paris Gare du Nord station, it was
a much longer journey than the hour and three quarters it
would have been by plane, but more time with Adams was
what Novak and Stella needed.

They took a small booth in the business cabin which
had glass doors that slid shut, leaving them in peace to
speak openly. Novak had purchased the other two seats in
the booth to ensure they would be left alone all the way to
Paris.

Stella had her phone out on the table for their Darkroom call to Diane back in New York. The pair took a bud
each of Novak's earphones so they could both hear over the
noise of the high-speed on the tracks, but also so Adams
couldn't hear what Diane was saying.

Stella had been the one to explain to Diane everything
that had happened since Moscow: Natalya still being alive;
her working with Andrei; the FSB's pursuit of them; their

escape to Germany; Natalya's abduction; Adams exposing Bill Rand's terrible secret; and finally Rand's demise.

When Stella was finished, Diane didn't say anything for a long time – long enough for Stella to check she was still there.

'I'm still here,' Diane answered.

The editor in her knew they'd landed another killer story. Her star reporters were looking at an espionage case that would make the FBI's Aldrich Ames and Robert Hanssen's spying for Russia look like fraudulent expense claims in comparison. There had been plenty within the intelligence community who had committed espionage over the years, but never a member of Cabinet with such high aspirations - and expectations – as Bill Rand. He was the highest-ranking spy in American political history.

But Diane knew that if they published a word of it, the attorney general – still reeling from the embarrassment *Republic* had caused the government with the Goldcastle affair – would go after them all the way to the Supreme Court before they even got a story to the printers.

Pressing forward and publishing online would bring huge consequences as far as access went. The entire government infrastructure would be closed off to *The Republic*, from star reporters, to junior researchers and interns. Diane had been around long enough to know you couldn't embarrass the government in such a way without consequences. Extraordinary allegations would require extraordinary proof.

'To be clear,' Diane emphasised, 'you have on record from Tucker Adams that Bill Rand, a presumptive nominee for the next Presidential election, was spying for some cabal of private interests.'

Stella confirmed.

'But Tucker Adams was a part of this Hilderberg Group as well?'

Stella hesitated. 'Senator Adams is...Hang on, Diane...' She took her earbud out and asked Adams, 'Senator. Would you mind giving us the room, please?'

He seemed only too happy to escape the conversation, and waited in the hallway outside.

Stella put her earbud back in. 'Sorry, Adams has stepped outside now...Adams is a part of Hilderberg, it's true. We know his father and grandfather were also members. But we don't know yet what exactly Adams has been doing on Hilderberg's behalf. This is the chairman of the Senate Intelligence Committee meeting regularly with deep state actors. That alone is a front-page story. We shouldn't forget that.'

Novak argued, somewhat brusquely, 'So we go with that, rather than the United States Secretary of Defense was complicit in the assassination of his predecessor, and has been spying for the deep state?'

'But all we've heard so far is Adams' side of things.'

'Stella, Adams isn't the one talking about using Stanley Fox to help steal the next Presidential election. We have Rand himself on record discussing that.'

Diane interjected, 'Hang on. Stanley Fox is still alive?'

Novak said, 'And being held somewhere by CIA, who have an operative working on behalf of Hilderberg. With Stanley Fox and his decryption method, they would have full access to every encrypted email, message, opposition servers, financial records, tax receipts, you name it. Enough to buy the next election. Stanley's too protected for anyone to steal him, and even if they did, there's no guarantee he would talk. The Russians might not be able to steal him, but they might be able to kill him.'

Diane asked, 'And how far back does this go for Rand?'

Stella consulted her notes. 'When he was elected to the House of Representatives. So about twenty years all told. That's longer than Robert Hanssen leaked classified FBI material to Russia. And what else is unique here is the way Hilderberg got Bill Rand on board. They were ploughing cash into his elections almost as soon as he was out of college, according to the files Adams has. You talk about playing a long game? Hilderberg committed hundreds of millions to Rand.'

'But how do the Russians fit into this?' asked Diane. 'We know Rublov, Omar bin Talal, and now Rand have been killed by this Russian assassin. So is it Russia or Hilderberg that's pulling the strings?'

Novak had to give the one answer that Diane hated the most. 'We don't know for sure,' he said.

Diane sighed in exasperation.

'Bill Rand had been pretty vocal about his position on Russia - he was in favour of raising tariffs and sanctions against Moscow. If the Russians found out that Hilderberg were going to back Bill Rand for President, they would certainly have motive for taking him out.'

Diane said, 'But Rublov and Talal were threatening to expose Bill Rand as a spy for Hilderberg. Why would the Russians want to kill them? It doesn't make sense.'

Stella raised her pen in the air as if to say, *that's exactly what I've been saying.*

Diane added, 'Right now you have a Grand Canyon-size hole in this story. And we're not going any further forward until it's explained. A government prosecutor would have a field day with this.'

'We're hoping to clear things up in Paris,' Stella said, trying to lower the temperature in the cabin.

Novak and Stella heard Diane dropping her pen on her desk.

'OK,' she sighed. 'Get to Paris and talk to Omar's editor. In the meantime, this is Downing Street all over again: so nothing in email. Stay offline. Got it?'

They each replied, 'Got it.'

'Especially with what I'm about to tell you: there have been some developments back here in Manhattan.'

'Like what?' asked Stella.

'Henry's been running some numbers and...it's not looking good. There's a very real chance we might run out of money. Soon.'

Novak asked, 'What does soon mean?'

Diane paused. 'Forty-eight hours.'

'When you say run out of money...' Stella trailed off.

Diane clarified, 'I mean, we have no money to pay our server, which means they might pull the plug on us. Everything's backed up, of course, but we would lose our entire online presence. Our website would disappear. Technically, we would cease to exist. Frankly, even if you bring this story home, I can't guarantee we'll actually have a *Republic* online or in print for you to publish it.'

Novak asked, 'What do we do?'

Diane gave the only answer an editor can give. 'Keep going. I need you to. And so does Natalya.'

After Diane hung up, Stella sat in stunned silence.

Novak pulled out his earbud and let it drop on the table.

For a moment, Stella thought he was going to cry. She put her arm around him. 'We'll get her back, Novak.'

'It's not that.' He looked away out the window, watching the countryside go past in a blur. He decided the best way was to just come right out and say it. 'I'm a father.'

Stella didn't know what he meant at first.

'Talya's daughter, Magdalina, isn't Viktor's. She's mine.'

'Oh, Jesus...'

'If Talya is sent to prison, I might have to move to Ukraine. I can't leave Magdalina alone. Talya's parents worked in refineries all their lives. They've been near death for the last twenty years. If they die, Magdalina won't have anyone. I can't abandon her, Stel.' He shook his head resolutely. 'I won't.'

Stella noticed the conductor in the hall asking Adams for his ticket. Adams didn't speak a word of German and so tapped on the cabin door.

Stella reckoned Novak could have done with another half an hour to talk, but reluctantly she waved Adams to come back in.

35

CIA SAFE HOUSE, FRANKFURT, GERMANY

The house on Wiesenau was close enough to the city centre to see the skyscrapers of the financial district near the European Central Bank, but still quiet enough that two strangers arriving on a Monday evening didn't attract much attention.

The safe house wasn't used often – mostly for Agency personnel coming in or out of Ramstein. It had a comprehensive telecoms set-up, armoury, safe full of unmarked bills for dozens of different countries, extensive wardrobe for every contingency, and a small kitchen full of canned goods and condiments.

CIA had bought up all five of the other apartments in the building so Agency personnel didn't have to construct legends in advance on the off-chance of an encounter with a neighbour on the landing. Meeting an endless series of strangers who didn't always speak German was not a good look for keeping a property low-profile.

The Frankfurt location also meant the safe house was often used at short notice: some had been known to arrive at the safe house gasping for breath, bloody, or wounded. For any agents in Western Europe the Frankfurt House, as it was known, was a true sanctuary.

Once they were inside, Rebecca headed straight for the telecoms equipment.

Sharp took out Gaspar's cloned SIM and connected it to a USB drive.

Rebecca's obsessive checking of her watch every five minutes hadn't gone unnoticed by Sharp.

'We'll get to him in time,' he told her. 'If we can connect to Gaspar we'll find out where your father is. He's clearly someone the FSB trusts. I'd bet on them sending Gaspar after him.'

Rebecca brought up all the historical data on the SIM card, then clicked through to live tracking, waiting for the signal to return from the satellite. 'Looks like he's somewhere over the Czech Republic.'

Sharp said, 'He must be heading back to Russia.'

Rebecca clicked again to update his position. 'Judging by his speed he must be on a plane. Are they keeping my father in a CIA black site?'

Sharp pursed his lips. 'It's not the right fit. The Eastern European sites are for enemy combatants. If your father starts to talk, they need tech equipment. Black sites are very bare bones inside.' Sharp stayed behind Rebecca's seat, trying not to crowd her. 'What do Gaspar's recent messages say?'

Rebecca filtered them by most recent. As the search spooled, she complained, 'Come on!'

The list compiled into a labyrinthine flowchart, connected by dotted lines and a network of pop-up windows that looked, to Sharp's eye, as though it would take weeks to decipher. The thousands of hours' experience Rebecca had with the ECHELON system meant she was able to swiftly zero in on the most pertinent messages.

She clicked into things then back out of them before Sharp had even read what had popped up, let alone drawn conclusions about their context or content. Such instincts had been finely honed from years of the highest pressure in GCHQ, sifting through data to find that single pearl of crucial information that can be the difference between a bomb going off or not. The kind of pressure that only makes you stronger each time you face it down.

This was Rebecca's place of business.

She pointed to the first suspicious message from Gaspar. 'This guy must be key. There's a ton of messages back and forth in Russian between Gaspar and this guy. He's based in London.' Rebecca made a flurry of keystrokes, bringing up a map of the U.K. 'Here...Kensington Palace Gardens.'

'Belchov,' said Sharp.

'Yeah.' Rebecca kept looking. 'So Belchov gets a message from this number here.' She tried to search further. 'Damn it. It's a burner, so we can't see the content of the message. But one minute later, there's a message from Belchov to Gaspar. It said: "We have SF's location. It's Metro. They can take him in transit."'

Sharp spotted it immediately. '"They". The Russians aren't sending Gaspar. They're sending a team.'

Rebecca drummed her fingers on the table, trying to think. Every second of a delay felt like a lifetime. 'So if Gaspar doesn't lead us to my father how are we going to find him?'

'What if we trace whoever told Belchov the location?' said Sharp.

'There's no other history there, no connections with any other phone we have.'

'That kind of information could only come from inside CIA. Either someone's been compromised or there's a mole.'

Rebecca insisted, 'We don't have time to worry about that. The location's the thing for now.'

Sharp pointed at the screen. 'May I?'

Rebecca wheeled her chair out the way as Sharp took over the keyboard.

He logged into the CIA counter-terror portal. Before it let him proceed, a warning flashed up on screen that he was entering an area only for those with Top Secret clearance.

'He said Metro,' Sharp mumbled to himself.

'CIA's hardly going to take him on public transport,' said Rebecca.

Sharp pulled up a list of all CIA detainee records. Every jihadi, bomb-maker, cartel boss, and hacker CIA had hoovered up into its black site system in the last six months. Considering that most people assumed the CIA extraordinary rendition programme had been killed off, the list was vast.

As Sharp navigated the purposely opaque list of detainees, he explained, 'When CIA makes a pickup, the Department of Defense creates an ISN – internal serial number – and the detainee goes into the system. Names are pointless, because you're relying on the detainee telling you. They don't exactly pick these guys up with passports on them. So everyone gets a number. Except this guy.' He noticed a detainee listed without a number. The only identifier was 'XXX'.

'Why would that happen?' asked Rebecca.

'There's really no reason other than the Defense Department doesn't want someone to be found. ISNs have to be assigned manually by someone on a computer.'

'So someone's chosen that. Bill Rand would have been in the perfect position to give that kind of order against my father.'

'True,' Sharp conceded. 'But it couldn't have been Rand who contacted Belchov earlier. There's also this...' He clicked into the file then circled the mouse around the "date of detention" cell. 'Recognise that date?'

The date meant more to Rebecca than anyone. 'That's the day when my father appeared at Tom Novak's hearing. But where was he taken to?'

Sharp bashed the ENTER button as the computer refused to grant him access to further details. 'This doesn't make any sense. I have full black site clearance.' Sharp picked up the phone. 'Screw it,' he said as he dialled.

'Who are you calling?' asked Rebecca.

'The only guy in CIA I can trust right now...' The other end picked up. 'Bob, it's Walt. About that favour you said you owe me. I'm calling it in.'

'What exactly are you calling in?' asked Bob.

'I need black site access for a particular ISN.'

'What is it?'

'Triple-X.'

There was a long pause at the other end.

Sharp said, 'Are you still there?'

'Yeah,' came the withering reply.

'You know who I'm talking about, don't you.'

Bob lowered his voice. 'Have you any idea what the director would do if he knew this conversation was happening?'

'I really don't know, Bob. I'm just a guy calling in a favour. The one that you owe me.'

'What do you want?'

'I want access to that detainee's records.'

Bob sighed. 'I could be fired for doing this.'

'Then you probably shouldn't tell anyone.'

There was silence. Then the sound of keys clacking.

Bob told him, 'You're in.'

The pop-up warning on the computer screen disappeared and Sharp hung up.

'Who was that?' asked Rebecca.

'Bob Weiskopf. My old boss at CIA Counter Terrorism. Three hundred thousand members of the U.S. intelligence community with Top Secret clearance, and I'm not one of them. He is.' The previously withheld information was now wide open.

The location of detainee XXX was listed as 'Camp Metro.'

'So it *is* a black site,' said Rebecca.

He did a search on the address. As the location gradually zoomed in, Sharp said, 'My God...it's in the middle of Manhattan.'

Rebecca remembered the phrase from Belchov's message. 'They said take him in transit. CIA are moving him.'

Sharp said, 'If we don't stop the FSB hit team, it'll be like your father never walked into that courtroom last December. And whoever is behind all this will likely walk away for good.'

Rebecca stood up. 'How quickly can you get us to New York?'

36

3RD ARRONDISSEMENT, PARIS – MONDAY, 8.27PM

Novak, Stella, and Adams headed straight from Paris Gare du Nord train station to the 3rd arrondissement on the right bank of the River Seine. Their taxi driver drove them with reckless abandon through the historic district of Le Marais' moodily lit streets, before dropping them two streets away from where they were really going. Novak didn't want their driver to know they were headed for *Provocateur*'s headquarters. Not least for the driver's own safety.

They followed the route on Novak's phone, taking them down a wide boulevard populated by quiet bars. The sound of French football commentary leaked towards the pavement.

It was still humid from the unseasonably warm afternoon. The three were overdressed after the chillier German climes. Novak and Stella carried their coats, while Adams wiped his forehead with a cotton handkerchief, sweat stains on his blue shirt and the sleeves rolled up.

He trailed behind slightly, constantly checking over his

shoulder. 'What's so crazy about this guy?' he puffed. 'What's his name again?'

Novak answered, 'Romain Laurent. He gave me one of my first jobs, covering riots in the Paris *banlieue* in the early two thousands. I was loud, brash, and thought I knew everything.'

'Was?' Stella said with a smirk.

Novak assured Adams, 'He's a legend.'

'Even I heard stories about him in London when I started,' Stella added.

'He's the son of some sort of French aristocracy, no one really knows for sure. He bought *Provocateur* when he was twenty-two years old and made himself chief editor. Seventeen of the twenty staff quit when he took over, but within a year it was France's biggest-selling satirical and current affairs magazine. They say he finishes the latest issue at eleven fifty-nine at night, smokes a cigarette, then at twelve oh one starts work on the next issue. He's probably the most demented workaholic in the industry.'

'Did you speak to him after Omar was killed?' asked Stella.

'I tried,' said Novak, 'but he never returned my calls.'

Rue Charlot was a classically Parisian backstreet: incredibly tight, barely two cars' width across, the buildings stretching up three, sometimes four, floors. Once Novak thought they'd reached the destination according to the map, he stopped walking then looked up at the building.

'Are you sure this is it?' asked Stella.

'I'm telling you, this is it,' Novak said, showing her the map. 'The most recent address online says it's here too.'

Stella grabbed the phone and did an internet images

search, comparing the pictures of *Provocateur*'s headquarters to what was in front of them. She turned on the phone's torch and shone it on the wall, illuminating a faint outline of letters spelling 'Provocateur' where they had been attached to the wall.

Without the lettering it now looked like any ordinary apartment entrance in Paris: a single door with multiple buttons to buzz the various residents.

All the buttons had names except for one.

Adams stayed back behind the pair, nervously checking they hadn't been followed.

There was no response from the buzzer.

'It's late,' Stella said. 'They must have packed up for the day.'

Novak persisted, pressing it again. 'Not Romain. This is practically breakfast time for him.'

'Look,' Adams said. He pointed up at a second floor window where someone was peeking from behind a curtain.

It was barely a sliver, but enough to see out onto the street below.

A few seconds later they were buzzed in.

As they trooped upstairs, Stella said, 'You'd think they didn't want you to know there was a magazine here.'

There were no markings on the front door. Not even a number.

Stella rapped on it, which echoed through the cavernous stairwell.

The door flew open and they were immediately greeted by a man in his late fifties with wild hair and a cigarette in his mouth. He was wearing a French national football team jersey (1998 World Cup winning-era), black jeans, and a tattered old dressing gown. He said nothing, holding a finger to his lips, then waved them in rapidly.

Once he had closed the door he threw his arms around Novak. It wasn't just the embrace of an old friend, it was the embrace of someone who didn't think they'd ever see them again.

'*Bonsoir, Monsieur Laurent,*' Novak said, recoiling from the stench of alcohol on him.

Romain reluctantly released Novak, then grabbed his left hand. 'Still no ring, huh? Have you got a woman at home?'

Novak couldn't help but cringe a little, 'Jesus, Romain...No. I don't have a woman at home. I'm busy working. Going to the apartments of old, drunk, French men.'

Romain held his hand out to Stella. 'Stella Mitchell, it is a pleasure of my life.' He frowned at Adams then asked Novak, '*C'est qui?*' ('Who is he?')

Adams smiled, then said in the most American French accent possible, 'Je m'appelle Tucker Adams.'

Romain seemed startled. '*Le sénateur.*'

Novak explained, 'He's helping us with our story. We thought you might be able to help.'

Romain tramped down the hallway.

As the trio followed, Stella thought how ludicrous it seemed that a nationally distributed magazine could be produced there. It was nothing more than a converted four-bedroom apartment, with two of the bedrooms serving as office space.

The curtains were drawn in every room, and there was a stale smell about the place, as if there hadn't been a window open for a number of weeks.

The walls had the most famous front covers of *Provoca-teur* mounted in frames on them. Most were caricatures of French politicians and public figures, but the one that stood out was their infamous Muhammad cartoon edition from several years ago. It had provoked protests and death threats against Romain, resulting in his having to go into hiding in the south of France for three months.

Romain wasn't short on hiding places. It was said the Laurents' wealth went as far back as the eighteenth century, escaping the French Revolution with their money, and fleeing to the high mountains of Switzerland.

Romain's mother died when he was eleven, after which his father – a prominent venture capitalist - became a recluse, drinking his days away at the family's remote chateau in the French highlands of the Massif Central. Romain distracted himself by buying *Provocateur*.

His days of success now seemed a long time ago.

Romain walked through the main office room - a large, high-ceilinged space with five computer desks gathered together in the middle of the room.

'I'm sorry,' he said, enunciating clearly, 'I can't help you.' He held his finger up while he put on a dim desk light, then turned on a record player in the corner of the room.

The speakers filled the room with the ecstatic opening chords of German-Romantic composer Richard Strauss's "Im Abendrot". It sounded like the gates of heaven opening up. The volume was already up high. Romain turned it up even louder.

He dashed back across the room then whispered between Novak and Stella, 'It is not safe to talk in here. We must go outside.' He waved them back to the hall, leaving the music running. Barely heard over the deafening operatic vocals, a neighbour upstairs stamped repeatedly on the floor, accompanied by exasperated shouts of '*Ça fait cent fois aujourd'hui! J'en ai marre de cette musique!*' – ('That's one hundred times today! I'm sick of that music!')

Romain responded by singing back the song's vocals at the ceiling, pausing between lines to take a fast swig from a two-litre bottle of vodka.

Stella and Adams didn't know what to do with themselves.

The sight of his former editor staggering around drunk in the dark apartment crushed Novak. He hadn't expected to find him in such a state. Of particular concern was hearing Romain so enthusiastically singing a song about loneliness and dying.

Romain grabbed a packet of Gauloises from the hall console table, then opened the front door. He beckoned the trio to follow him outside.

When Novak tried to ask something, Romain shushed him immediately. Only once they were in the open air did he seem at ease.

He lit a cigarette, exhaling with relief. 'I'm sorry, friend,' he explained. 'It is crazy here. I cannot be sure who is listening.'

'Who's listening?' asked Novak.

He laughed in a manic, desperate way. 'Isn't it obvious?' He sucked on his cigarette like it was delivering much needed medicine to his body. 'The Saudis, of course. They killed Omar, now they're coming after me. They have eyes everywhere, Thomas.' He said his name the French way, dropping the S. 'Eyes and ears.'

Stella asked, 'What did Omar find, Romain?'

He walked so fast the others struggled to keep up, his eyes darting around. 'A month ago, Omar told me he had the biggest story of his career. He said it was about a spy in the American government. Someone deep. And very, very high.'

'Did he say what he had or how he got it?'

'An MI6 agent had given him a dossier identifying the spy.'

Novak had the question on his lips, but Adams was first to ask: 'Did Omar tell you what was in the dossier?'

'He told me nothing. Except that he had something very valuable. And when the time was right he would tell me.'

'What about the British spy?' asked Stella.

'You are testing me, huh?' Romain took another tug on his cigarette. He tilted his head in the direction of Rue de Bretagne. He wanted the cover of the trees that lined the roadside all along towards the Bastille monument. 'His name was Colin Burleigh. Omar said Burleigh had the story, but he wanted another source before publishing. Then the Saudis got to him first. They've been after him for years. It was only a matter of time.'

Stella made eyes at Novak that he had to tell Romain.

Romain noticed the silence and slowed his pace. 'You know something I don't?'

Novak said, 'It wasn't the Saudis who killed Omar, Romain.'

He made a quintessentially Gallic shrug and pout. 'What are you talking about, of course they did. They admitted it.'

Adams joined in. 'The Saudi government doesn't mind

the world thinking that. It makes them look powerful like the Americans: sending assassins around the globe, taking out enemies.'

Romain protested, 'Omar was the biggest critic of the Saudi royal family. That's why we published him. Who else would want to kill him?'

Novak said, 'The Russians sent a man called Gaspar Nolé after him. We still don't know exactly why, but whatever was in the dossier must be very damaging to the Russians.'

Stella added, 'Burleigh gave the same dossier to Andrei Rublov, and Gaspar killed him too.'

'He won't stop, Romain,' said Novak. 'Now he's killed Bill Rand in Germany.'

Romain stopped walking. He flicked his head towards Adams. 'What are you here for?'

'I'm Tom and Stella's source,' Adams replied.

Romain's eyes widened. 'If you know who the spy is, why are you not dead too?'

Novak answered, 'There's a lot we still don't know. But we have to start by finding the Colin Burleigh dossier.'

Romain dismissed the thought with a wave. 'I wouldn't keep something like that in the apartment. It was so much more than the identity of the spy, *mes amis*.' He checked all around him, before whispering, 'It has everything. Omar said these people involved are operating at the highest levels of the British and American governments. There's only one place safe enough to keep such a file.'

'Where?' asked Novak.

Romain put his arm around him, still checking in all directions for a tail.

Stella took a silent cue from Novak's expression. 'Senator,' she said to Adams. 'Let's give them a moment.'

When they were alone, Novak held the collar of Romain's dressing gown. 'What are you doing to yourself? This is not the Monsieur Laurent I remember.'

'Maybe I have lost too much,' Romain replied. 'You of all people should understand that.'

'So you're quitting to drink yourself to death, is that it?'

'What else is there? You think you are safe?' He made a mocking pose flexing his biceps. 'Because you are a strong American? You want to win? You *can't* win. Not at this. You were the same years ago. Always wanting the biggest story.'

'And so were you,' Novak retorted. 'That's why I came to you back then. Now you've given up.' He hesitated for a moment. 'Just like your father.'

Romain paused, feeling his blood rise. 'What the hell did you just say?'

'You can't give up, Romain. And with every drink you take tonight, and tomorrow, and the day after, and every day you aren't publishing, you're giving up.'

'Ah, *merde*,' Romain swore, flicking his hand dismissively. But something must have sunk in. He seemed to wilt as he lowered himself to the kerb.

Novak sat down beside him. 'This isn't what Omar would have wanted.'

'I don't have the...' he gestured at his stomach, 'for the fight. Not anymore.' He had tears in his eyes. 'I don't want to feel like this anymore. I want to live, Thomas.'

Novak gripped Romain's forearm. 'This isn't living,' he told him.

'I know.' Romain wiped away his tears, checking how close Stella and Adams were. Too far away to hear.

'There's a bank in Geneva my family has used since the old days. I have a deposit box there. I gave Omar the passcode.' He took out one of his business cards and wrote the code on the back along with the address of the bank.

Novak reached out for the card but Romain didn't let go of it yet.

'Be careful, *frèrot*.' He smiled at his ironic use of the term.

Novak pocketed the card then clasped Romain's hand. 'I will, bro.'

Once Novak was on his feet, Romain glanced towards Stella. 'She is pretty, huh.'

Novak rolled his eyes. 'Could you be any more French?'

'You know you are the same as when you first came to Paris,' Romain said.

'Arrogant?' Novak chuckled, assuming Romain was messing around. 'Full of myself?'

Romain paused, then said in a voice that a father would use, 'Alone. There is more to life than this. I don't want you to end up like me, Thomas.'

The observation stung Novak. He didn't move for a few seconds, trying to think of a response. 'You should go home, Romain,' he said.

He took out a quarter bottle of whisky from his dressing gown. 'I'm going to sit here for a while.' He pointed up at the clear night sky. 'We are all in the gutter, huh...'

Novak smiled ruefully, remembering the Oscar Wilde quote they often said to each other in the old days. 'But some of us are looking at the stars.'

Romain held the bottle up, toasting him.

Novak didn't want to watch him drink anymore.

Once Novak returned, Stella looked at Romain worriedly. 'Should we be leaving him there?'

Novak kept walking. 'It's what he wants.'

Adams chased after him. 'What did he give you? Do we have a lead?'

'It could be the last piece in the puzzle,' said Novak. 'We're going to Frères Van de Velde in Geneva.'

37

For anyone else ping-ponging through major time zones as Walter and Rebecca had for the past two days, they would have been knocked sideways by the jetlag.

Instead, the pair were side by side in a four-seat booth, combing through the print outs of Gaspar and Belchov's phone records. Something about them was troubling Rebecca.

She sat back in her seat with a groan. '*Some*where in here there's a phone number for the mole inside CIA.' She looked at Sharp for confirmation. 'There's no way it could have come from anywhere else.'

'I'm with you,' Sharp agreed. 'Whoever told Belchov about Camp Metro should be considered a major threat. The problem is...' he lifted the considerable pile of phone records, 'these guys have been doing this a long time. They know how to cover their tracks.'

Rebecca leaned forward again, rummaging through the records. 'Fine. We'll do it the old-fashioned way: any number we don't have a history on, or know the identity of the caller, gets highlighted. I used to do this on my lunch break at GCHQ. I wrote a program that generated hundreds of thirteen-digit numbers, and duplicated only one of them, once. Then I had to find it.'

'Why?' asked Sharp, mystified as to why someone would put themselves through such mental torture.

Rebecca replied, 'In case I ever had to do this. Bruce Lee once said that he didn't fear a man who practised one thousand different kicks once. He feared a man who practised one kick one thousand times. This,' she tapped the pages, 'is the one kick I've been practising.'

If there was one thing Walter Sharp understood, it was the discipline to train one particular skillset for years in anticipation of the time you would need it in the field.

After half an hour Rebecca's discipline had paid off. She had uncovered an anomaly.

'Here.' She showed Sharp a circled number. 'This is the number that alerted Belchov that my father is being kept in Camp Metro.' She shuffled down four pages. 'And here it is again calling Belchov last week.'

Sharp examined it. 'But we checked that number against everything we've got on ECHELON. How are we going to find the caller without an existing ID?'

Rebecca somersaulted her pen down her fingers then back up again. 'Precisely,' she said. 'We look through every metadata listing against that phone and eliminate them one by one. Eventually, we'll find a link to someone we know. We have to.'

Playing Devil's Advocate, Sharp said, 'Unless it's a brand new burner. In which case the history will be meaningless.'

'Yes, well...let's just hope it's not a new burner then, eh.'

Whoever had been using the phone was trained in at least the basic aspects of modern grid-evasion: always taking the battery out when the phone was not in use, thus eliminating any geographical data; never using names in text messages; no internet data used.

But all Rebecca needed was one mistake. One little moment where something was overlooked.

'I've got it,' she said.

Sharp couldn't work out why she wasn't elated. 'What's wrong?' he asked.

'We've been had this entire time.'

'What do you mean?'

'We're looking for someone with Top Secret clearance who has had access to information on Camp Metro, right?'

Sharp agreed.

She showed him her laptop screen. 'They've been pretty careful normally. But here they called a landline.'

All Sharp could see highlighted was a string of numbers. 'What is that?'

'That's the coordinates of Kensington Palace Gardens. Specifically Yevgeny Belchov's landline.'

'Why would they do that?' asked Sharp.

'Because everyone slips up eventually. The call lasts for five seconds. No doubt Belchov telling the caller to get the hell off his landline. But look at the location of the caller.'

Sharp looked down at the next set of coordinates. 'Where is that?'

Stella clicked through, showing the coordinates on the map. 'Now look at the date and time of the call.'

It took Sharp a few moments. 'But that means...'

Rebecca got out of her seat and pushed her hair back. She had already moved on in her head to damage control.

'You said Novak sent you a message on OTR an hour ago. Where did he say they were going?'

Sharp double-checked his phone. 'Geneva. They have a lead on the final copy of the dossier.' Sharp could see the same problem as Rebecca. 'Shit.'

When she looked up, Rebecca was a picture of anguish. 'They're not going to get the dossier. They're walking into a trap.'

38

Novak, Stella, and Adams caught the first flight of the day from Paris to Geneva Airport, near the west corner of Lake Geneva. The border with France was so close that the airport actually crossed back into France at the north end of the runway.

Geneva had consistently been one of the world's most expensive cities for the past twenty years, and evidence of its prosperity was clear to see from the backseat of the taxi.

The architecture was a bold mix of period and modern, all immaculately maintained.

There wasn't a trace of litter anywhere. Everyone looked affluent and happy, basking in the glow of the city's late-winter/early-spring sunshine.

Lake Geneva sparkled from what seemed like thousands of different points on the water. To the south, the horizon was dominated by a snow-covered Mont Salève in France, towering over the compact city – not many European cities crammed so much into such a small space. And beyond that, Mont Blanc in the distance: the highest mountain in Europe.

In no time the trio were in the heart of the city, being dropped off outside a palatial marble building on the banks of the River Rhône. The building where Frères Van de Velde had first brought their banking empire to Switzerland at the turn of the nineteenth century – the bulk of the building still in its original marble, but with a slick, modern glass front.

Frères Van de Velde started in Paris in the early 1800s, advising the French government on gold buying. When four of the five Van de Velde brothers emigrated to America, they opened their first branch in New York. Within ten years, they had opened in London, Rome, Shanghai, Buenos Aires, and San Francisco.

After surviving the two world wars, Frères Van de Velde made its name in mergers and acquisitions, and investment banking.

In the early eighties, foreseeing a crash in the global financial sector, the board of directors reduced Van de Velde's exposure to the investment sector. As they watched their rivals fall one by one through the nineties, and eventually in the two-thousands – either dissolving into bankruptcy or bought over – Van de Velde had settled into a more boutique, private business. They concentrated on personal banking, handling large family estates like the Laurents'.

The interest and fees charged to accounts was enough to consolidate a turnover of close to four billion dollars U.S. a year.

They stayed out of the news, and out of the limelight. Just the way the board of directors wanted it. Because in the vaults of Frères Van de Velde lay some very dark, very unwanted secrets.

A doorman with a top hat opened the front door with a genteel nod.

There weren't any counters or desks to go to. Just a wide, open hall with marble pillars leading towards a staircase at the end of the vast room.

A man in a black suit descended the stairs, holding his arms out as if the pair had been long-awaited.

He said, '*Bon après-midi, Madame et messieurs. Je suis Christian Blanc. Je peux vous aider?*' ('I am Christian Blanc. How can I help you?')

Stella, who had the superior French in the trio, took the initiative and stepped forward, extending her hand. '*Bonjour, Monsieur Blanc. Nous avons un compte bancaire.*' ('We have a bank account.')

Blanc then did what Stella found most irritating after demonstrating she was happy to speak in a native language: he switched to English. 'How wonderful,' he said. 'It is always a pleasure to put a face to one of our guests.'

Stella thought Blanc had used the wrong word, but he hadn't. Guests was the term Frères Van de Velde always used for customers.

Blanc showed them to an anonymous-looking desk near the foot of the stairs.

Guards with transparent ear-pieces and dressed in tailored suits acted blissfully unaware of the trio's presence. They were anything but.

Half a dozen other customers were making their way in and out, speaking either French or German. A young woman in a Givenchy tweed suit seemed to pause at the sight of Novak, not being able to place where she recognised him from.

There was no doubt in Novak's mind why he had been recognised. 'Hey, how you doing...' he said, flashing her a smile.

Stella rolled her eyes at him. 'Jesus, Novak. Can we stay focussed here?'

Adams stared back at the woman, envious as to how Novak could garner the attention of such a beauty. He was so distracted he walked straight into an older man in a raincoat.

'*Merde*,' the man swore, straightening himself. '*Faites attention!*' ('Be careful!')

'I'm so sorry,' Adams said, flapping in apology.

Novak laughed to himself when he realised the woman had seen it all happen. 'You must get that a lot,' Novak told her.

Christian Blanc tried to be flamboyant with his body language, but it came off as stiff, like someone who had studied in the art of elegance rather than genuinely held it in his bones.

He led the trio to a desk where a clerk was sitting behind a computer terminal – its screen had a long visor over it, masking it from the guests' view.

Stella took Romain's business card from Novak. 'We'd like to access a safe deposit box.'

Blanc smiled warmly as he joined the clerk behind the desk, then took the business card.

The clerk said nothing and showed no expression as he keyed in the account number on the keyboard.

Blanc frowned a little. 'If I may, *Madame*, we recommend that customers do not keep account information written down. For security purposes.'

The clerk presented a tablet to Blanc, who held it out to Stella.

'And your password,' Blanc requested.

Following the password Romain had written down, Stella tapped it in: 'REGENCY'. She handed the tablet back to Blanc, who waited for the computer terminal to accept the password.

Novak and Adams glanced at each other in anticipation.

Blanc seemed to hesitate for a moment before smiling. He placed the tablet down, then brought his hands together in a silent clap. '*C'est magnifique.* That is all in order. Would you care for some coffee? Or we have some champagne upstairs?'

Novak was getting antsy, hands on hips. 'No, we're good,' he said quickly, then checked his watch. 'We're actually on a tight schedule...'

Blanc took his prompt and walked towards the staircase. '*Bien sûr...* If you'd be so kind as to follow me, please.'

Stella gave nothing away, but Novak was already feeling celebratory. He and Adams were far enough behind Blanc for him not to hear.

'Jackpot,' Novak whispered to Adams.

Adams, barely containing a giddy smile, patted Novak on the back.

Stella mumbled to Novak, 'Don't get carried away yet.'

Back at the clerk's desk the screen showed two different possible passwords for Romain's account.

The first was highlighted in green as "Normal Response": 'VERSAILLES'

The second was highlighted in red as "Threat Response": 'REGENCY'

The clerk got on the phone. '*It's Michel downstairs. An account has been compromised. Tell security to stand by.*'

The staircase turned sharply up to the right, revealing a secure, glass turnstile which required a swipe card from Blanc. There were security guards on either side of the barrier, and not the daydreaming sort.

The bigger one had cropped blonde hair and a face that looked like it was made out of granite. He stood with one hand wrapped threateningly around his other fist, poised. As the trio went through the secure barrier he pressed in his earpiece, as if receiving a message of some sort.

Stella was last, and noticed a small green LED changing to a red light once she was through, followed by a locking sound.

The only way out now was with a swipe of Blanc's card.

Stella stopped for a moment, then the guard said, 'Keep moving.'

Stella couldn't place his accent. European, yes. But not Western or Central.

Blanc told the guard, '*Il n'y a pas de problème, Frederick.*' ('There is no problem') Blanc then bowed apologetically at Stella. 'This way, please.'

They were taken through a vault door into a room filled almost floor to ceiling with gold-coloured safe deposit boxes. Some no thicker than a letter box. Some the size of a large desk drawer.

But once in the room, Blanc didn't stop walking. He

kept going to a door at the back. Novak, heading the trio, was unsure if they were supposed to follow.

'Your room is this way,' Blanc told them.

'Room?' Stella mouthed to Novak.

The door at the back led to a corridor much like a hotel's. There were rooms down each side, each with a door bearing a gold-plate with the name of the account-holder.

Blanc stopped outside Romain's, then unlocked the door.

He didn't open it, as per regulations. He took two steps back then told them, 'When you are ready to leave, simply close your door, and a guard will greet you here.'

The second Blanc left them alone, Novak opened the door.

He was the first one through.

As soon as he saw the contents, Novak mumbled, 'Holy...*shit*. Stella, what the hell is this?'

'I have no idea,' she replied.

The room was twenty metres square, and had a ceiling twice as high. The walls were soundproof brushed steel. The carpet a deep red.

The room was filled with antique furniture: desks, chairs, a leather chaise longue gifted to the Laurents from the court of Louis XIV. Stacks of paintings in their original frames were in racks against a wall. There were metal book-cases full of rare volumes. At a glance, Novak spotted a first-edition Charles Dickens *Great Expectations*, Mark Twain, Voltaire, Thomas Mann... Then there was a glass cabinet with one of Babe Ruth's baseball bats hanging upright in it.

'This place is a damn museum,' Adams cooed.

On the floor – like an afterthought – was a pile of red canvas sacks. When Stella nudged one of the sacks open with her foot and peeked inside, she saw that it was full of hundred-dollar bills. Each sack was close to one million dollars.

Overhead, an air conditioner hummed to keep the room at a consistent temperature of seventy-one degrees Fahrenheit, and relative humidity at fifty-five per cent: the ideal numbers for preserving paintings. Art galleries were in a constant battle to consistently hit such numbers, given the large influxes of people coming in and out of them. Romain Laurent's secure room had no such issues.

Novak could feel them standing in the centre of their story, his stomach in knots that at the sight of a simple manila file they could turn the political world inside out.

Adams was idly flicking through the paintings in the racks, then stopped on one. He stared at it for several seconds, then leaned closer to make sure his eyes weren't playing tricks on him.

'What is it?' asked Stella.

He exclaimed, 'It's a Van Gogh.'

Stella stood back from it, tilting her head a little. 'It looks like a Van Gogh. But I don't recognise it.'

It was a self-portrait of him standing in front of a field, holding art supplies. He had used his famous impasto technique: the thick layering of pastel so common in his most famous works.

Adams said, 'It's called "Painter on His Way to Work". Art historians thought it was destroyed by a fire in nineteen forty-five.' He looked up in awe. 'This could be worth one hundred million dollars.'

But the Van Gogh wasn't the only rare artefact.

As Novak rummaged through a stack of papers, he

came across the front page of a newspaper dated "June 28 1940".

The main photograph showed Adolf Hitler posing in front of the Eiffel Tower with Albert Speer, and a man the caption identified as Hugo Laurent. Hitler spent all of three hours in Paris. Some of which was spent in the company of Romain Laurent's grandfather and Nazi collaborator.

'That explains a lot,' Novak said to himself.

Stella was going through a box of papers on the floor and sat back on her knees, surveying the desks and dressers and cabinets around the room. Overwhelmed by the scale of the task in front of them, she threw her hands up. 'How the hell are we meant to find this thing? We could be here for days.'

Novak joined her. He said, 'If it's one of the most recent additions to the room, it's unlikely to be buried underneath anything.' He found a stack of folders sitting on their own on a corner of a desk.

The front of one of the files bore the official stamp of MI6.

'Stella,' Novak said in anticipation. He showed her the front of the file.

She nodded.

Across the room, Adams left the racks of paintings to join them.

Novak opened the file, coming across black and white photos of a young man, from what seemed like a surveillance photo. The man didn't seem aware he was being photographed. He mostly had his back to the camera, and the face was indistinct.

Under that, was a congressional campaign flyer from the nineties, the red and blue colours now faded. The font which had looked so sharp and modern back then now looked dated.

It wasn't the design that caught their attention.

'I mean, do you actually believe this,' Novak said.

Stella shook her head. 'Of course.'

The flyer read, "Adams for Congress".

Behind them, Adams was holding an automatic colt pistol - a Springfield XDS .45. It was only an inch wide with a three-inch barrel, making it one of the most reliable concealed carry weapons on the market.

Novak sighed in reluctant appreciation at the earlier hand-off in the lobby with the old man. 'That was real clean, Senator,' he said.

'Thank you,' Adams said. But now he had been unmasked he sounded even more vulnerable.

Stella thought back to Paris. She said to Adams, 'The way Romain reacted when you introduced yourself. It wasn't that he recognised you, your face. He knew your name. Omar told him not to trust you, didn't he. It was you all along,' Stella said, lifting her hands slowly away from the desk.

Adams said, 'I'm very grateful for you taking me to the last piece of evidence I need to destroy. Getting into this place was proving quite difficult. Even with a man on the inside.'

Novak faltered at the thought of all the carnage Adams had caused. 'You weren't helping Rublov. You were finding out how much he knew.'

After twenty years of keeping his secret from everyone, Adams was actually relieved to be able to finally talk to someone about it. Still, holding a gun at people was new territory for him. His hand was shaking, and lowered slightly as he spoke.

'I didn't want anyone to die,' Adams sputtered, barely able to keep himself together. 'That was their idea, not mine.'

'Hilderberg or the Russians?' asked Stella, turning her face away from the gun.

'Hilderberg?' said Adams. His hand now trembled in anger rather than fear. 'They wouldn't have pissed on me if I was on fire. Hilderberg wouldn't even put organise a goddamn fundraiser for me.'

Novak mocked him, 'What a tragedy.'

'Quiet, Novak,' Stella warned him.

'What the hell do you know?' Adams barked at Novak. 'You were the son of a fucking news anchor. Try being the son of an attorney general. I didn't have clowns at my birthday parties, I had former Presidents, Supreme Court judges, and commanders of NATO. Being a senator was like flipping burgers to my old man. So when the Russians came to me with an offer...I listened.'

'You sold out your own country,' Novak seethed. 'You were given every opportunity, every privilege America has to offer. Then you were handed a job with a six-figure salary, expenses, a car, a secretary, and a third of the year on holiday. Your country gave you everything, and you sold it out. You're a piece of shit, Adams.'

'Novak!' Stella snapped.

Frederick the security guard opened the door, also now pointing a gun at Novak and Stella. 'Is there a problem, Adams?'

'No problem,' Adams replied without turning around.

'Why haven't you finished them off yet?' Frederick bellowed.

'I'm handling it, Frederick,' Adams fired back. 'Wait outside.'

Frederick didn't budge, staying in the doorway.

Adams gathered himself, refocusing his attention on Novak. 'Tell me, Mr Pulitzer Prize: what do you think Bill Rand was going to do to the country come next November? The man who sold Stanley Fox out to Hilderberg. Yeah, that's right. Rand is the reason Fox has been tortured in some CIA hellhole. Without Fox, Rand didn't stand a chance. Look at Downing Street: he knew Hilderberg were going to have Simon Ali and Robert Snow killed, just to give him a *chance* at the Presidency and he went along with it!'

'Is that your pitch?' asked Novak. 'Tucker Adams: I'm slightly less criminal than someone else? You're like a drunk driver who swerves down a pavement, knocking down pedestrians, but manages to screech to a stop before hitting a baby in a pram. You grab the baby, then shout, "Look, I saved this baby's life!"'

'I *deserve* it!' Adams yelled, stepping closer.

Sensing Adams was losing control, Stella felt her hands turning cold and clammy, and her breathing quickened. But something inside her told her to ignore those things, to dig deep.

She could tell that Adams was gun-shy. And as she gathered control of her breathing once more, she thought of an angle to play. She said, 'What do you think the Russians will do with you once Stanley Fox is either dead or hidden so deep by the CIA that he's never found again? You're not going to the White House, Adams. Not without Hilderberg's backing. The Russians will send Gaspar after you as well. Can't you see? You've got nothing to offer anyone anymore. The Russians have only kept you alive so you could find this for them.' She raised the dossier. 'The second you hand it over to Lurch over there he's going to shoot you in the head.'

'Confident words for a woman with two guns pointing at her,' Adams retorted, trying to sound bold.

'Senator,' she said, trying to remind him who he really was, rather than a killer. 'The Russians just wanted to make sure Bill Rand never saw the inside of the White House. They did that. It's over.'

Frederick took several steps inside the room. 'I've heard enough of this. Finish them, Adams.'

Adams turned around. 'What?'

'You heard me. Belchov says you've to finish this yourself.'

'Why?'

'Because it's time you got your hands dirty. How can the FSB trust you unless you show you're willing to do whatever is necessary?'

Adams' aiming arm lowered slightly again. 'Please...don't...' His eyes filled with tears. His shoulders hunched.

Frederick cocked the hammer on his gun. 'Believe me when I tell you it's you or them.'

Finally Adams' tears spilled over. He lifted his free hand to wipe them away. 'I can't...'

Stella looked up and met Novak's eyes. They didn't have to say anything.

Frederick started to laugh, goading Adams. 'You're pathetic.' He shouldered Adams out the way.

Adams cowered backwards, gun now at his side. 'I'm sorry,' he told Novak and Stella.

They looked down and closed their eyes, not wanting the last thing they saw to be their partner shot in the head.

A first shot rang out, making Stella jump.

In the background somewhere, Tucker Adams let out an anguished cry.

Then a second shot rang out.

But Stella still hadn't been hit.

She opened her eyes again, seeing Novak in the same position, unharmed.

In front of them, Frederick was flat on his face on the ground. There were two gunshots in his back.

At the doorway Christian Blanc stood behind one of his security team – gun held out, aimed in Frederick's direction.

Tucker Adams was kneeling on the ground with his eyes closed, covering his ears. He had already tossed his gun to one side. 'Please,' he cried, 'I just want this to be over...'

Novak and Stella embraced harder than they'd ever embraced anyone else before.

'Are you alright?' Blanc asked, stepping past his guard.

'Yeah, I'm good,' Novak groaned, as Stella released him. The break in the adrenaline surge sent a wave of over-whelming exhaustion through him. 'You goddamn Swiss really are always on time.' He leaned on Blanc in relief, resting his head on his shoulder.

After Novak lifted his head off, Blanc waited until Novak wasn't looking to dust his shoulder with the back of his hand.

Novak called to the guard in tourist French, '*Garçon,*'

then pointed at Adams. 'Can you please put a pair of cuffs on that snivelling son of a bitch.'

Stella picked up the dossier from the carpet, then wiped some sweat from her face with her forearm. 'Monsieur Blanc, I've changed my mind.'

Blanc waited to hear the request.

'I believe I'll take that glass of champagne now.'

39

BUILDING 106, MANHATTAN – TUESDAY, 4.42PM

The silver ten-storey off East 54th Street in Manhattan looked like a normal shared office block. Every day hundreds of New Yorkers walked past it without a second thought. Bike messengers and couriers and postal workers stomped past with their packages and envelopes, and every once in a while one would wonder what actually went on inside 106.

The lobby was modest and plain. The front desk was manned by a security guard wearing an atypical blue uniform bearing the logo "City Security Services". There was a single elevator door and, beside it, a mirrored directory on the wall listing what companies were on which floor. But none of the companies were real: each one a CIA-owned shell company.

Architecturally, 106 was the equivalent of the espionage world's grey man: it blended in perfectly with its surroundings and raised no suspicions.

Rebecca had been trying both Stella's and Novak's phones since she'd identified Tucker Adams as the owner of the mysterious burner phone. He'd given himself away by calling Belchov from the one place Rebecca knew Adams was at the time of calling: mere minutes after meeting Andrei Rublov in Rock Creek Park.

'Anything?' asked Sharp.

'No,' Rebecca answered, pocketing her phone. 'There's nothing we can do for now. We need to focus.'

'Whatever happens in here, just act like it's exactly what you expect. The guards in here are going to be *on it.*'

When they entered the lobby the black operative in Sharp admired how well CIA had fitted the place out. It was the little details like the mirrored directory beside the elevator, which Sharp correctly guessed was actually a two-way mirror.

There were four other guards back there, and they unhooked their gun holsters as soon as he and Rebecca walked in.

In front of the guards in the hidden room was an overhead bank of CCTV screens showing high-definition images of the street outside, as well as heat maps of the figures going past. The cameras also acted as full-body scanners showing all metallic areas, anything with moving parts, as well as taking in heart rate and hot spots: all key indicators of a potential attacker.

The solitary guard at the front desk didn't look like a typical officer from Security Protective Services that guarded CIA facilities. That wasn't sufficient for 106 East 54th Street - or as it was otherwise known to those with sufficient clearance: Camp Metro. The jewel in CIA's clandestine crown.

Camp Metro guards were CIA Physical and Technical Security Officers. PTSOs. And were capable of much more than merely swiping entry passes and wishing people a good day.

The PTSOs for Camp Metro held certificates in Anti-Terrorism Force Protection; were trained in Technical Security Countermeasures; and installed and maintained all the intrusion detection systems, CCTV, and vehicle barriers on site. They weren't bad behind a computer either: able to navigate through CISCO and Linux systems; had expert-level networking experience; and were fully trained in both TEMPEST and COMSEC.

Every window in the building was bullet-proof and sealed shut. Even if someone were able to penetrate one of the floors above, all they would find were empty offices with cables and wiring hanging through the panelled ceilings.

The only floor that really counted in 106 was situated three floors under the lobby, and not even the PTSOs knew entirely what took place there.

'Top Secret' was a phrase that had been robbed of its import over the years. In the case of 106, the activities in the basement truly merited Top Secret clearance: the unauthorised disclosure of what went on there could be expected to cause 'exceptionally grave damage to the national security.'

They didn't let just anyone into 106. As Walter and Rebecca were about to find out.

The front desk PTSO asked, 'How you guys doing today?'

Sharp wasn't interested in the pleasantries. He recognised the sign-in setup from Camp Seven on the outskirts of Madrid.

The PTSO placed the tablet on the desktop then said, 'Please sign in.'

Sharp signed his name with his finger. The screen then changed to an image of the outline of a hand.

'And your hand,' the PTSO said. Until that point he had assumed Sharp was cleared personnel. His demeanour, tone of voice, and facial expression gave nothing away of any doubt or hesitation. He looked like every other Company operative that came through there.

There were no smiles or small talk like in the security gate queue at Langley. Compared to Camp Metro, Langley was a tourist destination.

Sharp placed his hand on the screen with frustrated inevitability. When the scan came back failed as he knew it would, his only option would be stubborn refusal and having to play the 'don't you know who I am?' routine.

The system took little time to identify Sharp's prints and spit back a refusal of entry.

The tablet screen switched to a red background, the words 'ACCESS DENIED' flashing in bold across the top.

Before the PTSO could say anything, Sharp stated, 'I don't have time for this, son. You wanna get me a screen that works.'

The guard held firm. 'Do you have an appointment, sir?'

Sharp leaned closer towards the desk. It was only a few inches, but it was enough to make the guard retreat by twice that margin. 'Your ass is going to have an appointment with the end of my boot if you don't figure out what's going on here. I'm SSO Walter Sharp and this is-'

Right on cue, Rebecca stepped forward. 'I'm Rebecca Fox from British Intelligence Internal Affairs,' she said. 'Under the British-American Intelligence and Diplomacy Act, I'm entitled to enter.'

'Not this facility, ma'am,' the PTSO replied, unflappable.

'What appears to be the problem?' asked Rebecca.

'Ma'am. I'm going to have to ask you to step-'

The elevator door pinged open, and out stepped Bob Weiskopf. He was in a shirt and tie, and holding a pastrami sandwich. He held his hand out in apology. 'Sorry, Nathan,' he called to the PTSO. 'That's my fault. I forgot to put Walt and Rebecca in my diary.'

The PTSO was firm even with Weiskopf. 'Sir. We have protocols here.'

'So do I,' Weiskopf replied, leading Walter and Rebecca towards the elevator doors.

'How you doin', Bob?' Sharp asked, masking the surprise and confusion he was actually feeling.

Rebecca played along seamlessly too, clutching her laptop bag, maintaining an officious air.

In the elevator Weiskopf keyed in a seven-digit code on the wall panel. He didn't have to tell either Walter or Rebecca not to say anything incriminating: they'd already spotted the cameras in there, and had correctly assumed there was also a microphone.

Once they reached the basement Weiskopf urged Sharp and Rebecca out quickly. 'We're good now.'

They walked along a corridor with an industrial feel to it: overhead pipes, leaking walls and puddles on the concrete ground.

'What the hell are you doing here?' Sharp asked.

'I might ask you the same thing,' Weiskopf replied. 'When I got your call from Frankfurt, I got an alert that you'd accessed the protected Camp Metro files. Everyone at director level gets them. Luckily they all think you were me.'

'There's no protocol for that on any other black site,' Sharp said.

'There is a reason for that, Walt.'

Rebecca said, 'You know who's being kept here, don't you.'

Weiskopf could see the tension in her face. How much it meant to her – to know. 'Your father.'

'Has he been tortured?'

Weiskopf paused. 'I can neither confirm nor deny any operations within this location to non-CIA personnel...'

Rebecca tutted.

But he went on, 'I can also neither confirm nor deny that the detainee known as Triple-X is being transferred to a CIA research facility in the Utah Valley to confirm the validity of his formula.'

'He gave up the formula?' asked Rebecca.

'The password that has access to it. The techs are running analysis on the code as we speak.'

'Bob, you can't transfer Stanley,' Sharp insisted. 'The Russians know he's here. They know he's being moved.'

'That's preposterous. They'd need a mole inside CIA to know that.'

'Or a mole who's chair of the Senate Intelligence Committee, and has Top Secret security clearance, and access to Camp Metro files.'

Weiskopf stopped walking. 'Tucker Adams.'

Rebecca said, 'He's been on the Kremlin's payroll for years.'

He started walking again. 'Son of a...'

They were fast approaching a black door at the end of the corridor.

Rebecca stopped Weiskopf. 'You can't let them transfer my father out of here. Please.'

'I only came here to protect Walt,' Weiskopf claimed. 'I don't have a dog in this fight.'

'I don't believe that,' Rebecca replied. 'Walt told me about you. What you've risked for him in the past.'

Weiskopf looked helplessly at the black door. 'What exactly do you want to do?'

'Help us break Stanley out,' Sharp said.

'This is the most secure CIA location on the eastern seaboard.'

'Just get us into his motorcade. We'll do the rest.'

Weiskopf looked at the door again, then at Rebecca. He could see the anguish in her face. 'I can get you five minutes alone with him.'

Rebecca didn't step back yet.

'And a seat in the car behind his,' he added, pushing his way past Rebecca. 'What happens after that is up to you.'

40

After giving their statement to the Swiss police, Novak and Stella took a private suite in Swiss Air's business class wing in terminal three. The glass-walled suite came with a desk and leather swivel chairs, high-speed broadband internet connection, printer, all the day's major international newspapers, and a wall-mounted television with access to CNN, BBC, Bloomberg, and Al Jazeera.

The pair had Novak's laptop open, spurning the broadband Ethernet cable in favour of connecting online via the hotspot on his phone, which carried a VPN to scramble their location. An airport internet connection was like hanging a flashing beacon around your neck, broadcasting a message to NSA saying 'Please listen to me'.

They were on a Darkroom call with Diane back in New York.

After Stella was finished reading through the most pertinent parts of the dossier, Diane leaned back in her seat. 'No one's going to escape the blowback of this one. The Senate, intelligence committees, CIA, the White House...'

'There's nowhere this doesn't touch,' Stella said.

'They'll be assembling grand juries for months.' Diane tapped her pen on her desk, lost in thought. 'What do you have so far in terms of copy?'

'I've just finished typing up a pretty solid spine,' answered Stella. 'We're going to need statements or comment from the State department.'

'And we need them before they can hide behind the usual "unfair to comment during investigation" horse muck.'

Normally the phrase would have got a laugh from Novak: Diane knew how ridiculous he found her insistence on never swearing. Particularly as he was so liberal in his own use.

He'd barely said a word since the call began.

'CIA won't budge,' Stella said. 'They're only good for a no comment at the best of times, but this…'

'Agreed,' Diane said. 'What about off-the-record?'

Stella looked surprised. 'You'd be happy with that here?'

'We have an ID on Adams from two sources who made direct contact with him. We have an official MI6 dossier on him: we're not looking for further confirmation. We're just looking to paint in the edges and give the government a chance to respond.'

Novak backed away from the desk. He couldn't hold his tongue any longer. 'It's not that simple,' he said. He'd been turning the problem over in his head even before the Darkroom call began.

'What's not simple?' asked Diane.

'The second we ask for comment from State, the

Director of the FBI will issue a national security letter, and shut this whole thing down.'

Stella said, 'This is too huge to keep a lid on, Novak. How can they do that?'

Novak reached for the TV remote and switched off CNN, which was running an obituary piece on Bill Rand. 'The FBI can issue NSLs for pretty much anything it wants. What's bad for us here is that they would definitely include a nondisclosure provision, as it could result in a danger to United States national security, or interfere with diplomatic relations. None of us are lawyers, but I think we can all agree that a Russian spy in Congress would probably cause some diplomatic issues.'

Stella argued, 'But surely with a grand jury investigation-'

Diane shook her head. 'Grand juries can be convened in private. And with a potential gag order against us, it would be a federal crime for us to even reveal we had been served with a gag order, let alone actually report the story that we had been gagged on.'

Novak added, 'There are Patriot Act orders that have been going for over a decade. There are tens of thousands of NSLs issued every year, and not one of them requires judicial review. I did a story on them eighteen months ago.'

Stella asked, 'Are you saying that we might be prosecuted for running this story?'

'No,' he replied. 'I'm saying we will. For sure.'

Stella retorted, 'Since when has that ever stopped us?'

Diane couldn't help but smile. 'I'll take this to legal. I'm going to have to figure out a way for us to publish this story in a way that doesn't close us down for good. Get back here safe.'

'We will,' Stella replied, noticing Novak's lack of response.

They shuffled slowly towards the gate as boarding for the Swiss Air flight to JFK began. When Stella felt Novak hanging back she knew what he was going to say.

Novak stared at a point on the floor, lost in thought.

Stella said, 'It's Talya, isn't it.'

Novak looked up. 'I can't leave her, Stella.'

'I'm not going to pretend to understand what you're going through right now. But what do you really think you can do for her? She knew the risks. We all know the risks we take, and we don't live in Moscow.'

'It's not just Talya,' Novak explained. 'Magdalina's about to lose her mother. She can't lose her father too. I can't stop thinking about all those nights I haven't been there for her. I know what it's like to have a father who wasn't always there. I'm not going to make the same mistakes he made. I-'

Stella interrupted, 'You're right.'

It took him by surprise.

'You're right. You should do whatever you have to for Magdalina. But going to Moscow for Natalya doesn't help her. Unless...' She broke off.

'Unless what?'

'Unless you love her.'

The call went out overhead that boarding was about to close.

She looked back at the gate, where the "final boarding" graphic had gone up on the monitor. 'I have to go,' she said.

Novak picked up his bag. 'You know if there was any other-'

'I know,' Stella said.

Novak made his way back to security, checking the overhead monitors for the next flight to Moscow.

41

HARRODS, LONDON – TUESDAY, 4.13PM

Yevgeny Belchov was sitting in the master barber's in The Gentleman's Lounge in Harrods, feeling restless. The problem with being a man of power was that you depended on others to carry out your instructions. It was rare to ever actually be in control of things. Most of Belchov's life now seemed to comprise of waiting for messages or phone calls to come through on burner phones.

He was reclined in an Alfred Dunhill leather barber chair that cost more than most people's cars. A vintage Leclerc 1971 champagne was airing in its glass. He should have been in a state of relaxation, in a world of luxury. Yet all Belchov could do was scowl at the 'hair expert' – it had been stressed to him they were definitely not a mere hair-dresser or barber – taking clippers to the side of Belchov's head with surgical precision.

Belchov had rejected the 'expert's' advice on a classic side-parting. Instead he demanded, 'Number three all over.' The same haircut Belchov had had since he was a teenager.

The hair expert stepped back when Belchov's phone rang. An anonymous number.

Belchov answered by demanding, 'What?'

There was a pause, then a voice in Russian. 'It's Ivanov.'

Belchov felt the blood leaving his face.

'Minister,' Belchov replied, shielding the phone. 'What can I do for you?'

'We've lost the Yank.'

'I'm sorry, sir?'

'The Yank. The Swiss have him in custody now. The dossier is out in the open. You told me you would take care of this. You told me you could be trusted.'

Belchov pulled his smock off and moved to a quiet corner. 'Minister, if there was anything I could have-'

'It's over, Yevgeny. You had a good run.'

Belchov turned to see a stick-thin blonde, no more than twenty, standing in the middle of the barbers with tears in her eyes. She was wearing a brown Prada coat that almost touched the floor.

Belchov held a finger up. 'One minute, Svetlana,' he told her.

'What's the matter?' asked Ivanov. 'Is she upset about something? A pretty girl like that won't stick around long if she can't buy anything. God knows she doesn't fuck you for pleasure.'

Belchov froze. 'You're following me? Following my girl?'

Ivanov laughed. 'Yevgeny, you're in London. You might as well be in Moscow for all it matters. Ask her what happened. Go ahead. I'll wait.'

Belchov put the phone against his chest. 'Svetlana, my

love,' he said still in Russian, rubbing her arm smoothly. 'What's the matter?'

She tried to speak in between her attempts for breath, crying pathetic, weak tears like a child. 'I saw a nice neck-lace, Yevvy. It looked so beautiful on me. Then your card wouldn't work.' She handed him back his black American Express Centurion card. It was much heavier than regular cards, made of anodized titanium. It was such an exclusive card, they were by invitation only.

Belchov kissed her forehead. 'I'll come upstairs and sort it out. Can you give me a few minutes?' He palmed her off to the hair expert. 'Go with Declan. He'll get you some bubbles.' He then went back to the phone. 'OK, I'm listening.'

Ivanov said, 'I guess I don't need to wait for you to check all your other accounts for you to believe me: you're broke, Yevgeny.'

Nearly three billion dollars. Belchov couldn't hide the desperation in his voice. 'Hang on, hang on, there must be something I can do. Some way to work this out?'

The pause that followed felt like an eternity.

'There might be something,' came Ivanov's coy reply. He was sitting in the FSB Director's office in Moscow, having a rare old time stringing along their patsy.

This was how they got them, the entire Russian political system: first, you got the businessmen to do all your favours, all your bidding. Then you gave them all the money, monopolised the businesses. Then you had them by the balls. Forever. Because you owned the banks.

'We need this story from the Americans to go away,' Ivanov explained. 'If you can stop it getting out...we might be able to find your money again. After all, it looks like some very strange transactions have taken place the last few years in your accounts. No one wants to see an ugly court case back here in Moscow. Money laundering brings such terrible prison sentences these days.'

Belchov had seen former associates fall away through the years. They never paid the right people off, or paid enough. The laundering or racketeering or fraud charges, or whatever half-baked crap they came up with always ended the same way: the state kept their power, and the billionaire ended up in jail.

Belchov was damned if he was going to end up in a jail cell. All of a sudden, the life of luxury – everything around him - he'd become so used to living felt temporary. They'd been smart and shown him how quickly it could all go away.

Belchov promised, 'I can stop the story. I know how.'

Ivanov chuckled. 'You have twenty-four-hours. I had better be impressed.'

42

On the other side of the black door were two PTSOs controlling access through another hallway – this one more like a corridor in a hospital, brightly lit with a linoleum floor. A series of gunmetal-grey doors lined each side.

From somewhere behind one of them there was a kind of wailing. Not of physical pain, but of mental anguish.

On each door was a white wipe board with the ISN of the detainee written in black marker. The stains of several serial numbers before were still visible underneath the current ones. Suggesting a long history of incarceration.

Rebecca, Walter, and Weiskopf were alone. The two men had seen it all before. The notion of incarcerating non-U.S. citizens in American detention centres – without charge – was old news to them. The way Weiskopf saw it, places like Camp Metro were a necessary violation: there was no doubt that some innocents would get swept up in the process, but the capture of the guilty offset that moral outrage. At least, that's how he justified it so he could sleep at night.

But to someone new to the world of black sites like Rebecca, it was truly shocking.

'How many are in here?' asked Rebecca.

'Twenty-one right now,' Weiskopf said. 'All of them will be shipped out somewhere else in the next week or two.' He walked them to a door at the end of the corridor.

The wipe board on the door read, "XXX".

'This is it,' Weiskopf said.

Rebecca seemed to freeze. She stared at the door handle. The notion that her father was just on the other side of a door a few inches thick – after so many years - was hard to process.

She was sixteen when he had been committed to Bennington Hospital.

Like an actor who blanks on their lines once the stage lights come on, Rebecca could no longer think of the many things she had planned on saying to her father should she ever get the chance to meet him again.

'We'll be right outside,' Sharp told her.

Rebecca reached for the door handle.

When the door opened she immediately felt cold air rush towards her: they had turned the air con to its coldest setting.

Stanley was sitting on a metal chair under a spotlight, the only light in the windowless room. He was shivering. His head was bowed, and had fallen to one side in exhaustion from sleep deprivation.

His hands and feet were manacled, linked to a chain bolted to the floor.

Stanley lifted his head, only vaguely aware of the door being opened. His eyes slowly met Rebecca's.

In that instant, all the speeches she'd been rehearsing

since she was sixteen went out the window. Her eyes were already full of tears by the time she reached him.

Stanley thought he was hallucinating from sleep deprivation, until he felt her arms around him. No memory could be that powerful, that vivid.

They held each other so tightly they could feel each other's bones.

'I knew it,' he croaked. 'I always knew...you would find me.'

Rebecca didn't want to draw attention to how cold it was. 'It's me, dad,' she whispered, rubbing up and down his arms. 'It's OK. I'm here.'

'I tried to...I tried...' He couldn't speak. He winced slightly from Rebecca's embrace.

She looked down, noticing deep brown and blue bruising around his neck and chest, beneath the low neckline of the linen smock he was wearing. The evidence of beating was obvious, but there was little evidence of the damage done by waterboarding, electrocution, sleep deprivation, and hunger: that was all behind the eyes.

She looked towards the door. 'We don't have much time. They're going to move you somewhere else, dad.' She whispered into his ear. 'I'm going to get you out. This will all be over soon.'

When she retreated, Stanley motioned for her to come back.

'I didn't want to lead them to you,' he said. 'I couldn't risk it.'

She crouched down in front of him, holding his hands. 'How much do you remember?'

He seemed confused at first, then a memory began to appear. 'I remember being in the study...I was working on the formula. I had been working so hard...I had been drinking too much. I just needed...I couldn't stand being in my head all the time...'

'I know, dad. It's OK.'

'I felt like...something broke. Inside my head. Then they took me away to that wretched hospital. But compared to this place...' He looked up at Rebecca in sudden horror. 'I left you alone. All those years...'

'It's OK, dad,' Rebecca said, rubbing his arm. 'You were unwell. Sam Sulley looked after me. Remember.'

'I never stopped loving you all that time, Becky.'

'I know, dad. I never stopped loving you. That's why I'm here.' She kept rubbing his arm. 'What about after that? Do you remember Bennington Hospital?'

'They kept giving me drugs. People from GCHQ came. They asked about my formula. I told them I had solved it. Then I remember the fire.'

'Where did you go? After the fire?'

'Oliver Thorn took me in.'

'Oliver...' Rebecca shook her head, replaying their conversation in the car.

'He was one of my junior researchers at GCHQ. A brilliant mind, Becky. I stayed in his attic for a number of years. He looked after me well. He'd check in on you, your ascendancy through university, then GCHQ. He told me you reminded him of me.'

Rebecca felt like a kid again. Always so pleased whenever someone commented that she was like her father. Rebecca stroked his hair as he spoke.

Stanley said, 'Oliver begged me to come out of hiding and meet you. But he didn't understand what they had done to me in Bennington. What I knew they might do to you as well...I could never let anyone ever hurt you, Becky. Not ever.'

'Did you stay with him the whole time?'

'Oliver was seconded to London, and I knew I couldn't go with him. So he fixed me a passport and I headed to Argentina.'

'What about Tom Novak and the NSA Papers?' she asked. 'How did you manage to leak it?'

He smiled for the first time. 'That was beautiful.' As he chuckled slightly he segued into a cough, which appeared to hurt him greatly.

Rebecca put her arm around him again. 'Is it your chest?'

'My ribs,' he said. 'I think one might be broken.'

Rebecca tried to bring him back to what he was saying. 'What was beautiful, dad?'

He smiled again. 'Oliver had managed to keep my GCHQ log-ins active all that time, so I saw the data that GCHQ and the NSA were collecting and I decided people had a right to know. So I leaked it. I went to Washington, and I paid a junior reporter from *The Washington Post* one hundred bucks to drop a memory stick with NSA files on the floor of the press room. Tom Novak was the lucky devil who found it.'

'You know, I helped them on their last story.'

He smiled with the kind of pride only a father is capable of. 'I know you did, Becky. I was so proud of you when I read your name in the papers.' He took hold of her hands, the colour seeming to come back to his eyes. 'You're the future now.'

'Of what?'

'Of fighting back! Against all this...rottenness. These liars. These crooks.'

'But they can't keep you here forever.'

Stanley squinted. 'As soon as they get a working model of the formula, they'll get rid of me.'

'You can't give up,' she implored him. 'I'm going to get you out of here. I'm a much more powerful person now. I'm in charge of a unit that investigates corrupt intelligence agents. I have contacts. Important contacts.'

'There's no one that can get me out of here except the director of the CIA.'

'What about the British government? I know Angela Curtis. If she knew you were here she would-'

Stanley leaned towards Rebecca, eyes widening in despair. 'Do what, Becky? Lloyd Willow and Teddy King orchestrated that entire attack on Downing Street. They assassinated a sitting Prime Minister. I'm nothing to them. They're not going to just hand me back. Not now.' He lifted his trouser leg, revealing dark-brown bruises all the way up his calves. 'The thing is, Becky. Everyone has a breaking point.'

Rebecca could hardly bear to look. Desperate to reassure him in any way she could, she told him, 'This is nearly over, I swear.'

Stanley shook his head. 'You don't understand...I gave them the password to access my decryption key. They have the formula.'

'Don't worry about that, dad.'

'I just...couldn't take the pain any longer.' He managed to lift his hands high enough to touch her cheek. 'But I have everything I need right here. You know, there's nothing more wonderful and terrifying for a father than seeing his daughter grown up. Yeats called it a terrible beauty. I never really understood the phrase until you came and sat here in front of me.'

Rebecca thought she might cry. It was everything she had ever wanted to hear him say.

He was struggling for breath now. It was the most he had spoken in months. 'When I was at Oliver's, I had a lot of spare time. He had the most wonderful library. I read all of Dickens, all of Austen, all of Dostoevsky. There was a passage in *The Brothers Karamazov* that reminded me of you.'

Rebecca felt like she was ten again, in front of the fire in her pyjamas on a winter's night, listening to her father's stories. 'What was it?'

Voices outside the cell door grew louder, the sound of PTSOs approaching, arguing with Sharp and Weiskopf.

Stanley knew their time was almost up, and looked towards the door.

Rebecca didn't want the moment to be over. She rubbed his arm. 'Hey. Forget about them. Tell me about the passage.'

'It was about the sun. And how even if you cannot see it for a moment, you still know it exists.' Another cough rose up through his chest. He steadied himself. 'All the time we were apart, I knew you were out there somewhere. Dostoevsky said just knowing that the sun is out there: that is what life is. That's what living is.'

Keys rattled in the cell door.

Rebecca kissed her father's cheek. 'I never left you, and you never left me.'

The cell door flew open, and in marched four PTSOs. 'Time's up,' one of them said. 'The detainee is being transferred.'

'Where are you taking him?' asked Rebecca, attempting to follow while the PTSOs blocked her path.

'Another facility,' one of them answered.

Stanley was dragged from his cell – bare feet trailing behind him – past Sharp and Weiskopf towards an elevator.

Sharp called out, 'Rebecca, we're in the following car.'

Stanley managed to look back towards her before the elevator doors closed. He called out, 'Grief will suck the life from you, Becky. It's time to let go. Live your life.'

On the corner of 55th and 3rd it was getting dark. A silver Jeep Grand Cherokee SUV waited with its lights off, pointed at the back service entrance of 106 East 54th Street.

A team of eight men sat inside, with a cache of FSB-issue PP-19-01 Vityaz submachine guns, Saiga 9mm carbines, side-arms of Serdyukov SPS 7.62 high calibre pistols, as well as a number of flash-bangs – and an RPG-32 anti-tank grenade launcher. Enough to overturn an armoured truck.

The men were professionals, but that didn't mean they weren't nervous. If a mission such as theirs went wrong, they knew they'd be fully denied by the FSB.

The truth was, if any of them were killed on the mission, it would be covered up by both sides. CIA wouldn't want to admit the FSB had been able to penetrate American soil any more than Russia wanted news of their own paramilitaries showing up dead on the streets of Manhattan. For such a scenario it would be understood that a mutually assured cover-up would be best for all concerned.

But if the men were hoping for a hero's funeral back

home with a coffin covered in flowers then they'd picked the wrong profession.

If their bodies even made it back to Russia in a body bag they could count themselves fortunate.

The point man in the front passenger seat asked the others, 'One more time: what is operation priority one?'

'Recover the weapon intact,' they all responded.

'What if priority one is compromised?'

'Destroy the weapon.'

The call came through in the point man's earpiece. 'In position?' the voice asked.

He replied, 'We're ready.'

43

The snow had been falling since Novak's plane landed barely an hour ago. One final chill of the winter gathering in Moscow's skies.

Novak had his hands in the pockets of his insulated jacket, his elbow joints locked out, arms straight as he huddled against the cold. It was a piercing cold that seemed capable of penetrating anything and everything.

He'd taken a locker at the airport for his backpack. He wanted to be free of impediments should he need to run. Looking for people in Moscow who are not meant to be found was a risky business. But Novak knew he had to do something to get Natalya back. Without her, he'd never be able to be a part of Magdalina's life.

One thing that struck him in the car park of Russia Now's HQ was a row of three identical black vans, their registration plates all part of the same series.

FSB? Novak wondered.

He unzipped his jacket once he got into the lobby of RN, shaking the snow off the shoulders.

'I'm here to see Viktor Karpov,' Novak said to the receptionist in Russian, then added, 'and no, I don't have an appointment, and no I don't care.'

The receptionist flicked cursorily through Karpov's diary. 'I'm sorry... Mr?'

A voice boomed down from the balcony above leading to the newsroom. 'Novak. Tom Novak.' It was Karpov. He waved Novak to come up.

The newsroom was a steady hum of activity - almost everyone was on the phone or typing. No one seemed to be paying any attention to the men in suits rummaging through Natalya's and Andrei's offices. Every drawer and box and cupboard had been turned inside out, their contents left on the floor.

Karpov strode casually through the newsroom, directing changes to his reporters' work after the slightest glance at their computer screens. He switched to English for speaking to Novak. 'I was wondering how long it would take you to get from the airport.'

'Is that supposed to intimidate me?' Novak asked. 'That you can have me followed as soon as I land.'

Karpov pointed his finger from one side of the room to the other. 'Nothing happens in this city without my knowing.' He went to his office, taking a seat behind his desk.

Novak stayed standing. 'Where is she, Viktor?'

Karpov made a tent with his fingers, tapping fingertips against each other. 'Straight to business then. I like this.'

'Where's Talya?'

Karpov shrugged. 'There was nothing I could do, Tom. She made this impossible.'

Novak pointed at him. 'No. *You* did this. And I'm not leaving until you tell me where she is.'

'Tom, I'm powerful man, yes? But there is only so much I can do in a country like this. Do you really expect me to fight for her?'

'She and Andrei found a story that no one else in this cesspit would ever have the balls to go after. Talya's a real journalist. She just never had a chance to show it. She's shown you now.'

Karpov laughed. 'Mister New York, you think you are so much smarter and cooler than us, don't you. You come here and think you know so much.' His humour turned quickly to anger. 'Let me tell you something, *chickenshit*. You wouldn't survive a year in Moscow.'

'I survived here much longer than that.'

'Oh sure, writing about anything except Russia.' Karpov puffed out his chest. 'What a big man you were. Coming to Moscow all those years. What did you do, eh? How were you so brave? You only write about Moscow when you're no longer here. Natalya did what she had to do to survive. But you corrupted her. You trained her to see corruption everywhere. And now look where it got her: the FSB are going through her office as we speak.'

Novak looked over, seeing FSB officers taking down Talya's large Russian flag from the wall. Behind the flag was her secret research from her work with Andrei's story. Hidden in plain sight the whole time.

Karpov came round to Novak's side of his desk, watching the FSB pull apart the rest of the room. 'The only thing Talya will be writing from now on will be her prison diary.'

'She's not yours.' He turned to face Karpov. 'I'm Magdalina's father, not you. And I'm going to get her and Natalya out of all this for good.'

Karpov laughed and went back behind his desk. 'It is so much bullshit to me. I always knew she wasn't mine.' He lit a cigarette then pointed it at Novak. 'Magdalina is scared of the dark. Just like her father.'

As Novak walked back through the newsroom, the video screen at the far end showed a live feed of RN's TV channel. The headline was in Russian Cyrillic, but Novak could read it:

"Terror in New York City."

The pictures were shot on a mobile phone a few storeys up, showing gunmen stalking the streets of Manhattan.

Novak switched his phone on as he ran downstairs. 'Shit,' he said, waiting for his 4G signal to connect.

He ran through the snow, out across the car park.

As his signal connected, one of the black vans sped towards him from the side. It skidded to a halt in front of him, then the side door flew open.

Before he could react, two pairs of hands grabbed him and hauled him into the van. A strip of black power tape was slapped over his mouth, and a hood was slid over his head. Someone snatched his phone from him.

His hands were cable-tied, and noise-isolating head-phones were put over his ears. The punches to his kidneys sent a rippling pain all down his side. He let out a cry but the sound simply bounced off the insulated walls.

Wherever the van was going, it was going there fast.

All Novak could think of was Karpov's remark about being scared of the dark. He was about to see first-hand just how dark the heart of modern Moscow could be.

44

THE REPUBLIC OFFICES, NEW YORK CITY – TUESDAY, 5.15PM

Diane was leaning over her desk fielding a conference call with the *Republic* legal team, when she noticed Stella arriving back in the office. And she was on her own.

Stella couldn't understand why it was so cold in the office. Everyone was wearing their jackets. Some even had scarves on. Stella blew into her hands. 'What's going on?' she asked a staffer.

'The gas was cut off,' he said, rubbing his hands in fingerless gloves together. 'Failure to render payment, customer services said.'

Diane stood up straight at her desk, wondering where Novak was. She told the conference call, 'Guys, I'm going to step out for a minute...'

Stella was already on her way to her.

Diane stopped in her tracks. 'Let me guess: Natalya.'

'I tried to talk him out of it,' Stella said.

Diane waved her into her office. 'I'll need to kick his sorry behind later. You should listen to this.'

Stella closed the door behind her.

Kevin Wellington of Bruckner Jackson Prowse, *Republic*'s lawyer, was speaking.

'...and that would only be if they don't have grounds. I'm afraid Tom called this right: the gag order can clearly be applied here. There's not a judge in the land is going to overturn a national security letter, and they will certainly not overturn the gag order.'

Diane came back on the call. 'But why doesn't the White House use these all the time if they're so easily applied?'

Kevin replied, 'Because a politician who's having an affair or cheating expenses does not constitute a threat to national security. But if the FBI is now investigating a U.S. senator spying for Russia, a nondisclosure will be upheld every time. If *Republic* even prints that they've been issued this nondisclosure then we can all pack up and go home. Because the federal government is going to own both us and you before the sun rises.'

Stella stepped a little closer to the phone speaker. 'This is Stella Mitchell, Foreign Affairs. Kevin are you saying this story is dead?'

He answered, 'I'm saying the story is dead until the FBI announces the investigation publicly, and names a suspect.'

Diane took the pen from behind her ear and tossed it down. 'By which point it will have leaked to every news organization in the country, because the FBI PR department is basically an F-word-ing sieve...'

Stella continued, 'And we'll have lost months of exclusives.'

Kevin couldn't hide the disappointment in his voice. 'That is the situation.'

Diane tried to maintain some resolve as long as Stella

was in the room. 'OK, thank you, Kevin, thank you, everyone. I'm going to need some time on this.'

She hung up the call.

The two women looked at each other.

'What do we do with *this* now?' asked Stella, placing the Tucker Adams dossier down.

Diane sighed in exasperation, turning to her office window. 'We can't print a blasted word of it. Who the hecker tipped off the FBI?'

Stella said, 'Adams? The Russians? After Geneva they must know how close we are now.'

Ever the one to right the ship, Diane said, 'We have to stick to the story at hand. Let's at least shore up what we do have. Tell me about Romain Laurent.'

'He's a solid secondary source on Adams. When Omar bin Talal told Romain about his story he didn't go into specifics about Adams, but Omar was adamant that should Adams ever come around he shouldn't be trusted. Romain says he'll go on the record for anything we need.'

'Then we at least have the inside track on why Omar was murdered.'

'That's not enough, though.'

The two women were suddenly distracted by a booming thud that sounded like it came from several blocks away. It was big enough to be felt underfoot, and shook the glass and jug of water on Diane's desk.

'What the hell was that?' asked Stella.

Diane then noticed several people running down the street. But not on the sidewalk: down the middle of the road, in between traffic, dodging and weaving through the headlights. From a few blocks away there followed the unmistakable sound of screaming.

A series of loud cracks then went off, one after the other. Within a few seconds they were much more rapid.

Diane opened the window to hear better. She'd spent enough time in warzones to know the sound. 'That's gunfire.'

In the newsroom, staffers flooded towards the bank of windows looking out onto Manhattan.

An intern rapped frantically on Diane's glass wall.

She pointed at the windows where they had a better view. The intern's voice quavered. 'They're shooting!'

Diane dashed for her intercom. 'Get me security in the lobby. Now!' She shouted to the newsroom, 'Everyone, back from the windows!'

45

Before the short elevator ride up to ground-level, the
PTSOs had changed Stanley into an orange jumpsuit. If
for any reason the unthinkable happened and he was able
to escape, he wouldn't exactly be able to blend in to a
civilian backdrop.

Stanley's feet were still chained to his hands. There were
three PTSOs on each side of him. By the look on Stanley's
face he barely understood what was happening. As far as he
was concerned, he had no life and it was never coming
back. Being locked up, sleep-deprived, and tortured, was his
future now. After so long, he had made peace with it.

Rebecca told him, 'We're going to be in the support car
behind, dad.' She stroked his face affectionately, trying to
awaken something in him.

'OK,' Stanley replied, forcing a smile for her benefit.
'Don't worry, kid.'

The PTSO crew and Stanley were joined at the underground service entrance by yet more PTSOs from the permanent security office.

'Have you ever seen such overkill for one sixty-two-year-old detainee before?' asked Weiskopf.

'Ye-ah,' Sharp drawled. 'I'm worried it's not enough.'

'What do you think?'

'I think the Russians will make their play in the first five minutes.'

'Would they really launch an attack in Manhattan though?'

'It's not about access or being able to sneak in. They need to go in hard and heavy, all lights on before they get to LaGuardia. They'll never be able to keep track of him on the other side.'

Weiskopf took a long, purposeful breath. 'If you were going to attack how would you do it?'

Sharp looked him in the eye. 'I'd go in hard and heavy with all the lights on in the first five minutes.'

An armoured truck was set up and ready to go, along with four unmarked SUVs, custom-fit for ground warfare.

The hardware on display was mindboggling. The tech gear and weaponry alone was worth high six-figures.

A helicopter could be heard circling above somewhere.

No NYPD personnel were being used for support, either on the ground or in the air. If there were any communication channels they couldn't control then CIA didn't want to use them.

Stanley was loaded into the middle SUV.

The SUV carrying Rebecca, Sharp, and Weiskopf would take up the second-to-last at the rear. Anywhere else was too tactically important to give up seats to 'tourists'.

The convoy of four SUVs set off, followed by the matte-black armoured truck. When the roller-shutter opened at the top of the short, steep ramp leading to the corner of East 54th and 2nd Avenue, the helicopter above became much louder.

Radios crackled with tactical info, and the helicopter team relayed crucial traffic flow updates.

The convoy couldn't run red lights, or break through traffic in any way. Just as CIA had no law enforcement authority, neither could it break traffic laws to transport a detainee, unless their operation fell under a U.S. Department of Justice investigation. And even then, no active CIA officers would be allowed to participate in the actual operation.

The PTSOs were on their own.

It didn't take long for them to be stalled at a red light. While they were stopped, Sharp's attention was caught by a silver SUV ahead. He bobbed from side to side, trying to see past the cars ahead.

'What's wrong?' asked Weiskopf.

'I bumped on an SUV over there. Its back window's down.' Sharp noted the temperature on the dash. 'It's only forty out...' he mumbled to himself.

Weiskopf was now equally tense. He knew if Sharp spotted something it was worth flagging.

Sharp called to the guards in front. 'Hey, have you got eyes on that silver Jeep ahead? Two o'clock. The Cherokee.'

The navigator complained to the driver, 'I love when tourists tell me how to do my job...' He asked Sharp, 'What about it?'

Weiskopf butted in, 'Just check it will you.'

With a sigh, the PTSO radioed ahead. 'This is Charlie unit. The silver Jeep, two o'clock. Get me eyes...'

The Alpha team in the lead SUV were tucked in behind the armoured Humvee. But before they could respond, Sharp saw something catch the light in the back of the Cherokee.

As the traffic lights turned green, Sharp could see the unmistakable outline of a shoulder-mounted missile pointing at the Humvee.

The call went out from Alpha team who also spotted it.

'Incoming!' someone yelled.

Everyone in the SUVs ducked below windscreen level but nothing was going to save the Humvee.

The front end shot up as if an IED had gone off under the front wheels, tipping it back until it was fully vertical. Then almost in slow motion it kept tipping back and back.

Alpha team immediately behind had to abandon their vehicle before they were crushed.

The Humvee finally crashed, roof-first, on Alpha team's SUV, crushing the entire front end.

Someone in Sharp's car called into his radio, 'We are engaged! Repeat, we are engaged and under attack...'

With just one shot of an RPG-32 the Russians had wiped out CIA's armoured Humvee, and Alpha team's SUV, leaving Stanley's SUV completely isolated and exposed.

The FSB agents swarmed in, seeming to come from every angle, unleashing shots from their Saiga 9mms. The streets, which were already chaotic after the RPG blast, were now an orgy of shoving and screaming. Terrified pedestrians crisscrossed and backtracked, not knowing where to run. Drivers at the intersection abandoned their cars, while others tried to smash and barge their way clear.

Sharp reached behind and grabbed three Glock 22s

from the weapons crate, handing one to Weiskopf and another to Rebecca.

'I need you,' Sharp told her. 'We're men down already.'

Rebecca looked at it in terror. 'I don't know *how* to shoot!'

Sharp opened his door to take up an offensive position. 'If any of them get close, just aim and squeeze.'

Weiskopf hadn't fired a gun in nearly fifteen years, but somewhere in his head his training came back to him. He took up the same position as Sharp, crouching behind his open door.

Rebecca stayed low in the backseat, focussed solely on what was happening up ahead in her dad's car and trying to figure out how to get to him.

The Russians advanced with perfect strategy for the situation, making use of the abandoned cars in the middle of the intersection: while cover fire came from behind, agents shot then ran, ducking behind car hoods. They repeated this process several times until all their principals were in position.

Seeing how organised the Russians were gave the PTSOs pause: they were on the back foot, with no clear exit strategy. They had not prepared properly.

An officer in Stanley's car told his colleague, 'We're in the shit.'

Shouting to be heard over the Russians shooting, he replied, 'Get in back! Secure the detainee!'

The PTSO scrambled into the backseat, just as a bullet shattered the windscreen. He covered Stanley and pulled him down behind the headrest.

The Russians had prime position, and could now simply overwhelm them with force and numbers. There were so many shots coming their way the PTSOs could only stand their ground.

Sharp and Weiskopf managed to crawl to the rear of Stanley's car, returning fire when they could.

The situation was made all the more difficult by the arrival of NYPD's Counterterrorism Bureau. They set up positions at CIA's nine o'clock, in between the warring units.

The Russians quickly turned their firepower on NYPD, setting off another RPG round. NYPD's first vehicles on the scene weren't nearly equipped to deal with an anti-tank missile, which decimated their entire front line.

The only sounds in the street were eerie, disembodied shouts in Russian, and the cracks of submachine gun rounds – the firing less frequent now as casualties grew.

'*Recover the weapon,*' the FSB point man yelled.

The PTSOs guarding Stanley came out from their cover points when another RPG hit. It was another devastating strike on Alpha team's SUV. This one was a direct hit on the fuel tank, which unleashed a fireball that stretched nearly two storeys high. The residual force of the blast flipped Stanley's car onto its side, sending Stanley tumbling upside down.

The other PTSOs were scattered around the vehicle like tenpins, unconscious.

The PTSO in the back with him was knocked unconscious, his arms dangling out the open rear door.

With bullets flashing past overhead, Stanley managed to crawl through the shattered trunk window. He could see Rebecca further back. He reached out in her direction, and groaned inaudibly for her.

The Russians descended on the car, taking out the PTSO guarding the front of Stanley's car.

Stanley was now alone.

'The weapon is out in the open,' the point man confirmed.

Sharp and Weiskopf could see the danger Stanley was now in.

'You're about to lose your principal!' Sharp yelled at the nearest guard. 'Flank them, quick.'

Sharp had a clean shot at two of the FSB, and took them out. The agent with the RPG turned it towards the SUV Rebecca was in.

She was still in the backseat and had no idea what was about to happen.

Sharp ran back and managed to drag her out as the missile screeched towards her. For a few seconds the explosion made Sharp and Rebecca weightless, sending them flying back through the air into the middle of the street.

Stanley was now a sitting duck.

A Russian grabbed the keys from a dead PTSO and unlocked Stanley's chains.

Stanley didn't fight the man, dragging his left foot behind which had been twisted in the aftermath of the RPG blast.

All the Russians had to do was cover the agent who was with Stanley.

Weiskopf was the only one with a glimmer of a shot: the FSB agent had Stanley under the arms, dragging him backwards, leaving only the Russian's head to aim at. Aiming through the shot-out windscreen, Weiskopf knew if he missed he would most likely take out Stanley in the process.

He waited for the perfect moment. Then fired.

The Russian collapsed from a direct hit in the forehead, dropping Stanley at his feet.

Stanley was left on his back, covered in blood. He tried to get up on his own, but he couldn't move. His ankle was twisted.

Backup had now arrived for NYPD, and their sharp-shooters started picking off the Russians one by one. Starting with the RPG shooter. Now it was the Russians who were surrounded.

Back at the intersection, Rebecca began to stir, managing to move her arms. She pushed herself up enough to lift her head, seeing her father sitting up on his own.

'Dad,' she called out. Like in a nightmare, she was screaming it, but what came out was barely a whimper. She tried again, managing to be louder this time.

Loud enough for him to hear her.

'Rebecca!' he yelled.

Three remaining PTSOs were now clear to advance to Stanley.

Stanley looked down. He knew it was over. CIA would take him back in again. And he couldn't face that. Not again.

Rebecca clambered to her feet and began to smile at him: he had survived. He was going to be OK.

'I'm sorry, Rebecca,' he shouted to her.

Rebecca didn't understand why he was apologising at first. Until she saw him crouch down and pick up the dead Russian's pistol.

'What are you doing?' she cried.

'It's the only way to keep you safe now, Becky,' he called out. His voice was feeble. Ravaged. Breaking. 'It's me they want, but they'll torture you too. There's nothing they won't do.'

'But you gave them the password already.'

Rebecca used up every last bit of strength, and it only got her two paces closer to him. She fell to her knees.

Stanley shouted, 'I only gave them a password for half of the formula. They'll realise before the end of the day. The real one is still in here.' He pointed the gun to the side of his head. 'And I know they have ways to get it out. Everyone has a breaking point.'

Weiskopf shouted from the side, 'Stanley, don't!'

Stanley wasn't even aware of Weiskopf's or anyone else's presence at the intersection. It was just him and his daughter. 'I've never been able to protect you,' he called. 'Until now. This is one thing I can do. As your father.' Stanley turned away from Rebecca with tears in his eyes. 'Don't look, sweetie. Don't look.'

There were screams from the buildings above, overlooking the road. The onlookers could see Stanley raise the gun to his temple.

It's often the case that suicides by bridge jumping are found with torn shoulders. Despite all the suffering and longing for it to be over, the instinct to stay alive remains powerful up until the last breath. But there is another – much less known - category of suicide: those who kill themselves even if they don't want to.

Stanley understood those feelings in that moment. He wanted desperately to stay alive. To walk on a beach again with Rebecca. To wander a bookshop. To read novels again.

But what he wanted more was for no harm to come to

his daughter. That overwhelmed any other desire he could ever think of.

Rebecca looked away and closed her eyes.

She heard the gunshot then the soft sound of him falling to the ground.

It was over. He was free.

And his daughter was safe.

46

The prison in Lubyanka was deep in the bowels of the FSB's headquarters, and had a history as infamous as anything in Russia's darkest past.

Set up in nineteen twenty the prison had housed famous figures such as revolutionary (or terrorist, depending who you asked) Boris Savinkov, and Nobel-winning writer Alexander Solzhenitsyn, who went on to survive the hellish Gulag in Siberia.

In Novak's cell he could feel that history in the walls. As if all the screams through the years had been captured and preserved in the concrete. Only the prisoners could hear them.

The cell was filthy. The dirt on the floor had been there for decades. A thin window near the ceiling let in just enough light to make you long for the outside world, but was tiny enough to make freedom feel impossible.

That was exactly how FSB wanted it.

Novak was hooded and barefoot. As he'd been ordered, he was crouching in the middle of the room in a ski stress position: his thighs parallel to the ground, the muscles burning.

Someone in good shape would be doing well to endure such a position for fifteen minutes before their legs gave in. Novak managed twenty-eight minutes the first time.

The second he hit the damp filthy concrete floor the cell door flew open. A guard marched towards him and shocked him with a cattle prod.

The second time Novak managed thirty-six minutes.

Whenever the prod made contact, Novak's spine stiffened, trying to go in four directions at once. Every nerve in his body lit up like a fireworks display. He twisted and writhed, trying to shake the pain out of his body. By the third time he was shocked, Novak understood that there was nothing you could do to get rid of it, to speed up the process. You just had to grit your teeth and wait for the pain to relinquish.

After the shocks, Novak became a Zen master of the ski stress position.

He shivered from head to foot. Not the muted shivering you get in your stomach during a cold walk home at night. It was a full-body tremor, coupled with the most intense stomach cramps he had ever experienced. His body was telling him to stop, to collapse. But that would only bring more pain.

After only a few hours of this, Novak felt the connection between his mind and body starting to strain. Like a boat tied to harbour with a rope that the sea kept tugging on. And the rope was fraying, one fibre at a time.

For a few minutes he had been gradually standing up a centimetre at a time, just to give some relief to his burning thighs.

As he heard the cell door open again, he lowered his body into a stricter position.

The chains around his hands and feet chinked together.

They hadn't put silencing headphones on him, so he could hear the arrival of another set of feet in the cell, but not the boots of the guard. There also came the sound of panting and groaning.

The guard pushed Novak back against the wall, collapsing back to a sitting position.

'*Rest*,' the guard said in Russian.

He heard a whimper next to him, 'Oh my God, Tom. What have they done to you?'

The guard whipped Novak's hood off.

Even in the darkness of the cell his eyes could barely take what little light there was.

The first thing he could make out was a hazy image of the guard leaving the cell. He had a balaclava on, and all-black military wear.

Novak squinted as he looked to his left, the light from the window temporarily blinding him.

Then his vision cleared as he felt his face being touched.

'Talya,' Novak mumbled.

She was chained too, but the pair were able to touch hands.

She had been stripped to her underwear. Her face was filthy and bloody in places from grazes and small cuts.

Novak wheezed, trying to clear his lungs. 'Are you OK?'

'I'm fine.' She whispered, 'What have they been asking you?'

Novak groaned as he sat up straighter against the wall to relieve his exhausted legs. 'Nothing. I keep asking them what they want, but they never say anything. What about you?'

'They want names. Everyone I worked with on the story. Anyone else Andrei associated with.'

'They raided your office. They found all your source material behind the flag on your wall.'

Natalya let her head fall back against the wall. 'You've got to be strong, Thomas. Don't tell them anything.'

'I won't.' Novak lifted her head slightly. 'Hey...I'm an American journalist. They're not going to keep me here longer than a week. Just long enough for the injuries to clear up before letting me go. Imprisoning an American journalist without charge would cause a diplomatic disaster for them. Then I'll get out and find Magdalina.'

'What about me, Thomas? No American diplomats are coming to save me.'

Two guards burst through the door. One went straight for Natalya, picking her off the ground like a play toy. Novak yelled, 'No!' and tried to kick out at the guard, but he couldn't reach him.

When Natalya tried to fight back, the guard gave her a short, sharp slap across the face with the back of his hand, leaving a bright red mark on her cheek.

The other guard booted Novak in the side.

As Novak writhed in pain, the guard spoke in English to him. He pointed his finger in Novak's face. 'What did you find in Geneva?'

Novak fought for breath. 'I...don't know what you're talking-'

The guard kicked him again. This time in the stomach, stealing every bit of oxygen from him.

The guard took out a phone and showed it to Novak.

'You're going to record message. You will tell the Americans to kill your story. You will tell them to hand over all copies of the dossier to us...'

Novak was already shaking his head.

'...or we will kill you.'

Novak kept shaking his head. 'Let me tell you something: Diane Schlesinger knows that if I need to take a beating for this story, then that's what I gotta do. You can take all the videos you want of me, she won't budge. She won't trade. She won't move an inch. You know why? Because she's Diane fucking Schlesinger. She's a mountain. And you ain't shit.'

The guard got up, throwing out his bottom lip, unmoved by Novak's dissent. 'This is fine. Interesting. But fine.' He snapped his finger at the other guard who picked up Natalya and carried her towards the door.

She kicked and screamed, her feet cycling in the air. 'Thomas...'

The guard with Novak explained, 'It is simple: make the video, and we don't spend the next three hours with the mother of your child...'

The fact that they knew about Magdalina shook Novak further.

Natalya kept kicking. 'Don't give them anything, Thomas!'

They took her next door and her shouts faded to nothing.

'Your choice is simple,' the guard told Novak.

The door closed with a crash and Novak was alone again.

47

EAST 54TH STREET, MANHATTAN

Rebecca perched on the back door ledge of an FDNY ambulance, with a blanket around her shoulders. Her face was patterned by the lights of dozens of police and EMS vehicles.

Staring into the middle-distance, her spell was broken by an approaching detective.

He checked his notebook before speaking. 'Miss Fox?'

'Yeah,' she replied in a far-away voice. It took her a moment before meeting the detective's eyes.

He chose his words not out of compassion, but because it was what he was told to say in a training seminar on grief management. His accent was pure New Jersey. 'I know this must be a difficult time, but I have to ask you a couple of questions.'

'You can ask but I won't answer.'

What little sympathy had been in his voice initially now vanished. 'We got a lot of dead bodies here. I need you to come down to the station to tell me how you were caught up in this.'

Rebecca reached into her jacket pocket and produced a burgundy passport that said 'DIPLOMATIC PASSPORT' along the bottom. 'And as the provisions of the Vienna Convention on Diplomatic Relations states, no diplomat will be liable to any form of arrest or detention. If you wish to question me you should contact the British embassy. Who will politely decline your request.'

Sharp, holding a bandage to his forehead and trying his best to suppress a limp, spoke from behind the detective. 'There a problem here?'

The detective handed back the passport. 'I suppose you're on the UN Security Council or somethin'.'

Sharp said, 'Good one.' He showed the detective his credentials on a small flip-down wallet. 'If I were you I'd check with Counterterrorism, who are actually in charge of this crime scene, before you start directing witnesses to your precinct.'

The detective retreated.

'You OK?' asked Sharp.

'I just wish they'd at least put him on a stretcher,' Rebecca answered.

Sharp did a quick one-eighty of the intersection, which was sealed off on all four sides by white tent walls. Bodies were covered in white plastic sheets; witnesses sat in dumbfounded at the sides, holding blankets around themselves.

Sharp said, 'This is a complex situation. CT's taking charge. It's going to take some time to clear up who all these people actually are. It doesn't help that at the moment all CIA has for a record of your father is three Xs on a piece of paper in Camp Metro.'

'It's so strange,' she said. 'I've been grieving for him so

long it's like I don't have any tears left. I can't remember the last time I cried for him.'

Sharp came round to sit next to her on the door ledge. He didn't have much in the way of advice or wisdom for such a moment. In his Midwest drawl, he declared, 'He did what he had to do.'

'I know.'

'Come on,' he said, limping up onto one foot. 'There's nothing we can do here.'

When they made it through the white tent wall, Rebecca noticed Stella waving for her attention in the crowd beside Diane Schlesinger.

Rebecca and Sharp pushed their way through to them. Almost everyone had their phones in the air, filming the chaos: the overhead helicopters, the constant sirens of ambulances coming and going, the arrival of more press with every minute.

'What on earth happened?' asked Stella.

Now that Rebecca was up and walking, she didn't want to stop moving. 'It was him, Stella,' she said. 'My father was alive all this time.'

Stella looked hopefully towards Sharp for an indication of where he was.

Sharp gave a quick shake of his head.

Stella put her arms around Rebecca, who seemed surprised at the embrace. She couldn't remember the last time anyone had held her. Now that Stella was, it felt like exactly what she needed. What she'd needed since she was sixteen years old.

Rebecca started to cry. 'I just wanted more time...'

'I know,' Stella said.

Diane turned away to answer her phone, having to

cover her other ear to hear the caller. 'No, I'm here with Walter Sharp and Rebecca Fox...Hang on, say that again, Henry...'

Seeing the moment between Stella and Rebecca, Diane gestured apologetically then held her phone up. 'Stella, we need to get back to the office right away.'

At *Republic* HQ Henry was pacing his office. His shirt sleeves were rolled up, and his tie was long gone. His hair was ruffled from running his hands through it.

Stella and Diane broke into a jog through the newsroom.

Henry motioned them into his office. 'Shut the door.' He turned his laptop around to face them, showing a video window. 'I received this about fifteen minutes ago. I had Kurt check it over. He said it's from an IP address in Moscow.'

Henry clicked to play the video.

It was shot on a phone, slightly pixelated from being compressed to make a smaller file that was easier and faster to send via email. It showed a dark, dingy prison cell and a female body in only underwear on the ground. The body was still.

Stella gasped. 'That's Natalya.'

Diane held a hand to her mouth, eyes half-averted from the screen. 'Is she dead? She looks dead.'

The person with the phone went in close to the face, showing a bullet wound in Natalya's forehead.

A narrator said, 'The next one is for Tom Novak. You have three hours to contact the number given to Henry

Self. If you talk, Novak dies. If you don't do as we say, he dies.'

The video ended.

'Was there a message with the video?' asked Stella.

Henry, still pacing around behind his desk, said, 'They want us to drop the Tucker Adams angle and pin everything on Bill Rand. And they say if we even think of running the Adams story in the future, every one of us will be killed like her.' He collapsed into his seat. 'I'm done. This magazine is done. I won't have anyone dying for a story. It's over.'

Trying to calm things down, Diane told him, 'Henry, this has just happened. Let's take a-'

'No, Diane,' Henry started to raise his voice, enough to make the staff in the newsroom notice. 'We're not going to wait a *second*. Tom Novak is in a goddamn prison cell somewhere in Moscow with a gun to his head. They've killed his ex. We nearly lost Stella to a gunman in London three months ago...' He swiped the air with his hand. '*Enough*!'

There was silence for several seconds.

Stella spoke first. 'I say we get him back. At any cost. I don't care. I'll swap with him if I have to.'

Diane said, 'This is an emotional situation-'

'He has a *child*, Diane,' Stella said. 'With Natalya. A little girl called Magdalina.'

Diane sighed. 'We've been through a lot. All of us, together. And I'm as desperate as anyone to get Tom back. But I think we have to consider what he would want in this situation. I mean, if their demand is that we print a story we know to be false, for a Hail Mary...If we do this and we *do* get Novak back, we have to consider what kind of reporter he'll be after he finds out we've given up the biggest espionage case in American political history.'

An intern – terrified at interrupting – knocked on the door. She was holding a note. 'I'm sorry, but Rebecca Fox is downstairs. She says she wants to give Stella the information she needs to make her deadline.'

'Thanks, Michelle,' Stella said.

Diane said, 'That's a woman downstairs whose father died all of an hour ago. She wants to help us finish this story. What do you say, Stel?'

She knew in her heart what the only answer could really be to the Russians. 'I think if we change a word of this story, Novak would rather be dead.'

'Stella. This is going to be the hardest deadline you've ever faced. But we need to extract our emotions from this one. There's never been a more important story for us to get right.'

Stella nodded.

'Go type up what Rebecca has for you.'

Henry was back on his phone.

'Who are you calling?' asked Diane.

Henry replied, 'Walter Sharp.' He nodded as he got an answer. 'Officer Sharp, this is Henry Self. We have a situation here. It's about Tom Novak.'

Stella was in full-on attack mode, standing over her desk with a cup of coffee that she was drinking like it gave her superpowers.

Rebecca sat behind, dialling into her Ghost Division portal on her tablet, pulling up all the relevant details Stella needed.

Diane clapped her hands. 'OK. Forget the NSL. Forget about grand juries and the FBI. What do we need to demonstrate in this story? First, that Tucker Adams was spying for Russia. We can prove that with the dossier. What do you have on Adams' history?'

Stella stopped typing and went immediately to her notes, taken during the flight from Geneva. 'Let me see...so at the Hilderberg meeting, Adams gave Novak and me a rundown of how Bill Rand's career had been shaped by spying for the Hilderberg Group. It certainly checks out. It's also clear from Adams' financial records that he too was backed significantly from early on. Once you know where to dig, the evidence is there. I mean, this is all long before the Citizens United decision in twenty ten, so he wasn't using Super PACs back then. All their donations are very traceable.'

'But Adams comes from money,' said Diane. 'He would have had access to political donors from his father-'

'No,' Stella corrected her. 'Adams told us in Geneva that his father never helped him. He took the money because he knew without it he had no chance of ever becoming a fraction of what his father envisaged for him.'

'So he made a deal with the devil, and in return...what?'

'When Adams was made chairman of the Senate Intelligence Committee, it couldn't have been better for the Russians. They had full access to classified American intelligence. And when word reached Moscow that CIA had got its hands on Stanley Fox, the Russians wanted Adams to help them...' Stella suddenly became mindful that Rebecca was sitting so close to her. '...stop Stanley's formula falling into CIA hands. But Adams couldn't stomach it. The Kremlin must have been pissed, and for a while it seems that Adams genuinely didn't know if he was safe or not.'

Diane said, 'But he was all that Moscow had.'

'Exactly,' Stella agreed. 'He was by far their biggest asset, and they weren't going to just throw that away. And then Colin Burleigh happens. Rebecca's the best person to fill you in on that.'

Rebecca looked up from her tablet screen. 'Colin Burleigh leaks the dossier to Omar bin Talal. Omar is killed in Switzerland and, given Omar's history, the entire world assumes it was the Saudi secret police that did it. We now know it was Gaspar Nolé. The problem for Moscow is, before Omar was killed he left the dossier in a safe deposit box owned by his editor, Romain Laurent. Burleigh then tries another reporter instead. This time, Andrei Rublov. Burleigh was stationed in Moscow for a while, and must have found out that Rublov had secretly been writing op-eds for a dissident website called *Exile*. Rublov then travels to Washington on the promise of meeting a source who can confirm the identity of the mole in Burleigh's dossier.'

'Tucker Adams,' Diane said.

Stella took over. 'And this is where things get murky. Novak and I have a theory.'

'Try me,' Diane said.

'We think Viktor Karpov was the one who told Adams that Rublov was onto him. Karpov is tight with senior Kremlin officials, and there are rumours he'll be the next Communications Director at the Kremlin.'

Rebecca added, 'With a little time I can match up phone calls between Adams and Karpov.'

Diane nodded. 'Then Adams meets Rublov...'

Stella said, 'He finds out how much Rublov knows, but I

suspect Rublov didn't tell him much. Otherwise Gaspar would have just stolen the dossier from him that night. So next morning, Rublov's car is remotely hacked and goes off the Arlington Bridge.'

Diane asked, 'And Adams really thought he could get away with pinning all this on Bill Rand?'

Stella said, 'If he got rid of all copies of the dossier, all that would be left would be a trail of dead bodies, and the evidence that Adams put together showing Rand to be a spy for Hilderberg. He'd be clear for a run to the White House, but he also wanted to bring Hilderberg down as payback for not supporting him all those years. That's why he turned to the Russians in the first place.'

Diane swept through her notes. 'And you're saying this Hilderberg Group is responsible for the Downing Street attack?'

Stella shifted uncomfortably in her seat, knowing what was coming. 'Essentially, yes...'

'Essentially?' Diane peered over the tops of her glasses. 'You're starting to sound like Tom. How do you know they're involved?'

Sheepishly, Stella said, 'Tucker Adams.'

Diane whisked her glasses off. '*That's* your source?'

'I didn't say we were *printing* that. I'm telling you what I have. Adams said Hilderberg helped facilitate the Downing Street attack in order to position Bill Rand as the new Secretary of Defense, in preparation for a run at the White House next year. That's what Hilderberg were meeting in Germany to discuss.'

Diane waited, making sure Stella was definitely finished, then let out a long puff. 'I don't know, Stella. I'm hearing "I think" quite a lot. And we have basically nothing concrete on this secretive Hilderberg Group.'

Stella didn't try to defend it. She knew Diane wouldn't be talked round on unsourced speculation.

'The main thread is definitely Adams. That's where all the sources are. Let's stick to that. But there's definitely legs in this connection to the Downing Street attack.'

Rebecca said, 'I might have something on that.' She scrolled through her tablet. 'Colin Burleigh is the key there: it can't be a coincidence that someone in the British intelligence services, as well as the Russians, wanted rid of Burleigh. My father told me that Teddy King orchestrated the Downing Street attack with Lloyd Willow. What if the Russians had something on King?'

Diane asked Stella, 'What are you thinking?'

Stella had a theory. 'The Russians might have blackmailed King to get rid of Burleigh.'

Rebecca suddenly seemed buoyed by a thought, her fingers zipping around her tablet screen. 'There was a phone call to Burleigh on the morning of the Oxford Street shooting. Since we have Gaspar's phone we have access to most of the big players working for Moscow. Yeah, look...' She passed Diane and Stella the tablet. Rebecca highlighted a selection of phone numbers on the screen. 'This one we know is Yevgeny Belchov, Gaspar's handler in London. And these here are calls made to Belchov's burner the evening of the Oxford Street shooting. The only number we don't have a record for is this one here.' Rebecca tapped on it for an ECHELON search, bringing up all the metadata. 'This same number that called Belchov also called Burleigh earlier that day. There are no other calls to Burleigh around that time.'

Stella could see the connection now. 'That was the call setting up the meet.'

Rebecca said, 'And Burleigh was told he was meeting me that evening. Which was false. Whoever called Burleigh that morning set up his murder.'

'Do you have a way of identifying the caller?' asked Diane.

Rebecca showed her the tablet screen. 'Working on it.'

Diane went back to Stella's first draft. 'We need to be careful when we keep saying "the Russians". What Russians are we talking about?'

Stella said, 'We don't know of individuals within the FSB, but Natalya seems to have suspected Viktor Karpov. She believed her office was being bugged.' Stella was struggling to find the relevant numbers on the ECHELON printout. 'Sorry, Rebecca,' she said, 'can you pull up recent phone calls to Viktor Karpov's burner? I only have until Friday here.'

'Two seconds,' Rebecca replied, altering the search date to also look at the last three days. 'Sorry. I spent so long looking at Belchov and Gaspar's movements...it looks like Karpov's been getting regular text messages every other hour.'

Diane looked up from Stella's draft. 'Who from?' she asked.

'Another unregistered number...' Rebecca tapped through the metadata. 'There's Moscow a week ago. But it jumps around a lot within Moscow. Brateyevo and Perovo districts.'

Stella recognised the name. 'Perovo. That's where Russia Now's offices are.'

Rebecca went on, 'Kapotnya, Sokolinaya Gora-'

'Wait,' Stella said. 'You said Kapotnya.'

Rebecca showed Stella the map of where the phone had been switched on. 'It's been a lot of places the last week.'

'What's the current location?' asked Stella.

Rebecca dialled into it. When the result appeared she mumbled, 'Oh, God.'

Stella checked, 'Is that live?'

'It's live,' Rebecca said through her hand. 'And it's accurate to within twelve metres.' Rebecca picked up her phone. 'I have to call Walter.'

48

It had been over an hour since the gunshot next door. The fact that Novak hadn't heard anything from Natalya since made him kick and scream. He wouldn't stop calling her name, and cursing the FSB, swearing reprisals if anything had happened to her. He knew he was playing into their psychological games, but he couldn't help himself.

Then his door opened, and a guard came in holding a phone.

The guard crouched down beside Novak who was pressed up against the wall.

Novak was hoarse. 'Where is Talya?' he begged. 'Please, just tell me. Where is she?'

The guard tapped on the phone to show Novak a video.

The same one sent to *Republic*.

As Novak realised what he was looking at, he kicked out hard enough for the guard to have to hold him down.

The guard shouted towards the door then made a 'come here' gesture.

The cell door opened.

After a few agonising moments Novak cried out when he saw the guards drag Natalya's body into the cell. The wound to her head had darkened and dried since the video was taken.

The guard grabbed hold of Novak's hair, forcing him to face the direction of Natalya. 'It is done.' The guard paused, holding up a finger. 'There is still time to do the right thing.'

The guard tapped on the phone, to a different video this time.

It showed a four-year-old girl being walked down a snow-covered street by an old woman. The person was filming covertly on a phone, following ten metres behind.

'You know who this is?' the guard asked.

Novak was shattered. He couldn't take any more. Emotionally, they had poleaxed him. Psychologically, he was in pieces.

He knew exactly who he was looking at.

The guard actually worried they'd escalated things too soon, and now Novak wouldn't be capable of coming to his senses to understand their demands. The guard slapped Novak's face. 'You are not paying attention. Look at the video...'

With tears in his eyes, Novak watched as the man filming pointed the camera away to his other hand, showing a gun with a silencer attached.

Novak shut his eyes again, unable to watch.

The guard slapped him, much harder this time. 'Hey! Listen to me: you have the power to save her life. A life you have never been part of. Do something for her for once. Spare her. Tell your editor to drop the Tucker Adams story. Adams told you it was Bill Rand.'

'Adams is under arrest in Geneva,' Novak spat. 'There's no way to make that work.'

'Adams will be released in the next two hours,' the guard replied. 'Bill Rand is already dead. He can be whatever you say he is now.' The guard swiped the phone screen so it was ready to record another video. 'I know it's not easy, but it is simple. Tell them to change the story or Magdalina dies.'

Novak shook his head at the impossible choice he was being presented with. A simple glance at Natalya's body told him the FSB were willing to do anything.

'Tell them,' the guard repeated.

Novak gritted his teeth. 'Diane...this is Tom. Please change the story. They're going to kill Magdalina. Please. Do whatever they ask you.'

The guard tapped Novak appreciatively on the leg then walked towards the door.

'Make the call,' Novak said. 'Call your man off.'

Another guard then appeared in the doorway and said something in Russian. He said it so fast Novak struggled to make it out. Something along the lines of 'Cancel it' or 'forget about it'.

'*Are you sure?*' the guard asked him.

The next part Novak did understand:

'*We're done. Our man in London has confirmed it. The FBI has gagged the story. We don't need him.*'

The guard beside Novak went to Natalya's side. 'Finally,' he said. 'We can get out of this shithole.'

Novak froze as he watched the guard pull Natalya's arm, and she slowly pushed herself to her feet.

When she was up on her knees, she dusted her front down.

The guard offered her a hand which Natalya looked like she was about to accept, then slapped him hard across the face with the front of her hand. 'Don't ever hit me again,' she seethed at him.

Novak thought he was going to pass out so much blood had drained from his face.

Novak sputtered, 'But...what about Magadalina?'

Natalya looked at the guards then at Novak. 'Who the hell is Magdalina?'

She took a wet wipe from one of the guards, and began wiping off the dried fake blood and dirt from her face.

Novak said, 'Talya...'

It was like she'd never even seen him before. In an instant, Novak felt their entire history together dissolve into nothing.

The Natalya he thought he knew wasn't real. And never had been.

49

PORTCULLIS AVENUE, MAYFAIR, LONDON – WEDNESDAY, 2.52AM

Teddy King trudged down the stairs of his three-storey townhouse, dressing gown flapping open around his bare legs. This had been his third attempt at sleep and he was now ready to give up for the night.

As he descended the dark wooden staircase - passing an extravagant modern art collection lining the walls - King felt the familiar vibration of his burner phone in his dressing gown. Each text message elicited a Pavlovian response in him, bringing a sense of dread and yet more tension to his shoulders.

There was a part of him that wanted it all to be over. But an even greater part of him wanted to survive. That was what he had done through the whole Goldcastle affair. While conspirators fell by the wayside, he marched on, maintaining his position of power.

He opened the door of his oversize fridge for a carton of milk. Before he closed the door, King asked the seemingly empty room, 'What are you doing here?'

The figure of Ant Macfarlane emerged from the

shadows at the back door. 'We need to talk,' he whispered. 'Is your wife upstairs?'

King snorted. 'She's on her usual thirty milligrams of Ambien. She won't be awake until long after sunrise.'

Macfarlane closed the kitchen door all the same. 'We had a deal. No fatalities.'

King poured himself a glass of milk then replied, 'Things change.'

Macfarlane struggled to restrain his volume. 'You said you were taking Burleigh in for *questioning*. That was an assassination. Not just of him, of my whole team.'

The glass chinked on the marble worktop as King set it down. He cleared his throat, then stepped closer. 'Anthony, we have a history. So I'm going to choose not to take this invasion of my home personally. But if it happens again...' he paused purposely. 'You know what resources I have at my disposal. And how willing I am to deploy them. Don't forget, you're the one who brought the Burleigh mission to Rebecca Fox's attention. You picked the team personally. All your people. That's why I've survived as long as I have.'

Not to be outmanoeuvred, Macfarlane countered, 'You're not the only one in a position to make threats, *Teddy*. I know how far back you and Stacey Henshaw go. Once you have that, it doesn't take too many leaps to connect you to the Oxford Street ambush.'

King, used to hiding behind a desk and a phone, had a terrible poker face. 'You've got nothing.'

'Really?' said Macfarlane. 'Were you careful enough to use a different burner phone to call Burleigh than the one you've called me on?'

King looked horrified.

'Because otherwise that number could be traced. And it

wouldn't take much work to draw some clear, simple lines between you and the Kremlin.'

King quietly seethed. 'Get out my house.'

Macfarlane didn't budge, enjoying that he'd pushed the right buttons. 'What have they got on you? It must be something big for you to risk all this. You were in the clear after the Downing Street bombing, even after your own boss, Foreign Secretary the right honourable Nigel Hawkes, was sent down for conspiracy to murder. The Russians have proof you were involved, don't they.' Macfarlane could see he had King right where he wanted him. 'That's why you went after Burleigh. He had evidence of what you'd tried to pull off with Hawkes: a coup against Simon Ali. That would be the end of you.' He leaned in. 'You're going down for a *very* long time, King.'

King picked up the glass of milk and smashed it on the tiled floor. He raged, 'Get the fuck out of my house, you ungrateful piece of shit! I'm putting the call out for a bullet in your fucking head before sunrise...'

Macfarlane turned and left, a warm smile on his face.

50

Diane was in with Henry trying to explain the Natalya situation. Stella sat on the edge of her desk, facing away from Rebecca.

'You can't blame yourself,' Rebecca said.

As an ambitious reporter with hopes of becoming an editor herself someday, the Natalya deceit was a savage blow to Stella.

She said, 'I can handle looking like a fool in front of Diane and Henry, but this will shatter Novak. I know it.' She pushed herself off the desk, reliving all of her and Novak's mistakes. 'I didn't do what you tell every rookie: believe what is demonstrated to you, not what you want to believe.'

Rebecca finished tapping on her tablet then looked up in regret at Stella.

The one last hope Stella was clinging to was about to evaporate.

'Anything?' she asked.

Rebecca replied, 'I've checked. There's no record of Viktor and Natalya's divorce.'

Stella slumped against the desk again.

'That's not all, I'm afraid,' Rebecca added.

'What now?'

'I was checking hospital records about Natalya's apparent shooting. Then I got to checking further back.' She paused. 'Natalya's never had a baby.'

Stella closed her eyes. 'Of course. Novak and I always wondered how she ended up working with Andrei. She and Viktor must have been together on this right from the start.'

'Latching onto you guys in Moscow was the perfect cover for her to find out how much you knew.'

Stella couldn't help but admit it. 'She played this perfectly. She knew Novak would go after her. Giving them the hostage they needed.' She groaned. 'Poor Novak. I don't know how he'll ever get over this.'

'You'd be surprised what you can get over,' Rebecca said.

Diane suddenly threw the door open. She was slightly out of breath. 'Stella,' she said. 'Come with me.'

She and Stella ran to Henry's office.

Henry was standing in the middle of his office, reading through the finer detail of a letter. He held it in the air once the two women arrived.

Stella assumed it was a letter terminating her contract.

'This is it,' Henry announced with finality. 'It's done.'

'Mr Self,' Stella said, 'before you fire me I'd like to apologise personally for the-'

Diane interrupted, 'Stella.' She shook her head.

'Fire you?' Henry asked Diane, 'What the hell's she talking about?'

Realising that Diane had kept the error from Henry, Stella said, 'My mistake. It doesn't matter.'

It was already out of Henry's mind. He had bigger fish to fry. 'We're officially shut down on the story. We now have both the gag order and national security letter.'

'So it's time to discuss next steps,' Diane said.

'I don't understand,' said Stella. 'What are we discussing?'

Henry's eyes darted from Diane back to Stella. 'How soon until the story is ready?'

'I'm just polishing,' Stella answered.

Henry asked Diane, 'Is that a reporter euphemism for "ask me again in three days"?'

Diane assured him, 'For anyone else, yes. For Stella, that means it's ready.'

Stella said, 'Though I'm not sure why I've bothered. We can't put it out.'

Something about Diane's expression told Stella something else was cooking.

Henry put his hands on his hips, a determined look on his face. He spoke to the phone on his desk. 'Are you still there, Kevin?'

'Yes, sir,' Kevin replied.

'Why don't you get Stella up to speed.'

Kevin explained, 'The gag and NSL stops *Republic* from publishing or reporting in any way, or telling someone down the street in a coffee bar what story we have, how we got it, or who it involves. It's a long strip of black power tape across all your mouths.' Kevin had a two-thousand page volume on federal criminal code in front of him. Specifically the section on Title Eighteen. He paused for a sip of coffee – his sixth cup of the day – while he found the relevant passage. 'However. If your only goal is simply publishing the story, then there *is* a solution, but you're not going to like it.'

'Try me,' Henry said.

'Maybe,' Kevin suggested, 'this should remain between yourself and Diane for now?'

Stella turned to leave, but Diane put her hand out to stop her.

'No,' Diane said. 'Stella's senior staff.'

Kevin said, 'OK, but I need you to understand I could lose my job over this...'

Half an hour later Henry was in the conference room, looking exactly like someone who had been awake for twenty-six hours. His face was pale, and he looked genuinely haunted. It had been at least a dozen hours since he'd even thought about food.

Before beginning the conference call, Diane waved him over. She did up his top shirt button and put his tie back on.

'I don't want you looking desperate,' she told him. She then placed her hands on his shoulders. 'This phone call is probably going to decide the fate of this magazine. There are fifty-four staff writers and researchers and interns and editors who have your back. This is what you *do*. You've made deals your entire life.'

Henry laughed. 'Diane, no one in the history of media has ever made a deal like the one I'm about to make.'

Diane gently patted his cheek. 'Exactly. You're a fucking legend, Henry. Bring this one home.'

Henry pursed his lips.

Once Diane left, it was just him, a telephone, and a long conference table.

One by one the contacts came on the line, checking in with sighs and frustrated hellos. Each one of them wanting Henry to know how late it was, and how his proposition had better be good.

On the line were the chief editors of the major American newspapers, and directors of every print media group that mattered. It was crucial that it was only print he was talking to. If the plan worked, digital would take care of the rest for him.

Henry began, 'Folks, I'm going to keep this brief. Anyone who knows me, knows I tell it like it is. Tonight, I have one of my chief reporters, Tom Novak, being held by the Russian security services. He has by any standard been tortured, and threatened with execution. All because of the story I'm about to give you all.'

David Sheinberg, chief editor of *The Washington Times*, asked, 'What do you mean "give"?'

Henry replied. 'This evening, *Republic* was given a gag order attached to a national security letter from the FBI. They're investigating our claims that an American senator has been spying for Russia for the past two decades.' Henry was ready to continue, but had to stop to let the scandalised murmurs peter out. 'We have sources that I, and Diane Schlesinger, trust. They're solid. It's a good story. But we can't run it.'

One of the editors, well-versed in the particular legal framework, knew what Henry was about to offer. 'You're giving the story away.'

Henry wasn't sure if he'd impressed them, or brought ridicule on himself. 'If I could briefly quote from the gag order provisions: "a court can order parties to a case not to comment on it but has no authority to stop unrelated reporters from reporting on a case." You and your teams are all unrelated reporters.'

Sheinberg, closest in political leanings to Henry, offered his take. 'If you give the story away, what's in it for you, Henry?'

'The truth,' he replied simply. 'Guys, look at where we are. There's barely a White House briefing these days without a false statement. I mean, statements that hold no basis whatsoever in fact. And I don't give a shit about whose side you're on. Republican or Democrat. I'm not against either. I'm against lies. And I'm for the truth. And this gag order is against the truth.'

Someone had already heard enough, saying, 'Good luck, Henry. But you made your own bed on this one. I'd sooner not join you in jail.'

Henry glanced at the phone, expecting to see further lights for open lines blink off. Most of them held on. 'Does anyone else want to bail?' he asked.

'Go ahead, Henry,' said Kelly-Anne Hopkins, director of the right-leaning media group that owned *The Republic*'s old nemesis *Bastion News*. 'We're listening.'

Bouyed by Hopkins' surprising support, Henry went on. 'Enough's enough. If we all stand up as one, point to this story and say, "this happened", what are they going to do? They can't throw us all in jail.'

Someone jeered, 'There are no guarantees.'

'That's right,' Henry conceded. 'There are no guarantees I could make that would be worth a damn. That's why I'm asking you to put aside any personal differences any of you might have with me. Lord knows this would be an ideal opportunity to stick the knife in. What I'm asking you is, don't do that. Don't let them win. Because if they win this time, they could be beating you next time. And it'll be easier. Because we'll all be more scared than we are now.'

Sheinberg said, 'Henry, have you considered that you can't even disclose that you're subject to a gag order. Have you checked with your lawyer whether giving us this story violates the order?'

'I have. And it does.' Henry found himself smirking. 'It very *definitely* does.'

Sheinberg laughed. 'I'm no lawyer, but I don't imagine yours is going to be around for long letting a major client end up in federal prison.'

'Funny. That's exactly what he told me twenty minutes ago. That's also why I'm the only one standing in this room right now.'

'I don't know,' someone else said, 'I'm going to have to check with my legal team before I even accept any source material from you, Henry.'

Hopkins asked, 'What I want to know is: does Diane Schlesinger back the story?'

'She does,' Henry said instantly. 'And I can tell you that-'

'I'm in,' Hopkins replied.

Henry was stunned into silence.

'If Diane is in, then I'm in,' Hopkins repeated.

Sheinberg then said, 'Screw it. I'm in too.'

'I'm in,' someone else said.

The dam had been broken. Everyone piled in with how they wanted to report the story, and how it could work.

It was still all theoretical, but Henry had done all he could do so far: not fall at the first hurdle.

He stood there listening to the best minds in American journalism going at it. Everyone talking over each other, discussing strategy.

Henry turned to Diane who was standing outside and smiled at her.

Stella, who had been monitoring things from behind the glass wall of her office, stepped out to the hallway to confer with Diane.

'How's it going?' asked Stella.

'So far so good,' Diane answered. 'The lawyers are wading in now. So that's costing about five hundred bucks a minute. I tell you. Thirty years in this business, I've never given a story away. I'm sorry it has to be yours and Novak's.'

Stella said, 'It's OK. I'd rather our doors open tomorrow morning than Novak and I get some retweets and Facebook likes.'

'I have a feeling you'll get plenty of those tomorrow regardless.'

Stella smiled.

Diane looked back towards Stella's office. 'Where's Rebecca?'

'She went downtown. There's paperwork that needs signed before she can arrange bringing Stanley Fox's body back to England. The gall of these people: CIA arrests him, illegally, holds him without charge. Tortures him, and now that he's dead everyone's suddenly very concerned with paperwork. The director of the CIA is going to have some tough questions to answer in the next few days.' Prompted by Diane's silence, Stella asked, 'You don't think so?'

'I think these people have got away with more than anyone ever thought possible.'

Stella let a few seconds pass before asking the question she had really left her office for. 'You'll tell me when you know something about Novak, right?'

Diane kept looking into the conference room. 'I think the less I say about that the better.'

'I don't need specifics,' Stella said. 'I just want to know the best people are on it.'

Diane turned her body slightly towards Stella. 'Walter Sharp has made arrangements. I knew you wouldn't accept anything less. None of us would.'

Stella laid a hand on Diane's shoulder. 'Thank you,' she whispered, before returning to her office.

51

He had been beaten, threatened, and imprisoned, but the overwhelming emotion Novak felt was humiliation. He had done the one thing he always swore he never would: put personal feelings above a story.

If it had been anyone other than Natalya, Novak would never have marched so blindly into the trap.

He had fallen for some admittedly creative theatre of Natalya's – and Karpov's – and for what? Another shot at love? At redeeming a relationship that had never really been a relationship in the first place. All those moments of intimacy he thought he was getting with her in their Moscow days together: that was never really her. And the supposedly 'new' version of her – dedicated, idealistic – was just another version of that.

Novak felt like a fool. He'd not only jeopardised his own life, he now had to worry about Stella, Diane, and Henry back in New York.

Novak's spell of self-reprisals was broken by a guard bursting in to the cell and whipping Novak's hood off. The guard was silent and mesmerizingly strong. He pulled Novak to his feet and carried him out to the hallway into the cell next door.

The floor was covered in plastic sheeting, and at the centre of the room was a wooden chair.

Until that point the FSB had shown little concern for cleanliness, so Novak knew the sheeting meant only one thing: he'd be leaving the cell wrapped in it.

Of course, Novak thought, *they can't admit they have me. So they'll make me disappear instead.*

A guard shackled Novak to the chair. As much as Novak fought and tried to break free of his restraints his adrenaline reserves lasted only a few seconds before an overwhelming wave of exhaustion hit him.

How long had he been held now? Ten hours? Twenty? Three days? There was no answer that could surprise him. All he knew was that the sun hadn't been up for long.

Three other guards came into the room, all masked.

One of them told Novak, 'Time is up.' He then nodded to another guard, who marched forward and took out a gun.

Novak braced himself, closing his eyes.

Suddenly, out in the hallway there was the sound of running and men shouting.

The guard in charge directed his staff to check out the disturbance. When they opened the door there were more FSB agents running through the hallway. One of them stopped at the door.

'Colonel,' the man explained breathlessly, 'there's been a security trip on the third floor.'

The colonel took one look at Novak, then at his men. 'Secure him. I'll check it out.'

Once the others had gone, one masked man was left with Novak.

He kept an FSB-issue MP-443 Grach pistol trained on Novak's chest. If anything were to happen, the guard wasn't going to mess about with head shots in a struggle. He'd take a nice big, easy target like a torso all day long.

The guard chuckled. 'You think you're getting out of here?' He shook his head. 'You're never getting out of here. Not standing up anyway.'

Exhausted, frightened, and shaken, Novak found himself grinning back at the guard. Why, he couldn't say. There was something about being in that room, in that particular situation that felt familiar. He'd stared death in the face so many times in Iraq and Afghanistan. The difference was he hadn't had time to stare into death's eyes and figure out if he had the stomach for the fight or not. There were RPGs that had screamed achingly close overhead to his military Humvee. An IED that took out vehicles behind and in front of his. It was only once those confrontations were over that Novak realised how close to death he had come.

This time, Novak was being invited in to death's waiting room; he knew how it would happen and where; and that it wasn't far off.

There was an image he couldn't get out of his head. What he had imagined Magdalina looked like. The child's face had so quickly become a part of him, thinking that she was out there in the world somewhere, needing him, and that he hadn't been a real father yet.

In the quiet moments at the Grand Hotel, lying next to Natalya in the darkness, he'd thought about what wisdom he would try to impart to his new daughter. How he would make up for their lost four years. Now that the lie had been revealed, the sense of responsibility hadn't left him.

Novak flicked his head at the guard to get him to come closer. 'Please...I can't talk,' he mumbled in Russian.

The guard stepped tentatively towards him, staying an arm's length away with the gun still on Novak's chest.

Novak tried to say something else, but it was inaudible. Then his head fell to one side.

The guard flicked with his boot at Novak's foot.

No response. It was like he'd passed out.

When Novak felt the guard shoving him on the shoulder, Novak sprang back to life, looping his shackled arms over the guard, snaring his aiming arm.

The guard toiled to free himself, letting off a shot into the floor. Novak held on for dear life, but he hadn't thought through any plan beyond the grappling stage. Even if he managed to totally disarm the guard, he was still shackled in the belly of FSB headquarters with no idea how to get out.

He kept wrestling and holding on, looking desperately towards the door.

There was no move Novak could make, stuck in no-man's land in the middle of the locked cell. Confusion and panic started to rise in Novak as shouting in the hallway got closer to the cell. There was an argument going on between the FSB agents.

A call went out on a radio in the hall: 'We need backup in here immediately!'

The guard shouted for help.

52

In a third-floor apartment off the corner of Ostozhenka Street – the most exclusive and expensive residential street in Moscow – the curtains were closed on all the windows. That was how Gaspar liked it, regardless of the time of day.

He only wanted the outside world to be a part of his life as and when he decided. Since he was a little boy he had preferred a dark room, isolated from reality.

The whole apartment was old-fashioned, with high ceilings and ornate cornicing, but with minimalist, modern furniture. Belchov had arranged it for him: a gift for a particularly risky series of jobs.

The living room was in darkness, except for the glow coming from the sixty-inch television, where a Blu-ray of *No Country for Old Men* played in dubbed Russian.

Gaspar slouched in the middle of the sofa, sinking into the soft cushions, a girl on each side of him.

The one to his left was falling asleep, her arm sliding on top of his.

He retracted his arm violently and snapped, 'Don't touch the watch.'

On the enormous glass coffee table in front of them was a silver tray with a small mountain of coke on it. Enough to last at least a week between the two girls (and they were definitely girls, not women; the agency Gaspar used didn't have anyone on their books over twenty).

Three bottles of Cristal had been finished. Not that Gaspar drank. Or snorted, or did any kind of drugs. His first – and last – drink had been when he was fifteen, but he had hated the sensation of not feeling in control.

Now that Natalya had been delivered back to Moscow, the plan was for him to make use of some vacation time. Moscow was the safest place in the world for him. He could do anything, be arrested by anyone, and he knew the Kremlin would take care of it. Using the language from the Scorsese films he'd grown up with, he thought of himself as a made guy. An untouchable.

There was nothing for him back in Paris where he'd grown up – in the 93, the notorious banlieue rife with poverty, radical Islam, and gangs.

In Paris, the rich were in a different class. They looked down their noses at you. They lived on a higher plane. In Moscow, any old riff-raff could be a billionaire. You didn't even need to be smart. You just had to be in the right place at the right time. Like he was, when he met Yevgeny Belchov in a French nightclub: the night he'd saved Belchov's life.

The rich in Moscow didn't put on airs and graces when they spoke. If they were a street kid, they still spoke like a street kid when they had eight figures in the bank.

'Do you want to screw?' drawled one of the girls, eyes rolling about in her head.

Gaspar recoiled at the stench of cigarettes from her breath. He reminded himself to stress non-smokers to the agency next time.

Much to his relief the phone started ringing, which gave him an excuse to stand up. 'Why don't you go for a sleep next door.'

He answered the phone in the kitchen.

'Gaspar,' came the urgent voice at the other end. It was Belchov. 'We need you at Lubyanka! Someone's trying to break out the American.'

Clear-eyed and with nothing dirtier than caffeine in his system, Gaspar grabbed his jacket and went straight out the front door.

It would be nearly two hours later that either of the girls noticed he was gone.

53

More shots were fired in the hallway as Novak continued grappling with the guard in his cell. Novak didn't know much about hand to hand combat, but he knew enough to not give up his back to the guard. Walter Sharp had once told him that the second you have your back to a guy it's twice as hard to re-establish control.

Novak managed to turn the guard, now looping his hand shackles around the guard's neck. The guard knew he was in deep shit: no weapon, his back given up, and standing in the middle of a room.

Novak pulled as hard as he could, choking the guard out. Novak felt the guard's lower body loosen around the knees, ready to give way.

Once the guard passed out and dropped to the ground, Novak found the keys to his shackles in the guard's pocket and unlocked himself.

Just as he was feeling the cut marks on his wrists, the cell door flew open. A man in a balaclava wearing all-black combat gear and holding a semi-automatic rifle appeared in the hallway. He did a quick sweep of the cell, clearing his blind spots in the corners.

Novak was about to reach for the pistol on the ground.

Then the man said in an American accent, 'We're getting you out of here.' The operative shielded Novak on the way out of the cell and led him back up the hallway, rejoining the rest of the masked team. He told Novak, 'Don't get too comfortable. The real shit's out there.'

The team surrounded Novak and marched him through the labyrinthine corridors of Lubyanka. They charged through like they'd rehearsed it for days on end, when they'd only memorised the maps they'd been given in their briefing barely an hour earlier.

On the way they passed bodies of FSB agents they'd taken down on the way in. The rules of engagement had been set out very clearly in the briefing: they weren't to shoot unless fired upon themselves.

The CIA's men were ghosts. Men with no histories or paperwork. No birth certificates, drivers' licences, spouses or children. Everything wiped. For ninety per cent of the year they lived in the shadows, under aliases, fake IDs, ready to get to work whenever necessary. The only questions they ever asked were 'What is the target?' and 'Where?'. Whys never came up. That wasn't their job. If any of them were caught, there was no backup team ready to deploy. No safety net. They'd be stuck there, tortured until any and all intelligence was finally cracked out of them.

An auxiliary FSB team scrambled to catch up with the Americans, taking whatever shots were open to them. Bullets sparked on the metal staircase as CIA descended towards the side exit onto Ulitsa Bol'shaya Lubyanka.

The point man busted through the door, waving the team into the two waiting SUVs. No one celebrated as the doors closed and the drivers hit the gas. They were too professional for that. And in any case, the rapidly accelerating Audi S8 behind them suggested their troubles were far from over.

The navigator up front in the lead car got on his radio. 'We've got possible interference, nine o'clock. Black Audi.'

The point man in the back of the rear car with Novak said, 'Eyes on him.' He reached across to put Novak's seatbelt on. 'Hold on,' he told him, 'this could get rough.'

Novak reached for the grab handle above the window.

Gaspar had speared his way across the city to Lubyanka, six kilometres in heavy traffic, having to take a long detour around the Kremlin, in just under twenty-five minutes. But it helps when you're in a car that goes from zero to sixty in three point three seconds, and you're not afraid to use pavements or take shortcuts by driving the wrong way against traffic.

Gaspar was in direct communication with the FSB's comms centre via a hands-free earpiece.

'Black SUVs on Ulitsa Bol'shaya Lubyanka towards the river,' they told him.

Gaspar didn't need to reply. He spotted a tiny gap between a bus and two taxis. He floored the Audi and it shot through the gap like a rocket, but there simply wasn't enough space to clear the front wing of the turning bus. Gaspar braced for the impact as the Audi glanced off the bus. The car fishtailed from side to side. Gaspar somehow got back under control, then floored the gas again.

Overhead, a police helicopter joined the pursuit. As the

call went out on Moscow police radio, every patrol car in the area wanted a piece of the action too.

As much as the driver in the lead CIA car knew the route, nothing could replace Gaspar's intimate knowledge of Moscow's road system, knowing all the areas he could run off the road and gain a little more momentum.

As CIA made a sharp right on the Embankment running alongside the river, Gaspar saw an opportunity while the Americans turned the corner. There were no buildings blocking sight of the apex of the corner, so Gaspar would have a clear shot - at least for a few seconds.

The car was being flung around so violently that Novak felt like he was on a theme park ride. It was thrusting and braking with more force than he had ever felt in a car.

As the CIA cars made power slides around a ninety-degree corner, Gaspar hung out his window and took aim at the rear windows of the trailing SUV – knowing that was where the Americans would put their most valuable assets.

Gaspar got off three shots, blowing out the right-side window. It would have made a solid head shot if Novak's head hadn't been ducked down by the point man who had anticipated the danger.

The lead car wasn't going fast enough for the point man's liking. 'Get on the fucking gas!' he shouted on the radio.

Gaspar mounted the pavement, which allowed him to clip a good chunk off the apex. The solitary pedestrian there, waiting to cross the road, managed to throw himself out of the way just in time.

Now the road was wider. Faster.

Gaspar gripped the steering wheel a little tighter.

The helicopter's searchlight was now all over the top of

the CIA cars. Across the river, there were half a dozen patrol cars, ready to cut them off by shooting across the Bolshoy Moskvoretsky Bridge.

In the background, St Basil's Cathedral was lit magnificently in the dawn sky. But all anyone in the vicinity was paying attention to was three cars at the centre of a breakneck chase, pummelling their way through the early Moscow commute.

CIA had to rely on brute force more than agility, side-swiping any traffic in their path if it meant maintaining their lead which was closing by the second.

Gaspar now had clear shots to the back of Novak's SUV. After two shots, the SUV's back window shattered, showering Novak and the point man with glass.

Novak cowered in the backseat, feeling helpless and nauseous as the car flew from side to side.

The point man managed to fire back, but was far warier than Gaspar of taking shots with civilians around.

Two patrol cars had crossed the bridge and now set themselves up as a roadblock ahead against CIA.

The lead car navigator shouted, 'Brace, brace, brace...'

The patrol cars crumpled as the lead SUV ploughed through their front ends: their weakest part. The impact meant Novak's SUV now surged to the front, carving a path south along the river.

The navigator in Novak's car radioed: 'We've gotta shift this guy and this helicopter if we want to make it outta here.' Surveying the map in his lap he got back on the radio. 'OK, hard right coming up...'

They took the slip road off the embankment, driving away from the river.

The navigator shouted, 'Coming up: hard left, hard left against traffic!'

The Bolshoy Kamenny Bridge went over the embankment and across the Moskva River. But the CIA navigator had realised they could only get on there by turning onto the wrong side of the road.

The driver was met with a wall of headlights and a cacophony of car horns. Somehow he managed to avoid a head-on collision, but there were plenty of wing bumps as he fought his way through.

All the two CIA cars were doing now was clearing a path for Gaspar, who kept hanging out his window to take shots whenever he could.

He was right up the backside of Novak's car by the time they were halfway across the bridge, bumping and nudging it at an angle, trying to spin them out.

With no barrier between the lanes, CIA finally managed to get into the correct flow of traffic and upped their speed again.

But Gaspar's proximity had allowed him to shoot out the trailing car's tyres.

'We're out, we're out!' the navigator radioed, his voice filled with fear.

Still travelling at speed, the SUV spun across the left side of the road, back into the path of oncoming traffic. It came to a halt in the middle of a lane where a lorry couldn't get out of the way in time. The SUV was obliterated.

None of the CIA team stood a chance.

Now it was just Novak's SUV and Gaspar. And half of the Moscow police force.

They charged down Leninsky Avenue, one of the widest, fastest roads in Moscow.

The navigator no longer had to worry about his radio. He shouted back to the point man and Novak, 'We're going to take the tunnel. It's our only chance to lose them.'

The Third Ring Road tunnel was a nice idea, but to get onto it from Leninsky Avenue meant going against the flow of traffic again.

In the circumstances, it was their only option. The police had closed the gap to Gaspar as well, and the helicopter was going to cling to Novak's SUV all the way out of Moscow if necessary.

Gaspar pulled up alongside them, aiming at the back-seat passengers rather than the driver. In an evasive move, the CIA driver hit the brakes, dropping back several car lengths.

As the chase went on down into the tunnel, the helicopter peeled away.

Coming towards the chase were more Moscow City Police cars, filling the tunnel with blue flashing lights and sirens.

Gaspar slammed on the brakes, leaving him side by side with CIA.

Out of bullets now, Gaspar tossed his gun on the floor. He jerked the steering wheel hard left into the SUV's side. But CIA had the heavier vehicle and didn't budge.

The point man now had a chance to get some shots at Gaspar.

Gaspar slowed, weaving in behind the SUV, ducking from one side to the other, robbing the point man of a clear shot.

The CIA driver could see a pool of water up ahead, glistening under the lights.

'Hold on,' he called back.

Novak could sense his entire life playing out before him. All those near-death escapes in war zones, bombs, IEDs going off; ambushes and death threats; barely surviving a sniper in Berlin with Walter Sharp just a few months earlier. This time, it felt like it really could be his time to finally go.

You can only ride your luck for so long.

But it wasn't luck that was going to get him out of this one. It was the keen eye of his driver.

Purposely taking a track towards the water pool, the driver hit the gas again.

It was now a straight drag race before they reached the waiting Moscow police ahead, who had formed a barrier with their patrol cars right across the road. Two cars deep. There would be no battering through them this time.

Gaspar peered at the CIA driver with nihilistic eyes. '*Je m'en fous!*' ('I don't care.')

It meant nothing to Gaspar if he died in that moment. He had never expected to live past eighteen.

He went hard on the gas, close enough to the SUV to nudge its back bumper. Just what the CIA driver wanted.

Tunnels in Moscow had a habit of leaking. And in the sub-zero temperatures it created fatally hazardous conditions. Especially at the speed Gaspar and CIA were going.

The driver readied himself, keeping a close eye on the frozen puddle. Then at the last possible moment, he turned hard right, pulling up the handbrake.

Gaspar sped straight on. He was on top of the ice before he knew it. The car turned weightless underneath. In panic Gaspar snapped the steering wheel left, then right.

Neither move did a thing. He slammed the brakes. Nothing happened.

The police by the patrol cars could see what was happening, and bailed to either side of the tunnel as Gaspar skidded helplessly towards them at nearly sixty miles per hour.

He ploughed straight through the centre of the patrol car barricade. The airbags exploded in both the front and sides on impact, but they felt like brick walls to Gaspar.

The CIA driver righted the SUV, then accelerated through the gap in the patrol cars that Gaspar had forged.

Once they had made it up the runway and onto the main road, the driver lowered his speed right down to forty and slotted in with the merging traffic.

'We're good,' the driver confirmed.

The point man brushed the window glass off Novak's shoulders, passing him his earpiece.

'My CO wants to talk to you,' the point man said.

Novak, still gathering his breath, popped the earpiece in.

'Can you hear me?' the voice at the other end asked.

'Yeah,' Novak groaned, holding his head. When he retracted his hand he saw blood.

'It's Walter Sharp,' he said. 'My extraction team is taking you to a safe location.'

Novak wheezed in relief.

Sharp said, 'You're coming home, Tom.'

Back in the tunnel, Moscow police ran to the wreckage of Gaspar's Audi, expecting to find a dead body.

At first, all they could see was twisted black metal and flames licking up around the driver's seat.

Gaspar hung over what remained of the dashboard, his entire head drenched in blood.

A patrolman shouted, 'Get an ambulance!'

Gaspar tried to move his arm, then groaned, '*Je m'en fous.*'

54

Everyone in the *Republic* staff knew something big was happening, they just didn't know what. Henry, Diane, and Stella were the only ones on the inside, shuttling between each of their offices, carrying pieces of paper back and forth.

Henry had been on an endless series of phone calls for several hours. The scale of what exactly he was trying to coordinate was beyond anything any single editor or owner had ever attempted.

For the length of time Henry had been awake he should have been on his knees. Instead, he had never felt so jacked. No amount of coffee could replace the feeling of adrenaline flowing through his body at that moment, on hold with all six major media magnates that had agreed to his plan.

'I know, Peter,' Henry explained, desperate to deal with the five other blinking lights on his phone, 'but it has far less weight if it's not all the same. That's the whole point.' After an exasperated pause, Henry added, 'You're about to sell

ANDREW RAYMOND

the most copies of the *Post* since nine eleven. I'm handing
that to you on a plate. In return, as a near-bankrupt magazine owner, I am asking for not one single cent. Peter, for
the love of all that is holy: use the same headline as
everyone else...' He switched to the line for David Sheinberg of *The Washington Times*. 'David, I'm back...No, only
you can set the front page...Why? Because if word gets out
before printing, this entire thing collapses. The only thing
we have going for us is total secrecy.'

Across the hall, Diane was line-editing over Stella's
shoulder as she wrote: about the most uncomfortable conditions under which anyone could write a story.

But there was no alternative. They were out of time.

Stella paused typing while she waited for Diane to catch
up. She sat there pensively, staring at the screen. She listed
the flaws Diane would no doubt find in the work. Every
word and phrase now seemed transparently pedestrian to
Stella, lacking clarity or purpose, shifting focus from one
paragraph to the next, her adjectives too weak...

Diane suddenly declared, 'It's perfect,' then pointed up
the page. 'OK, one last check above the fold.'

Henry shouted from his office, 'Diane! Time!'

'It's coming,' Diane shouted back, eyes locked on the
computer screen.

'Rublov should be above there,' Stella suggested.

Diane said, 'We'll dilute the headline if you put him any
higher.' She paused, thinking it over one last time. 'No, this
is it. We're done.' She then bellowed to Henry, 'We're done!
Tell them it's in the air now.'

Henry raised his arms in victory. He could finally
hang up.

Stella sat back in her chair, finally realising she'd been hunching her shoulders for the past two hours.

She stared at the audacious headline, struggling to take in the enormity of what they'd put together. It wasn't just the story. It was the format. The whole enterprise.

Kurt knocked on the door but hung back. 'Is this a bad...?'

Diane waved him in. 'What is it?'

He handed her a folded note. 'You said you wanted to know when it came through.'

Diane looked at it, then told Kurt, 'Thank you.' She handed the note to Stella.

"Tom Novak just left Russian airspace."

Stella looked over at Henry standing alone. 'Should we go over there?' she asked.

Diane said, 'In the last hour, he's sent himself to prison and bankrupted himself. He could probably do with some friends right now.'

When the two women reached his office Henry was smiling. He held up a piece of paper. 'Have you seen this? Tom's coming home.'

'We saw it,' Diane said.

Henry took a long breath, looking out his office to the newsroom. 'I'm gonna miss this place.' He turned to the two women. 'I'm gonna miss working with you guys. We had a real good run.'

'It's not over yet,' Diane said, in hope rather than belief.

55

Without fail, every morning Parker Newton, chief of staff to the President, was first to arrive in the West Wing of the White House.

Cleaners were still vacuuming the carpets in the bullpen where the President's staff, speech writers, and assistants worked.

Newton always carried a flat white from Lacy's on Lexington Drive, along with a blueberry muffin which he'd consume while going through the day's security briefing, the daily diary, and the morning papers.

After setting down his muffin, Newton turned his attention to the pile of newspapers on his desk, left there an hour earlier by an intern.

As soon as he saw the headline, Newton dropped his coffee, which bounced off the corner of the desk and spilled all over his Italian leather loafers. Newton was barely aware of the mess, but at least thought the worst of the shock was over.

Then he noticed the other front pages underneath.

'What the f...' He lunged for the phone, dialling star-1. 'It's Parker. You need to wake him.'

Newton's secretary appeared in his doorway, still wearing her coat, wondering what was going on. Parker tossed the papers out across his desk for her to see. He covered the mouthpiece, telling her, 'Get the director of the FBI on the phone.'

It took the secretary a moment to snap out of it before nodding.

Parker went back to his phone call. 'I know what time it is, Scott. Get in there with hockey pads and a helmet if you have to and wake the fucking President, or I'll do it myself.'

56

A news distribution van pulled up at Monty Delvechio's news stand with a screech. Fred the driver jumped out the already open sliding driver's door. He was running late and getting frustrated.

'Hey, Monty,' he called out somewhat irritably, while doling out the piles of banded newspapers.

Monty was flipping up the front awning of his stand with a pole, and didn't notice the papers at first. 'You sound harassed, Fred.'

Heaving the newspapers out the back of the van, Fred groaned, 'Running late.'

Monty put down the pole almost in slow motion. He bent down to examine the front pages, noticing they were all exactly the same. 'Is this right, Fred?'

Fred complained to himself, 'I don't write 'em, Monty. I just deliver 'em.' He hopped back into the front seat. 'Have a good one.'

As Fred drove away, Monty moved the top pile, seeing the same front page design and even the same headline on the New York Express and the Daily New Yorker. Both of them with the same single story on a full page.

'What the hell...' Monty mumbled as he unfurled an Express. He did the same with a Times, and then a Post.

A headline in bold capitals took up the entire space above the fold:

"GOVERNMENT GAGS THE REPUBLIC FROM REVEALING SENATOR TUCKER ADAMS IS RUSSIAN SPY."

Below the fold carried a picture from Geneva of Adams in handcuffs, his face twisted as he shouted at the photographers.

Rue Charlot, 3rd Arrondisement, Paris – Wednesday, 11.41am

Romain Laurent was asleep on the floor next to his bed, in the position he'd fallen asleep in six hours ago: lying on his front.

His phone pinged with an email, wrenching him out of sleep. A sunbeam was streaming in through the window, and had turned the bedroom into a greenhouse.

Romain struggled to his knees so he could open the window and let some fresh air in. He hacked and coughed out the window, feeling his hangover already kicking in.

He picked up the phone to see what idiot had woken him up.

It was an email from Benoit, his pony-tailed senior editor.

The subject line said:

Have you seen this?

The email had a link to Agence France-Presse's take on

the Tucker Adams story, which included a subheading on
Omar bin Talal.

Romain read it with his mouth hanging open, and a
cigarette in his hand which went unlit until he'd finished the
entire story.

'Son of a bitch,' Romain said. He suddenly remembered about the cigarette and lit it.

He quickly dialled Benoit on his phone.

'Benoit!' he whooped. 'They did it! Thomas, and
Stella!'

Benoit replied, 'They credited Omar in the byline. Did
you see?'

Romain looked across the room at the bottles of vodka
he'd bought the night before. Stocking up so he wouldn't
have to leave the apartment all day.

He couldn't help it. He started to cry.

'Boss,' Benoit said, 'Are you OK?'

Romain pulled himself together. 'I'm fine. Yes...I'm
fine.'

'Do you want me to do anything?'

Romain lit his cigarette. 'Call the staff in.'

Benoit nearly fell over. 'Are you sure?'

'Yeah,' Romain said. 'Call the staff in. It's time to get
back to work.'

He hung up without even a goodbye, then took the
vodka to the kitchen. He unscrewed the caps then emptied
the bottles down the sink.

Romain said with determination, 'Yes, Thomas. I've still
got some fight left in me.'

57

THE REPUBLIC OFFICES, NEW YORK CITY

The switchboard had taken so many calls once the newspapers hit the streets that they had to redirect to the newsroom. *The Republic*'s website had crashed three times since the story went live, as Henry's collaborators had agreed to send all their traffic to them. Everyone wanted to see what *Republic* had to say. But it wasn't long before the FBI had blocked it, flagging the homepage with a National Security notice.

It didn't really matter at that point: the story was still being shared all over the internet and social media. And there wasn't a thing the government could do about it. Just as Henry had envisaged.

He was alone in his office, flicking through news channels.

Kevin Wellington knocked gently on his door, holding his briefcase. 'I got here as fast as I could.'

Henry, still facing the television, said, 'It's on every channel.' He turned around. 'We made it too big to ignore.'

Kevin closed the door behind himself. 'Diane said she spoke to you.'

Henry muted the television. 'Uh huh.'

'We don't have much time.' Kevin opened his briefcase on Henry's desk and took out some papers. 'You should probably call your family-'

'I've called them.'

Kevin nodded. 'Should I talk you through what's going to happen next?'

Henry moved towards the window, surveying the bustling streets below. 'Please.'

'You'll be charged with violation of a federal nondisclosure agreement.'

'How bad?'

'Three years. You'll do eighteen months but I'll get it as close to sixteen as possible.'

Henry thought it might have been worse. 'What about you, Kevin?'

'I'll be fired by the end of the day,' he replied, unfazed. 'I recommended that one of our biggest clients commit a federal crime. I'm told the partners would really rather I add billable hours than do that.'

Henry chuckled. 'We could never have got the story out without you, Kevin.'

'Don't feel too sorry for me,' Kevin replied. 'I'll have a dozen job offers by the end of tomorrow.'

'How long before the police get here?' asked Henry.

'My contact says they should be here in about ten minutes.' He paused. 'You should know there's some press outside. I'm not the only one with a police source apparently.'

Henry turned around and straightened his tie. 'I'm ready.'

He walked out to the newsroom, where phones were ringing off the hook. He stepped up on a chair and whistled. 'Could I have everyone's attention, please!'

Stella and Diane both hung up the phone calls they were taking. The newsroom was still awash with ringing phones, so Diane made a throat-cutting gesture at reception, then pointed at her ear.

The receptionist cut all calls, leaving the newsroom in silence.

'Thank you, Diane,' Henry said, smiling. 'As you all know, we were hit with a national security letter from the FBI and a gag order. We managed to circumvent this by handing over Stella and Tom's story...' Henry stopped, noticing Novak appear at reception.

He wandered in slowly, not wanting to distract from proceedings but it wasn't long before the staff started applauding at his presence. He had a black eye, large bruises on one side of his face, and barely healed cuts from his temple all down to his jawline. His left arm was in a sling.

Henry called out, 'Tom Novak, everybody!' He led the applause, and whistled again.

Stella ran towards Novak, knocking him back a step as she embraced him. Even though he winced from the pressure on his arm, Stella chided him, 'You crazy bloody twat.' She put her arm around him as they listened to Henry.

He pointed at the pair. 'Those two right there. That's what I wanted to tell you about. Tom Novak and Stella Mitchell have made *The Republic* what it is today. Sadly, I'm not sure what exactly will remain of it come tomorrow. My lawyer's advised me that the police will be here any minute to arrest me for violating the gag order. Having made other reporters aware of the story in the first place constitutes a violation of the gag order. So I'll be arrested. And I'll be jailed. Even with a full confession and a plea deal.' He motioned again at Novak and Stella. 'But when I see the courage that these guys and the rest of you have shown, from the NSA Papers, to Goldcastle, to Downing Street, to this: all I feel is gratitude. I might be about to become a felon, but at least I'll be able to look my kids in the eye someday and say that for a small part of my life I got to work at *The Republic*. And together, we stood up for something. We did what we thought was right. And we never backed down.'

Behind reception, the elevator doors pinged. As Henry expected, out stepped half a dozen uniformed police and three detectives. One showed a warrant to the receptionist, who pointed in Henry's direction.

The staff broke into applause, growing louder as the police got closer to Henry.

Kevin stood by Henry's side as the detective read him Miranda. But the applause and cheering for Henry grew so loud, the detective had to shout to be heard.

'...You have the right to an attorney. If you cannot afford an attorney...'

Novak and Stella cheered him as he was led past in handcuffs. Henry winked at the pair.

58

Rebecca knew as soon as she opened the door of her apartment that there was someone already in there. Her mail, which had been accumulating since she left, had been pushed back towards the wall from the door opening.

Whoever was there wasn't interested in keeping it a surprise.

'I knew you'd come for me anyway,' a voice called out from the living room.

Rebecca felt for her phone in her coat pocket, then pressed and held in the standby button on the side of her phone, which she had turned into a shortcut for switching on her audio recorder.

As she rounded the hallway into the living room, Rebecca said, 'I won't be the only one coming for you.'

Ant Macfarlane sat in the slimline chair across the room. He was wearing a collarless leather jacket and jeans. 'I'll go quietly,' he said. 'But I think so long as you're recording me from your pocket we might as well get some things on the record.'

Rebecca set down her phone on the glass coffee table between them.

'I heard about your father,' Ant said. 'I'm sorry.'

'Suddenly you care about loss of life?' asked Rebecca.

The accusation appeared to sting Ant. 'I didn't know King was going to do that to Burleigh, or any of the others. You must believe me.'

'What did he tell you? Let me guess: he was just going to bring him in for questioning. That no one would be harmed. I suppose he showed you evidence of Burleigh's guilt?'

'Yeah.'

'You gave King the cover he needed to set up the op that would assassinate Burleigh. You handed me that op, personally. I trusted you.'

Macfarlane's voice cracked a little. 'And I trusted *him*.'

'So is this your last goodbye before disappearing off into the sunset with Stacey Henshaw?'

'Henshaw was working with King. I don't know what he promised her, but I don't expect to ever hear from her again.' He reached into his jacket pocket and put down a memory stick. 'And if she were still around, she certainly wouldn't give you that.'

'What is it?' asked Rebecca.

'It's why King needed Burleigh killed,' Macfarlane answered. 'The files the Kremlin was blackmailing King with. They were stolen in a hack two months ago. The files prove King and Willow not only knew that Senator Tucker Adams was spying for Russia, but that they approved of it and aided Adams' continued success. It's the evidence that you and Angela Curtis need to prove that there was an alliance between Teddy King and Lloyd Willow to assassinate Simon Ali, and install a puppet Prime Minister to replace him. It's everything you need to end this.'

He stood up, putting his hands in his pockets.

'You should run,' Rebecca warned him. 'They'll kill you for helping me.'

Ant stopped in the hallway and said, 'They can try.'

59

FLIGHT 243, SOMEWHERE OVER THE ATLANTIC OCEAN –
TWO DAYS LATER

Novak and Stella were in First Class, the overhead lights dimmed for passengers to get some sleep on the transatlantic flight from JFK to London Heathrow.

Stella had been trying in vain to plough through the emails she'd received since publication of the Tucker Adams story. Every hour brought a fresh landslide of more. Her inbox was now at four hundred unread messages. She looked up from her tablet, stretching her neck.

She noticed Novak staring out the window, his tray down, food uneaten.

'You OK?' asked Stella. 'You haven't eaten since lunch.'

Novak tried to smile. It wasn't nearly as convincing as he thought it was. 'I ain't hungry.'

Stella took his roll and buttered it. 'You'll sleep better if you've had some carbs,' she explained.

Novak could tell she wouldn't take no for an answer. He finally broke into a smile and took a bite.

Stella asked, 'What do you think will happen to Natalya now?'

Novak shrugged. 'Her cover's blown now, which I'm guessing won't please the Kremlin. I suspect she might have faked one too many deaths for her own good.'

'What about New York?' asked Stella, turning away from the aisle. 'What about *Moscow*? How can either side keep that quiet?'

'Mutually assured denial: it's not in CIA's interest to point fingers at the FSB for Stanley Fox's death, and vice versa for kidnapping me. Life just goes on.'

Stella passed him her tablet. 'Not so much for Teddy King, though.'

The picture showed King being led away in handcuffs from the front step of his house in Mayfair. The headline said: "Teddy King arrested for conspiracy to murder and treason."

Novak handed back the tablet. 'Sharp got word to me before we took off. Glen Fallow's been charged with holding a foreign citizen without charge and assault and battery.'

'He should have been charged with manslaughter.'

'Sharp was pushing for it, but it was never going to happen. How is Rebecca?'

Stella shut off her tablet screen. 'She's been offered a month off on compassionate leave, and I'm sure she'll take none of it. She tells me big changes are coming for Ghost Division.'

'Oh yeah?'

'Apparently Angela Curtis is keen to expand the unit.'

'What kind of expansion?' asked Novak.

'She's holding exploratory talks with CIA about an American arm of Ghost Division. Seems that the New York situation with Stanley Fox was enough to push the President over the edge. Rebecca will be heading up in the UK. Walter in the States.'

'I guess that was inevitable. The last six months have seen more security breaches in British and American security services than ever before. I'd bet on things getting worse before they get better.'

'What makes you say that?' asked Stella.

'We've been thinking about this too small, Stella.'

'You want to go after Hilderberg, don't you?'

'Don't *you?*' asked Novak. 'They probably would have got Bill Rand into the White House. You saw the people at that meeting: they have people everywhere, Stella. Now they've lost their candidate for the White House, what do you think's going to happen?'

'I doubt they'll go gently into the night,' Stella said. 'But if we go after them, we can be under no illusions about what they're willing to do.'

Novak looked dolefully out the window. 'I just don't know if I have the stomach for it.'

'What are you talking about?'

'Stella, you're going to be a great editor someday. But that's not for me. I don't know if I still want to be running around with a backpack and a notepad when I'm fifty.'

Stella paused, looking at him with care. 'Is this about Natalya?'

Novak liked how easily Stella could see through him. 'It's funny...ever since I started in this business I always assumed I'd never be a father. It never even entered my head it was something I could do. I was twenty-two, charging around Latin America, the Middle East, Eastern Europe, trying to shine a light on things no one knew about. I thought it was so great that I wasn't tied to anything. At a moment's notice I could go anywhere. Report on anything.' He broke off, looking down into his hands. 'But when Talya told me we had a daughter together...I wasn't scared like I thought I would have been. When I realised she'd lied to me, I actually felt like something was missing from my life. I always assumed that reporting would fill any kind of void. But when I thought I was a father, I was willing to walk away from everything else. I mean, is this what I'm risking my life for? A story? What impact am I really making in the world? I'm thirty-six. I've got no real friends. An apartment I'm never in, with a mortgage I can't afford. And it's a miracle either of us has survived the last six months.'

Stella thought about it. 'Because it's what we *do*, Novak. Love is for other people. This, *Republic*, breaking stories, this is what we love. And nothing else makes sense the way this does. Look at what we've done in just the last six months. We've got some of the most powerful people in the world on the run, Novak. Our Tucker Adams story sold more newspapers since World War Two.' Stella sighed. 'But then, I've never been so in love with someone that I'd be willing to risk my life the way you were - just for a *chance*, a shot in the dark, of getting them back. If you're capable of that...' she raised her hands slightly then let them drop. 'You're going to be just fine.'

Novak, still looking out the window, reached for Stella's hand and held it.

60

Yevgeny Belchov was sitting on the floor of his now empty living room, drinking a bottle of vodka, when the doorbell rang.

His security detail had been removed, now that he had no money to keep paying them. Every other service and luxury he'd grown accustomed to had been taken away. Even the electricity had been switched off, leaving the iron gate in his driveway stuck wide open.

He didn't recognise Novak and Mitchell when he opened the door, squinting against the harshness of the sunlight: he hadn't been outside in two days.

'If you're after money you're too late,' he barked, hiding half in profile behind the door.

'Mr Belchov,' Stella said, 'we write for *The Republic*.'

'You two are a pair of maniacs, you know that. You better come in but they've probably seen you by now.' He left the front door open, and wandered back to the living room, swigging his vodka as he went.

Willing to take their chances, Novak and Stella went in.

What struck them first was the vast emptiness of the enormous house. There wasn't a single piece of furniture left in the place.

'Who's watching you?' asked Novak.

'Who else? The FSB, numbnuts.' Belchov stumbled back to his resting place on the floor. 'You see what they do to me? Reduce me to a schmuck, like the Jews say.'

'You must have known this might happen someday,' said Stella.

Belchov shrugged. 'You say one word, you fall out of favour, and,' he clapped his hands, 'game over. One phone call to the bank is all it takes. Assets frozen. Repossessed. You should have seen this girl I had here. Svetlana. She cried for this diamond necklace like it was a drowned child. I swear to God you've never seen a performance like this in your life.'

Stella crouched down to get at Belchov's eye level. 'Mr Belchov, we have phone records linking you to Teddy King of MI6.'

Belchov nodded enthusiastically then broke into a laugh. 'That fucking *mu-dak*.'

Stella turned to Novak, who translated for her, 'Shithead.'

She went on, 'We also have phone records linking you to Tucker Adams. Do you have any comment on that?'

Belchov's smile vanished. 'Fucking Americans,' he spat. 'I tried to tell the Kremlin he was more trouble than he was worth.'

Stella said, 'We know that the Kremlin wanted rid of Stanley Fox. There are eight FSB agents sitting in a morgue in New York City with nowhere to go.'

Belchov parroted the official line. 'There is no direct

evidence linking those men to either the FSB or any other...'

Stella gestured that she didn't need to hear anymore. 'Yeah, I heard all that already on Russia Now. All we want to know is what you had on Teddy King at MI6, and who gave the order to have Stanley Fox killed.'

Belchov laughed. 'She doesn't want much, does she,' he said to Novak.

Novak stone-faced him. 'Don't look at me, pal. Stella's asking the questions.'

'If you give us a name,' Stella said, 'we can make yours disappear.'

Belchov took a drink.

'King is in custody now. Do you honestly think he won't talk? You must know he'll pin anything he can on you. Or do you think a jury will believe a disgraced Russian billionaire?'

Belchov struggled to his feet with a heavy sigh, then wandered to the living room windows holding his bottle. He nudged a shutter on the wooden venetian blinds down, seeing a black Jaguar parking up across the street. He knew who was out there, and what was going to happen once Novak and Stella were gone.

Belchov smiled. 'Like it matters, huh? My life is already over.' He took a long drink. 'You know, I told them to kill you.'

Stella checked herself, as if looking for damage. 'Better luck next time?'

Belchov laughed. 'It wasn't personal, young lady. You understand.'

'I don't hold grudges, Mr Belchov,' Stella said. 'I write headlines.'

Something about the veiled threat got through to Belchov.

'They've made a stupid mistake,' he said. 'They've taken away everything I had.'

Stella quoted, '"When a man has nothing to lose, he's never been more dangerous."'

Belchov nodded appreciatively. 'You know Solzhenitsyn. Very good.' He looked towards his empty bookcases.

Stella and Novak could tell Belchov was on the verge of giving them the last few diamonds he was still in possession of.

'Tell me about Adams first,' said Stella, nudging him over the line without him even realising it.

Belchov said, 'Adams was never meant to become our puppet in the White House. He was spying for us, and he gave us plenty. But the Kremlin always wants more. It wasn't enough just to have a spy in Congress. Now they wanted the fucking White House. It was ridiculous. Then Bill Rand came along, and everything went to shit.'

'He became the new favourite with the Hilderberg Group,' Novak said.

'Exactly. Adams got resentful. Then this Stanley Fox appeared. Imagine you have to stop a nuclear bomb going off, and if you fail, it will go off every day, for decades. Except you will never fully understand how much damage it's done, or how much money it has cost you. That's what Stanley Fox was.' Belchov shrugged. 'He had to go. That was it.'

Making sure they got what they really came for, Stella asked, 'What about Teddy King?'

Belchov laughed. 'Ah, Teddy. We couldn't have got to him without Adams. He used his Congressional security clearance to access NSA, then broke into MI6's database in their Washington substation. We sent him in to look for compromising material on King when he was moved from MI5. We didn't expect to find a smoking gun linking King to Lloyd Willow and Nigel Hawkes and Goldcastle. We had *everything.* So we sent a man to King. King understood the situation. So he agreed to help us with our problem: get rid of Colin Burleigh.'

Stella went in for the kill. 'One name, Yevgeny: who gave the order to kill Stanley Fox?'

Belchov needed one more drink before he said it. 'Boris Ivanov. Everything went through him and the Ministry of the Interior.'

Novak couldn't help trying for the cherry on top. 'What about the assassin?'

Belchov was adamant. 'No. You don't get him. Not for anything.'

'What, do you owe him your life or something?'

Belchov surprised him by saying, 'I do. And I'll never forget it.' He took another drink. 'Go on,' he said. 'You got what you wanted.'

On the way out the driveway, Stella held her fist out at Novak. 'Game, set, and match,' she said.

Novak looked over his shoulder at the Jaguar again.

Stella said, 'Don't leave me hanging, Novak.'

He finally noticed her fist and touched knuckles. 'Sorry.'

'That's what I'm talking about,' Stella enthused. 'That's how we do things in Kensington.'

Novak laughed.

Gaspar waited until Novak and Stella were gone, before

limping across the road. Underneath his coat his right arm was in a sling, and he wore sunglasses to hide the bruises on his face.

Belchov had left the front door open. Running was pointless now. He sat in the middle of the living room floor with his back to the door.

When he heard Gaspar's footsteps approaching, Belchov made a request:

'Do me a favour, my boy. Make it fast.'

Gaspar kept his free hand in his coat pocket. 'I want you to know I'm grateful for all you did for me,' he told Belchov.

He closed his eyes. 'I'm grateful to you too, Gaspar. I never forgot that night we first met. But now you have your orders. I know it's never pers-'

Before Belchov could get another word out, a bullet entered the back of his head. It exited his forehead, sending a sharp stream of blood forward across the floor.

Gaspar was on the phone before he had cleared Belchov's driveway. He'd received a message from control.

It was a picture of Natalya. The message with it said: '*Next.*'

61

Angela Curtis was sitting alone in the Pindar secure briefing room when Rebecca Fox entered. Like being summoned to the principal's office, she held back, knocking on the doorframe.

Curtis took off her reading glasses and beckoned her in. 'Rebecca, come in.'

'It's just us?' Rebecca asked, looking around the vacant seats.

Curtis said, 'I thought I'd take the opportunity for a one to one.'

Rebecca took a seat.

'I'm sorry about your father,' Curtis said. 'I want to repeat my offer of compassionate leave.'

'I appreciate it, Prime Minister, but there's work to be done.'

'Indeed. That's what I wanted to talk to you about.' She passed her a piece of paper inside a manila envelope. 'It's time to start over.'

'Start what over?'

'Ghost Division. If the events of the past week have shown anything it's that we are in the grip of a full-scale crisis in the intelligence community. A Prime Minister and several MI6 operatives assassinated. Corruption. Cover ups. Leaks. We're in crisis, Rebecca. That's why I'm issuing sweeping new powers to Ghost Division.'

Rebecca started to read the planned proposals. 'Warrantless wiretaps. Internet browsing histories. Phone calls.' She lowered the proposal then cleared her throat. She didn't know quite how to put it. 'Prime Minister, I'm not qualified to offer a political opinion. But I would strongly advise you to destroy this and don't let anyone ever know it existed.'

Curtis was taken aback. 'And why is that?'

'You're declaring war on your own intelligence agencies.'

'Rebecca, you're the only one I trust, and I need you by my side. This is the biggest year in my political life. And believe me when I tell you that some of the changes I'm going to bring in are not going to leave me very popular with the establishment of this country. I'm asking you and Ghost Division to protect the British people.'

Rebecca took a long intake of breath. 'I don't know what to say, Prime Minister.' She stood up and held out her hand. 'It will be an honour.'

Curtis smiled and shook Rebecca's hand warmly. 'That's the answer I was hoping for. Go home and get some rest.'

Rebecca dropped her head to one side, like she had a better idea. 'Actually, I thought I'd get back to Thames House. There's still a lot of other leads in the metadata on Gaspar Nolé's phone.'

Curtis put her reading glasses back on with a smile.

Rebecca was in the tunnel heading back towards the MoD when her phone rang.

It was an anonymous number.

'Hello?' Rebecca answered.

'Rebecca. It's Oliver Thorn. I need to see you. It's rather urgent.'

Rebecca checked her watch. 'I need to get back to Thames House, Sir Oliver. Could you meet me there?'

'We can't meet there,' he replied sharply. 'It might not be safe.'

'Might not be safe? What are you-'

'It's about Angela Curtis, Rebecca. I need your discretion. Can I trust you?'

Once Curtis was alone the intercom went.

It was Roger Milton. 'Prime Minister, I have a call-'

'Not right now, Rog,' Curtis replied.

'Not to the switchboard. To my mobile.' He urged her, 'You should take it.'

Curtis took off her glasses again. 'Who is it?'

He paused. 'It's Jozef von Hayek.'

After a brief hesitation, Curtis said, 'Patch him through.'

A Flemish accent filled the briefing room from the intercom. 'Prime Minister,' von Hayek said. 'This is a call I've been looking forward to making for many months now.'

Curtis replied, 'And one I've been looking forward to taking for even longer, Mr Chairman.'

'As you know, the Hilderberg Group has been watching you for some time now. We'd like to invite you to one of our gatherings. An informal affair, you understand. After such nastiness last week.'

'I'm flattered you believe I fit the bill, Mr Chairman.'

'If we didn't think so, we would never have moved the pieces so decisively in your favour. With every day that's gone by we become more certain we made the right choice.'

'It's certainly going to be a big year ahead. If I can help in any way-'

Von Hayek cut her off. 'Angela, with respect. What we have planned is so much bigger than that.'

Curtis rose from her seat, laying her hands on the table top. 'What did you have in mind?'

'I told you six months ago that we would get you into Downing Street. And we did. But this is just the beginning. That's the thing about power: no one gives it to you. You must take it for yourself before tyranny decides for you. Your great-grandfather understood that better than anyone else. And now the time has come for someone to complete Friedrich Hilderberg's great work.' he paused. 'Are you ready, Prime Minister?'

Angela Curtis began to smile. 'I'm ready.'

THE END

Novak and Mitchell return in *Traitor Games*.

ENJOY CAPITOL SPY?

YOU CAN HELP WITH JUST A MINUTE OF YOUR TIME...

If you enjoyed *Capitol Spy*, it would be a great help to me if you left a rating or a brief review on Amazon.

Most major publishers spend a huge amount of money on marketing, and to get books into the hands of reviewers. I might not have that ability, but with a minute of your time, you can get something that money cannot buy: word-of-mouth support.

If you would like to leave a rating or review, just head over to Amazon and search for "Capitol Spy Andrew Raymond". There will be a link on that page to leave a review.

Many thanks,

- Andrew

GET EXCLUSIVE NOVAK AND MITCHELL MATERIAL

You can keep up to date with my latest news by joining my mailing list. It's rare for me to email more than once a month, and you also get a Novak and Mitchell reading pack with some very cool exclusive content.

If you would like to find out more about the mailing list, head over to:

andrewraymondbooks.com

Finally, and most importantly, thank you, dear reader...

I've worked late into the night, and got up long before dawn to write this book. A number of you have watched my books find a bigger and bigger audience in the last few months. It's been so nice to share that with a lot of you.

In the last few months, *Official Secrets* became the UK's No.1

Political Thriller, and at the time of writing has been a best-seller in various charts for three months and counting. Something I never thought would happen. I'm very grateful for that kind of support.

If you would like to get in touch on Facebook, you can find me at:

facebook.com/andrewraymondauthor

Alternatively, I'm always glad to receive emails from readers at:

info@andrewraymondbooks.com

NOVAK AND MITCHELL WILL RETURN IN *TRAITOR GAMES...*

Until next time,

Andrew Raymond

- Glasgow, Scotland

AUTHOR'S NOTE

The Minister of Interior Affairs is often referred to (what British or Americans would recognise is head of domestic or 'home' affairs). The actual ministry in Russia is called Internal Affairs. But given the connotations this has in the West of an investigative unit of the police, I decided to make a small adjustment to the minister's title for the sake of clarity.

As readers of *Official Secrets* might remember, I switch between the British and American spellings of 'defence/defense' only when referring to an official government position. So it is the U.S. Secretary of *Defense*, and the British Ministry of *Defence*.

For me, the actual title or position cannot and should not be changed to suit one's British-English or American-English preference. By doing this, I seek to show respect to both countries' traditions, even if it might appear jarring to someone on either side of the Atlantic. Unfortunately, for anyone writing in English this is not an easily resolved dilemma!